# THE LORD OF TERROR

A FANTÔMAS DETECTIVE NOVEL

BY MARCEL ALLAIN

*Bibliographical Note*

This Antipodes edition, first published in 2016, is a republication of the work first published by David McKay Co., Philadelphia, in 1925. The original translation has been altered to reflect modern spelling and usage.

ISBN 978-0-9966599-3-2

# Contents

# THE LORD OF
# TERROR

## 1. Sheer Impossibilities

Fantômas!… Ten years ago, fifteen years ago soon—it was in 1911—that brigand's name, that name so mysterious, so sinister, was on everyone's lips, haunted every man's thoughts…

Fantômas!… Slowly, sitting alone in a darkling room, when the fire is dying and the night falling, first locking and double-locking your door, utter those three syllables! They evoke a sense of mystery. They recall to memory a nightmare that endured for months, for years, that obsessed the whole world!

Fantômas!… The fellow was nowhere and everywhere at once. Nothing was secure from his enterprise. Nothing could be safeguarded against his rapacity. He mocked the strongest safes. The most elaborate precautions but moved his mirth. He was the "Robber" of the storybooks, the redoubtable master of men's lives and fortunes…

Fantômas!… Again is seen that vague, sinister figure—black clothes, black hood, slender hands in black gloves, everything as before, and, unforgettable, the same stealthy walk and flaming eyes—eyes now grim and menacing, now ineffably scornful…

In Paris, into the best guarded flat, in the suburbs, into the most carefully locked house, in the provinces, in the open country where sturdy watchdogs guard the slumbers of the inmates, the man could force his thievish way. People well remembered, just when and how it pleased his criminal caprice…

Fantômas!… No human being surely—rather Robbery personified, Pillage incarnate, Felonious Audacity in the flesh, the very Genius of Evil.

*     *     *     *     *

"But come, who and what is this man?" A Minister of State asked the question one day. Strong in his consciousness of power, he affected to see in this monster only a common lawbreaker. But the police officer to whom the statesman had put the question replied:

"Sir, it is… He! the all daring, the all capable. There is nothing he cannot do!"

"Nothing he cannot do!" The detective who said the words was named Juve… At his side, at his invitation, stood a young man, who nodded his head in agreement:

"Yes, nothing he cannot do," he echoed the words. The young man was the journalist Jerome Fandor…

Fantômas!… Juve!… Fandor! The three names are mutually complementary. You cannot mention one without mentioning the others. It is a special privilege of the land of France to give birth, always in times of crisis, to the sons she has need of. Free, triumphant, ever elusive, never to be identified, unique, there was Fantômas… To do battle with him, to answer his insolent challenge, Juve and Fandor.

Juve? A police officer, the King of police officers. No, not one of those secret agents whose task is doubtless useful, but whose very trade is one of dissimulation and deceit. No, but a fighting man, a soldier of a sort, the man who dared to say: "Nothing Fantômas cannot do!" the man who threw down the gauntlet to the Prince of Thieves!

Fandor? A journalist, the reporter who is bent on knowing, even when his life may pay forfeit for the information he craves, the writer whose pen obeys his thought and is ready to confront every peril.

Juve? A man of forty, adroit, astute, subtle of mind, tenacious of purpose.

Fandor? Twenty-five—all the fire of reckless daring, all the lightheartedness of youth.

Juve? Fandor? Two friends… and Fantômas, the enemy, their common enemy…

Oh, the astounding memories those names call up! the rage that filled the city when a fresh atrocity of the master's was made public and Juve and Fandor were stated to be in pursuit of the malefactor and straining every nerve to checkmate his plans!

"He?… or they?" men asked each other, "which will win?" But the struggle was never-ending. Victory only hastened on another engagement. Fantômas invariably escaped. Fantômas was never caught, never actually taken, the mask never once torn from his face.

Then one day, like a sleeper awaking from a horrid dream, humanity threw off its panic terror.

Juve and Fandor had brought Fantômas to bay on board one of the powerful steamships that make swift passages across the Atlantic, linking the shores of France and America. The *Gigantic* had left Le Havre and was at sea when Juve passed the word to a tramp she fell in with off Newfoundland: "He is with us. He will not come ashore alive, I take my oath to that!"

Then, six hours later, a brief cable was dispatched from the Nantucket light-ship, a message none has ever forgotten: "S.S. *Gigantic* a total loss. Juve, Fandor and Fantômas among the dead."

At first men seemed dumbfounded. Dead? Dead in a terrible, but commonplace catastrophe, these heroes of melodrama? Dead in one common tragedy, he, the thief, and they, the champions of duty? But before long the truth had to be admitted. Survivors, picked up by shore boats, gave details. Juve, remaining on board, had gone down with the ship at the very moment he stood face to face with Fantômas and revealed his identity. Fandor had been thrown by Juve willy-nilly into a boat, but the boat had capsized. Rocked in the cradle of the deep they slept the sleep that knows no waking…

No, none could ever forget these telegrams that arrived one after another and the universal commotion and excitement they caused. True, the public mourned Juve and Fandor. Each man seemed to have lost one of his own nearest and dearest… But oh! the merciful deliverance of the disappearance of the odious brigand! Once more security reigned in every home. A common dread was ended forever. Yes, the man was dead. Never again, as the door opened, would He appear behind it. Never again, at the end of the garden, at the corner of the next street, would His grim figure spring up! With him had vanished Terror… How sweet the sense of safety, how comforting the certainty of reprieve!

Ten years and more had gone by since then. Now the ugly memory was dying out, a memory none wished to keep alive.

Alas! a tragedy is brewing! After truce, the battle is renewed!… Is He come to life again?… But that is a question we shall not answer. The problem that confronts us is too hard for one man's solving. To do that calls for united effort, for the combined acumen and courage of all… It is an exact, detailed, impartial inquiry, a grim, uncompromising inquest we are about to institute before the eyes of our readers. Let them study the question; they will pronounce judgment, they will discern the truth, and then…

But who is our informant, we shall be asked—a logical demand! Yet it is one we cannot answer. No, not yet!… Later on, perhaps?…

Best not anticipate therefore. Here, in plain words, are the facts:

That day, leaping from his car, which had just stopped before the door of the modest dwelling he occupied at Passy, Comte Léon de Vautreuil, holding in his arms a sort of box or casket, ordered his chauffeur:

"Drive to the garage, Jean. I shall not be going out again. Tomorrow we'll telephone you your orders."

The Comte spoke in a ringing, cheery voice. Cheery too the way he wheeled lightly round on his heels with the quick alertness of a healthy man of fifty or so. Comte Léon de Vautreuil? Under the name, which we disguise a little—the reason will soon be apparent—our readers will no doubt guess a familiar personality… An attaché of yore in Russia, the gentleman in question has now, it is true, quitted the diplomatic service, but his entertainments, his luxury, are widely known, no less than his inexhaustible charities. Moreover, is he not the father of the lovely Josette de Vautreuil, the recognized queen of all the elegant dissipations of Paris?…

The Comte strode across the pavement to his door and was ringing the bell when a stranger, very respectably dressed, stepped forward and halted beside him.

"You have something to say, sir?" questioned the other, and the man proceeded to explain:

"I have brought, Monsieur le Comte, the insurance policy relating to your new motor."

"Very good!… You have the papers with you?"

"Yes, but I want your signature…"

"In that case, let us go into my study."

A footman had meantime opened the door. Rapidly the Comte, still carrying his casket, threw off his overcoat and hat in the corridor on the ground floor and opened a door, which as an old-time diplomat he always kept locked, and invited the stranger to enter.

A couple of minutes later the official had taken his departure, not having been one second alone in the room. Taking the needful documents from his pocketbook, he had handed them to his host and, the signatures duly affixed, he made for the door with a polite bow.

"Louis, show the gentleman out," Léon de Vautreuil gave the order to the footman.

This done, the erstwhile attaché returned to his study, crossed the room, opened the bolted door of another smaller apartment, and called in a cheery voice:

"Josette, Henri, my children, come see what I have brought—a box that contains over ten millions worth of diamonds…"

It was at most five minutes the Comte had been at home. He alone was in possession of the keys of his study. No one had entered unaccompanied by himself. *He* had never left the room…

In the little chamber adjacent the two young people he had addressed, his daughter Josette and her fiancé Henri Tardoux, sprang to their feet and hurried to the door. But on reaching the threshold, they halted in alarm, transfixed by amazement… The Comte stood by his desk, his face as pale as death, his limbs trembling. With outstretched arms he pointed to the door communicating with the corridor, muttering in a hoarse voice:

"There, look there! Look there!"

On the white panel of the door, a writing stood out, perfectly legible, for it was traced in printed characters and in red ink:

> If you wish to save your life and the lives of those dear to you, you will hand over to me voluntarily half of the diamonds entrusted to you.

There was no signature…

For some seconds a heavy silence reigned in the Comte's working room. Each was striving to unravel the mystery of this strange message. What exactly did it mean? How could it have been written there? Henri Tardoux was the first to recover some degree of calmness. A friend of his fiancée from boyhood onwards and looked upon by M. de Vautreuil as a son, he need not fear being indiscreet. More than that, as assistant to Marsouval, the famous savant and a noted scientist, himself trained in habits of accuracy and precision, he was always wont to act calmly and logically. The young man demanded:

"Now, father, to begin with, what diamonds do you mean?"

"Diamonds I have here… in this box… They have been entrusted to me by Russian refugees to be sold…"

"They were entrusted to you secretly?"

"Secretly, yes!… Nobody could possibly be aware of the thing… at least I imagine so."

"And no one had protested against the sale?"

"Oh, nobody!…"

"Then this writing must have been done by some bad character?"

"But no one of the sort could have got in here, by God!"

As he spoke these last words, Léon de Vautreuil raised his arms to heaven with a gesture of impotent anger. Moreover the ex-diplomat must necessarily have been greatly upset to allow himself even the mild oath he had just indulged in.

But Henri Tardoux fell silent. His prospective father-in-law's remark had impressed him strongly. Better than anyone he knew for certain that the study was always kept locked. How then allow that a robber, whomever he might be, could have found his way into this well-guarded room without leaving any trace of his doings?

After a brief moment for reflection, Henri Tardoux went on:

"Anyhow, father, seeing the writing is there, somebody put it there... So..."

"So?..."

"So we must discover who... You've had no one here?"

"Yes, I have—an insurance official. But I never let him out of my sight. What's more, the writing is not a foot from the floor... and I'm positive he never stooped down."

"Never mind! Suppose you phoned the company?"

But casting a look at his timepiece, the diplomat objected:

"Too late now—ten past six. The offices will be closed."

"Besides," he insisted, "it's not that fellow at all. Devil take it, I must have seen him writing. Evidently someone got in while I was away."

"But, father," stammered Josette, "that's impossible. Louis was outside in the corridor all the while... Henri and I, we've been together in the small salon for the last four hours. So both doors have been continuously under observation..."

"And no visitor has called?... no tradesman?"

"At the front door, no. At the kitchen door I cannot say... But Victoire has never left her kitchen..."

Without answering the girl, Léon de Vautreuil left the room, making almost a run for the kitchen regions, presided over by a stalwart cook, a female "cordon bleu," one of those worthies who carry on the fine old traditions of French good living.

"Victoire," panted her master, "has anyone been? have you had any tradesmen in? Answer me, look sharp! It's vastly important."

With arms akimbo and quite unconcerned—the woman had been in the same place twenty years and knew she was above reproach—Victoire retorted:

"Anyone been here? My word, no, not so much as a cat. Barring Bouzille, of course... But why ever does Monsieur ask the question?"

But the diplomat was off again:

"Bouzille—who's Bouzille?"

"My odd jobs man, to be sure," declared Victoire, "a half-witted creature I've employed these last five years to stack the coals and get the wood."

"A laborer in fact."

"A fellow does odd jobs, as I'm telling Monsieur—a Jack-of-all-trades, why certainly!… Says he's a 'finder of articles lost or mislaid,' a 'dog's funeral-furnisher,' a 'drowner for life-savers to rescue'… A shuffler, eh? Well, well, knows his own business best, I reckon."

"Victoire, listen to me! This fellow, this Bouzille, did you let him out of your sight for one second?"

"One second, why no, sir. And for why, because I had nothing for him to do today. I plunked him outdoors right away—beg pardon if I talk too free, sir."

Léon de Vautreuil stayed to hear no more. Followed by his daughter who had accompanied him, he returned to his working room, where he found Henri Tardoux, thus left alone, on his knees examining the mysterious writing through a magnifying glass.

"Nobody has been!" announced the diplomat. "Louis, no less than Victoire, is above suspicion… It's maddening, maddening!"

Then suddenly, laying his hand upon his brow, Léon de Vautreuil added:

"Anyway, it's a little joke I mean to see to the bottom of, I take my oath to that!… You are dining here, Henri?"

"Impossible, father, I have a course of lectures to prepare…"

"Goodbye then, my boy… I'll leave you with Josette. We'll see you again, tomorrow, won't we?"

As he thus changed the conversation and in a way dismissed his daughter's lover, leaving the investigation they had started unfinished, Léon de Vautreuil displayed a feverish haste. In fact no sooner were Henri and Josette out of the room than the diplomat sank seemingly exhausted into an armchair.

"Heavens! am I going mad?… A dreadful thought has just

flashed across my brain!… But no, it cannot be! 'He' is dead, dead and done with!…"

Then springing up again and running to the casket, he opened it with trembling fingers. The box was intact. The diamonds had not been touched.

"I was afraid," muttered the Comte. "Yes, I was afraid—and I am afraid still!"

Then, opening his safe, he laid the jewels on one of the shelves and relocked the triple secret safety-locks with the most minute care.

Meantime, in the adjoining room, Henri Tardoux, already oblivious of the mysterious incident that had occurred, was taking leave of his fiancée, scolding her a little the while:

"Come, promise me to be sensible!" he scolded the girl. "I don't want to see your eyes red any more… You promise?… Very good, I trust you, dear!"—and two minutes after receiving the promise, he was gone.

Oh, no! don't think there was any serious quarrel. Nothing of the kind. If Josette's eyes were red, this was because the child, of a highly impressionable nature, could not get over the loss of an aunt who had brought her up and from whom she had been parted a week before on the old lady's sailing for Brazil on important business connected with family money matters.

Josette's persistent grief seemed exaggerated in Henri Tardoux's eyes—and it may be he was not far wrong. Making his way home to the Villa Montmorency, this little house he occupied at Auteuil, he rapidly ate the dinner served by the old manservant who made up the whole domestic establishment, and entered his drawing room, now transformed into a laboratory and crammed with books and scientific apparatuses. Then he fell to thinking about Josette's sorrow:

"Truly, I should never wish," the young man growled, "even in thought, to insult an old lady. But, all the same, I cannot understand Josette's keen regret for that rather cross-grained individual, who did all she could to annoy us. Mlle. Eléonore was a curse—and that's the plain truth!"

Lighting a cigarette, he proceeded:

"She made a point of managing everything, meddling in everything, criticizing everything… Upon my word, I cannot regret her departure!… Josette may very well have been upset as she watched the steamer leave harbor with her aunt on board; well and good! but to burst into sobs every time she sees one of her portraits, that's a thing I can't stomach!"

And with a sudden laugh, the young man extracted a photograph from his pocketbook as he resumed:

"True, the portraits of my lady Eléonore must be getting scarce! Every time I come across one, I pocket it—one less chance of seeing Josette in tears!"—and gazing without the smallest twinge of conscience at the fruit of his dishonesty, the young man observed:

"This photo is the most like the original, I think, of any in existence. That comic little hat, that quaint hooded cape, those prying eyes and sly smile… it is Eléonore de Vautreuil to the life!"

But next minute he was repentant:

"After all, I'm in the wrong. The woman deserves respect, her faults were those of her years, and old age is venerable. Moreover, I am indebted to the old lady for one happy moment, the moment when I saw her go, when I watched her boat steam out of harbor! Now I know her to be on the open sea, thousands of miles away, I ought to be indulgent to her weaknesses. So I wish you a good passage, Mademoiselle Eléonore!"

*       *       *       *       *

Still smiling, Henri Tardoux laid the picture on his table, intending to deal with it later, and buried himself in a scientific volume. Suddenly he looked up, startled by the sound of footsteps, light but distinct, that had reached his ears. But his servant had gone home and he believed himself to be alone in the house.

"Theodore?… is that you, my man?" he demanded, raising his voice. "Are you still here?"

There was no answer, but the noise went on. Next minute the door opened slowly… Henri Tardoux was on his feet in an instant. His heart stopped dead, a cold sweat broke out on his brow, in sheer amazement at what he saw. The person who had entered the room, who was moving towards him, before whom he fell back in consternation, he recognized at the first glance, he knew her no less by her clothes than by her face.

Yet it was impossible—he was convinced it was impossible—that she could be there!

It was the traveler returned! It was Mlle. Eléonore de Vautreuil, whom he himself had escorted to Le Havre, whom he had seen depart with his own eyes, who was at sea at that very moment in mid-Atlantic!

*     *     *     *     *

At the moment, in the brief instant when he recognized the woman he had seen with his own eyes starting on her travels, Henri Tardoux, his face as white as paper, asked himself the question: was he not losing his wits? This was his first thought. Eléonore de Vautreuil was thousands of miles away, on the open sea. It was therefore impossible she could be there, standing before him, in his room. An impossibility *is* an impossibility. If he thought otherwise, it meant he was going mad. *But* this impossibility was there before his eyes! And as he gazed at the figure, he could neither deny nor doubt the reality of what he beheld!

The figure was advancing, her feet scarcely brushing the carpet—was close upon him!…

Doubt was no longer possible, and the young man strove to explain the thing as a case of mistaken identity. It was not the returned traveler, this old dame who stood there—it was someone else like her! But no mere likeness could have deceived his senses. He had known Mlle. Eléonore since childhood, no mistake was possible.

Or was it a hallucination? But this hypothesis was equally untenable. He was too keenly aware of what was happening. He compared the portrait on the table with the face before him. No mere hallucination could have endured the test.

What was it then? A spasm of anguished fear, a mortal

terror, shook him, and he asked himself:

"A ghost? was it a ghost, a phantom, a spirit materialized?"

But Science, noble, self-respecting Science has never accorded her sanction to the belief in spiritual visitants from another world, abandoning such chimeras to charlatans, sciolists, pseudoscientists out for self-advertisement and notoriety.

Meantime Mlle. Eléonore had reached his desk. Standing there and lightly bending over it, poising a pencil in her hand, she seemed to be trying to write, without succeeding…

Then the young man revolted against the witness of his own eyes. What he beheld was an impossibility; therefore, he told himself, "I do not see it! I am in a bad dream." But he was a brave man, and pulling himself together, mastering his panic, he resolved to convince himself of the error of vision he was laboring under.

In a toneless voice he called:

"Mademoiselle!" and again, "Mademoiselle!"

But his visitor did not seem to hear. Then he took a step forward, and suddenly, firmly believing no one was there, that he was the victim of a mistake, he raised his fist and dealt the phantom a mighty blow.

He thought to strike the empty air, but his fist fell on a body—a human body! More than that, there, before his eyes, staggering under the weight of his blow, the apparition sank, a helpless mass on the floor, without a cry.

Henri Tardoux could control his nerves no longer, and knew not what he did. Striding over the body of his victim, he fled from the room, slammed the door behind him and turned the key in the lock.

*   *   *   *   *

Next minute the young man had left the house and was running through the deserted streets of Auteuil, making for the station of the Ceinture railway. The weather had changed. A fine, cool rain was falling which calmed his excitement.

"I am only fit for Charenton!" he exclaimed suddenly. It was ten o'clock at night or thereabouts, and here he was, hatless, in slippers and indoor lounge coat, wandering about out of doors. He would go back home; but no, that he could *not* do.

"No, no!" he reflected, "I am not mad, really. Yet I have locked up at home… someone who is not there! I will go on to Rippert's house. He will go back with me—and see what I have seen!"

And as he hurried there, he recalled the details, at once positive and self-contradictory. He was convinced that Mlle. Eléonore was on the sea. He had himself escorted the traveler to the ship, he had seen her set sail…

And yet, and yet he *knew* his fist had actually struck somebody… and this somebody he was convinced was Eléonore de Vautreuil—which was impossible!

Louis Rippert, Assistant Secretary in the office of the Prefecture of Police, was one of Henri Tardoux's best friends, though their characters showed marked points of difference. While Marsouval's assistant was sober-minded, hardworking, scornful of all frivolous amusements, the public servant was, on the contrary, a lighthearted pleasure-seeker, devoted to fashionable entertainments and elegant dissipations.

Returning from a dinner at the club wearing his dinner jacket, vexed at having to give up his game of bridge to devote the evening to a tedious report, Louis Rippert at the same moment his friend was gazing at the most baffling of apparitions, had just reached home in anything but a good temper.

"Here I am, Mary," he said, accosting the pretty, smart maid who had run forward to open at his ring. "Anything new? No one rang on the phone? And the dog?"

At the same time his eyes explored a dark corner of the entrance hall, where a dog kennel could be vaguely discerned. But the girl had her answer ready:

"Dead, sir!… The poor beast suffered dreadfully…"

"And the vet could do nothing?"

"Nothing, sir. Monsieur Barbézieux said he had been called in too late…"

Without deigning an answer, the young man, greatly put out by his dog's death, his friend and fellow-sportsman, was turning to enter his working room when he asked suddenly:

"What have you done with him? We must phone…"

"No need, sir. Bouzille, the dog's undertaker, has removed the body…"

"The 'undertaker'… what yarn is this you're telling me?"

"Beg pardon, sir, but the neighbors have nicknamed him that. When a dog dies, he takes on the job of getting rid of the carcass for the animals' masters… So I thought…"

But a loud peal of the doorbell interrupted the young woman's discourse, and two minutes later Louis Rippert was questioning his friend Henri Tardoux in bantering tones:

"Hello, old man! What the devil's up? In your slippers? without a hat!… and your teeth chattering? Speak up. My word, you make me feel uneasy."

The other had thrown himself into an armchair. Sitting there, elbows on knees, head between his two hands, he replied in a hollow voice:

"Listen to me, Louis, I *am* going to speak. But you mustn't think I'm mad…"

"Mad?"

"Yes!… I am not mad! I'm not!… But…"

"Come now, look me in the face! Have you been drinking?… What is happening?"

"My dear old Louis, there's something happening I dare not tell you in words… Come with me, and you will see for yourself."

"See what? and where are you taking me?"

"To my house…"

"To your house? and what's going on at your house?"

"What's going on? Why, this: I've just downed with a blow of my fist somebody who can't possibly be there!—my fiancée's aunt, Eléonore de Vautreuil, yes, Eléonore de Vautreuil, who sailed for Brazil, as I told you myself!"

But at this announcement Louis Rippert could not help but laugh out loud.

"*What* did you say?" he demanded. "Good thing you warned me you weren't mad!"

All the same, three minutes later when, point by point, with that precision and particularity of detail which only men of science can compass, Henri Tardoux had recounted to his comrade the incomprehensible adventure that had befallen him, Louis Rippert had, for all his skepticism, felt his mind troubled… Not of course that for one instant he took for gospel the story told him by Josette's fiancé! He could not, and would not, believe that Mlle. de Vautreuil had visited his friend's house. No, the impossible could *not* happen! Yet he was bound to admit that his companion was in full possession of his senses, that he was in fact neither mad nor drunk!

"Do you realize, I ask you," the young man of science insisted. "I hit out… she fell… Yet I know she is not there, she cannot be there at all!"

Meanwhile Louis Rippert was pacing the room excitedly.

"My dear fellow," he kept repeating, "it cannot have been Mlle. de Vautreuil you struck, that is out of the question. You suffered hallucination? hmm, not likely!… However, you are right, we must know the truth. Let's go then, by all means… just a moment to get a revolver and…"

"A revolver?… what for?"

"Why, to kill her, by God! this too enterprising traveler!"—and Louis Rippert indulged in another guffaw.

But his friend protested. "No, no," he begged him, "leave your gun behind. I'm thinking… Yes, it *was* she. I feel certain now of what I say… And an accident quickly happens. You might fire in your agitation and kill her."

"But you say she's on the high seas?"

"But she's there, I tell you—without being there at all!…"

Then, dumbfounded at what he was saying, the statements he heard coming from his own lips, Henri Tardoux struck his forehead wildly as he cried:

"I've lost my head, I admit I have. I'm going out of my mind!"

To tell the truth, Louis Rippert too was beginning to ask himself fairly and squarely if his old friend's reason had not suddenly gone under, when piercing screams, outcries of the wildest terror startled the two young men.

"Good God! It's Mary!" cried the girl's master, who had instantly recognized his servant's voice. Then, pushing his comrade to one side, the Assistant Secretary, foreboding some unknown catastrophe, dashed out into the corridor, yelling:

"Mary! Mary, I say! What is the matter?"

The words froze on the young man's lips. Stretched on the floor of the anteroom, his young handmaid was writhing in the crisis of a fierce attack of hysterics… Near her, looking confused and embarrassed, stood an old man, a beggar in appearance, muttering unintelligible explanations.

Louis Rippert had had no time to gather the meaning of the strange scene when, with a terrible cry and a face convulsed with fear, he found himself knocked over, hurled to earth, struck full in the chest—by a dog!

It was a superb spaniel with a lovely black and white spotted coat. Evidently mad with delight, the animal, after making its spring at Rippert's shoulders, was now frisking round the room, waving his bushy tail and yapping with pleasure.

"My dog!… my dog Cheeper, that was dead… Yes, it *is* Cheeper!" stammered the Assistant Secretary in a toneless voice.

Then the beggar was heard protesting against things in general:

"You trust old Bouzille… Why, here's a pretty go, my word!… Ain't I the fellow what finds articles lost?—and I've found your pup again, I have!… But there, if as how the dog's got to be lost again, why, I'm in that job too."

So saying, Bouzille took a step to his rear, and slipping through the half-open door, effected a judicious, silent and rapid retreat.

Not a doubt but the resurrection of the dead dog (but had the beast ever been really dead?) would have struck an infinitely less tragic note in the minds of all who were later on to seek the explanation of this fresh mystery, if they had been aware how Bouzille, as he made off, shook his old sides in a fit of silent self-satisfied merriment.

"To think of it!" he was muttering to himself. "Sure enough, I can't make a guess what's happened… Anyhow I know enough not to worry my head about it all! Dead dogs come to life again indeed! There's only damned fools… or your scientific guys to believe such tales!"

Bouzille was a hard judge of humanity, and entertained a special contempt for men of science. But doubtless he had his own good reasons for being skeptical as to Cheeper's resurrection.

## 2. Common Sense to the Rescue

Whether it was that Bouzille had blabbed or Mary had failed to hold her tongue or Rippert and Tardoux had neglected to maintain a proper reserve, anyway the fact remains that next day the peaceful suburb of Auteuil was literally overwhelmed by an invading army of reports, and the evening papers had hardly left the compositors' hands before they were snatched up by eager readers. As universal as the public curiosity was, however, the contents contained but little to satisfy it. *La Capitale,* that usually well-informed organ, simply confined itself to the report the bare indisputable facts, offering no explanation and not so much as suggesting any hypothesis to account for them.

"Dumbfounded to see his dog alive, when a few moments before he had been informed of its death, Louis Rippert," so read the account, "immediately telephoned to M. Barbézieux, Veterinary Surgeon of Nanterre, who at once confirmed the fact of the animal's death, which he had himself witnessed. Abandoning all attempt therefore to fathom the mystery, Louis Rippert and Henri Tardoux proceeded to the Villa Montmorency, where with feelings of alarm and distress that may well be imagined, they found the Lady Eléonore de Vautreuil still lying in a dead faint on the floor."

And the reporter responsible for the article proceeded to give a string of fantastic details:

"After receiving first aid from the two young men, the lady in question recovered consciousness. Then, still without a word, her face haggard, her legs trembling under her, she appears to have left the house, crossing the garden, gaining the street, and taking the road leading to the Étoile…

"Mlle. Eléonore, followed by the two young men, who all the time kept asking themselves if they were really in their right senses, seemed to recover her strength in the fresh night air, and suddenly starting off at a rapid pace, reached the Rue de l'Assomption at Passy where she rang the doorbell of M. Léon de Vautreuil's house, her brother with whom she used to live before her departure for Brazil…"

The paper declared—and we may readily believe the statement—that the maddest of mad scenes had signalized the traveler's return to the domestic hearth…

"One extraordinary, one fantastic feature," continued *La Capitale,* "is that Mlle. de Vautreuil, who nevertheless appears to lie in complete possession of her wits, does not utter a word and makes ineffectual efforts to write. Moreover, it is utterly impossible to come near her; the presence of a human being at less than a yard from her person seems to cause her intolerable agony… Those who have seen her, the doctors who were called in, are lost in vain conjectures as to what they call a phenomenon of hypersensitiveness.

"It should be mentioned," proceeded the article, "that both the family and the police (informed of the facts the same night) have instituted inquiries and that these two lines of investigation have given precisely the same results!

"The shipping agents are positive of their facts: Mlle. Eléonore de Vautreuil undoubtedly embarked on the steamship now at sea. The pilot, the last man to leave the vessel, actually spoke to her when she handed him letters to take ashore, letters that reached their destination in due course. Furthermore, though unfortunately the vessel is not provided with a wireless installation of long range enabling immediate communication to be opened with her, still she has a less powerful set that was utilized by the passengers to send telegraphic messages to another ship passed at sea and which brought them to France, where she was bound. Two of these telegrams were from Mlle. de Vautreuil! No doubt, we repeat, can be entertained as to the lady being actually and assuredly on the open sea…

"And yet she is also at her brother's house!

"How is this possible? She alone, perhaps, the heroine of this inexplicable adventure, would be in a position to explain. But, dumb and incapable of writing, doubtless as the result of the nervous shock experienced, will she ever be able to answer all the questions one would fain put to her? We cannot tell.

"Nor can we tell indeed how M. Louis Rippert's dog that died was able to come back alive to its master's house. The beggar Bouzille states that he saw the animal barking at the door and that under cover of night, not recognizing the beast as the same dog whose body he had thrown into the Seine, he confined himself to ringing the bell in hopes of getting some trifling tip. Is the man speaking the truth, the whole truth?"

Modestly enough—but no reader could take it amiss—the article ended with an admission of incapacity to understand the case.

"We relinquish all attempts to explain the facts," declared *La Capitale*. "They are manifestly outside the domain of common reason. Science alone, which does not accept miracles, might be in a position to speak, but science says nothing, only ponders and waits. We must imitate her patience."

But for the public, this demand for patience was precisely what the public would not accept! It was indignant that in presence of such mysteries no plausible explanation should be forthcoming…

While the doctors kept obstinately silent, and while the police declared, not without truth, that they had no concern with the business, having received no complaint and being unable to regard as an offense against the law the fact of being in two places at once, a swarm of journalists continued to besiege Léon de Vautreuil's house. Finding the door shut and admission refused, they indulged in the wildest fancies.

"My master has nothing to add to the article that appeared in *La Capitale*," declared Louis, heedless alike of the prayers and the threats of the newspapermen.

Forty-eight hours later, two camps had formed in the newspaper world, the serious journals recognizing the miraculous and inexplicable side of the circumstances, while organs greedy for scandal, in order to appear extra well-informed, left it to be understood that Mlle. Eléonore's journey had been all a presence, that a "family drama" explained what seemed inexplicable, and that, all said and done, there was nothing to hinder Léon de Vautreuil being a murderer, Henri Tardoux his accomplice, and Louis Rippert their dupe.

*　*　*　*　*

This "reasonable" explanation was as a matter of fact no explanation at all. The appearance of Mlle. Eléonore, not to mention that of the dog Cheeper, failed to become any more comprehensible by presupposing the guilt of the ex-diplomat. It was not a case of a live woman "too few," but of an absent woman "too much." Whether or no, public excitement grew greater day by day and compelled Henri Tardoux to form a definite resolution. Coming to the Rue de l'Assomption, he sought out the Comte.

"Father," he began, "have you noticed the state of nervousness Josette is in?"

"Yes, not a doubt of it, she is upset…"

"And is in danger of falling ill. Don't you think, sir, a journey…"

"Why, certainly… But where to? and who would go with her?"

"Her English governess in the capacity of chaperone… and I to protect her. Suppose you persuaded her to go to Marseilles, sir?"

"To her cousin's wedding? But will she agree?"

"If I beg her to, yes!"

*　*　*　*　*

Three days later, Josette was settling down at the Hôtel des Alliés in the pretty and stirring town of Marseilles, under the respectable wing of her duenna and the tender protection of her fiancé.

In fact Josette had agreed to the expedition with a very good grace. Greatly upset by the sudden reappearance of her aunt, quite incapable of bearing the sight of the old lady without a grievous strain in her woman's nerves, she had readily and gladly admitted that a period of moral rest would do her a great deal of good.

Mental repose, well and good; but was she destined to find this at Marseilles?

After unpacking her trunks and making the most comfortable arrangements practicable in a hotel bedroom, Josette, passing through a small sitting room adjoining, tapped at the door of the room occupied by her lady companion:

"Madame Smith," she asked the Englishwoman, "will you come and have a cup of tea? I am going to ask Henri to join us."

Fond of good things and greatly enjoying the journey, Mme. Smith eagerly accepted the invitation and made haste to follow Josette, who going back to the small salon telephoned to Henri Tardoux whose room was right at the end of the hotel.

"Hello! I'm quite settled in, Henri... I'm having tea with Madame Smith... Will you come up?"

Then, when the young man accepted, she added:

"Bring the papers with you, please. I can hear them shouting the evening editions..."

One thing is very certain. At that moment Josette was a hundred miles from suspecting the face of embarrassment her lover pulled on hearing the last words. The papers? No indeed, it was just the papers Henri Tardoux, in his anxious solicitude for his fiancée, was least desirous of letting Josette see... *He* had read them! He had them before him now. He could not take his eyes off them. No, these were certainly not the things to give Josette.

Yet these papers contained no sensational details relating to the mysterious occurrences in the 16th arrondissement. But there *was* something else—lengthy articles devoted to a certain impressive anniversary. Was it not, in fact, on that day ten years before that the loss of the *Gigantic* had stirred all the world to an indescribable excitement?

With touching unanimity, the journals, one and all, had devoted their first pages to the task of recalling bygone memories. They actually published, in default of Fantômas' portrait—who could boast of possessing that?—two photographs of the unfortunate friends, Juve and Fandor.

"The two greatest police officers of the time," the description read, "the only two men on earth who could have unraveled the Parisian problem of the reappearance of Mlle. de Vautreuil."

"No, I will not take the papers up!" Henri Tardoux made up his mind to that. "No matter. I will pretend I have forgotten them! Besides, will Josette remember to ask for them?"—and as a matter of fact Josette never did remember.

Pouring out the tea as she welcomed her fiancé with a smile, she asked him:

"Are you satisfied with your room, Henri? Mine I find just perfect. And then look what a fine view I have. I can see from my window right to the old harbor…"

"Oh, but you must be mistaken," objected Henri. "We are at the other extremity of Marseilles."

"Yes… but from this height. Anyway come and see. No, not there, in my room."

The young man got up, and while Josette went on filling the teacups, stepped into the next room.

*     *     *     *     *

But when Henri Tardoux returned to the small salon, his face was livid and he was trembling in every limb.

"What is the matter with you? Good heavens! What is the matter?" demanded the girl.

"Nothing, nothing!" stammered the young man.

"But you are deadly pale. You are trembling, Henri. You have seen or heard something?"

"No, no! What fancies are these? I swear you are mistaken!"

But he was so obviously not speaking the truth that turning pale in her turn, Josette too sprang up and rushed into her room.

She was expecting to see some appalling spectacle, but without guessing what it could possibly be… She found nothing uncommon, nothing extraordinary. The room was in the same orderly state she had left it in, once her unpacking was completed.

 

"Henri! I don't understand!" she was beginning. But Josette's cry froze on her lips. Hurrying back into the small salon, she saw her governess apparently in a state of terror. The woman was alone!

"Henri?… where is Henri?" the girl asked.

"Gone!" groaned Mme. Smith.

"Gone where?… what did he say?… answer me, I beg you."

The worthy woman was choking. She could barely articulate:

"He said… he said… well, he said: *Another* mystery to drive us all mad!'"

## 3. Two Heroes Demand If They Are Really Themselves

Mme. Smith was quite right in her report of the words uttered by Henri Tardoux as he fled from the room. Such indeed were the expressions the young man had used—these and no others. If these words were strange, in fact almost incomprehensible, Henri Tardoux's behavior was more extraordinary still.

Rushing in frantic haste to his own room, he extracted a pair of excellent field glasses from a traveling bag. Then, still at a run, he mounted to the top story of the hotel, and, reaching a point exactly above his fiancée's rooms, stepped out onto a terrace dominating the building. The view was indeed fairy-like, but Henri Tardoux paid little heed to the view, no doubt of that! Clapping the glasses to his eyes, he proceeded to examine the roof of an adjoining building that lay at quite a short distance from his point of observation, the same roof he had looked at from Josette's window.

On this roof two men in a half-recumbent position were staring at each other, so it seemed, with unbounded aston-ishment. Nay, he did more than see them; he knew them… His stupefaction grew more and more intense, and his face assumed a ghastly look as he muttered:

"Now it's dead men, dead men alive! dead men come to life again! I could swear it!… But I'm going mad surely, going mad!"

Now, if Josette's fiancé, witness of a prodigy undoubtedly startling, doubted his own sanity, the two men whose awak-ening he had just been observing, appeared every whit as un-certain as he was regarding the state of their wits. Dressed in sporting kit, easy fitting and more comfortable than elegant, both men displayed features equally indicative of energy. Though of different ages—one might be near on fifty, the other appeared just thirty—both, it was plain to see, were strong and vigorous individuals.

But now they looked stupefied by sheer amazement. A moment before they were lying motionless and asleep. The noisy horn of a motorcar had roused the younger of the two companions from his slumbers. Scarcely had he raised himself and sat up, however, before his comrade too had lifted his head.

Minutes passed, minutes that seemed hours, while the pair stared into each other's eyes in speechless wonder... Suddenly breaking the quiet of the high, airy roof where none could hear them, they spoke:

"Juve!" panted the young man.

"Fandor!" returned the police officer.

Then, as though the sound of their own voices had definitely roused them from the lethargy that benumbed them, they spoke in spasmodic jerks.

"But then, I'm not dead? So you saved me, did you, Juve old man?"

"But then, you dragged me off the sinking ship, Fandor? But... but..."

And they fell silent again; and then they started afresh: "So then, in God's name! where are we?"

More and more confused, the pair looked about them right and left.

"A roof!" exclaimed Juve, "we are on a roof!"

"Marseilles!" cried Fandor. "That's Marseilles, those shanties there! not a doubt of it!"

Presently, after another silence:

"But we're dead, by God!"

At this Fandor broke suddenly into a great peal of laughter.

"Dead? Not me! Or else it's not such a dreadful thing to be dead! Speak up, Juve, do *you* understand the business? We went down with the *Gigantic* and now we find ourselves atop a house... We are drowned off Newfoundland... and we pop up again at Marseilles. It's beyond me, Juve, old man!"

But, if Fandor with his usual nonchalance found it in him to joke, if he roared with laughter, albeit a merriment that sounded a trifle forced, Juve for his part had suddenly fallen serious. Smiting his brow, he brought out in a hollow voice:

"And Fantômas, God's mercy!… Fantômas? Is *he* dead… is he dead, I ask you!"

With the air of a man recalling precise memories engraved forever on his heart, Juve concluded:

"Let me think… Yes, the boat was sinking… we, Fantômas and I, were in a cabin… the water was already pouring in, while the man was telling me a string of silly, nonsensical lies… that he was my brother! I think I can hear him still… And I wanted to laugh… My brother! why, I never had a brother… And then—and then…"

"And then, Juve?"

"And then I died, God Almighty! I choked and died! I am sure of it!"

"As sure as I am, Juve, that I was in the boat you pitched me into… Helene, Fantômas' daughter, was beside me… Another lifeboat crashed into us… And I too am convinced I died! absolutely certain!"

Then, once again, the two men scrutinized each other, bewildered, dumbfounded to such a degree they thought again they were losing the power of reasoning… Were they not sure and certain of what they told each other? Had they not, both of them, the clear and definite memory of their death agony? And yet, after dying in the shipwreck of the *Gigantic* off Newfoundland, here they were alive on a housetop in Marseilles!

"Juve," exclaimed Fandor suddenly, "there's one good thing I can tell you…"

"Namely, Fandor?"

"Namely that all this makes no difference."

"Makes no difference!"

"If we *are* dead, we're dead men in quite excellent health! And so, suppose we shift our quarters? I'm hungry, I am."

Laughing, the journalist sprang up, and Juve, following his example, also rose to his feet.

"Curse me! but you're doing the young man, you are, in the other world," observed Fandor. "A cyclist's rig? You and you the serious-minded Juve!"

"None of mine," protested the police officer furiously.

"Nor mine neither, this lounge suit," declared Fandor. "Well, well, to be dressed gratis would appear to be a boon reserved for the departed… Come on to breakfast. I'm hungry enough— to buy me back to life again!"

And leaving Juve staring, Fandor, feeling it was out of the question to comprehend on the spur of the moment their miraculous adventure, made for a dormer in the roof.

"We must get through that, Juve," he proposed. "Look, it opens into a maidservant's bedroom. A moment to break open the door and we're on the stairs leading down into the street. No fear of being taken for burglars, I imagine. Being dead, we should be inviolate, eh?"

No sooner said than done, and five minutes later the two friends reached the Canebière.

"Marseilles! Yes, we really and truly are at Marseilles," grunted Juve in a morose voice.

"Oh, never a doubt of it!" echoed Fandor; "too strong a smell of oil to make any mistake about that. How about a fish breakfast?"

"If you like… You've got the money?"

Juve had been searching his pockets—in vain.

Rapidly Fandor followed suit.

"Not a sou!" he announced.

Next moment he seized his friend's arm convulsively.

"Oh, look, Juve, look there,"—and this time Fandor was in no joking mood! His voice had suddenly grown so hoarse as to be hardly audible.

"What is it? what's wrong with you?" demanded his companion.

"There, there! see that paper?"

Fandor was pointing to a sheet displayed in front of a newspaper kiosk showing a headline printed in heavy type:

*"Anniversary of the Death of Juve and Fandor."*

"Anniversary! anniversary!" stammered Juve, struck with fresh bewilderment. "But we've been dead a long while then! A week maybe?"

With one accord the two friends dashed for the kiosk and, panting with excitement, began to peruse the journal, a giddy sense of frantic bewilderment growing in them as they read. Yes, it was verily "the anniversary" of their death that the paper was celebrating! Were those not their portraits displayed on the front page? And the contents of the article increased their amazement still further. It was admirably well informed, giving chapter and verse for every detail. Point by point, in fact, it corroborated their own recollections.

"Peace to the ashes of these heroes!" the writer wound up. "Juve, going down with Fantômas, will have had the consolation of witnessing the irremediable defeat of the Genius of Crime. Fandor, drowning in the icy waters of Newfoundland, cannot have regretted his share in the glorious fate of the man he loved like a father!… Yes, peace to their ashes! It is ten years since their death, ten years since the *Gigantic*…"

But at this point Fandor stopped dead. Gripping his companion's arm, he screamed:

"Ten years, Juve!… Ten years ago? No, no I say. That is too maddening to think of! It's a misprint… it's… it's imbecile!"

Fandor hesitated no more. There, in the open street, yielding to his devouring curiosity, he snatched the paper and bolted with it in his hand. Twenty yards further on Juve overtook the fugitive. Nobody had noticed the theft; there was no pursuit of the thief.

Fandor was now paler than ever:

"Juve," he questioned, "what year are we in?"

"Why, 1911, bless my soul!"

"Look there, it says 1921. It is ten years sure enough since the *Gigantic* went down! It is ten whole years we have been dead!"

Then Juve tore the paper out of Fandor's hands where he stood pointing to the date.

"Nineteen hundred and twenty-one," intoned Juve, "nineteen hundred and twenty-one! And the paper records our death as happening ten years ago? And we died off Newfoundland, by drowning? And we turn up again on a housetop at Marseilles!"

Clenching his fists in a frenzy, Juve uttered a single exclamation expressive at once of bewilderment and despair:

"I don't understand!" he groaned. "I can't understand."

Then suddenly, as Fandor sank on a bench, his head between his hands, his mind lost in anxious thought, Juve took up the paper again and ran his eye over the pages a second time:

"Fandor! Fandor!" he shouted, "read here, this column—'The Mysteries of Auteuil.'"

It was a concise summary of the strange circumstances surrounding the reappearance of Mlle. Eléonore and of Louis Rippert's spaniel. Then, as Fandor, after reading, looked up at his comrade with a questioning gaze, Juve resumed in a hollow, distressed voice, a voice that no longer trembled, however, but was firm and confident.

"Fandor, you understand now?… Fandor, the Paris mysteries, our reawakening… You must know that one word only can account for it all?… one name only… You guess what name!"

"Yes," said Fandor gravely.

And that word, that name, shuddering, but with flashing eyes, Fandor pronounced:

"Fantômas!"

*　　*　　*　　*　　*

How indeed could the young man fail to divine Juve's thoughts? Was he not forced to the same conclusion? Was it not inevitable that he and all the world should recall at this crisis the tragic figure of the legendary, the dreaded Fantômas?

Yet scarcely had Fandor uttered the grim name before he seemed to regret having spoken it:

"Juve! Juve!" he protested, "this is midsummer madness! Fantômas is dead."

"Same as we are, Fandor."

"Well, yes!… same as we! And dead men don't come alive again. And common sense, good sound common sense…"

"Indeed, my lad!" interrupted the other, "indeed I think it the very moment to call in common sense to the rescue! I think… and I am afraid!"

"Because, Juve?"

The police officer looked his companion frankly in the eyes:

"Because," he spoke gravely, "because if Fantômas is dead—dead like ourselves… well, I am afraid, I tell you! Oh, with you, I don't try to hide my thoughts, not I!"

And truly, was he not justified in his fears? The mere suspicion that Fantômas might appear again alive and terrifying was a sinister omen. Juve had shuddered, Fandor was biting his lips till the blood came.

"Juve," resumed the journalist, "first and foremost we must understand… conjecture… find out…"

"What?"

"How we can be alive again!"

"Oh, that, that is not impossible. It is not even difficult… Now, listen, Fandor. Remember, I assert nothing—I only suppose, I frame a hypothesis… Well then, the *Gigantic* went down…"

"Ten years ago!"

"Yes, ten years ago! The *Gigantic* went down and we, you and I, lost consciousness… we thought we died. Now grant me this: once unconscious, we might, you and I, have been picked up, eh?"

"Who by, Juve?"

"By a steamer?… by an airplane, if you prefer?… Fantômas was aboard the *Gigantic.* Is it inconceivable that he had prepared the catastrophe, brought about the shipwreck—and called rescuers to the spot?"

"No, Juve, no!… But go on."

"Well, then we are saved by his confederates… Now, have you thought of this, how a patient under chloroform remains to all appearance dead all the time he lies asleep? And this lasts hours. And, if he is fed, even mechanically by forced feeding, is there anything to hinder its lasting days?… weeks?… years?"

"So you believe…"

"I believe nothing; I suppose… Another thing, Fandor, do you know that without recourse to chloroform, simply by pressure exerted on certain nerve centers, doctors have in some instances put patients to sleep? Have you never heard of the case of the dervishes in India who go on for months in a sleeping state, to all appearance dead? Need I remind you of the case of 'famous sleepers,'—the sleeping woman of Thonelle, who awakened twenty years after she had gone to sleep? and who had no remembrance whatever of having been asleep?…"

"But then, Juve, you think it possible…"

"Listen, I think it possible that Fantômas was able to rescue us; possible that, having us at his discretion, he was able to keep us in a state of sleep as long as he wanted; possible that eventually he had us deposited on the roof where we woke up…"

"But Fantômas hates us. He would have killed us a hundred times over!"

"But if he had need of us? of our lives?"

Fandor vouchsafed no reply. His mind revolted at the idea. The thought that Fantômas had held him for ten long years at his mercy exasperated his nerves. Moreover Juve's last words, words the police officer had uttered in an agitated voice, froze him with dread. If Fantômas had saved them, if for ten years running, by some devilish contrivance or other he had thrown them into one of those dreamless sleeps which the learned instance as having occurred at long intervals, if in the end he had suffered them to awake there, at Marseilles, was it not certain he was pursuing some appalling aim? The young man shut his eyes. He was as intrepid as Juve, no personal peril could unman him; but he recoiled before the atrocious horror of this threat— Fantômas free, alive, resuscitated, ready to renew the struggle, to reopen the black list of his crimes!

"Juve, Juve!" stammered the journalist, "your coolness is beyond me!… If Fantômas is alive, *I too* am mortally afraid!"

But now Juve shook his head in mockery:

"Afraid? We are afraid? A fine thing that! Come, come, there is no time for fear! If Fantômas is alive and safe we must track him down, capture him, drag him to the scaffold… that and nothing else! There has been a truce; now the fight starts afresh. Forward to the fray!"

Juve stood up. He was very calm now. Everything appeared to him so certain.

Meantime, Fandor, still on his bench, had picked up again the stolen paper and was rereading the article devoted to the Paris mysteries.

"Granted, Juve," he remarked, "this hypothesis of a long sleep is plausible as regards us—you and me. But it would offer no explanation of the reappearance of this Mlle. de Vautreuil. And the dog? A vet certified its death… Then again, Henri Tardoux is Marsouval's demonstrator—a man of science. He asserts these facts, and *he's* no charlatan surely!"

"My dear boy, I said nothing about that. I supply a solution of our own case, nothing more. As for Mlle. Eléonore's case, I said the word *'Fantômas'*; it is a line of inquiry to follow up…"

"Forward, then! You are right, Juve!"

"Forward! yes, forward's the word, Fandor!"

But the journalist had not yet left his seat when he broke into an oath:

"God's truth! Juve, but it's Paris we must make for!"

"Why, certainly! Where's the difficulty?"

"And the cash, Juve? and the tickets to take?"

"Bah! they'll help us."

"Who?"

"I'll go to the Prefecture and make myself known."

"And they'll tell you you're dead! And they'll lock you up, for sure! Have you anything better to propose?"

"Perhaps… Yes!"

"What's your plan?"

An ironic smile flitted across Fandor's lips:

"Juve, my dear good Juve, I don't know you now! What the devil is come of your cogent logic, your sagacity, your subtlety, your detestable character in a word?"

And while Juve shrugged his shoulders impatiently, half-vexed at his companion's banter, Fandor continued:

"My turn now to call in common sense to the rescue! Good Lord! Juve, you mean to make yourself known?"

"Undoubtedly."

"To proclaim you are alive?"

"Why not?"

"Because it is playing the enemy's game, Juve! Yes, just that!"

Then, without giving the other time to protest, Fandor went on explaining:

"Fantômas made us pass for dead? Very good! Suddenly he restores us to life. Tell me, man, doesn't that prove that our lives have become necessary for his purposes?"

"Why, yes!… But…"

"There's no 'but,' Juve! If Fantômas brings us back to life, *my* idea is we should die again. That's the best way to balk his projects, the best way to upset his plans. Then, once well dead, there'll be nobody to plague us, if I may say so. We shall be free—free as shadows! You don't think my notion a good one?"

"I do think this, you're no fool, my boy! Only, if we stay dead, how about the financial question? Credit's not given to the departed, eh?"

"Quite true… but I have another idea…"

"Another?"

"Yes, another! Juve, just give me a couple of minutes to think. Either we shall have earned good money between now and this evening, or I don't know my own trade."

Meantime, resuming his perusal of the "daily," Fandor with puckered brows busied himself in examining the news of the day.

"At the Prefecture, Juve, you see for yourself," he explained, "they'll ask you a heap of dangerous questions. Not so in a newspaper office. It is not the custom there to interview the fellows who supply a bit of interesting copy. Well, by God! it's only a matter of discovering the stuff to make a fine scoop for me to earn…"

But Fandor cut his sentence short.

"Gracious goodness!" he groaned, "just think what I'm reading!"

"What is it now?" quavered Juve.

"There's been a war! France and her allies have whipped Germany. Alsace-Lorraine is ours again!"

"You're dreaming, sir."

"No, sir, nothing of the kind. It all happened while we were dead! Oh! when a man comes back from the other world, it does strike him forcibly what an ignorant savage he is!"—and Fandor forced a laugh to hide the intensity of his feelings, the triumphant delight that thrilled him.

There had been a war. The country had taken its revenge for the ignominious defeat of 1870. The lost provinces were French once more. In a moment, proud satisfaction intoxicated Fandor like strong wine.

"War!" growled Juve the while. "Ah! suppose now it was because of the war that Fantômas has been shamming dead? Suppose he had a tragic part to play in this world drama?"

"We will discover that, Juve! We will search and find out… Pending that, I want stuff to make salable copy… Ah! listen here!"—and the young journalist's voice rang out loud and clear while he brandished his newspaper proudly in the air.

"*Arrivals and Departures in the Fashionable and Tourist Worlds…* At the Hôtel des Alliés I find the names of Monsieur Henri Tardoux, Mlle. Josette de Vautreuil… Juve, Juve old man, what say you to that? Without humbug, isn't that a stroke of luck, eh? You can guess what I'm going to do, can't you?"

"God! yes, you're going to interview these travelers?"

"Without a moment's hesitation."

"And then? You're not thinking of asking them to pay for our tickets?"

No, nor even for a breakfast, though my stomach's as hollow as a drum—it does give a man an appetite being dead!… Then, Juve, then I will sell my report to one of the daily papers."

"Without signing it, Fandor?"

"Yes, that is so."

"In that case your man will kick you out of doors as an impostor. He'll take you for an impostor right away. Do you suppose an editor who doesn't know you will listen to your revelations for two seconds?"

But Fandor only shrugged his shoulders with an air of mockery.

"What a peevish fellow this old Juve is!" he exclaimed with a covert grin. "Barely risen from the grave, he turns on his cynicism again! Deuce and all! now's the time to smile, man, and think nothing's impossible. Look here, Juve, I'll wager you they accept my copy."

"On the strength of your pretty looks?"

"On the strength of my headline."

"So you've got a headline?"

"A marvelous one! A headline to bowl over all the editors of all the papers in this world. This is it: 'Is Fantômas Resuscitated?'"

Though not a journalist and incapable like Fandor of appreciating all the value of a telling heading, still Juve nodded approval.

"Now," cried the young man, folding up the stolen paper from which he had extracted so much information all important to the two derelicts, "now, no more talk, Juve. To work now! We've played at being dead long enough… You'll wait for me here?"

"In front of the Bourse in two hours, if that suits you."

"Agreed,"—and pivoting on his heels, Fandor set off hotfoot in the direction of the Hôtel des Alliés. He had noticed its signboard as he and Juve first left the house on top of which they had awakened.

At that moment Fandor was happy and full of confidence. Doubtless he could easily guess how a fearful struggle was to begin afresh, how once again they must fight Fantômas—but the tragic prospect did not depress him. To run into danger, to affront peril, was this not in his eyes the very charm of life? To hunt down the notorious brigand, was this not the call of duty, his first and foremost duty?

And yet, as he made off, an eager, triumphant figure, Juve could not refrain from a shrug of the shoulders:

"The gallant fellow," he muttered to himself covertly, "always the same! The devil's own energy, and not a bit of prudence! He's mighty proud of his discovery that we ought not to reveal our resurrections. A fine game that! Am I not bound, first thing, to put myself in touch with the Investigation Department? Am I not out to gather all the information possible to help me fathom Fantômas' plans—short of asking him to tell me his secrets as a favor?"

Without more hesitation Juve, his comrade once out of sight, hurried away towards the Offices of the Criminal Investigation Department, which at Marseilles, as at all seaports, was a highly important institution.

All the same, Juve would have been very surprised, no doubt, if at that moment he could have known the nature of the journalist's lucubrations…

"Good old Juve," the young man was telling himself with a smile, "surely he's not his own man yet… Not make ourselves known? A first-class ticket that! But, just the other way round, I'm going to make a point of telling my name… Anyway, if Fantômas is plotting vengeance against us, it is I he'll attack in the first place. Thus Juve will have a respite for a bit. That's all that's needed,"—and once more in Jerome Fandor's eyes there gleamed a lightning flash of steadfast determination and unbounded energy.

"The fact is," resumed Fandor, "reasonable as are Juve's suppositions, there is no proof that they are really justified… Is Fantômas alive? Does he know we are safe and sound? Was it he who dumped us like inconvenient bales of goods on the roof there? Mystery, always mystery!"

Mysteries which Jerome Fandor was still far from having fathomed when he reached the door of the Hôtel des Alliés.

Most people would have gone in there and then, but Fandor first slowed down his pace, then strolled by, casting curious glances into the interior of the building.

"Let us show our strategy," he muttered. "Let's study the ground. After all, this hotel is damned near the roof where Juve and I came to life again… Is that a coincidence? is it an accident—done on purpose?"

But pass up and down as he might twice over before the main door of the Hôtel des Alliés, he noticed nothing that struck him as interesting. The entrance hall was almost deserted. In one corner the liftboy was teasing a kitten. Back to the wall, the porter in a gold-laced uniform was reading a newspaper, looking half asleep. Outside the door a waiter was polishing the brass label of a mailbox, while a few steps away, a cripple, a hunchback, who appeared to be a paralytic as well, was sorting out a whole collection of postcards, plans and guides to Marseilles in the little handcart in which he sat huddled up.

"Peace, perfect peace!" approved Fandor. "Let's venture in!"—and he made a step forward.

Alas! as the journalist was on the point of crossing the threshold, he was to learn to his cost how hard it is to preserve an incognito for a man who at one and the same time is dead, alive, and famous! The eyes of the paralytic had hardly met his before the cripple turned pale:

"Mercy on us!… Why it's… it's…"

Beside him the waiter threw up his arms to heaven. "The dead man!" he yelled… "the dead man in the paper!"

Much annoyed at this fashion of announcing him adopted by the hotel servant, whose amazement and consternation were indeed quite comprehensible, Fandor could not check a grimace expressive of anything but satisfaction. He had never craved notoriety, or even fame, and without a doubt this quasi-posthumous celebrity was infinitely disagreeable to him. To make up one's mind to stay dead and then to hear one's resurrection proclaimed in a sounding voice was vexing to a degree. Stopping dead, the journalist protested:

"Hush, man! hold your tongue. Have you gone mad? Are you speaking of me?"

But denial was all in vain. Scared and trembling, the porter now ran up, waving the paper he had been reading, on the front page of which the young man's portrait was displayed, surrounded by a deep black border. The resemblance was perfect, there was no denying it!

"Jerome Fandor! Jerome Fandor!" stammered the man. "It is you for sure!… It is…"

"It is idiotic!" the journalist broke in. "I am not I!… There! you understand? that's plain enough, I suppose?… So now tell them to show me up to M. Henri Tardoux or Mlle. Josette de Vautreuil. That's all I ask you." But Jerome Fandor was pursued by ill-luck. Scarcely had he uttered his protest, and a poor one at that, before another cry rang through the entrance hall.

"It *is* he," a man's voice declared, "Jerome Fandor! No, I was not dreaming, I was sure of it. Josette, you see that, don't you?..."

The journalist turned, and next instant a young man and a girl, issuing from the lift, made a rush towards him. Now Fandor's face wreathed itself in smiles. He bowed, hat in hand, as he asked:

"Monsieur Tardoux, no doubt?... Mademoiselle de Vautreuil? May I beg the favor of five minutes' conversation?"

Thereupon, in the small salon into which Henri Tardoux and Josette led the journalist, followed a bewildering scene of incoherence and confusion.

"They told me I had been dreaming!" declared Tardoux, "and I almost believed I had... I saw you two on the roof... But the paper said you were dead... but the whole world..."

"Oh! let's leave the world out, Monsieur Tardoux. The world is very ill-informed. Besides, I've not come to see you to talk about my own doings. No, it is Mlle. de Vautreuil I wish to speak to you about."

However, it called for all Fandor's talents as an interviewer to induce Henri Tardoux and Josette to tell him the facts of the Auteuil episode. Startled as they were to discover that Fandor was alive, the two fiancés would only too gladly have changed places and overwhelmed the journalist with questions.

"Look here," Fandor besought him, "we will discuss all that presently, shall we? For the moment only one point is urgent... Is it a fact that Mlle. Eléonore is in Paris?"

"Certainly!"

"In that case she never left her brother's roof?"

"But she did!"

"Yet if she is on the sea, she cannot be at the same time at Passy."

Nervous and embarrassed, Henri Tardoux could only shrug his shoulders.

"Sir," he retorted, "I could quote your own example to prove that the impossible is sometimes possible!… I doubt, though, if you caused yourself to be taken for dead voluntarily?"

"That is so."

"As likewise Juve, the police officer… Well, the case is different for Mlle. Eléonore, just as for my friend Rippert's dog. No trickery can be imagined. But listen to the whole story,"—and concisely, though clearly, Henri Tardoux related the facts as they had occurred, ending up: "Well then, that's all… Oh! just one word more—Jerome Fandor's questions I have been willing to answer, but I beg of you not to let this amazing story go further. Mlle. de Vautreuil, my fiancée, has been, is still indeed, seriously upset by the thing, so I would rather…"

But the other was not listening—he was thinking:

"Yes, Juve was right, this case of Mlle. Eléonore, as also that of the dog, bear no resemblance to our own…" Aloud he remarked:

"One thing is certain; the lady is now in Paris… Therefore I say she has never left off being there, for it is impossible to be in two places at the same time…"

"But it is, by God! there are the facts for you!"

"No, in the Devil's name! The facts are false!"

"Monsieur Fandor, I assure you solemnly Mlle. Eléonore is on the high seas…"

"Monsieur Tardoux, you believe what you say, I know, but believe me, it is silly to say anyone can be on the seas *and* in Paris!"

The two men were getting warm. Fortunately Josette intervened:

"Henri! Monsieur Fandor!" she besought them, "I cannot bear this disputing!" adding with a smile: "Monsieur Fandor, is there anything else you wish to know?"

But now the journalist was angry with himself for his sudden loss of temper. His nerves must indeed have been on edge to make him so far forget himself!

With a look Fandor asked the girl to excuse his heat. "You are right, Mademoiselle," he admitted. "I had no business to contradict the gentleman the way I did… What would you have?

The whole affair is one to make us all lose our heads… Just tell me this—before, hmm… before your good aunt's return, had nothing particular attracted your notice? Had nothing out of the common occurred at home?"

"No," replied Henri Tardoux.

"But yes," Josette contradicted flatly—and paying no heed to the black looks her fiancé gave her, the girl related how an extraordinary inscription had been traced on the panel of a door.

"Of course this has no connection with my aunt's reappearance, but still…"

"But, Mademoiselle, on the contrary it explains everything! I beg and beseech you, one detail more. The insurance agent your father saw, has he been found?"

"No, Monsieur. The insurance company has failed to identify him."

"Then he was the culprit?"

"Certainly not. The insurance policy he brought my father was just the regulation policy. If the agent has not been found, this simply means it must have been a case of one employee taking over another's duty to oblige him, and this being forbidden, the former naturally refused to incriminate himself."

"Naturally? You think such conduct natural?… But no matter… About the inscription itself? What ink was it written with? You are a chemist, Monsieur Tardoux; have you analyzed the impress?"

"No, no!… I never thought of it."

"Never thought of it!"

"What use would it have been?"

"This use, if the ink had been copying ink, I should have said the insurance man carried, glued on his boot, a rubber pad smeared with glutinous ink, and that it was with this pad that, standing up all the while and talking to Monsieur de Vautreuil, he stamped in the writing without seeming to do so. A petty, obvious trick, eh? Quite simple—as the man never stooped, it was pretty certain M. de Vautreuil would stick to it he was innocent!"

"But you would make the fellow out to be a criminal. In that case he could not have produced the genuine policy, could he?"

"Why not? Come, come, this is just childishness! Yes, the man was a criminal. Seeing that the thing was well worth trying, he had made his preparations… A difficult job truly to get taken on in an insurance office, then to supply a colleague's place and say nothing about it afterwards. Never fear, the fellow would prove the best of employees! I'll even bet he didn't resign his post right away! No, not such a fool! No doubt, he stuck on a fortnight or so and then bolted!"

With which, giving a savage frown, Fandor made his bow, turned on his heel and exit, tossing back a curt "good day to you!" As he recrossed the entrance hall, he growled up:

"Charming girl, that Josette de Vautreuil! But her fiancé, is he a knave or a fool? that's the only question… As for my article, my headline's to be modified—instead of *Is Fantômas Resuscitated?* it'll read *Fantômas Is Resuscitated!* So there you have it!" Had he then guessed the truth?

Suddenly he started violently. Behind him a man's voice hailed him by name.

"Ah! now who else has recognized me?" thought Fandor wheeling round, only to stop dead in sheer amazement. The man who had called after him was the paralytic!

Propelling the box on wheels that served him as a vehicle with a will, the cripple was making good running down the slope of the Avenue and had quickly caught up the journalist.

"What do you want?" Fandor asked him.

"To get you to touch my hump! They say it brings good luck… But no, must be serious. I was to give you a message."

"What message?"

"The gentleman would like to speak to you…"

"The gentleman?"

"Yes, the young man you've just parted from. He told me to overtake you and explain to you how he could not well answer your questions before his fiancée, but that he was waiting to see you now… My! but he looked worried!"

"Why didn't he try to catch up with me himself?" muttered Fandor, involuntarily thinking out loud. "Henri Tardoux's proceedings were in no way strange in themselves; the only surprising point was that he should have commissioned an intermediary…"

"Wait!" the paralytic went on, "that's not all. So that the young lady will not see you talking together, the young man has hidden. But I know where, and I'll show you the way there."

"So be it, off we go!"

## 4. The Man Who Refused to Come to Life Again

Fandor's brow cleared. The last detail he had just learned explained many things to him and let him guess many more. Henri Tardoux must have had grave reasons for hiding from Josette the interview he asked for. It was therefore quite natural he should have sent a message to Fandor instead of joining him in the street for fear of being seen.

"What the devil is he going to tell me, or confess to me?" Fandor asked himself—and with a purely instinctive gesture he clapped his hand to his pocket, where all his lifelong he had carried a revolver. Alas! the pocket was empty.

"Annoying!" muttered the journalist. "But, I still have my fists… one man's as good as another. And then, I am all wrong perhaps?"

The hunchback was hurrying on in front. Instead of entering the hotel, he hurried past the main door and turned to the left into a side alley:

"This way, sir, if you please. The young man is hiding over there…" Stopping in front of a low-browed door, the paralytic asked Fandor:

"Will you open the door? The handle is too high up for me."

"Here you are!" assented Fandor… and then he gave a yell. As the door opened, the cripple gave him a violent push that sent him flying forward, to find nothing beneath his feet. The door gave on a deep cellar. It was dark as pitch and was used probably for storing the hotel comestibles.

Fandor pitched over headlong and crashed on the stone floor. But two seconds more and he was up again and on his feet. Bleeding, bruised, almost stunned, the young man explored the darkness with haggard eyes.

"Nothing!" he groaned, "and nobody!" In fact, he could see nothing and hear nothing. Be sure his heart beat furiously in his breast, but never a qualm of fear! It was an attempt on his life, a dastardly attempt, but he was well used to such eventualities. Quick as lightning Fandor reflected:

"Should I shout for help? No, not a doubt of it, precautions must have been taken. I would not be heard… Best wait!" But Jerome Fandor had to wait, to remain there motionless, searching the night. Seconds passed that seemed interminable. Then the gloom seemed to grow less dense, the darkness less complete. A vague glimmer of diffused light modified the blackness. His eyes perhaps were adapting themselves, the pupils dilating.

But suddenly the young man started back, an exclamation of surprise escaping him. Crude, startling, half-blinding him, a shaft of light had shot forth, the dazzling beam from a projection. It came from one corner of the cellar and its rays were concentrated on a single point. And there was nothing at that particular spot—nothing but a chest half full of a kind of coarse, black powder. In his surprise, Jerome had fallen back a pace, but next instant he repented this rearward step, resolved to advance and commenced to do so. But the unhappy man was not to complete that first step. In the full blaze of the light, with a tigerish bound, a human form, the outline of a man, had sprung into view.

Then indeed Jerome Fandor felt his heart stop dead, while he clenched his fists in mad anger… He had recognized at first glance that outline, that mysterious, tragic, appalling figure. He could give it a name. The man before his eyes he knew instantly to be none other than the Genius of Evil, all daring, all powerful, truly entitled the Lord of Terror.

"Fantômas! Fantômas!" stammered Fandor, his eyes riveted on the apparition. Completely clad in black silk tights that molded his body from head to foot, that shrouded him in darkness, that confounded him with the night, his face concealed by a mask from which only shot the fierce flame of his burning eyes, the man formed a picture baffling description. How to know him again, once his black envelope was stripped off, his mask removed?

"Fantômas! Fantômas!" reiterated Fandor. He never hesitated to give the wretch his name, the monster whose staring eyes fascinated his gaze. Had he not seen the same form many times rise thus before him, at once mysterious and recognizable?

And at the same time as horror-struck his lips articulated the dreaded name, Fandor was asking himself:

"He? Is it indeed he? Is he come to life again? Is this possible?"

Alas! he had no time left him to think… As if he had read in the journalist's face the thoughts that whirled through his brain, as if he guessed that, his surprise abated, Fandor was going to act, the Man in Black in a toneless, expressionless voice, disguised and coldly mocking, broke the grim silence:

"Jerome Fandor, good day!" he began scornfully. "Is it your good pleasure we converse?"

Then with a swift gesture he pointed, and went on, his tone brief and peremptory:

"Look! Do you understand? One rash act and five hundred innocent souls perish; the hotel blows up!"

Already Fandor was crouched to spring. Heeding only his gallant impulse, he was on the point of leaping at his enemy's throat and engaging him in a struggle to the death. But the vile creature's words nailed him to the spot. The Man in Black was stooping. In his hand, waving towards the brown powder in the chest at his feet, flickered a tiny flame.

"Gunpowder!" he announced. "Dare to move, to take one step, and I swear I will set it alight."

What could Fandor do? Despicable as Fantômas was, he was no coward, fear had never yet checked his plans.

"He will fulfill his threat!" thought Fandor, his mind sick with anguish. "The hotel is full of travelers and servants… What must I do?" He was a brave man and he longed to risk all. He would die, and others with him, yes, but Fantômas would perish along with them…

Yet Jerome Fandor never stirred… Fantômas? but was it really Fantômas who stood there? The Master Thief having dis- appeared, might not another criminal have had the monstrous audacity to claim the heirship to his villainy, to claim the inheritance of his sinister fame, of his grim record of weeping and mourning and gnashing of teeth?

Fantômas?… Ah! if it was Fantômas, Jerome Fandor's duty perhaps was to defeat him at all costs, to sacrifice the wretch who would perish in the explosion… To spare him, to let him live, was it to precipitate countless other catastrophes, to involve yet more victims? But yet, *was* it Fantômas? Beneath that mask and that black envelope *who* was hidden?

Still motionless, Fandor suddenly screamed:

"If I am to spare you today, I will meet you again tomorrow! Curses on your head, Fantômas!"

Imperiously the brigand interrupted:

"Do not talk foolishness, Fandor… I am not Fantômas…"

"You are not?…"

"Hush! No, I am not Fantômas, I cannot be Fantômas… Fantômas is dead!"

"Where is the proof?"

"Everyone says so…"

"The same was said of me and of Juve."

"Yes, but Juve and Fandor will certify the death of Fantômas—and the world will believe them!"

"It is an order?"

"An order!"—and uttering each word singly with startling emphasis, the Man in Black pronounced:

"Juve and Fandor are alive. Juve and Fandor will know that unprecedented events are occurring. Juve and Fandor will inevitably hear how Fantômas is recalled to life… I demand that Juve and Fandor certify, affirm, proclaim that Fantômas is dead! They will say this, and men will believe them. They must make men believe. They must do this… for, if they are not believed…"

"If they are not believed?"

"I will avenge myself on them!"

"They do not fear you!"

"Then they shall die!"—and the Man in Black went on in the same measured tones:

"Peace or war! Juve and Fandor can take their choice. Peace, if they confirm Fantômas' death…"

"Never!"

"War, if they speak out…"

*　　*　　*　　*　　*

The Man in Black had uttered these final words in a tone of implacable resolution, but it did not appear as though Fandor was impressed thereby. He answered:

"The choice is made. It will be war!"

But hardly had he pronounced the words of defiance when a peal of laughter escaped the other and a sudden darkness took the place of the blinding light of the projector. Fandor had sprung forward instantly, but he grasped only empty space! The Man in Black, familiar with his surroundings, had easily escaped.

The Man in Black?… Fantômas?… No, Fandor doubted no longer. He was convinced he had just encountered the terrible brigand. Could he be deceiving himself?

Groping round, at last he discovered a door, left the cellar and, wandering by devious passages, reached a stairway, which he mounted. Five minutes after, coming out into the courtyard of the hotel, Jerome Fandor found himself the center of a group of scullions idling there, who stared at him inquisitively, evidently surprised at the sight of his torn clothes and disheveled appearance.

"Ah, Monsieur," cried one of these young rascals, "look, somebody's pinned a paper on your back." This Fandor snatched off and scrutinized, panting with excitement. It was entirely blank—at first… Then, little by little, in the daylight, by slow degrees it showed sundry black marks. A second or two more and Fandor deciphered a word written in sympathetic ink now coming out. One word only, but a word of stern defiance, of grave import, of promise and of menace, a word that well summed up the full audacity of a desperate criminal, the word ULTIMATUM!

But no sooner had the young man cast his eyes on the message than he broke into a roar of laughter, shrugging his shoulders scornfully. He was a man ever ready to confront the most fearful danger, to accept the most daunting wagers of battle, but not one invariably scrupulous to observe the conventions of polished speech. For reply to this "ultimatum" addressed to him, the journalist too on his side found a final word to sum up all his thoughts as adequately, as comprehensively, as the one the man he called Fantômas had used to express *his* mind:

"Swine!" said Fandor, and that was all.

Then, calm as if he had not just engaged in a first skirmish with the Lord of Terror, he walked out of the Hôtel des Alliés to rejoin Juve and hold council with his ally, and this done, to sit down and write his "copy," that was to supply the indispensable sinews of war.

However, Jerome Fandor was not destined to meet Juve quite so soon as he had hoped!

## 5. Juve Is His Own Man

While the journalist was prosecuting his investigation, Juve had made his way to the offices of the Marseilles Criminal Department.

"They'll pull a fine face, the fellows at the 'shop,'" he was thinking, "when I send in my card to the Chief. Good! All the same they'll not be a bit more surprised to see me alive than I am myself not to be dead!"

After five minutes' quick walking Juve reached the official headquarters, mounted to the second story and entered the anteroom leading to the private office of the Inspector-in-Chief. In this outer room an usher was dozing, who, hearing the newcomer's footsteps, started up, rubbing his eyes, and addressed him in the peevish voice of a man unexpectedly disturbed:

"Where are you going?… Who do you want to see?"

"I would like," answered Juve, "to speak to the Inspector-in-Chief… He is in his room?"

"Don't know!… You have an appointment?"

"No!"

"Then make a proper request… write… or see the Inspector on duty…"

"My good man," insisted Juve amiably, "I have business with the Inspector-in-Chief… Take my name in to him… I think he will see me."

As he spoke he picked up a visiting form lying on the usher's desk and wrote down his name on it.

"There, my fine fellow," he thought to himself, as he handed the paper to the other. "You're going to have the surprise of your life when you see who I am!"

The man simply read what was written and got up slowly from his seat.

"Juve?" he remarked. "Oh! it's you, Juve? Should have said

so!… The Chief's expecting you… I'll go and tell him,"—and he went up and knocked at the door, without seeming to suspect that it was Juve who had jumped with surprise at his words, so utterly dumbfounded as to doubt the evidence of his ears. What! his resurrection did not strike this underling with amazement? What! he was "expected"?

"I was ready for anything," thought Juve, "but not for this!"

His reflections, however, were quickly interrupted. After a momentary disappearance in the adjoining office, the usher came back, leaving the door open.

"You can go in, sir!" he said.

Juve stepped forward. Inside the room the Chief Inspector was seated behind a monumental desk, busy signing a pile of letters without so much as lifting his head, like one who attaches little importance to the visit he is receiving.

"Good day, M. Juve," he said casually. "Please, come in… No doubt you didn't come yesterday… There, I'm at your service… Oh! have no fear. I've kept my word. No trap is laid for you… I am all alone!"

Instinctively Juve bent his brows at this, while he scrutinized the room with looks of suspicion. He knew the habits of certain of his colleagues too well not to believe just the opposite of anything they told him. His host professed to be all alone? Then where had he hidden his men?

"I congratulate you!" resumed the Chief Inspector. "You've put on poor Juve's face to a nicety—fit to deceive anybody… However, let's come to business. Who are you, and what do you want? Let's play an open game, eh?"

Juve was more and more bewildered. He was too cool a customer, however, to lose his head, even on an occasion like this.

"My dear colleague," he replied amiably, "may I ask you in the first place why you congratulate me? I am not over and above clear as to that, I can assure you… I've put on Juve's face, you say? The queer thing would have been if I'd done the opposite. I have 'put on' my own face, thank you! And why? because it is my own face, by God! I *am* Juve…"

"Come, come!"

"Excuse me, but I must insist. I am Juve, and I know nothing whatever about a missed appointment yesterday."

"But you asked me to grant you an interview."

"I? Never!"

"Very good, very good! Now listen, let's not waste time… You refuse your name? As you please. Only, let me inform you once and for all that I am not your dupe. Juve, the real Juve, the great Juve in a word, has been dead these past ten years… Therefore…"

"You are mistaken. Juve is alive. I am Juve."

"The obstinacy of the man! You want to see me angry?… No, no, never fear, don't be alarmed. Come, better look at this map. There, there you have the banks of Newfoundland—and that's where Juve died, in 1911, along with Fandor and Fantômas… Besides, just read today's paper. There, can't you see it's not worth your while to pretend you are Juve? Damn it all! Let's talk like men of common sense!"—and getting up and slapping his visitor familiarly on the shoulder, the Chief Inspector continued:

"You're a joker, eh? Now mind you the police are not the people to talk balderdash to?"

By this time, in spite of himself, Juve was getting a trifle ruffled.

"My good colleague," he snapped, "talking of balderdash, give me the proofs that Juve, Fandor and Fantômas are dead."

"The proofs?"

"Yes. Were their bodies ever found?"

"Fandor's, no!"

"But Juve's? Fantômas'?"

"Why, you must know that! Yes, *their* bodies were found."

"When?… and by what were they recognized?"

"Come, you're going too far, you know! My patience has its limits… Fantômas was known by his wearing his black tights; Juve, by papers he carried in his pockets. The bodies were picked up by an American liner."

"The heads were there?"

"But…"

"My dear sir, examine the archives… For my part, I strongly suspect these bodies were headless. You will see how in that case all the supposed identification was deceptive? The bodies recovered were faked—that's all there is to it! To dress up a dead man in black and stuff papers in the other's pockets, why, it's just child's play."

"And that proves you are Juve, does it? If you are Juve, what the devil has become of you since 1911? There, my fine fellow, explain that, will you? How did you escape in the shipwreck? How…"

"I know nothing about it!"

"Really! Then, in that case, you came to life again yesterday?"

"This morning!"

"On purpose to come here? Well, you must suppose me a born fool! And this resurrection, by what miracle was it worked? Explain!"

"How do *you* explain the Paris incident, my worthy colleague? It's not possible to explain every mortal thing on earth!"

"Excellent! I was waiting for that! But since you are Juve, the real Juve, *you* can fathom the mystery, I suppose? Juve cannot be nonplussed, seems to me? Go on, I'm all attention!"

The official was enjoying his bout of banter. Juve got up:

"As a fact, I can explain everything—and in one word—Fantômas is at work!"

"He is not dead?"

"No more dead than Fandor, or myself! However, that's not the question…"

"And what *is* the question?"

"My dear sir, I came here simply to make myself known, to establish the fact of my resurrection and, before going on to Paris…"

"To ask for assistance, I take it?"

"Precisely!"

"Well, my good fellow, you are going a bit too fast, as they say. There's just one thing missing in your little story—and that is one scrap of probability. Now a piece of advice; take it to heart. If in five minutes from now you haven't altered your tone and attitude…"

"If, that is, I haven't admitted I am not Juve?…"

"Exactly!… And I do beg you to drop joking."

"You'll have me guillotined, eh?"

"I'll have you locked up… You understand?"

"Perfectly."

"Then, make up your mind! Who are you? What do you want?"

"Beg pardon! One other detail: you refuse to hear me any more? You refuse to verify in what condition they profess to have found the dead bodies of Juve and Fantômas?"

"Oh, ho! You're cross-examining me?…"

"And you refuse to inform me under what circumstances you have been in communication with an individual other than myself who gives himself out to be Juve?"

"Yes, I refuse. Please understand this has ceased to be a laughing matter."

This last threat was readily explainable. Fully persuaded he had to do with an impostor, genuinely convinced that Juve, the great Juve, had died ten years before, the Inspector-in-Chief was driven to the immediate conclusion that he had at last triumphed over his troublesome visitor.

Juve, as though overwhelmed, had sunk into an armchair and sat covering his face between his hands, for all the world as if he could not tell what countenance to assume.

"You understand it is high time to stop your jokes?" again asked the Inspector-in-Chief. "Answer!"

Juve's answer was short and sharp:

"No, it is high time for me to act,"—and he acted there and then with disconcerting rapidity. Springing up, he drew his hands from before his face—and leapt upon his colleague.

The Inspector-in-Chief had had no time to put up a defense before he received a terrific punch on the jaw. Like a lump, without a cry, the official crashed to the floor. Never had a boxer in a great match been more quickly and more decisively knocked out! The man lay unconscious while Juve straightened himself and, shrugging his shoulders, adjusted his necktie, which was a trifle out of place.

"So there," he told himself plainly, "Jerome Fandor, madcap as you deem him, has seen clearer and judged more correctly than 'the great Juve,' as men call him. What a lesson in modesty!" Laughing quietly to himself, he continued his soliloquy with all the tranquillity of a person who is in no sort of hurry, and who feels no vestige of uneasiness.

"Never mind, I find Death has not stiffened my joints too much! Certainly I have put on flesh a little and must go in for a bit of exercise to get my form back. But all the same, there's not much to complain of! My word, but it did me good to touch him off so prettily, that dunce! It was like the Juve of former days, that was!… Yes, I am my own man again!"

He laughed again, well pleased with himself, then went on with his soliloquy:

"Of course, to fell an Inspector-in-Chief is not quite the proper thing… But, but what else could I have done? The fact is I was going to be mixed up in a silly business. I would never have gotten this high and mighty official to admit that I had allowed myself to come alive again. My word! I have done the right thing in closing the incident!"

"Now another thing!" he interrupted his reflections. "I should like a trifle of money… Hmm, I'm sorry to have to steal it. But there, all's fair in love and war. If Fandor were with me in this little job, he'd make fine fun of my scruples." However, Juve's own scruples cannot have been very terrible, for soon he was carrying out his project. Without the smallest shame he went through the unconscious man's pockets and took possession of his purse and pocketbook.

"The main point," he went on, "is to know if I shall find a sufficient sum… Oh! ho! hardly a millionaire my fine friend! Twenty-seven francs in his purse—and paper francs! I won't get very far with that… Unless the pocketbook's got a surprise packet in it for…"

But Juve never finished his sentence… Such was the perfection of his training as a detective that, without his ever giving it a thought, his senses were always on the alert. If now he gave a sudden start, it was because, in spite of the heavily padded doors of the working room he was in, Juve had just caught a sentence spoken in the adjoining antechamber.

"For the Chief," he heard the voice of the man on duty saying, "very good, I'll take it in…" and footsteps approached.

The police officer pulled a wry face.

"Good Lord!" he muttered, "if that fellow comes in, if he sees the state the Chief's in, goodbye to my little plans!"

"But how stop the man from entering the room? For all his cleverness Juve was bound to confess he saw no possibility of evading the hideous dilemma he was in. Where could he hide the body of the Chief? With his keen eyes he searched every corner. How often, in circumstances as grave, had he not in the last rapid survey seen something hitherto overlooked that was the means of his salvation?

Alas! this working room was deplorably empty. A bookcase, a file, a chair or two, a desk, an armchair, formed the whole furniture of the place.

"In two seconds I am caught!" Juve muttered to himself. But two seconds were amply sufficient for this prince of detectives. Never yet had he taken longer to surmount the worst predicament! At the very instant the usher laid his hand on the latch of the first of the heavy doors, Juve took his decision.

"The simplest measures are often the best," he told himself. "Let's shove our man under the desk… and face it out!"

Grasping the Chief Inspector by the shoulders and sliding him along the polished floor, Juve dragged him beneath the big desk.

"The feet stick out!" he noticed. "No matter. I'll hide them."

The usher entered and at the first glance saw Juve. The latter was seated in a great leather armchair right in front of the piece of furniture under which his victim lay.

Never so much as turning his head, with a slow and perfectly natural-looking movement that an actor of genius would hardly have ventured on, he let his right hand fall in such a way as to drag over the accusing feet a newspaper he had picked up from a rack and hastily opened. Without his voice betraying the least agitation Juve now remarked, pretending he had made a mistake:

"Back already, sir? You haven't been long!"

Then turning round to look, he corrected:

"Oh! I beg pardon! I thought it was…"

"The Chief?" said the usher. "He's not here then?" The worthy man had only to take another step and he would have seen his master!

But Juve never turned a hair. "Double or nothing!" he thought to himself. "Victory is the prize!"

He answered, still in a quiet voice and suppressing a yawn:

"He's just gone out."

"Gone out! which way? I've never left the anteroom…"

"My word!" declared Juve, "I never noticed which way he went out… that way, I think."

"By the door? It's bricked up!"

"By some other then…"

"There is no other!"

Juve felt a suspicious look fixed on him. He yawned again, then speaking more quickly than ever:

"Why, then you must have left your post or been asleep, if you didn't see him!"—and yawning for the third time fit to dislocate his jaw, he added:

"He's coming back shortly anyway. If anyone asks to see him, you can say he'll be at liberty soon. I have only a couple of minutes more to end my business with him."

A critical moment! The man seemed uncertain what to do. Suddenly he announced:

"It's for a dispatch by pneumatic which has just come… Here it is. I'll tell him when he goes by again… Funny all the same I didn't see him when he went out."

No answer was needed, and Juve took good care to make none. While the fellow was making for the door, after depositing the dispatch on the desk, Juve slowly raised his paper again as if to resume his interrupted reading. A moment later, however, he was far from preserving the same phlegmatic and nonchalant mien. The instant the door was closed, he was on his feet.

"In three minutes that idiot will raise the alarm. Very good! in three minutes I shall be far away! Now to empty the pocket-book. Capital! five hundred francs… Now time to be off!"

He was already halfway to the door when his eyes fell on the dispatch the attendant had brought in.

"Good heavens!" swore Juve. "The thing can't be! That writing?… Not a doubt of it, the detective had experienced a prodigious shock, for the man who just before had shown such calmness, was now trembling.

"Good heavens!" he repeated. "Yes! I must know for certain. I have a right to know, and it is my duty to know."

Even as he spoke he tore open the envelope and drew from it a sheet of flimsy covered over with minute writing.

"This beats everything! The thing's incredible, inconceivable! The colossal insolence of the wretch!"

Juve felt no scruple in reading the communication, a document so amazing in fact as to justify his curiosity in taking every means to satisfy itself. The contents read as follows:

TO THE INSPECTOR-IN-CHIEF:

Sir—In final reference to our previous communications, I have decided to put before you an ultimatum of sorts, and of the most unequivocal nature.

Circumstances indeed have led me to reveal in plain words a fact I have always hitherto concealed, to wit that I am a criminal. So now I can speak and act freely and I am taking advantage of this freedom.

Sir, you have for the past six months been the fortunate husband of a charming wife, a woman you positively adore. Happy marriages are few and far between, but yours has been one of them. Now weigh my words carefully.

Either you send, this very day before three o'clock, to me—I mean to the address I have given you—a sum of fifty thousand francs…

Or I will wreak on you the most drastic of reprisals;—with your own hand—mark what I say—with your own hand I will so contrive that you will murder your wife, the adorable Kate you love so fondly.

It is of course, needless, I imagine, for me to add that I am always serious in business dealings, and that my plans are always so carefully laid that nothing and nobody can hinder their realization.

Never attempt, therefore, when you send me the sum I demand, to set a trap for me. I am aware that is the first thought that will occur to you as a police official, but there is no trap wherein I can be caught. Nor yet attempt to protect your lady wife, or even merely to warn her.

I am one it is not good to play with, and I trust my name is sufficiently familiar to all the world to convince you that the best part for you to choose is once again to carry out the order I beg leave to give you. Submit, sir, submit with a good grace! And indeed, what are fifty thousand francs when it is a question of saving your wife's life, and sparing yourself the commission of a crime as dreadful as it is inevitable?

I rely with the utmost confidence on your common sense, and remain your very obedient servant.

Arrived at the last sentence of this astounding composition, Juve stood like a man turned to stone, petrified by amazement and, it was plain to see, by fury.

"By God!" he roared, "by the Lord God!… And it is signed, signed in full! The wretch has dared…"—but he could not finish. Generally speaking Juve was a quiet man, but this quietude, this apparent calm, really marked a fiery spirit. At times he had sudden outbursts of anger, more alarming by far than the everlasting outcries of weak, nervous natures.

As he prepared to leave, he added:

"After all, it is my fault, the Inspector-in-Chief, the addressee of this communication, is precluded from taking action; wherefore, in common fairness, it is incumbent on me to replace him. Oh! there can be no possible doubt about that. It is a question of moral obligation!"

He seemed beside himself, and his rage was not without some justification. The message he had just read and which he was carrying off with him was signed in a name and description that constituted a defiance of unparalleled insolence. It was signed: "Inspector Juve."

Such was the audacity of the thing, so convincing a proof

was it of consummate impudence, that Juve could hardly be mistaken as to the identity of the writer. Despite the use made of his own name, he felt no doubt of the true personality of the sender of the message he was stealing.

"Between us two now, Fantômas!" he thought. "The game has begun. The stakes are wagered. We shall see who is going to win!"

After opening the door, he half turned again and once more assuming a voice of the utmost calmness, he pretended to speak to someone still in the room:

"Very good, sir! You may depend on me."

Then he walked gravely past the usher, not without noticing again the way the latter looked at him askance. "Go on, my fine fellow!" Juve laughed to himself. "Have your suspicions, by all means! Give the alarm! You don't teach an old monkey to pull faces. I've run in too many folks in my time to let myself be nabbed!"

He was in the street two minutes later. Right before him was a clock over the door of a school. The hands marked three o'clock exactly.

"Damn!" swore Juve softly—and relaxing his pace, he sauntered nonchalantly away.

## 6. Proofs That Prove Nothing

Whether right or wrong in his suspicions regarding the identity of Fantômas with the Inspector-in-Chief's mysterious correspondent, Juve knew this much for certain, that the threatening letter he had intercepted included both true statements and false allegations. It was authentic, to begin with, that the Inspector-in-Chief, Juve's victim, was head over heels in love with his wife Kate, an English governess whom he had first met by chance, and who nowadays was not a little proud of having become an Inspector-in-Chief's lady. It was equally undoubted that the said official did not deem it possible that anybody better than his lovely Kate could be found in the world, and that, to save the latter the shadow of an annoyance, he would have thrown himself into the Seine, delighted to drown for the sake of the woman he loved!

Of a fair height and a putty brunette complexion—henna and peroxide, it may be, had something to do with the color of her hair—madame had fine eyes, a tiny mouth, a caressing voice—and the worst character on earth! Well aware that she was the adored darling of her great lump of a husband, Kate took full advantage of the fact for the satisfaction of every caprice. Though by no means a rich man, the Inspector never protested. All the bills that poured into the house were duly met, and when his purse proved inadequate to meet the demands, he would bring out his checkbook, encroaching on his modest bachelor savings.

Now the writer of the letter signed "Inspector Juve" certainly appeared aware of this state of things, but on the contrary it would seem that the unknown correspondent was a trifle premature in declaring that, if at three o'clock to the minute he had not received fifty thousand francs in gold, a tragedy would follow… As a fact the fifty thousand francs had of course not been sent by the hour named, inasmuch as Juve had whipped off the blackmailing missive, and all the tragedy that was staged at the Inspector-in-Chief's domicile consisted in the bewilderment of Madame Kate's little maidservant and an animated dispute on the landing outside the flat with the delivery agents of a big shop dragging after them an enormous roll of carpet.

"Go on!" asseverated the poor child, "I tell you it's not for here! Anyway, if Madame had ordered a carpet, I would have known about it!"

"Beg pardon!" protested the head man, "the name and address are all right, ain't they? *Madame Kate Morand,* eh? Very well, then we have to leave it here—and here it is!"

"But, gracious me! you've mistook your house, you have!"

"Well, and what's the matter to you, by God? It's paid for! Best take it in."

This last argument was so cogent that the little servant suddenly gave in.

"Well, have your way then!" she agreed. "Lordy, how silly I am! Of course you'll come back for your carpet, if it's not right. Pitch the thing down there, and be done with it!"

Then, in a rage, the girl turned her back and made for her kitchen, while the four men triumphantly lodged their lumpy package against the wall of the vestibule.

"Good night to you, my dear!" the head man called out. "We're off now,"—but the girl vouchsafed no answer, and the profoundest quiet settled down again in the house.

The profoundest quiet? Yes, in the gloom of the ill-lighted room no sound could be heard—just at first. But presently, at intervals, softly, slowly, a slight rustling noise became audible. Were the carpets—there must have been two, corded together—were the knots badly tied, were they coming undone?

There was this faint rustle, and simultaneously in the half dark of the corridor, a vague something, a black shadow, black as night, was stirring. The vestibule was quite small. It communicated by folding doors that were never shut, with a second room, as confined as the first, which Kate Morand called her drawing room, because it contained a piano, a couple of armchairs, a low, narrow ottoman and an india-rubber plant decorated with a bow of cherry-colored riband.

The light was far from good in this inner room, the window shutters being closed. How then see distinctly and realize what was afoot, happening with an almost miraculous rapidity? Suddenly the mysterious shadow, the black, slender, tall, supple, silent figure, glided from the vestibule into the salon, crossed the room and slipped behind the heavy curtains hanging before a window. Another rustling, and all fell silent again.

Two minutes later, hardly more than that, the maidservant was hurrying to the outer door, which she threw open in answer to her mistress's vigorous pull at the bell.

"Take care, Madame," the girl warned the newcomer, "the place is choked up with carpets."

"What? what do you say?" the Inspector's lady demanded in surprise.

"I'm warning Madame. Quite easy to take a tumble over them carpets they've brought."

The other looked quite amazed. Casting a glance at the bales blocking up her anteroom, she protested:

"But I never ordered the things! What's it all about?"

"Madame, it's paid for."

"Well, it's a mistake. I'm not expecting anything of the sort. You should have refused to take them in, you silly girl!"

"I did, Madame… but…"

"Enough, enough! You deafen me. I have a frightful headache. The shop will send to recover the carpets, and that'll be the end of the matter. Now go!"

The good lady took off her hat, threw it haphazardly on a chair—she was not a careful person—and departed for the drawing room, while the little servant, concluding her mistress was "suffering with her nerves," made haste to disappear. Thereupon her mistress lay down on the ottoman, shut her eyes and tried to get to sleep, for it was quite true she was afflicted with a racking headache.

"It's that bouquet my husband made me carry," she thought to herself. "The flowers had too overpowering a smell. He can never choose anything right. Oh! how my poor head aches!"

Lying full length, she stayed quite still for five minutes, then suddenly sat up, half opening her eyes.

"What is it moving in the room?" she asked herself, and casting a sleepy look around the empty salon, proceeded:

"You'd think there was an animal shut in… a cat perhaps?… Oh! my poor head!"—and shutting her eyes again, she yielded to the drowsiness that oppressed her.

As a fact there was no animal shut up in the room. The slight noise the woman had heard had its origin in something much more serious than a cat's gambol. Softly, very softly, the window curtains were drawn aside. Then a man had left his hiding place behind them, a figure whose aspect was even more astounding than alarming. He wore a dark costume of very elegant cut and carried a soft felt in his hand, but his face was covered with a mask of black velvet that effectually concealed the features. Slowly, deliberately, the figure stepped up to the sleeping woman.

"Madame!" he accosted her, and she sprang up instantly and saw the stranger, who saluted her with a profound bow.

"Sir!… But… how…" she stammered in amazement. Then a little scream escaped her. She had caught sight of the mask the intruder wore.

"Oh! who are you?" she quivered. "Who let you in?"

Then she stopped, laying a finger on his lips, her strange visitor whispered: "Hush! not a sound… But first and foremost, Madame, let me assure you of my deepest respect. You have nothing untoward to fear. I merely wish to have a moment or two's conversation with you."

Kate was still stunned with surprise as the unknown continued:

"You run no danger… none. But you desire to know my name? Alas! Madame, that is precisely what I cannot tell you!… No matter! rather than refuse your wish, I will tell you this much—believe it or not, as you prefer—Madame, this morning, I was visited by a journalist, a young man of talent… Well, he informed me, without a smile, that he recognized in me Fantômas!… Shall we say then that I am Fantômas?"—and as he pronounced the dread name, the unknown seemed to smile…

*　　*　　*　　*　　*

On first hearing the stranger speak, Kate Morand had trembled violently, for did the mere name of Fantômas not justify her terror? But soon she regained her serenity. Her visitor was extremely polite and perfectly respectful. How could she believe him to be the infamous brigand?

"Monsieur," Kate spoke in a faltering voice, "if it is a joke…"

"Precisely so, Madame!" the unknown cut in, "it is a practical joke I want to play on your husband… I can count on your help?"

"But, Monsieur, I don't understand one word…"

"Of what I'm saying? Alas! again, I cannot give you any explanation… Anyway, what matter? See here, tomorrow you will bless me… Why certainly! for tomorrow when you discover what all this means, you will realize how your husband has spent fifty thousand francs to assure your tranquillity…"

"You speak in riddles, Monsieur."

"Well, yes, but I do it with a purpose. Just let me act, Madame, and never try to fathom my intentions… I merely repeat, I will do you no harm… and that it is all by way of being a jest…"

But now Kate had good reason to be afraid. Swiftly, though without a sound, the unknown had drawn a fine cord from one of his pockets and a silk handkerchief from another. Before the Inspector's wife could guess what her visitor would do, he had tied her hands and gagged her!

"Madame!" this surprising personage then addressed his victim, "your pallor reveals your agitation, and, believe me, I am grieved to see it. But I swear once more…"

But breaking off abruptly the scoundrel burst out in a fit of smothered laughter:

"She's fainted!" he cried, "fainted away!… Oh God! so much the better! She will be none the worse afterwards, and this way I will not have to explain to the good lady how, though she has nothing to fear from me, she may well have everything to dread from her husband!"

Again the fellow chuckled maliciously. Truly, who else could it be but Fantômas who acted with such audacity combined with such amazing coolness?

"Let's waste no time," the wretch suddenly went on. "It would be vexatious if the maidservant surprised us. To work! It's only a matter of a few minutes more."

So saying, the fellow stooped and lifted the fainting woman—Kate Morand was no featherweight—from the ottoman on which she had fallen and walked off with her in his arms, moving noiselessly, for his boot soles were thickly padded with felt that completely deadened the sound of his footsteps. Quickly he reached the anteroom—and then the same rustling began again, the dull sound of carpets being rolled up and tied together. Neither eye nor ear could detect that anything was amiss.

Ten minutes later—it was twenty-five minutes after three—a ring summoned the maidservant to the door again:

"Oh! it's you, is it? I knew you'd be coming back! They weren't for us at all then, them carpets, eh? Look, there they are… But, whatever you do, don't make a row, anyway! My missus is asleep…"

The maid, on opening the door, had found herself face to face with four sturdy fellows. These were none other than the same men who had come a little while before to deliver the redoubtable carpets.

"Yes!" announced one of them. "Another silly blunder!… In our shop that's what the clerks are always doing—a damned lot of fellows they pay handsomely to do nothing! Not like us poor devils, tramping upstairs and downstairs to haul goods about for pennies a day! Come on, hurry up, my lads… Good evening to you, mademoiselle!"

The men hoisted the heavy bales on their shoulders and, still growling and grumbling, tramped downstairs and left the house, while the maidservant went back to her kitchen, stepping on tiptoe so as not to wake up her mistress and incur another exhibition of that lady's nervous tantrums.

*     *     *     *     *

But if the fair Kate was a nervous wreck at that moment, be sure the good city of Marseilles held another individual in a similar condition of more or less acute nervousness—and that individual was Juve and no other. Noting the time by a neighboring clock and realizing that the moment fixed upon by the scoundrel who signed his messages with his own name was close at hand, Juve had slackened his pace and dropped into a saunter. This by no means, however, implied that the police officer was idle or indifferent. Heavens, no! Under his calm exterior, Juve was boiling with rage, but he was well aware that success is reserved for such as can master their feelings, and he was a past master in that art.

Juve never let the offices of the Criminal Department out of his sight. Strolling quietly up and down before the house, he kept his eyes fixed unobtrusively on the building.

"If only I knew what was going on inside," he muttered—and he grinned with rather a wry mouth as he asked himself if they had discovered his victim yet, the unfortunate Inspector-in-Chief.

He was not left long in doubt. Barely a quarter of an hour had passed before a motorcar drew up to the curb and stopped in front of the official headquarters. A clever-looking middle-aged man sprang out and disappeared hurriedly under the porte-cochère.

"Good! the doctor. They've called the doctor by telephone. In five minutes we shall see something happen. Four or five fellows will come scurrying out…"

But he had overestimated the interval. Three minutes only had elapsed when four shady-looking individuals—recognizable a hundred yards off as detectives—appeared on the threshold and hailed cabs.

"The four in question," grinned Juve. "Of course my victim has spoken, and following the good old police routine, he's sending off his four satellites to the railway stations and quays for outgoing vessels, not to mention the cafés and other places of amusement, to hunt for 'Juve.' And, of course, it never once occurred to anybody that 'Juve,' not being a born fool, was sure to have hidden just where they'd never look for him, that is, close to the Department headquarters! Yes," he went on, but he was frowning now, "they're not after me, and they won't catch me. But, after all, what's that matter? What *does* matter is that Fantômas has threatened the Inspector-in-Chief, and that, little suspecting his telegram is in my pocket, he'll move heaven and earth to exact the penalty he claims. Will I be able to stop him?"

Almost out loud and quite unconsciously to himself, Juve continued soliloquizing. To all ordinary apprehension, this message, telling the Inspector-in-Chief that he would kill his wife with his own hand, was a pure piece of braggadocio, but Juve thought otherwise. In his eyes the true author of the threat was Fantômas—and did he not know what appalling ruses Fantômas was capable of?

"Anyhow," he reflected, "while my own interests bid me stay here under the eyes of the police so as to be sure of those gentlemen not seeing me, my duty to others makes the same course of action imperative. I am bound to safeguard the In-spector-in-Chief's wife. Now I don't know the woman, and I don't know her address! All I do know is that she's in danger of being killed by her husband… So, to save her, all I have to do is to shadow the husband… But what is the fellow going to do? If he doesn't come out of doors, how is he going to kill his wife punctually at four o'clock? Or will she come to see him at his office? Hmm, I wouldn't much like that. I don't quite see myself accosting the pair hat in hand and warning them—'Sir, Madame, take care, don't go killing each other!' This time it would be a case not of jail, but for a straitjacket!… Ah! twenty to four! only twenty minutes left!"

He drove his nails into the palms of his hands. The more he thought, the more he became convinced that Fantômas' threat—it was certainly Fantômas who must have written the message—could not be an empty one. But how, how would the Lord of Terror bring about the tragedy he had planned? This "how" tortured Juve.

Next moment, however, he gave a sudden start. A step could be heard under the archway of the porte-cochère, rapidly approaching.

"The doctor going away again no doubt?" thought the detective. Yes, it was indeed the doctor, but he was not alone. At his side, talking amicably with him, was Juve's victim, the Inspector-in-Chief.

"Capital!" thought the police officer, "a rapid convalescence! Well, that being so, all my scruples vanish. Ho, ho! they're off by motorcar. Lucky I went through his pocketbook. I shall be able to treat myself to a joyride too."

The doctor, in fact, was taking the Inspector-in-Chief in his own private car. The latter had just lit a cigarette and seemed in excellent spirits.

"Go along, my good sir! Smile and look pleasant, do!" growled Juve, hailing a taxi. "You don't know the danger your wife is running, but I know!"—and he ordered the driver:

"Follow that car. Follow it up fairly close, but without attracting attention. Police business, my man!"

The chauffeur nodded without saying a word. Vaguely, as he looked at his face, the worthy man had told himself that he knew the face. But it never occurred to him that he had seen it that very morning in his newspaper in the article about the anniversary of Juve's death.

"Righto!" was his only remark, and one after the other the two vehicles got underway.

Juve was calming down. "My friend is not driving," he reflected, "so, he's not going to run over his wife. So, I needn't worry till he arrives at his destination. Where is he going, I wonder? Home? Hmm, hardly likely. We're making for the Parc Borély. Is he going to treat himself to a drink by way of a pick-me-up?"

Along the broad avenues leading to Marseilles' magnificent promenade the doctor's car put on speed. Other flyers too accompanied or overtook and passed the medico's car, all taking the same turnings and apparently following an identical route.

"Oh God!" thought Juve, "there must be some official ceremony on. That's where my man is going. And I know nothing about it, just out of the grave as I am…" But this time Juve's smile was a little forced. The idea that the Inspector-in-Chief was going to attend some official ceremony, inauguration of a statue, or laying a foundation-stone—was not much to his taste. Doubtless, it was not to be supposed that the Inspector's wife would mingle in the crowd, but it was equally certain that under shelter of that same crowd Fantômas might easily conceal his movements—and once more he asked himself the question, how was the threatened tragedy to be brought about?

"A speech," pondered Juve, "a speech may be deadly, but it doesn't kill, and if not a speech, what else is there the man can be up to?"

However, there was nothing to help him guess the truth from the inadequate premises which were all he had to go on. So he resigned himself to waiting. Detective officers of genius are always careful not to build up theories in advance. Patience and watchfulness, indefatigable and increasing, are their best weapons.

However, in this case Juve was not destined to remain long in uncertainty. Like flies round a honeypot, the automobiles, slowing down to a walking pace, gathered thick around the entrance of a temporary erection on the confines of the Parc Borély. Doors swung open, handshakes were exchanged between arriving guests, a hurrying crowd thronged within, showing their cards of admission to two officials at the door. Juve rapped on the window of his cab and sprang out. Relying on the doctrine that nobody would ever think of recognizing him within two steps of his victim, he took no measures whatever of concealment and advanced boldly towards the entrance doors.

"What's going on in there?" he asked a loiterer, putting on a simple, countryfied air. The man looked at him in amazement.

"What's that? you don't know? Why all the papers have been talking about it for the past week. It's the inauguration of the Ex-Trench Officers' Club."

"Oh, is it? Well, my word, I didn't know. I've only just arrived in Marseilles… Then there'll be speeches and a banquet and champagne drinking, eh?"

"Why, certainly!"

"And dancing with the pretty ladies who are invited?"

"Not a bit of it! It's what the paper said themselves—the rule's not polite. No, women are not admitted! not even the President's lady."

"Well, well!… Thank you, sir!"

"Don't mention it, sir!"

Juve moved away. No one was a better hand than he at getting an unsuspecting witness to supply him with essential facts. Now he was thinking.

"Women are not admitted. Then my friend, the Inspector's wife, can't be there. Yet it's three minutes to four, and in three minutes she is to be…"

But once again he stopped dead in the middle of his reflections, such a spasm of consternation seizing him that he seemed momentarily paralyzed. A shot had rung out, loud and unmistakable.

"Ah! the unhappy lady!" groaned Juve. Instinctively he had jumped to the conclusion that the horrid catastrophe had actually occurred. It was only reasonable to think so!

All the same, not a soul save himself showed the least sign of surprise. In spite of his agitation he remarked the fact. Then, pale but mastering his emotion, he hurried to one of the men on duty at the gate.

"Where have they got to in the ceremony?" he demanded. "Who was it fired? Tell me quick!"

The official looked at him in surprise.

"Where have they got to?" he spoke at last. "Why, they must be at the inauguration of the shooting range… But what's that to do with you… Hi there! where are you off to?"—and the man bolted after his questioner. Juve, running like a madman, had darted forward, scampering through the porchway and shouldering the doorkeepers on one side.

"Stop!" yelled the official, "stop! Your card?"

Juve turned round. "Idiot! my card… my card?" Then suddenly bethinking himself, he fumbled in his pocket.

"There!" he cried… "And shut the doors, I tell you. Let nobody go out."

In a second, in less than a second, he had recovered his self-possession. A card? they were asking for his card?—and by the Lord, he possessed the most efficacious passport man could have. In his hand was the pocketbook stolen from the Inspector-in-Chief. He opened it, took out his victim's badge, and flourished it in the air… Was Fantômas not bound to be there? Rapidly he gave his order:

"Nobody is to go out! nobody!" Then he was off again, still at a run.

In three steps the police officer was across the little forecourt and at the door of the building itself. A closely packed crowd was gathered inside. Groups of men were laughing and joking and sampling the champagne. It seemed an impossibility to break through the gay throng, but Juve, still at the run, pushed his way impetuously through every obstacle, regardless of the abuse that greeted his rude onslaught.

He heard nothing, saw nothing save, at the far end of the great flag-draped hall, a group of people gathered round a man standing at the entrance to the shooting range.

"Your turn, Inspector!" a voice was saying. The individual addressed half-turned around and Juve recognized the Inspector-in-Chief. He was just taking a Lebel rifle handed to him, leveling the weapon, aiming, on the point of letting loose at the distant target.

"Stop! stop!" yelled Juve—and with one bound sprang at the marksman's shoulders and tore the gun from his hands, hurling it to a distance.

"Stop!" he panted. "You are going to kill your wife!" The confusion was indescribable, the scandal too monstrous for words. A dozen stalwart hands had gripped Juve, almost before the unhappy Inspector recognized him.

"You!" he stammered.

"Yes, I… I who am saving your wife's life!"

"My wife? my wife? But where is she?… You're mad!"

"Four o'clock is striking!" announced Juve. "Listen, I say!… Yes, where is your wife? Behind the target, by God! I'll swear to that!"

The words seemed so incomprehensible that at first no one appeared to grasp their meaning. Then a dozen excited onlookers vaulted the barrier and ran to the butts.

They were back in no time. "No, there's nothing, nothing but sand…"

"Sound the sand!" vociferated Juve.

But an employee stepped forward. "It's not worth the trouble," the man declared. "I've never once let the workmen out of my sight, they've only this minute finished the butts… There's nothing but sand and a pile of very old carpets. They put 'em there, so's we might recover the bullets and sell the lead to be recast…"

"Unroll those carpets!" ordered Juve. He spoke like one possessed. At each fresh statement a flash of intelligence lit up his eyes. No, he did not know—but he guessed. His logical faculty was his guide, a guide that could not lie.

"You are mad!" the Inspector-in-Chief reiterated. "And besides that, the man gives himself out to be Juve…

"Juve! exactly so!" the detective confirmed his words. "Now, unroll those carpets! Damn it, you can talk afterwards…"

He seemed sure of his facts. Excitement rose to fever pitch, you could have heard a pin drop.

The carpets were brought…

*      *      *      *      *

It is very certain that, supposing Kate Morand's little maidservant could have seen these lamentable rags now, stained as they were with sand and torn to ribbons, she would never have known them as identical with the silken Smyrna rugs that had lain for a brief while in her master's rooms. Yet they were the very same carpets.

The proof of this was swiftly forthcoming—the tragic proof. Scarcely had the rolls been undone before a cry of horror escaped every throat. Inside these lamentable rags was hidden a woman, none other than pretty Kate Morand… Fainting, bound hand and foot, gagged, the wretched woman seemed dead already. Yet, when the Inspector-in-Chief, with a cry of horror, dashed towards his adored, the latter, revived by the fresh air, stirred feebly. Already too a doctor was pressing to the front, pushing back the throng of curious onlookers.

"Give her air!" he ordered. "Keep calm. I answer for the lady's life, but we must take proper precautions."

The crowd drew back. Such was the shock all present had experienced that not a word had yet been spoken. Thunderstruck, the Inspector-in-Chief, paler than the victim herself, was leaning against a wall, muttering:

"And I was just going to fire!… and I would have killed her!… killed her with my own hands!"

Then he seemed to wake from a nightmare and sprang forward, shouting: "Juve! Juve, I say!"

"Here!" replied that officer in his calmest voice. "One moment, and I'm with you… But I was dying of thirst!"

Juve alone of all that crowd had kept his head. While everyone else seemed to have taken leave of their wits Juve had gone off calmly to the buffet where he imbibed a glass of champagne and treated himself to a sandwich.

"Incredible how hollow a man feels after ten years in the grave!" he was saying. "Well, now to reassure my good friend,"—and he walked up to the Inspector-in-Chief, holding out his hand.

"There, let's make peace! What, you won't! Nay, don't say anything yet. I must first put you in possession of the facts. Now read that dispatch—came by pneumatic tube. Why, yes, it's a telegram I pinched after I'd shown you my talents as a boxer. And, by the by, here's your pocketbook. I've not spent a great deal so far. Still I've got a cab waiting at the door, and the taximeter must be running up. If you'll be so good as to pay my driver, we'll settle up afterwards, eh?"

Only, if Juve appeared all the time to be perfectly calm, it became more and more manifest that nobody could understand a word he was saying. Excitement, far from diminishing, was actually increasing.

"But this is sheer nonsense! simple craziness!" thundered the Inspector in sudden fury. "This telegram is signed by you!"

"Certainly it is! but it was not I who signed it."

"Who did then?"

"My dear sir, presently, by ourselves, in your private room, I will tell you."

"But then, how did you know?…"

"Bah! we are of a trade, you and I, are we not? I thought things out! I followed you!… Knowing what you were threatened with and seeing you with a gun in your hand, it was no work of wizardry to guess the truth… and you can see for yourself how that proves…"

"Proves what?" panted the Inspector-in-Chief.

"That I am Juve—the true Juve, by God!"

The detective spoke in all sincerity of heart. Knowing that he was "himself," he thought he could not but convince his auditors. Alas! he was forgetting how incredible, how stupefying his statement was. For a moment the Inspector-in-Chief gazed at him as if struck dumb. Then he shuddered from head to foot as though shaken by an electric shock.

"Juve is dead! ten years ago!" he shouted—and in a voice of fury he gave the order:

"Seize that man! Handcuff him!"

"But… since that proves…"

"Bah! your proofs are no proofs at all!"

Meantime around their Chief constables in plain clothes had already gathered on the prowl. In a twinkling two of them had slipped the bracelets on poor Juve's wrists.

"Come along!" they ordered. "March!"

Juve protested vigorously: "What now! let me be heard at least!"

"Not here! in private, yes. Now get on!"

Two minutes later Juve and the Inspector-in-Chief, the Prefect by his side now, found themselves in a small office, safe from popular curiosity. The fair Kate, conveyed there in a motorcar, had made a succinct statement. She was entirely out of danger now and was recovering her serenity.

At once the Inspector-in-Chief took up his parable afresh.

"Listen," he declared, addressing Juve, "you have saved my wife's life. But that proves nothing whatever. You saved her life *too* cleverly. I tell you, you saved her because you *knew* she was there. And you knew that because… because it was you who carried her off!"

The Inspector-in-Chief failed to observe the mocking smile that hovered about his prisoner's lips. Juve in fact was beginning to enjoy the game prodigiously. Heaven! could he not easily enough conjecture his adversary's line of reasoning? It was so eminently the sort of theory to fascinate a mind trained in police routine!

"Why yes, they're going to tell me it's all a clever plot… that I abducted the woman… that I wrote the telegram… that after that I saved Madame's life… all this by way of making myself important!"

Aloud he remarked: "And my personal appearance? Come now, yes or no, is my face Juve's?"

"Juve is dead! he died on the banks of Newfoundland! You are like him, amazingly like him, but…"

"But is all you can say. Now, my dear sir, I am sorry to contradict you, but I am not *like* him! I *am* Juve, and I am going to give you another proof. I am dead, you say? I died along with Fandor?"

"Undoubtedly!"

"Well, I am going to confront you with someone who is just exactly as much like Fandor as I am like Juve! There, what do you say to that? An extraordinary likeness, well and good!… But two?"

The inspector had turned pale. "I don't believe you," he declared. "I defy you to show me Fandor."

"Very well, let us go to the Bourse. He should have been waiting for me there for the last ten minutes,"—and Juve got up. He was fully persuaded now that his identity would be quickly established. The police might indeed stick out for their theory of a "startling likeness"; still they would be forced to find another explanation when a likeness every bit as "startling" should be established with Jerome Fandor.

The Inspector-in-Chief however did not budge.

"Take you to the Bourse?" he growled. "Upon my word, no!… I don't know who you are, but anyway you're a dangerous character, and I've no mind to facilitate your escape. Besides which, it's needless. The telephone's there. I'm going to send an officer. Jerome Fandor is too well known for an inspector not to spot him, if he's waiting for you where you say."

Juve willingly agreed, and a moment later the order was given by telephone, in answer to which an inspector set out from a police station near the Bourse in search of the journalist. Five minutes a ring-up announced the emissary's return.

"Hello, hello!" shouted the Inspector-in-Chief in an excited voice, springing to the instrument. "Well, have you found him?"

After listening for a moment, he hung up the receiver and turning to Juve—

"Nobody! no Fandor nor anybody like him at the Bourse," he declared with a taunting laugh. "Come, come, this farce has lasted long enough!"—and this time it was he who stood up and Juve who remained seated.

"Nobody?" exclaimed the detective. "Certain your Inspector hasn't made a mistake? sure he looked carefully?"

"Oh, certain! All he saw was a messenger boy from *La Capitale* strolling about outside the railings. There's no one else waiting there."

"My dear sir, in that case let me use the telephone and call up *La Capitale*. The paper has an office here?"

"Yes… but…"

"But don't you understand? Well, now you're going to— Fandor has been *La Capitale's* best correspondent. If he's not at the rendezvous, it's because he's run to the office of the paper to write an article… If there's a messenger boy in front of the Bourse, that's because Fandor is very sure that, seeing the lad and his cap with the journal's name on it, I shall guess he's there to tell me he'll be back soon. Anyhow, you will see…"

Juve spoke so quietly and with such an air of perfect confidence that, in spite of everything, the Inspector-in-Chief began to feel doubtful. All his common sense protested against his *soi-disant* colleague's claim. He would never be persuaded that Juve and Fandor were not dead, but could he, or ought he, to reject a possible means of arriving at the truth?

"Well, ring up *La Capitale* then!" he agreed. "But you're only trying to gain time really…"

"Wrong there, my good colleague! My own idea is I'm wasting it,"—and calmer than ever, Juve waited to get connection. Then:

"Hello! is this *La Capitale?* I want to speak to a young man who has just brought in a sensational article. Put me through to the Editor…"

Three minutes later Juve, smiling broadly, handed one of the receivers to the Inspector-in-Chief.

"Here! listen!" he bade him. "It's well worth hearing,"—and he spoke into the instrument:

"Hello! is that you, Fandor? You know my voice? Will you be long? I want you here…"

Then the Inspector-in-Chief could hear a cheerful voice answer:

"Hello! it's you, Juve, is it? No, five minutes more and I'm done!… I'm hatching a stunning article, at forty sous the line, if you please! I'll stick in another fifty lines and I'm with you! I've news to tell you too. I've seen him… Yes, *him! him!* the man risen from the dead!… Where are you?"

"At the Borély, Fandor… and under arrest!… The bracelets on my wrists!"

"Impossible!"

"Taken for an impostor, my lad! Accused of being like 'the genuine' Juve… That's why I want to demonstrate that you are like 'the genuine' Fandor! Will you hurry up, please. You must ask for the Inspector-in-Chief's prisoner."

A peal of laughter came from the direction of the telephone:

"Collared, old man! So they've collared you! Oh, ho! but that's a joke! Another fifty lines to pop the news in… Why then, the man's a 'loony,' is he? Your Inspector-in-Chief, an imbecile, a born fool! Wait one moment, and I'll hop into a taxi, and bring him my face!… All the same, old man, I'm cold to the heart because of *him,* to know he's alive. I could swear to that, else I should be laughing like a schoolgirl for the fun of it all! Be with you in no time…"—and a click announced that Fandor had hung up.

Juve hung up his receiver, then turning to the Inspector-in-Chief, whose face expressed absolute bewilderment:

"Well?" Juve asked him.

"I'm going mad, I'm going mad!"

"Which means you are beginning to believe me?"

"No!… no! You are dead…"

"Then I'm a dead man who's longing for a cigarette! In the silence of the grave I quite forgot to buy some… You haven't got any?…"

"Here, take one," the Inspector replied in a dull, toneless voice like a sleepwalker's. The conversation he had listened to had not convinced him yet, but it had increased his confusion of mind. How sure of himself Fandor seemed to be! And still, common sense told him… Meantime he had drawn a cigarette case from his pocket and laid it on the table.

"Dear friend and colleague," Juve continued, "I'm trespassing on your kindness, but I should like a light. I haven't brought any matches with me from hell."

Striking one from the Inspector's box, the amazing man added:

"Now a last request. If you were really obliging, you'd have these handcuffs taken off me."

"Off with them!" the official ordered a constable.

"Thank you!" smiled Juve. "That's better. Now tell me, is it far from here to the offices of *La Capitale?*"

"No, a quarter of an hour's walk…"

"Then, granting Fandor makes haste to get done with his article, he may be here in half an hour?"

"Yes."

"Well, we'd best wait for him."

"That's so. We will wait."

"You don't care to talk, I can see," observed the detective. "No, don't protest. It's very natural. So, I'm going to read this paper. It has an obituary notice on the late Juve, which makes amusing reading for me, you can see that!"—and more and more unruffled, Juve buried himself in the pages of a Marseilles daily, while the Inspector-in-Chief stood passively by, apparently overwhelmed by circumstances.

Meanwhile time was slipping by. A clock hung on the wall in the little office where they were. It struck the half-hour. Then it struck six o'clock. Juve looked up quickly. "It's long waiting!" he observed.

"Very long…"

"Fandor should be here surely?"

"That is just what I'm thinking!"

"He must have been delayed…"

"Or he has preferred not to come…"

"You mean to say?…"

"I mean to say that I am convinced now!"

"Convinced of what?"

"Convinced that your accomplice has chosen to cut and run," concluded the Inspector-in-Chief with a scornful laugh.

Juve made a last appeal to his patience:

"I hear what you say. But grant me just a quarter of an hour's grace! At forty sous the line Fandor could not help drawing out his stuff. But he will come. Are we to go on waiting?"

"So be it!"

Once more the two men fell silent. Only as the time of waiting grew longer and longer, Juve felt his anxiety getting more and more acute. Why had Fandor not hastened to answer his call? Why had he not come hot foot to his friend's succor? It was only in jest of course that Juve had accused him of spinning out an interminable article. Fandor was not the man to condescend to such devices, especially when he knew he was expected. Must it be supposed then that some accident had happened to him?… Some accident… but what sort of accident?

Juve was now frowning, his preoccupation very evident.

In front of him, on the contrary, the Inspector-in-Chief stood with a bantering air of triumph. The journalist's absence proved the truth of his suspicions that the *soi-disant* Juve and Fandor were nothing more than common impostors.

He got up briskly. "Your quarter of an hour is gone!" he announced.

"It is."

"And the *soi-disant* Fandor is not here!"

"I admit it."

"Then…"

"Then phone to *La Capitale,* and ask what has become of him…"—and again unhooking the receiver, and ringing up the editorial department of the paper, the Inspector-in-Chief questioned:

"Hello! I should like to know if M. Fandor is still with you?"

He listened to the reply, thanked the speaker, and turning to Juve:

"Gone!" he declared. "He went three-quarters of an hour ago! So, you don't laugh?"

As a matter of fact Juve had turned pale, Fandor had left the newspaper office! He had not arrived at the Parc Borély!… Why?

"You don't laugh?" repeated the Inspector-in-Chief. "Well! that's because you realize at last that your story won't hold water. My good man, your accomplice has left you in the lurch!… Now, why ever did you tell him you were in the hands of the police? You must have known he would take to his heels. Come, let's be done with it. You confess, eh?"

Juve was livid… Fandor had not got to him! Why, why? Who had risen up in his path? Who had barred his way? Who?

Involuntarily, in spite of himself Juve answered the question by a name, a name at which for all his courage he shuddered, for no man is courageous where the life of those he loves is at stake.

At the last words of the Inspector-in-Chief he raised his head.

"Sir," he declared, "I confess nothing… But I ask you a favor,

I beg and beseech you to grant it, in the name of your wife whom you love, and because *I* love Fandor. Handcuff me again; send ten officers to guard me; only let me go to the offices of *La Capitale*. I *must* know what has become of Fandor, I must! You cannot refuse me… I am Juve—and I confess I am afraid, terribly afraid!"

Such vivid emotion indeed vibrated in the detective's voice that the Inspector-in-Chief was himself moved.

"Very well," he gave his decision. "My wife is alive, thanks perhaps to you… I will have you taken there… Only…"

"Only?"

"Only, after that they'll take you to headquarters, and I will have you locked up… I am not your dupe!"

"You will do with me what you will. So be it!… But now, quick, let us be off!"—and in two minutes more the cars were on their way.

The Inspector-in-Chief returned straight to his office at the Criminal Department, while Juve, handcuffs on wrists and guarded by four officers, was taken to *La Capitale*. Was he destined to recover traces of Jerome Fandor there?

## 7. Between You and Me, Fantômas!

After hanging up, Jerome Fandor, regardless of his promise to Juve not to lose a second in coming to his rescue, had devoted two full minutes, if the truth must be known, to giving rein to his boisterous mirth.

"Juve collared!" he grinned. "No, it is *too* funny! Anyway, it'll teach him to what comes of not listening to my advice! What the devil has brought him at loggerheads with the police? Didn't I tell him to lie low? But no matter, it's a thundering lark!"—and he started laughing again.

Jerome Fandor had never been the man to encourage dismal thoughts. Brave to rashness, capable of every sort of reckless daring as of every form of self-sacrifice, the *beau idéal* of the reporter who risks his life with a smile to win the glory of sending in the first sensational wire, he had learned how to look on the bright side of things and find the grotesque and amusing side of every accident.

The thought that Juve, the great Juve, the King of the detectives, the man all the world revered for his adroitness, had got himself jailed by provincial police officers, struck him as comic to the last degree.

"Now let's get done!" he muttered. "Four lines to wind up with… then I read the stuff over, take it in to the Subeditor, pocket the cash, and away I go to the Borély to rescue Juve…" For a while, however, he stuck fast, pen in air, searching for the telling peroration to bring his copy to an effective close. Not so easy to find, the clear-cut downright phrases that tomorrow were to thrill all the world, to inform the universe in words of gay defiance that the Great Terror was to begin afresh.

The journalist wrote slowly, erasing and correcting painfully:

"At the last minute a word on the telephone informs us of Juve's arrest, mistaken for an impostor by the Marseilles

Criminal Department. A common incident. Nonetheless Juve is Juve, even as I, Fandor, am myself. Whence have we come back? Whither are we going? I do not know. No man knows. But Fantômas is come to life again… and so are we, Juve and I. There is nothing to add. Our readers will draw from the facts stated whatsoever conclusions they may think fit."

"There!" Fandor said softly to himself, "that's clear and precise. Not another word wanted!… Let's just read through again…"

He was sitting all by himself in a small, quiet room, where a clerk had installed him a little before. To tell the truth, he had at first found some difficulty in convincing the editorial department of his identity. No doubt the provincial editor had been prodigiously astonished to receive a visitor who addressed him as "my dear colleague" and informed him he was Jerome Fandor, "the Jerome Fandor, deceased ten years previously" and that he knew nothing whatever of what he might have been doing all that time! But folks are not so particular in newspaper offices as in the police, and Fandor had given such good proofs of his identity by showing his familiarity with newspaper work and demonstrating his close connection with the Paris head-quarters of the journal that the Editor of the provincial issue had eventually resolved to recognize him.

"Do me a screed!" he had told him. "Say what you like in it, but I give you fair warning—I shall put a ten-line paragraph at the head of your stuff advising the public that *La Capitale* has opened our columns to you without the smallest guarantee of authenticity… You accept on this condition?"

"Oh God, yes!"—and the worthy Fandor was at this moment actually putting the finishing touches to the said "screed," re-touching a word here and a sentence there. Moreover he was laughing consumedly at certain passages.

"To think of my readers' faces!" he was thinking, "the faces of them when they come to digest my scribble!"

Truly he little suspected, poor man, as he sat there doubled up with open-hearted merriment, that at that very time a tragedy was playing, a tragedy in which the principal part was his, and the most sinister part, that of victim!

In a house contiguous to the building containing the offices of *La Capitale* a window had been shut down ten minutes earlier, and an unknown hand had immediately drawn heavy double curtains across it. The curtains were lined with a dark, practically black, material. How then, even if he had looked up from his work, even if he had been able to scrutinize this closed window, could Fandor have made out the man, clad in black from head to foot, wearing close-fitting black tights, his face hidden by a black mask, who had glided in front of the curtains in question, and now, standing motionless and indistinguishable against the dark background behind him, held a pair of binoculars to his eyes with which he stared straight into Fandor's room. While the journalist could see nothing of the unknown, the latter missed no single movement of his victim. The room was blazing with light and Jerome Fandor made no attempt to conceal himself.

Scarcely had Juve's friend turned the second sheet of his "copy" before the Man in Black muttered to himself:

"Seven pages more to revise… Two minutes on an average per page. He'll be at it for another quarter of an hour… Add five minutes for a talk with the Editor… five minutes to go to the cash-office for his money… I've five and twenty minutes to the good. Excellent!"

The Man in Black left the window, parted the heavy curtains, and glided back into a room plunged in absolute darkness.

"Tommy!" he called.

"Here, master!" said a child's voice in respectful tones.

"I am going downstairs. In three seconds I shall be at the bottom. Pay attention! Has Léon been told?"

"Yes, master!"

"Then, don't move. Only you will come when I whistle. You understand?"

"Yes, master!"

"And you will know the individual?"

"Oh, yes, certainly, master."

"Then obey, be faithful… and remember that if I can reward

like a king, I can also punish in fearful ways!"

"But, master, I…"

The lad fell silent, in amazement. The electric lights had suddenly flashed forth again in the room… and the room was empty… absolutely empty. The Man in Black was gone without a sound to betray his footsteps. "Oh!" the young rascal breathed a sigh of relief, "for my part, I like it better when *he's* away. It just takes away my breath to feel him near me… The Man in Black? yes, that's how he likes to be called! Well, other people may do as they like; my notion is he'd turn round all right, if you called out Fantômas after him!"—and the young scamp tried to laugh. He was a lad of twelve or thirteen, with a thin, pale face and the shady look of a street Arab. All the same he was very smart in a magnificent livery in which he seemed to be a trifle uncomfortable—trousers, tight-fitting, frogged jacket, round cap cocked over one ear, on which brightly polished brass letters glittered like gold. A messenger boy doubtless.

Looking round the empty room, empty save for one dilapidated straw-bottomed chair, the youngster went on:

"So, he's taken his traps with him, eh? his soft hat, his overcoat, his boots? My word, a quick dresser!… Hmm, must listen in. He's going to whistle."

At the same moment from under the porte-cochère of the house a well-dressed man emerged—soft hat, long furred greatcoat, tortoiseshell eyeglasses, full moustache and beard, he might be a business man, a ship owner, a middle-class gentleman of sorts. He carried under his arm a dispatch case bulging with papers. Crossing the street deliberately, he entered, with a brisk step and cigarette in mouth, the entrance lobby of the *Capitale* offices.

"Messenger! Hi, there! Messenger," he called.

"Sir?" answered a voice, issuing from under a staircase, where the rascal had retired for a few minutes' surreptitious nap.

"Sir? you want to see?…"

"You, you young varmint! Here, take this letter! You're to deliver it at once. You know the place, don't you? Well, what now, you stare at me as if I were the Pope!"

"But, sir… the thing is… I'm on duty. I don't know if…"

"If you can go away? Stupid! I'm your master."

"My master?"

"Oh, ho! my pretty boy, you want proofs, eh?… I am Monsieur Henri. Yes, the Chief Editor from Paris… There, look!… Why, yes, you're in the right. You're bound to make sure!… Now, are you satisfied?"

The lad was more than satisfied. This gentleman he did not know, but who claimed to be his master, had just given him convincing proof. Opening his dispatch case, he had shown him engraved on the leather flap inside, an inscription that filled him with the greatest wonder and respect. The unknown was indeed Monsieur Henri, and the youngster was ready for anything. Monsieur Henri, the Editor-in-Chief from Paris, had every right to order him about for sure. It was the Boss—"the Boss of all Bosses!" he exclaimed to himself. Then aloud:

"I'm off, sir!" he added briskly.

"Good! You know where the street is?"

"Far end of the town, sir, yes!"

"Well, away with you, my fine lad. I'll tell 'em upstairs you're gone." But the boy was gone already. With one bound he had mounted his bicycle and was off, pedaling with all his might.

Thereupon "Monsieur Henri" turned quickly on his heel and regained the sidewalk. Quite unruffled, he now whistled shrilly. Almost instantly a lad ran up, the same who just now had been talking with the Man in Black.

"Quick!" whispered "Monsieur Henri," "to your post! The fellow will be here in a moment. Whatever happens, do it properly, do it successfully!… or else…"

His eyes flashed. His blazing pupils gleamed with so lurid a light that the boy turned pale with fear.

"Master!" he protested feebly.

"Hush! When I raise my arm, he's there. So watch out!"

*     *     *     *     *

Upstairs, meanwhile, the editorial sanctum, Jerome Fandor

was taking leave of the Editor of the provincial issue.

"I may count on you then," he was asking the latter, "to inform the Paris Chief of my resurrection?"

"Monsieur Henri, you mean? or Monsieur Dupont de l'Eure?"

"Monsieur Henri? Never heard of him! Can't have been there in my time—before my death!… No, wire to Dupont de l'Eure."

"In two twos, by wireless, I'll ask him…"

"By wireless? Why, what's that?"

"What's that! Just telephoning without wires of course."

Jerome Fandor broke into another peal of laughter.

"By the Lord! I'm not up to date," he exclaimed. "That's a positive fact?… But there, I'm chattering, and Juve will make me jump if I'm late. My dear colleague, till we meet again! I'm off… Oh! the cash-office, if you please…"

"On the right, the door yonder."

"Thank you! Just time to pocket my 'boodle' and jump into a taxi. Then I 'clear' Juve, and all away for Paris…"

Jerome Fandor wrung the Editor's hand for the last time and departed, disappearing into the cash-office without giving a thought to what the other might be saying behind his back.

As a matter of fact the Marseilles journalist was not altogether easy in his mind.

"Is it the man?" he soliloquized. "Is it really and truly Jerome Fandor?… Hmm, it doesn't look like it, but I wouldn't stake my life on it… Anyway this much is certain, his article is startling. What a fine story, by God! Tomorrow we shall be printing off to the tune of three millions!"—and he went back to his desk.

No, he was not convinced, any more than other people, that it was Jerome Fandor he had just been talking to. A resurrection such as this left him very skeptical; but could he refuse the sensational report he was going to telegraph to Paris?

At the cash desk, sublimely indifferent as to whether or how far his stuff was taken for gospel, knowing as he did that he would have the last word, Jerome Fandor presented the voucher he had been handed.

"There, sir," he addressed the cashier, "I'll take it in gold louis, if you please."

"Oh, come! Gold! You're asking a bit too much."

"Well, then, crown pieces, just common five-franc pieces!"

"Why not American dollars, say—or English sovereigns!"—and the clerks handed him a wad of tiny banknotes with a curt, "There's your money."

Fandor looked at the notes with a bewildered air. Like Juve, the currency of the day left him wondering.

"Come on, I'm behind time," he said to himself. "Paper louis should be as good as the other sort, I suppose. Let's take them and go,"—and he bowed and made for a neighboring staircase. "Hurry up!" he told himself. "Juve must be in the devil's own temper by now. So much the worse for him, that's all. Tonight in the train I'll undertake to make him laugh a bit."

Four steps at a time Fandor flew down the stairs. He felt light as air, with good money in his pocket. Suddenly a small boy in messenger's uniform stood in his path. "A cab, sir?"

"You've got one then?"

"The rank's not a dozen yards away."

"Run then!… What, you're not gone yet?"

The lad, however, deserved no reproach for tardiness. In one bound he was across the lobby and through the entrance doors. Two seconds more and the humming of a motor became audible.

"The cab, sir,"—and from the step where he was perched, the youngster sprang to the pavement and opened the door of the vehicle.

"There you are, Colonel," Fandor cried, jocosely, handing the lad his tip. "Now, driver, Parc Borély. Stop at the Ex-officers' Club! You know it? Very good, and drive your hardest, my man!"—and Fandor got in.

"Ah!" he said in surprise, "the curtains are down. What an idea!… My word, but she can travel, this old bus." The taxi was going full steam ahead in fact, so fast indeed that Fandor had some difficulty in shifting the blinds over the windows which he had found closed.

"Devil take those contraptions!" he grumbled. "They're

always out of order!"

Then, with a brisk oath: "Damnation! a tire gone! It only wanted that to get me there quick!" He had caught a characteristic whistling sound, the noise a pneumatic tire makes when pierced by a nail and rapidly going flat. Next moment, however, he corrected himself:

"But no! I'm a fool. From inside I couldn't hear a noise of that sort. No, it's not a puncture…"

He waited another moment, noted that the taxi was traveling as fast as ever, but he still heard the same whistling sound.

"Anyway something's escaping. I'm not going crazy, I suppose?" He listened more carefully, but could not guess… No, he could not guess what was happening—at first…

But suddenly he sprang to his feet and turned pale, swearing and cursing!

"Why, what? In God's name, what is it?"—and he sniffed the air inside the cab. "Smell of bitter almonds! an acid smell! cyanhydric acid! I… I… But I'm choking, choking!"

Next instant he could not draw his breath, a hideous burning pain tore at his lungs, his brain reeled, while red lights danced before his closed eyes. With a last desperate effort he half rose, seized the door handle and tried to open it, but it was locked. Then he strove to break the glass, but his strength was gone. His arm refused to move, it seemed to weigh a ton. And still that hideous scorching in the lungs and still the red lights careering before his sight.

"They're murdering me!" the unhappy man cried, his voice rattling in his throat, "or at least they're doping me!"

Then a word, a name shuddered on his lips:

"Fantômas! Fantômas!"

*     *     *     *     *

The victim fell back on the seat of the carriage, speechless. Blood flowed from his nostrils. A reddish foam gathered on his lips. His chest was heaving.

On his box outside, two minutes later, the chauffeur stooped over and closed a tap: "There we are!" he muttered. "The fellow's got his dose by now. No need to empty the reservoir, eh? What's left may be used again… And such an easy dodge—a bottle of compressed gas, a hole with a pipe passing through it… childishly simple, by god!… Ah! there's the master!"

The driver pulled up. At the corner of an avenue stood a man and a lad waiting.

"Done it?" questioned the man.

"Yes, master! For sure he must be sound asleep by now. You could fire off big guns without waking him!"

"Then drive on! We're going on the box with you."

"You'll be more comfortable than inside!"

"Why, yes! Only hold your tongue. Get on! I don't like chatterers!"—and with the word the taxi got underway again.

…It was the very moment when Juve was beginning to opine that Fandor was taking an unconscionably long time about answering his summons.

*　　*　　*　　*　　*

"Now for the last time—are you Juve? the genuine Juve? and Fandor is really Fandor?"

"Certainly!"

"You won't say different?"

"I will not say different!"

"Well, my good man, you've got a bigger impudence, all to yourself, than all the longshore loafers in Marseilles put together! Don't you agree with me, you fellows?"

Three salvoes of hearty laughter saluted this question. In the conveyance that was taking him to the *Capitale* offices Juve had to undergo yet another cross-examination and listen with much bad language! Little he cared at that moment whether they believed him or whether they deemed him an impostor. What troubled him was not his personal safety. Sooner or later he would get back his own identity. What upset him was Fandor's non-appearance. What had happened to his lifelong comrade?

So Juve answered absentmindedly the question put to him by the four police officers told to guard him.

"Jerome Fandor is Jerome Fandor," he told himself, "and that means youth, gaiety, gallantry—and recklessness, mad recklessness! Who knows what new impish trick he has invented? What new enterprise he has been trying? Ah! the villain! I'll pay him out for all this anxiety!"

But one of his conductors was tapping him on the arm: "So, Monsieur Juve, so you went down off Newfoundland in 1911, and you wake up here, in Marseilles? Come now, you must see the thing's not believable."

"Well then, don't believe it."

"That means you confess."

"*I* confess? Never!"

"Still, our Chief himself, and he's no fool…"

"Leave your chief out of the question, my good fellows. He's got nothing to do with it. Rather tell me if we have still far to go."

"Go where?"

"To *La Capitale*."

"Lord, no!… Look, there it is."

"At last!" sighed Juve—and he leapt from the vehicle rather than got out. All his anxieties in fact were over now. The place looked eminently peaceful. It reeked with the smell of printer's ink that is the characteristic perfume of all newspaper offices. Men in blue overalls were coming and going. A messenger boy was dozing in a chair. Everything breathed security.

"I was wrong to torment myself," thought Juve. "Fandor is upstairs there, I wager, having utterly forgotten about me in the fever of composition"—and never once remembering his handcuffs and the effect the sight of them must inevitably produce, he addressed the messenger peremptorily:

"Young man, show me the way to the Editor's room."

"What!" the lad nearly jumped out of his skin, "a prisoner! and you're asking…"

"For the Editor, yes! Answer my question!… Or better give him my name. There, go and tell him it is Juve, Juve the police officer."

"The dead man!" the youngster shuddered from head to

foot, "the dead man all the talk's about!"

"Yes! Good God, but I've had enough of hearing it said I'm dead!… You go and tell him it's Juve, Juve alive and kicking, and that he wants to see him. There's no need for you to *understand!*"

Amazed and bewildered, the boy said nothing, but climbed a staircase and vanished. Then suddenly his voice was heard coming from the upper regions:

"You're to come up, sir!"

And as he mounted from floor to floor, Juve could hear the great man rebuking this unfortunate subordinate:

"What! you have the impudence to shout like that? You can't go down for the gentleman?"

"I'm dead beat!" the boy was answering. "There was a gent sent me off to the other end of Paris—to an address that don't exist! I'm done, sir! My legs are all gone no how!"

But Juve stopped his ears. The young messenger's woes left him cold. And then, no sooner had he reached the landing followed still by his fourfold bodyguard, by no means disposed to lose sight of him for a single second, than a loud cry greeted his arrival.

"Ah, great God!" exclaimed the Editor, where he stood on the threshold of his den: "Juve now, after Fandor! It whips creation! An impossible likeness!"

Then, falling back: "Come in," he invited. "Ah! you're a prisoner!"

"Yes," returned Juve, "and I've been waiting for Fandor to come to release me. You've seen him, haven't you?"

The Editor appeared to hesitate for a moment:

"You ask if I've seen him?"

"Why, yes!… Well?… Now, what's the matter now? Come, come, you've surely seen Fandor? I phoned him here…"

"I have not seen him!" replied the Editor crisply.

"Not seen him!"

"No!"

"Still… but just look here. Half an hour ago they phoned me back that he'd just left your place. Then he must have been here! Speak, man, speak for God's sake! Why do you pretend you haven't seen him?"

"Because I *could* not have seen him!"

Juve felt his hair rising on his head. Again he had the uncanny impression that he was up against some monstrous, incomprehensible adventure… He could not doubt the fact that Jerome Fandor had come to the *Capitale* office, inasmuch as he had himself telephoned him there. That the Editor had received his visit, this was equally impossible to doubt, since the Editor had announced his departure. Then what did this declaration mean: "I have not seen him." Why this falsehood?

Juve passed his hand over his brow on which drops of sweat were trickling. In a rather hoarse voice he insisted:

"Come, sir, your words mean something serious. I haven't explained myself yet—I am anxious about Fandor. I am here because I am afraid he may have been the victim of an attempt on his life by Fantômas. There, you see for yourself I am letting you into important secrets. Now answer me. These gentlemen with me are police officers. Neither Fandor nor I have anything to conceal… You understand me, I think? Why say you have not seen Fandor?"

The Editor's eyes never left the other's face. Slowly and deliberately he replied:

"Because I *could* not have seen him."

"*Could* not?"

"No!… No more than I *can* see Juve."

"What?… you say…?"

"I say that Juve and Fandor are dead!… And that those who pretend to be their incarnations are swindlers!"

"Swindlers!"

"Yes, and I hold the proof of it…"

"But you are mad, mad as a hatter!"

Juve was getting angry. For the Editor to refuse to admit that he had seen Fandor, because Fandor was presumed to be dead, was his business; he had a perfect right to his skepticism. But for him to assert that he held *the proof* that Fandor and he were swindlers, no! he could not allow that. He shouted:

"Give me your proof!"

"Very good, here it is,"—and with cold precision, while the officers of the Criminal Department pressed near him, deeply interested, he walked to his desk and taking up an envelope, held it out to Juve.

"Open that!" he told him.

Already Juve had torn the envelope half in two the quicker to see the contents.

"Well?" he demanded, as he drew from the envelope ten blank sheets of paper.

"Well, Juve, you don't understand now?"

"Not a bit!"

"Yet, it's perfectly simple. Listen to me: a young man presented himself here, a fellow as closely resembling Fandor as you resemble Juve..."

"Why certainly!"

"He proposed to write me a sensational piece of stuff. Its heading read: 'Fantômas has come to life again!'"

"'Has'... not rather: 'has he'?"

"'Has' come to life again. He affirmed the fact..."

"Then?"

"Then I accepted the proposed article, and offered the young fellow a price—a high price. We clinched the bargain. An hour after, my young man, who had been taken by my orders to a private room, handed me an envelope with the words: 'Here's my contribution.' I gave him a voucher on the cashier, and he took his departure."

"Well? where does the swindle come in? You've got the article?"

"No!"

"How no?"

"I've got nothing. The fellow was a swindler. The envelope he gave me I opened, and I've just handed it to you. It held nothing but blank sheets of paper!"

"Blank sheets of paper?... these blank sheets?"

"Yes! I had been swindled. Therefore the man I had received was not Fandor. Fandor, when he was alive, was an honest man.

He would never have played such a trick."

But for once Juve found no answer. The adventure now revealed to him threw him so completely off his balance that he forgot his other anxieties. Was mystery after mystery inevitably to follow to bewilder his wits? At the same time it was quite true that Fandor was not the man to do anyone out of a few louis like this!… And yet it was he, he Fandor, who had been at the *Capitale* offices.

Suddenly Juve looked up: "Excuse me! One word. Did Fandor give you an explanation of what his article contained?"

"No!… why?"

"Did he inform you what it was that justified his assertion that Fantômas had come to life again?"

"No, again.… But I don't see…"

"You can't see, sir! Well I'm going to show you! Can you take me to the room where he worked?"

"Certainly. Come…"

The journalist got up, and was on the point of leaving the room when the door opened and three young men entered:

"Now tell us, sir! Without humbug…"

"In a moment, gentlemen, in a moment!" broke in the Editor. "I'm busy,"—and repeated his invitation to Juve.

Still accompanied by his four bodyguards more and more intrigued, and escorted by the Editor of the provincial issue of *La Capitale,* Juve a moment later found himself in a small glass-partitioned room:

"It was here the self-styled Fandor wrote…"

"Very good!" Juve thanked him. "Now, look !"—and without the smallest hesitation he seated himself at the desk that stood in the middle of the apartment. Picking up a pen lying on the desk, dipping it in the ink and taking a sheet of paper, he announced:

"You see I am writing, don't you? Look, I am writing: 'Fandor was really Fandor.' Do you see?"

"Yes, of course!… After that?"

"After that? Nothing. I fold the paper. I put it under cover. Look, there's the envelope. Let us go back to your office now."

"So be it! But still I don't see…"

"A moment's patience! just a moment! This way, isn't it?"

Two minutes and the four officers, Juve and the Editor were back in the latter's private room. Then at last the imperturbable detective gave some tokens of excitement.

"Now!" he declared, "it ought to be ready now. Open my envelope, sir!"

And there and then a cry of amazement escaped the Editor's lips. The sheet of paper on which with his own eyes he had seen Juve write the line he had read was blank, absolutely blank."

"Now you understand?" Juve demanded quietly, "you understand, don't you?… No? Then I will explain: Fantômas— yes, I say plainly Fantômas—Fantômas knew that Fandor had discovered his existence. Fantômas knew that, as sure as fate, Fandor would make for *La Capitale,* his own paper, to write his revelations on the point. Fantômas did not wish these revelations to appear, so Fantômas, or his accomplices—he has plenty—put sympathetic ink in his inkwell—sympathetic ink, the stuff that fades out when it dries. Come, you understand now? Fandor really wrote his contribution. He handed you his envelope, in all good faith, but when you opened it, all was blank. So there you are!"

At that same minute the door again burst open. This time it was a compositor, who popped in his head.

"Sir," he appealed to his chief, "sir, you know about it? No?… Well, it's just maddening. All the copy they send down to us fades out. The ink is 'faked,' the men say."

"Tut, tut!" cried the unhappy Editor in dismay, and half beside himself he slammed the door, then stepping back to Juve with outstretched hand:

"You forgive me?"

"Of course I do!"

"So you *are* Juve? It was really and truly Fandor?"

"Why, yes!"

"And you say Fandor has disappeared?"

For once Juve lost his air of assurance. For a while, as with unerring perspicacity he fathomed in a moment the snare with

which Fandor had allowed himself to be entrapped, he had forgotten his anguish. Now, with redoubled force, it was tearing
fiercely at his heartstrings. Yes, Fandor was right, Fantômas
had come to life again. Everything proved it. Moreover, had the
journalist not said so himself? and Fandor was not one to speak
at random. How indeed fail to see Fantômas' hand in this clever
trick of the sympathetic ink? Who but he could have contrived
and carried such a thing out successfully?

"So *he*," Juve reasoned, "did not wish the article to appear.
It follows *he* was certain to stop Fandor from rewriting it. It
follows it was *he* without a doubt who prevented Fandor from
going to me." With paling cheeks poor Juve thought on:

"Yes, Fantômas, the Lord of Terror, the Genius of Evil, the
King of Horrors, was capable of anything! What might he not
have done with Fandor, now that the journalist was a stumbling
block to the realization of his grim projects?

With choking voice Juve asked:

"When did Fandor leave here? Were you the last who saw
him?"

"I think so… Yes!… But wait, we will ask the messenger,"—
and he rang the bell. A moment later he was questioning the
boy, who had hurried to answer the summons:

"My lad, you saw Monsieur Fandor leave, eh?… You know
who I mean, don't you?"

"Surely, sir! But I didn't see him. I was gone on an errand."

"On an errand? Who for? What time was it?"

"The time? that I can't say… But Monsieur knows quite well.
It was Monsieur Henri who sent me… All the same it was a
false address… Listen, sir, here's what Monsieur Henri said."

"Monsieur Henri? What Monsieur Henri? Not Monsieur
Henri from Paris, I suppose?"

"Yes, it was, the Boss, sir!"

"But I never saw him!"

"Why, he went up to you."

"You're dreaming!"

"No, sir, I'm not. Why, I wouldn't believe it was him at first.
Then he showed me his dispatch case. His name's on it, so

there!”

All the while the boy was speaking, Juve was pacing the floor restlessly, his face alternatively paling and flushing red.

“Allow me!” he begged, and began in his turn to question the boy:

“My lad, you know this Monsieur Henri by sight? No?…”

“I’d never set eyes on him before, sir!”

“Then anybody, no matter who, could tell you it was your master?”

“But… the dispatch case?”

“Costs fifty francs, a dispatch case does!… And the address he sent you to was bogus?”

“Yes, there’s no such number.”

Juve turned to the Editor. “Open the envelope,” he said. “Yes, the envelope given this youngster to get him out of the way.”

“Be it so! but there’s bound to be nothing inside, if it was not the real Monsieur Henri?”

“Open it, open it!”—and the Editor did as he was bidden.

“Mercy on us!” he groaned the next instant. Between his fingers trembled a sheet of paper. It bore, written in pencil, these two lines, which the Editor read out in a shaking voice:

> My advice to you is not to try to recover trace of Fandor. That might cost him his life. Hear and obey. Farewell!

“No signature!” concluded the journalist with a groan. Juve had fallen back into a chair, burying his face in his hands. His voice was shaking with sobs as he replied: “No signature? No! no need to sign that. He knew sure enough the message would reach me. Yes, he knew that sure enough… *He* did… Fantômas did!”

And for once in his life, unashamed, Juve burst into tears.

*     *     *     *     *

For the moment none dared stir in the Editor’s room.

The tears of a man like Juve are a terrible thing to witness. They manifest an overwhelming emotion, and emotion is infectious.

Doubtless in the last few minutes the Editor of *La Capitale* had become convinced that he was actually in the presence of the veritable Juve. But the four officers of police still fought against admitting the fact. Meantime all held their breath in suspense. In the little room hovered an invisible shadow, imperious, menacing, a shadow none could locate precisely, but which each and all could divine—*his* shadow, the shadow of Fantômas, of that master of cruelty, no atrocity could balk of his purpose. Lo! the nightmare that had held the world palpitating in terror was to begin afresh! Fantômas was alive again!

Juve wept on. For himself he would have felt no fear. He was indifferent to all else when he thought of Fandor's danger. Where was his "little lad"? What peril was it precisely that threatened him? How could he be saved? But Juve was too much a man of action to give way for long to profitless discouragement.

"No," he told himself, "the first engagement of a war does not decide the victory,"—and this war was only beginning!

Juve sprang up. His eyes were dry now and his face impassive. "Very well," he declared, "I will save Fandor, and I will win the day over Fantômas!"

With a whimsical smile he turned to his nonplussed bodyguard: "Say, gentlemen, you're taking me back to the Department?"

"If you wish… yes!"

"Let us be off then!"—and turning to the Editor—"Sir," he said, "I take it you don't any longer now accuse Fandor of having swindled you."

"Why, how can you say such a thing! Monsieur Juve, you'll shake hands with me,"—and the two men clasped hands in a cordial grip.

Then the journalist: "One word more! What am I to publish?…"

But Juve stopped him with a decided gesture:

"Nothing, by God! nothing! What's gained by giving the enemy an official account of his victory? No! not a word of all this in your paper. It's best so. The public will know things quite soon enough… And it will be Fandor, I trust, who will supply it with needful and proper revelations."

"You are quite right."

Thereupon the car that had conveyed the prisoner and the police officers to *La Capitale* set off again immediately on its way and presently pulled up at the door of the Criminal Department headquarters.

"Of course you wish to see the Chief?" one of the officers asked.

"Yes, and at once."

"Very well, follow me,"—then, after a moment's hesitation, the man amended: "Follow me, *Monsieur Juve.*"

The party plunged into a dark and fetid stairway. Halfway up, before a door in the wall, three of the four inspectors surrounding Juve halted.

"Not worthwhile all of us going up, eh? You're enough by yourself to keep an eye on the prisoner?" one of them asked another, the officer in fact who had just addressed Juve by his name.

"Yes, certainly! See you again!"

Alone now with the only remaining member of his bodyguard, Juve pursued his way upstairs. He said no word, but it was plain his mind was working feverishly. The smallest petty details noted in the course of his visit to *La Capitale* passed in review before his mind's eye, were pigeonholed in his memory and definitely assigned each its own proper degree of importance. It was only by such calculation and classification he could hope to find the clue whereby to save Fandor's life.

Deeply absorbed as he was, Juve was vaguely conscious of being conducted by the officer accompanying him into an anteroom where an usher was seated at a table, reading a sporting paper with the deepest interest. No less vaguely he heard the dialogue that ensued.

"Say, Charles," asked Juve's companion, addressing the attendant, "is the Chief within?"

"Yes, but ever so busy."

"Oh, no matter for that."

"Yes, but it does matter... I give you fair warning, he's in a stew..."

"All right, all right! But the business brings me here brooks no delay. Go and tell him... He'll see me."

"I tell you he won't."

"I tell you he will."

Then Juve suddenly woke up. He had distinctly heard the last words of the usher, spoken in the positive tone of a man certain of his facts. The fellow had said:

"The Chief will not see you right away. I tell you again—he is engaged in an important interview... Well, if you must know, he's with a ghost—an uncanny business! He's with Monsieur Juve!"

"He's with Monsieur Juve"—the very words Juve had been expecting, watching for on the usher's lips. The Inspector-in-Chief was with "Juve," while he, Juve, was in his anteroom, the handcuffs still on his wrists! He could have cursed with rage. He could have screamed with annoyance. But not a muscle of the great detective's face quivered. Juve remained absolutely impassive. Better still, with a look of supreme authority, a look of compelling moral force, Juve imposed silence on his dumbfounded companion. The cry of terror that had risen to the officer's lips froze in the utterance. He could only stammer painfully:

"Oh! he is with Juve!... well, well?"—and he seemed to be searching the real Juve's face to learn what he was to think of it. Unfortunately for him, the worthy man was not to see Juve's face at all clearly. Taking advantage, indeed, of the fact that the room was only dimly lighted by a single gas jet, Juve had stepped back and bending his head the better to avoid being seen, he was tiptoeing to the door of the private room where *another Juve* was interviewing the Inspector-in-Chief.

Another Juve?... Oh, the King of Police Officers felt no doubt! This "other Juve" he could readily put a name to!—and his every nerve quivered with rage, and every muscle tautened. There, he was there, in that room!

"It's not long they've been together," added the usher, addressing the police officer. "But the Chief saw him at once. And when I showed him in, I saw immediately there'd be a rumpus in a minute! The boss threw up his hand to heaven. Then, upsetting his chair, he sprang forward, while he waved me from the room and banged to the door. Yes, my own idea is, there's going to be the Devil's own dance presently,"—and the fellow laughed a thick laugh.

As a matter of fact the fellow was perfectly right. When "Juve" was announced, the Inspector-in-Chief had naturally supposed this was the individual who had saved his wife's life and whose return he was impatiently expecting. Consequently his surprise had been extreme and his bewilderment no less on observing that the person coming towards him, a free man, without handcuffs and unguarded, was another Juve, a duplicate Juve.

Doubtless the two were much alike. Doubtless they might have been confounded by anyone else, but not by a police officer. Certain details immediately struck the Inspector-in-Chief: those iron-gray locks, a wig?… And the nose, the thin, straight nose, cleverly modified by makeup?… And the determined, energetic mouth, painted in with lipstick?…

He had little time, however, to scrutinize more thoroughly the face that seemed at the same time familiar and unknown. The Juve standing before him bowed curtly and at once began to speak.

"My dear sir!" he announced, "I am come to see if you are a fool or an intelligent human being!" adding with great rapidity: "I have asked you, under penalty of your wife's death, to send me fifty thousand francs… You have not done so… I have therefore given you proof that I am not to be mocked, and if your wife is not dead, that is because I willed it so… Now my patience is run out… Give me at once, at once I say, the contents of your service chest that is in that safe… Or…"

"It's enough to drive a man mad!" the Inspector-in-Chief told himself. "That man is not the Juve who saved Kate's life! In that case, why, the other, the Juve who did so, was surely his accomplice?"—and to gain time, he demanded aloud:

"Or?…"

"Or I am here to kill you—of course. And I shall clear out your safe myself. So choose!"

But the Juve who spoke in this way with an air of calm effrontery, had possibly reckoned without his host. If not very intelligent, the Inspector-in-Chief was at least no coward. Barely had he heard the threats addressed to him ere he rose to the occasion. Gathering himself together, he sprang forward with the suppleness of a tiger, leaping at the throat of the man trying to intimidate him.

"Scoundrel! Brigand!" he yelled.

But not another word. The man, with splendid promptitude, had merely taken a step to one side to dodge the attack. Then, quicker than lightning, he had hurled him against the wall and clapped a revolver to his head.

"One word," he said dryly, "and I blow out your brains! Now, your keys!"

He was victorious! A victory short and sharp, but short-lived. The same instant, driven in by a mighty blow, the door flew open, half torn from its hinges, and a voice of thunder pealed:

"Between you and me, Fantômas!"—and handcuffed as he was, Juve, the real Juve, sprang in. With one bound he hurled himself at the villain whom he had not hesitated to designate by the name of Fantômas.

Nor did Fantômas—but was it indeed *He*—hesitate an instant. With a crook of the legs he sent the Inspector-in-Chief rolling on the floor. Then, revolver in hand, he faced his new assailant.

"Between you and me, Juve!"—and he seemed on the point of firing.

A second more and, not a doubt of it, Juve would have fallen, his brains bespattering the carpet.

Not so! Juve was not the man to hesitate—a moment's hesitation and he was a dead man—he threw himself full length on the ground, and twisting with the adroitness of an acrobat, he dealt his opponent such a kick the wretch's bruised and shattered hand dropped his weapon.

"Between you and me, Fantômas!" repeated Juve triumphantly, and he was on his feet in an instant…

Too late!… The pretended Juve was no longer in the room!

Oh! the two enemies, Juve and Fantômas, were well worthy of each other, capable, the first for duty's sake, the second for his own vile ends, of the maddest deeds of daring and address.

In one step the man was across the room and had leapt on the sill of the half-open window. From the roof above dangled a rope. A coincidence? No, coincidence is not so propitious as all that. The rope was there of set purpose. By the time Juve reached the window, Fantômas—it was he, it could be no other but *He*—had grasped the rope and was sliding down it at a giddy speed.

"Damnation!" swore the police officer. Down below in the street stood a hay-wagon, driverless and apparently derelict. It was in it the scoundrel fell—softly, and in an instant had leapt to the ground with a laugh. Further on a motorcycle was leaned against a shopfront. The fellow raced to it, mounted and away with a salvo of explosive laughter.

"But we can kill him, kill him!" the Inspector-in-Chief was vociferating behind Juve's back. He had got to his feet, picked up the brigand's weapon and was taking aim.

"Idiot!" screamed Juve, and snatched the revolver out of his colleague's hands at the exact moment the motorcyclist disappeared round the corner of the street.

"Idiot!" repeated Juve, furious. "Why, man alive! It's ourselves you're after killing!"

The scene presented at that moment in the Inspector-in-Chief's office was, for all its tragic seriousness, farcical in the extreme. So swift had been Juve's entrance, so rapid the would-be murderer's departure, that no one had had time to intervene. Still the policeman and the usher had rushed pellmell into the room, only to stand in the middle of the floor paralyzed with astonishment, mouths wide open and eyes starting out of their heads.

The Inspector himself stood silent and panting for breath. At last the official found his voice.

"Idiot?" he asked. "Why idiot?… I could have killed him!"

"Really?" sneered Juve.

"I am a first-rate marksman!"

"Delighted to hear it!… And you shoot with Fantômas' revolvers?"

Then, without waiting for an answer, Juve held out his manacled hands to the astonished police officer: "There, my friend, just knock those bracelets off. You have your Chief's permission…"

The Inspector-in-Chief nodded assent. He had not a word to say. Juve's last remark had put the lid on his bewilderment. In a timid voice, while Juve was chafing his wrists numbed by the pressure of the handcuffs, he asked: "If I shoot with Fantômas' revolvers? No, of course not! But all the same, you don't imagine, do you, he carries dangerous weapons?"

"For those who use them, why, yes!"

"Eh? what do you mean?"

Juve showed signs of a sudden, momentary peevishness: "Why there, can't you understand *anything*? Come, did you really suppose it was you Fantômas wanted to murder? or that he was after your safe and the paltry fifty thousand francs in it?"

"By God! yes, I did!" stammered the Inspector-in-Chief.

"What foolishness!" Juve proceeded. "Little Fantômas cared about you! It was I he was expecting, yes I! I! He knew very well they'd be bringing me to see you. He was pretty sure that, finding a bogus Juve was talking to you, I should force my way in come what might. You were only the pretext to bring about our meeting… Do, pray be logical! Fantômas has captured Fandor to hinder the journalists proving that he, Fantômas, was alive. Now is it likely he would leave *me* in peace? Was he not bound, as sure as fate, to try to kill me?"

"To kill you? you? Why…"

"Why, yes, to kill me! You're of no account!… Only, luckily, I knew this much, that you don't disarm Fantômas unless he wants to be disarmed… His revolver? I snatched his revolver from him, did I? Bah! that's exactly what he wanted! That's what he played for! Look you! Come along and you shall see if I'm not right." So saying Juve stooped and picked up the weapon dropped by the brigand. Then he laid it on a chair and taking a piece of string from the official's desk, tied it to the trigger.

"Come along!" he repeated, "let's get outside the room. There, look. Now, do you begin to understand?" Arrived in the anteroom he order his companion to stand at a distance and pulling the string, fired off the revolver.

The trap was manifest to all, the terrible trap Juve's marvelous sagacity had frustrated. The instant the striker met the cartridge the weapon, the muzzle of which had evidently been plugged, burst into a thousand fragments. If, in the heat of battle, Juve had picked it up and fired—and it was twenty chances to one this would have happened—he would have been killed!

"Are you convinced now?" he demanded, and the Inspector-in-Chief gasped:

"By God, sir! you are Juve indeed. Oh! forgive me! I put myself under your orders… I… I…"

"Telephone!" ordered Juve in a peremptory tone, recovering all his calmness. "Tell them at the railway station to have a prison coach ready, and give me four officers. I shall take the first train to Paris."

"But why this prison van? this escort? You are Juve. Why should I keep you prisoner?"

"Of course," returned the other. "But, you see, I don't intend to be murdered in the night. This way I shall be safe, especially with a bodyguard of four. I want to sleep, and I want to live… I want to live to save Fandor!"

## 8. A "Very Nice" Young Man!

The precautions Juve had taken in having a special coach reserved for him and demanding the escort of four Inspectors of the Marseilles Criminal Department, were these really necessary? Truly it did not seem so. The journey was absolutely uneventful in nothing whatever differing from any other, and when at last the train drew near Paris, Juve might well believe he had for once been too prudent.

Suddenly the train began to slow down, whistled off the signals, and presently rolled majestically into the terminus. Without a moment's delay, having all the look of a man determined not to lose a second, Juve unlatched the carriage door and sprang down on the platform.

Behind him the four guards immediately formed up. Then Juve broke into a sudden peal of laughter.

"Poor devils!" he grinned. "Blind men who think they can see through a brick wall. Ah! the wiliness of the Force!"—and he laughed harder than ever.

No, indeed! It was from no motives of "prudence" Juve had demanded the luxury of four traveling companions and a special coach all to himself. It was simply and solely because he had perfectly well guessed that the Marseilles Criminal Department still entertained doubts as to his identity. It was because, by no means desirous of being conveyed to Paris in the guise of a veritable prisoner, he had, by claiming escort, anticipated the fears of the Inspector-in-Chief. Moreover, the astute detective knew quite well that the Inspector who accompanied him had strict orders not to lose sight of him without special instructions from the Police. Above all, he felt persuaded that, while his train was on its way, the electric telegraph had been busy announcing his resurrection, stating the hour of his departure, mobilizing all the forces of the Paris Department.

"Oh, ho! the Police!" laughed Juve to himself. "Police, thy name is red tape!"—and still grinning at his own parody, the great detective alighted. Then he stopped dead: "Well, well," he muttered and paled visibly. On the platform, ten yards from him, just facing the spot where the prison coach had come to a halt, stood a short man, a slim figure in a black greatcoat, a hard felt hat pushed rather to the back of the head and eyes that glittered strangely behind a pair of glasses riding on the bridge of a sharp, thin nose.

"The Chief! Monsieur Havard! He's not changed one atom!"—and deeply moved, his heart beating fast, Juve sprang to greet the able Head of the Department. Yes, he had had an intuition, almost a certainty, that he would be there. Surely, in learning of Juve's resurrection, M. Havard must at first have feared he was going insane. Then, with the utmost haste was he not bound to have come to stand there, keen as ever, peering into the face of this dead man they told him was come alive again?

Juve was within arm's length when he addressed him with a "Good day, Chief!"

At this, going white as paper, M. Havard recoiled...

"You, Juve!... You! By God! then it's true, is it? You here? you...?"

Calmly, knowing well the affection the great man bore him, Juve took the other's arm and drew him apart.

"Certainly!" he declared. "Certainly it is I... I myself and nobody else. And here's the proof. You remember, Chief?"

M. Havard seemed to have been actually watching for the words...

"Remember what? Hmm... what do you mean?"

Slowly and deliberately Juve spoke:

"This is what I mean, Chief—Je-do-ea-tide-ra-phi-sicca-o-de-ve-ca-di!"

No sooner had the old detective uttered the cabalistic and apparently meaningless syllables than M. Havard threw himself into his arms and pressed him to his bosom:

"Juve! Juve! good old Juve! So it *is* you! Good Lord! to have mourned you as dead for ten years, and to now see you again!"

At this point Juve turned to the four police officers standing by in bewilderment at the unexpected recognition:

"You don't understand, gentlemen?" he asked them. "The syllables I have just pronounced seem absurd to you? Well, they are not absurd at all. They merely constitute tokens of recognition agreed upon between M. Havard and me! Being known only to us two, they clearly prove who I am,"—and turning again to M. Havard: "You'll give them leave to go now, won't you, sir?"

"Why, of course!"

"Off with you, gentlemen. My compliments to Marseilles when you get there!…"

Then, without giving them a second thought, Juve drew M. Havard away:

"Your car?"

"In the station yard."

"You'll drop me in passing?"

"Where, Juve?"

"As if you didn't know, sir!"

"Then you think *he* is in it?"

"Not a doubt of that!"

"But you need rest?"

"After ten years being dead? Not I!"

M. Havard ordered his chauffeur to make for Auteuil, and then, as the vehicle rolled lightly in that direction, Juve proceeded to give his companion a concise summary of the events that had occurred at Marseilles, winding up with the words:

"You see, sir, doubt is now impossible. Fantômas is alive again. Yes, alive again like Fandor and myself… Fandor is in Fantômas' hands. It is Fantômas who…"

"Fantômas!" broke in M. Havard in a low, rumbling voice as if he were thinking aloud and speaking simply for his own ears. "Fantômas! Free again, so it would seem? Let loose again on Paris, on mankind?"

Presently, laying a nervous hand on the other's arm: "And you are prepared to begin the war afresh?"

"Why, of course, sir!"

"And you suspect…?"

"Sir, I should like to have details about the Auteuil mystery."

But for once M. Havard hesitated about an answer. Since Juve had joined him, he had gathered from the detective's brief allusions that the latter firmly believed he saw the hand of Fantômas in these events. But was he not perhaps mistaken? With some hesitation the Head of the Criminal Department admitted:

"Yes, I too had thought it possible. Yes, I too believed so for a moment. But now…"

"Now?"

"Now? Hmm… Well, now, Juve, I'm not so sure! A woman appears to be in two places at once… a dead dog, or one taken for such, has turned up again alive… Yes, it's puzzling enough! But why must Fantômas be mixed up in it? What's mysterious is not necessarily criminal."

"No, sir! But what's mysterious is always disturbing. Common sense bids us refuse credence to such miracles. They invariably conceal some trap or other."

"But you yourself, Juve… and Fandor? and Fantômas? All that's miraculous enough surely…"

But Juve was ready with his answer:

"We? oh! for us, we were not dead. We only passed for dead—and that's not at all the same thing. It admits of explanation. But, devil take it, neither Henri Tardoux nor the vet were crazy, I suppose? Mlle. Eléonore is on the high seas, that's unquestionable; while the dog, till proof to the contrary, must be considered dead. Now, seeing that the facts as they stand seem to lead to a nonsensical, an impossible conclusion, it is logical to conclude that these facts are false—or that they have been manipulated with some sinister purpose."

M. Havard said nothing, and Juve went on:

"So this is what I think in a nutshell: Mlle. de Vautreuil who is on the Atlantic is not in Paris! If the dog was dead, the dog cannot have come alive again. That I say, and that I stick to! If the contrary seems to be true, that's because Fantômas wants it to…"

"Fantômas? but why Fantômas?"

"Who save he, sir, would ever have thought of such things?"

Again M. Havard found nothing to say. Juve was a first-rate hand at drawing conclusions there was no disputing. Who, indeed, save Fantômas could have conceived the idea of establishing the presence of one and the same person in two places at once? Who save *He* could make believable the resurrection of a dead animal? Still, for all that, the clue was very slender…

Juve proceeded to ask for further details:

"Wealthy, this Comte de Vautreuil?"

"Very. Entrusted moreover with a whole boxful of diamonds to sell—to the tune of millions, it appears."

"Oh!" was all Juve said, apparently not much impressed by this piece of information. "And Mlle. Eléonore?" he went on. "What does she say? or does she still refuse to speak?"

"Yes, still refuses to say a word, and impossible to come near her, into the bargain. The doctors say the woman has suffered some fearful shock…"

"Oh God! but doctors are past masters in the art of talking without saying anything!"

"And that it was this shock that brought on her state of abnormal sensitiveness. When anyone goes near her she seems to experience positive pain, just as if they had struck her. The condition is one known to science. The medical books quote instances. It even appears to be curable, with time."

"Better wait then!" said Juve banteringly. "Now, sir, suppose you put me down at Montmartre, instead of taking me to Auteuil. I've got to find myself a lodging… Hmm, three rooms quite enough—two for Fandor, one for me."

"What say? Fandor? But poor Fandor…"

Juve's eyes twinkled:

"Fandor?… Ah, yes, you are anxious about him? I anxious? Not a bit now! In a word, he's a very nice young man, Fandor is! Who'd want to hurt him? Fantômas? Why, yes… but still… I'm leaving you here, sir. I'm going to take that tram."

No explanation was forthcoming, but M. Havard knew his

man. He knew better than anybody it was no good asking Juve to explain anything once he deliberately and purposely adopted an enigmatic attitude such as this.

"As you please, dear boy!" the Chief agreed, and stopped the car. "We shall see you at the Department?"

"Yes!… you reinstate me, eh?"

"Can you ask such a question?"

"Thank you, sir! thank you!"—and clasping M. Havard's hand, he shut the door, and the car continued its course.

But the great detective did not go far. He was at the Rond Point des Ternes, and making for a seat, he sank on the dirty bench:

"I couldn't stand anymore, no! I could not. I was fit to burst! Asinine staff like that when it's Fandor's life at stake, when each second that passes means his death perhaps!"

Juve clenched his fists, and shrugging in a fashion far from respectful towards M. Havard, went on:

"And he knows there's a box with millions in it, and I've just told him I am convinced Fantômas is come to life again!… Is the man blind?"

Then he sprang up again, his forehead wrinkling in anxious thought. If Fandor had been near his friend, he could not have failed to guess that at that moment Juve was planning some desperate project, that in the detective's subtle brain a ray of light was dawning.

"To work!" Juve exclaimed, and set off, turning his back on Auteuil and making for Montmartre at a rapid pace. As he went he was muttering to himself:

"Fandor! Fandor! Ah, if only I knew exactly what is the danger you run!"

*　　*　　*　　*　　*

At this same moment when Juve was suffering torments of anxiety as he thought of this dear comrade in so many struggles and so many dangers, Fandor, very much alive, but mad with rage, was foaming with impotent fury! Yet he was being very well looked after. He was in no pain. He was actually safe from all immediate danger. To all appearances Jerome Fandor was the object of such elaborate precautions that he ran no risk even of injuring himself by giving rein to his anger.

In the Marseilles goods station a hospital nurse, in white from head to foot and looking very smart in the becoming costume of the Ladies of the Red Cross, was walking beside a wheeled hand-litter which a railway employee pushed along and in which lay Fandor, dressed in a coarse blue gown, gagged and apparently incapacitated from stirring a limb…

Railwayman and nurse were chatting together:

"So, Mademoiselle, you're not afraid then to do your work?"

"Afraid, I afraid? Good Lord, no!… Why should I be afraid, tell me!"

"Well, there's the mad patients, nasty that, eh?"

"Only when the fit's on them."

"Yes, but you never know when it's coming on, ain't that so?"

"Why yes, of course!" the nurse agreed. "Now look you, that patient there has a horror of being shifted. So you see, they've just clapped the straitjacket on him."

"So's the fellow can't do a thing?"

"Oh! not a thing! You can see for yourself, his legs are tied fast with that strap, his arms secured by that buckle that holds 'em behind his back. Can't budge an inch!"

"For sure! and he can't give tongue neither, with the gag."

"Oh! the gag's only to stop him making a scandal. It's a young fellow his family's having brought back to Paris. Seems it was a fit of despair drove him off his nut. You can understand, in the train, we couldn't well have him yelling out; would have scared the passengers. So they just shoved the muzzle on, but it's only for the time being."

"Poor devil!" the railwayman summed up the situation. The "poor devil," Jerome Fandor to wit, was indeed to be pitied. His indignation had reached such a pitch that he felt he must choke with rage. Yes, he was mad, but it was with fury.

Was it not appalling to be tossed thus like a rag on a handbar-row, to see himself dragged along amid a throng of well-meaning people and not be able so much as to cry, "Help!"? "It is

Fantômas has got me! Fantômas who's bidden them put the straitjacket on me! Fantômas who makes out I am mad!… But there, even if I could cry out, nobody would believe me, oh God! Whatever I screamed out they'd set down to my being a madman!"—and he ground his teeth.

The poor fellow's situation was indeed deplorable. On waking from a long spell of unconsciousness—how long a spell he could not tell—he had found himself thus tied up and gagged, unable to raise a finger or stir a limb. He was in a sort of coach-house or shed, lying on a blanket spread on the ground and close beside a motor ambulance.

"Is this a nightmare?" had been Fandor's first thought, but very soon he realized that he was not dreaming. While in a second or two his memory was beginning to come back to him, and one by one he recalled the incidents attending his resurrection, his subsequent investigations at the Hôtel des Alliés and finally his visit to the Editor's room of *La Capitale,* the door of his prison opened.

"Fantômas! I am going to see Fantômas!" had been Fandor's first thought. What he did see was the entrance of a hospital nurse and a chauffeur—accomplices doubtless of the scoundrelly malefactor, as Fandor instantly divined.

But what were they going to do with him? The journalist had felt them lift and carry him to the motor ambulance, which presently drove out of the coach-house, which stood in a plot of waste ground, reached the busy streets of the city, and climbing the hill leading to the railway station, entered the premises devoted to goods traffic.

"Wherever are they taking me?" Fandor asked himself. He was soon to learn. Coming to a halt with his hand-litter, the railway employee stopped in front of a first-class carriage standing on a turntable.

"There you are," he announced. "You see I was right; the coach *wasn't* coupled to the Paris train… But you can get in and settle yourselves, you and your loony. That's the compartment, can't be no mistake. Look, see the chalk mark—'Reserved: Hospital Service.' It's for you, never fear," and the man started off on an endless string of explanations:

"To begin with, when the train's got to pick up sick folks, dead cases that is, or dead 'uns, or murderers perhaps—special passengers in fact, it's always in our goods yard they load 'em up… There, look for yourself, the whole side in these special compartments opens all of a piece… Now, I'll just hitch the poor devil up. Once in, he'll be a bit more comfortable… And, I say, best be quick about the job. There's the engine coming to back you into station… Heave ho! There you are!"—and Fandor felt himself hoisted up, shaken about, and finally rolled over onto the narrow invalid couch of a specially appointed hospital carriage.

In another half minute there was a loud clash of metal as the locomotive struck the buffer, driving the coach back a half-dozen yards.

"There!" sang out the railway man. "Now they're going to back you into the station and couple you up to the express. Good night, Mademoiselle! A pleasant journey to you!"

"Goodbye," replied the nurse carelessly, adding sotto voce: "My word! I thought you were never going."

Meanwhile Fandor was getting more and more exasperated. All this idle chatter he had been listening to made him feel sick. Could any woman be so base as to play the odious part this creature was playing?

"As for you," Jerome Fandor swore to himself, "if ever I come across you, I promise you I'll make you dance a little dance of my own contriving!"—and he made a violent effort to twist his body round, trying to secure at any rate a rather less uncomfortable posture. This he had by no means succeeded in doing when he found his wardress bending over him, and made the only movement it was possible for him to make, viz., raising his eyes to her face.

"My dear," the woman addressed him in a half-mocking tone, "I'd best give you fair warning here and now. I have my orders, dreadful orders. If you stir, I am to give you an injection with this syringe… So, I don't think I need say more. You understand?" Yes, Jerome Fandor understood perfectly. If he was not "good," they would poison him! Oh, yes, it could mean neither more nor less than that, the nurse's little speech of admonition. The woman went on:

"And I'll tell something else into the bargain. You are not mad. I know that! *He,* your captor and keeper, is quite well aware of it too. What he means to do with you, I don't know. But, at any rate, he's not in the train and you have nothing to fear from me.… You are a very nice young man, I can see that. So, keep quiet, go to sleep! No good to be got by kicking up a shindy to no purpose. Tomorrow we shall be there… Good night!"

All the time the woman was speaking, Fandor felt his fury getting fiercer… "He had nothing to fear," "*He,* his captor, was not in the train," "He was a very nice young man, and he would be wise enough to keep quiet…" The wretched man longed to protest against each and all of these declarations, even at the peril of his life. "He had nothing to fear?" A lie! How could he fail to guess the fate in store for him?

"His captor?" But that was Fantômas. He had gathered that much! Why not say the name straight out?… "He was not in the train,"—nay, would to God he were! would to God that hated form might suddenly appear in the carriage! At any rate Fandor would be out of suspense, would *know* he was condemned to die.

Next minute he wanted to laugh. Why the devil did the nurse tell him he was "a very nice young man"? What a funny thing to say! "A very nice young man or a very bad young man, a good boy or a naughty boy,—if only I had my hands free for ten seconds, my guardian angel would precious soon see what a 'very nice' young man is capable of!"

But alas! to all appearance Jerome Fandor was not so soon to have his hands free—were it only for ten seconds. The carriage was alongside the platform now, and was being coupled up to the train, while Fandor could hear the farewells exchanged between passengers and friends seeing them off. They were on the point of starting. He muttered:

"And Juve is bound to suppose I am still at Marseilles, and is likely going to scour the whole town in search of me. To think I cannot leave him the very tiniest clue!"

Tied down on his pallet-bed, reduced practically to all but absolute immobility, just able, and that was all, to move his head, Fandor relapsed into a condition of despairing calmness. His passion was exhausted, and reason was reasserting its sway—and to reason was verily a sorry business in his present plight. "Where are they taking me?" he asked himself. "To Paris? Yes, no doubt. But Paris is a world in itself. And what do they mean to do with me? Why has Fantômas attacked me so immediately after I had come to life again?"

But now Fandor accused himself of a lapse of logic. He knew the answer to the question. Had he not received an ultimatum? Had he not refused to submit to the demand of the Torturer?

"Well and good!" he decided, "Fantômas is taking his revenge. But I have no regrets. If I am killed, Juve is still there to avenge *me*."

*     *     *     *     *

A shrill whistle, followed by a loud hissing of escaping steam, and the train had started. Now each turn of the wheels was taking him further and further away from Juve, his only hope, for Juve alone knew his identity, alone knew of his resurrection.

Presently, slowly and patiently, he managed to turn round a tiny bit.

"So," he said to himself, "my wardress is reading, is she? If she were a kind woman, she would read aloud." Next moment he saw he was mistaken. "But, no, she's not reading, she's asleep, she's actually snoring. Oh! tired, my good woman, tired out, eh?" He came to a rapid decision: "Suppose I took the opportunity not to be 'good'. Suppose I set about a survey of my surroundings. One never knows, it might come in useful."

Calling up all his energy, straining every muscle, attempting the impossible, he managed at last to turn over on his side, so that he could see something more of the compartment in which he lay a prisoner.

After a careful inspection of whatever he could see from his new position, he concluded:

"Nothing worth looking at there; not the faintest chance of escaping," and with another desperate struggle, he twisted half-round on his other side.

"Let's have a look this way too," he muttered. "At least it'll be a change. Besides, you never can tell. Best look at everything!"

No indeed, "you could never tell." The young man had barely completed his change of posture before he beheld something that interested him to the last degree.

"No, it can't be!" he cried. "That would be too good to hope for!... And even if it were so, I could never profit by the chance,"—and, his breath quickening, he panted with suppressed excitement.

For the third time he put out all his strength and succeeded in turning a little further on his side. He did so with the utmost possible circumspection, for he knew that, whatever happened, he must avoid waking his wardress. No doubt the wretched woman had deemed it unnecessary to keep a really strict watch on her prisoner, convinced as she was that he was quite incapable of moving. But all the same how providential her slumbers were!

Now he could see better, and all but gave vent to a cry of joy.

"The gas!" he thought. "Evidently we are in an old-fashioned type of carriage, lighted by gas. Yes, gas! And gas can stifle,"— and he laughed to himself behind his gag.

And then yet again he essayed, patiently and painfully, to turn over a little further still.

"Yes, it is certainly gas burning there... But here, close here, what is that?"

With starting eyes Fandor was gazing eagerly at a slender pipe running along the partition. This was what he had caught sight of and what had roused him to such vivid interest.

"I wonder," he whispered to himself, "if it *is* the gas. Hmm, one ought to try. But then, it may not be. And besides, I myself would be the first victim, if I did succeed."

"But no," he went on, "it's as simple as how-do-you-do. A child would think of the dodge! With a scrap of luck, I shall bring it off,"—and again he gave an amused laugh behind the gag.

"After all what do I risk? Dead tomorrow or dead today, what's the odds? My heirs won't be a bit the poorer."

And he smiled at the quaint conceit, as he added:

"Anyway I was dead the day before yesterday! Why worry about such a trifle? I know what it means, don't I?"

Surely Jerome Fandor exaggerated when he declared "a child" would have thought of the dodge he had just mentally decided on.

Bound as he was, feet and hands firmly tied, what profit could he hope to derive from the discovery, surely common-place enough, he had just made, to wit, that the carriage was lighted by gas?

For all that Fandor did not relax his efforts. Slowly, patiently, persistently, with infinite precaution, he set to work. Resting on his heels and head only, straining and stretching, making a spring of his body, he contrived to shift his position a little on the bed and worm himself up against the partition, his back towards it, his face to the carriage door.

Then his face hardened with a look of firm determination. "Now," he told himself, "the time's come to do a bit of damage to the Company's property… and to risk the syringe! So be it! Nothing ventured, nothing gained—and there's something I very much want to have."

A short second longer he seemed to hesitate, then evidently coming to a final and definite decision, he proceeded to carry out his scheme—an odd scheme indeed, that appeared little likely to lead to any important result. Fandor raised his head. The instrument with which he had been gagged was evident-ly a contrivance used in asylums for the insane and no doubt bearing the name of some celebrated specialist. It was fastened by a sort of buckle of nickel of quite a solid construction.

This massive buckle the journalist now utilized as a hammer. With a vigorous movement of the head, at the risk of injury to himself, he brought it with great force against the carriage window.

"Nothing happened so far!" he muttered. "Let's try again," and at the second attempt things went better, the glass was starred.

"Once more!"—and he struck again. This time, the glass was partly shivered, cracked, but still holding to the frame—railway-carriage windows are made of good, thick glass—the pane looked as if it had been broken by a bullet or a stone. It was holed in fact.

"And through the hole," Fandor told himself, "air comes in," as was indeed self-evident. But the journalist's object was a good deal more than merely to improve the ventilation.

"Well," he went on with his soliloquy, "my sweet nurse is still—I mustn't say snoring, that wouldn't be polite… Charming creature! I wouldn't wake her for the world. A 'very nice' fellow like me should always be courteous to ladies. However, suppose I go on with my little business."

Once more with a series of snakelike contortions, he shifted his position more to one side on the bed. His hands were secured behind his back by two straps firmly stitched to the sleeves of his straitjacket, but his fingers were free, and taking advantage of this, he made a further exploration of the ground. Slowly, with infinite pains, he groped about the surface of the partition, feeling for the pipe that had drawn his attention before.

"There!" he said at last, "there's the fellow… Well all that's left now is to get down to business."

But it was a forlorn hope, what he was attempting—for shifting his position on the bed, Fandor had noticed that the brass tongue of one of the strap buckles was up. This tongue he meant to force against the gas pipe so as to pierce the metal with the point.

At first the thing seemed impossible. The point kept slipping over the rounded surface of the lead and could get no bite on it. Then the train had speeded up, plunging full steam ahead through the darkness, and Fandor, balanced precariously with his back to the partition and shaken by the jolting, had little control over his movements.

"Good Lord! but I'm clumsy!" he growled. At long last, however, his patience was rewarded. The point of the tongue bites on a lump in the metalwork, catches in a slight dent.

"Now for it!" thought Fandor. "Austerlitz or Waterloo? God help me, as He helped poor Latude!"—and he worked with all his might and main. Was it to be victory or defeat?… Now he could feel the point pierce the lead, and he set to work to enlarge the hole.

Yes, the victor of Austerlitz's luck was to be his! So well he worked—and the property of the Company was so ill-found—that suddenly the pipe broke apart at a join.

Almost instantly a strong stench filled the carriage. The gas used for lighting, stored in a reservoir under compression, spread swiftly through the confined space of the compartment, making the air unbreathable.

"So there," growled Fandor, "one profits by the lessons one's been taught. After all, I'm only repeating the adventure in the cab. No doubt Fantômas used a more powerful, more poisonous gas, but there I do my best with the means under my command. Good! Now let's take our proper precautions. Clap your mouth to the hole, dear boy! Clap your mouth to the hole!"

He felt as happy as could be, convinced he was going to carry out successfully the impossible escape he had contrived for himself with such desperate recklessness.

"If the good lady who does me the honor to keep guard of me doesn't wake up, if she just quietly stifles, the 'very nice young fellow' will be bidding her a polite farewell in another ten minutes!"—and he laughed with satisfaction behind his gag. The gas, in fact, was, now pouring into the carriage, was rapidly rendering the air absolutely unbreathable.

But Fandor was taking no risks. Profiting by the judicious preparations he had prudently made, he had glued his lips to the fracture in the glass and was breathing the fresh air outside. The nurse, on the contrary, still fast asleep, was, all unconscious of her danger, inhaling the poisonous atmosphere.

Still might she not wake? Would she not make some struggle to save herself?

Suddenly Fandor heard a groan. Placed as he was, his forehead pressed to the glass, he could not see her. His heart contracted.

"Game's up?" he asked himself. But second after second passed, seconds that seemed interminable.

The groaning stopped. "That ought to have done the trick?" he calculated. "But there, I don't somehow want to kill her. She's a woman after all,"—and inhaling a deep mouthful of good air, then holding his breath, he turned round…

If the woman was still asleep, if she had fainted, Fandor might count on getting safe away…

*     *     *     *     *

A single glance reassured him. The felonious hospital nurse had slipped half off her chair. With eyes closed, a pallid face and arms dangling, she had let fall the book she was reading before dropping off to sleep, and now lay inert and motionless.

"So there!" thought Fandor approvingly, "yes, a highly dangerous thing, gas! 'Never leave your regulator open,'—that's what the Company's notice says."

But it was no time for laughing and joking. Now Fandor set to work with feverish haste. The journalist whose lips ever wore a merry smile, whose tongue was ever ready with some droll phrase, some amusing quip in the midst of the worst perils, had his serious side too, could prove himself energetic and carry through the boldest, most audacious decisions.

"To work!" he cried, and no longer having to fear his companion's awaking, he began the task of releasing himself. Another man might have found it a hard job. He made light of it with his characteristic adroitness. He finished breaking up the windowpane, chafed through the straps at his wrists against a jagged piece of glass still sticking in the frame, and his hands once free, was not long in removing his gag and untying his legs.

"Ow! but that's good," he cried… "But now let's see to the good lady there. Won't do for the fresh air to wake her up too soon."

Through the broken pane, in fact, the gas was fast escaping and the atmosphere becoming breathable again. Fandor took the hospital nurse in his arms, lifted her gently and deposited her on the invalid couch.

"There you are!" he soliloquized. "Doubtless, Mademoiselle, you'll have a bit of a headache when you wake. But I've a notion you won't take long in making up your mind. Indeed I wouldn't be surprised if you laid a complaint against me. Now you'll please excuse me, I'm going to be a bit indiscreet. Fact is, a trifle of money I must have." The nurse had slipped a small traveling bag under the seat. This Fandor opened without the smallest scruple and set about an inventory of the contents.

"Three hundred francs," he noted, as he came upon a well-filled purse. "Excellent! Fact is that's just about all I need… And a revolver! Ha, ha! That may come in useful!… Ah! and what's this note here?"

His face suddenly lit up. The note he had found was merely a scrap of paper that must have been rolled up into a ball and on which was typewritten the following message:

> Juve has left for Paris. His identity is to be established. He knows nothing about the Fandor business. Carry out my orders to the letter.

"So," grinned Fandor, rubbing his hands in delight, "Juve is in Paris. Why, that's good to hear. We will come together again to a certainty."

Re-closing the bag, Fandor now proceeded to strip off his straitjacket and the blue canvas trousers he was wearing. Underneath this asylum rig he still wore the costume he was dressed in when he first regained consciousness in Juve's company on the Marseilles housetop.

"So, we're all ready now, I think we may safely say. Here goes then, for the cinema act!"—and vouchsafing no explanation of this somewhat cryptic utterance, he was making for the carriage door when he stopped suddenly.

"On second thought, no!" he muttered. "No, I can't behave

like a cad and leave my guardian angel in a hole. Must play the game and do what we can to mitigate the horrors of her awakening!" Doubtless at any other time Fandor would not have acted like this. Face to face with a woman who was indisputably an accomplice of Fantômas, he would have felt no scruple about securing her person and delivering her over to justice. But did not present circumstances render such a course out of the question?

"They believe me dead—everybody does," he reflected. "Besides, I was put on the train as being a madman. If I show I am alive, if I announce that I am Fandor and that it is Fantômas who has given me out as insane, why, it's as plain as a pikestaff the public will just shrug its shoulders and they'll clap me on my straitjacket again!… Thank you, but I'm not taking any!"

Fandor hesitated no more. He just tore out a blank leaf from a memorandum book he found in the wretched woman's bag and scribbled in pencil the following ironical message:

"Received the sum of three hundred francs, which I undertake never to repay," signing at bottom: "A very nice young man."

"There," he observed, "with that little document to show, my wardress will be in a position to get Fantômas to reimburse her—if she sees fit to demand it!"—and cracking with laughter, he quitted the compartment for good and all, opening the door, letting himself down onto the step and gripping the handrail running along outside.

To Fandor an acrobatic feat such as this was child's play. To clamber along a train in motion, even an express train, was not a thing to give him pause. Still, this was not enough…

"The thing is, to get off the train," the young man was telling himself, "and I should prefer doing it without attracting attention. Discretion is one of the virtues I flatter myself I possess. Come, no shirking! A cinema stunt it must be—of a sort to make Pearl White and other admired screen stars turn green with envy!"

"Now! now's the time. If I don't break my neck, it's only my lucky star I'll have to thank for it!"

The express was still running at full speed. Ahead of the embankment an iron bridge could be made out, that appeared to be rushing to meet the train.

"No need to chicken out!" Fandor encouraged himself. "A bridge should be across a river… a river can be dived into, and when you know how to swim—a very useful accomplishment swimming…"

He did not finish the sentence. The moment the train emerged on to the metal flooring of the viaduct, Fandor took his leap—and as luck would have it he had timed his spring exactly right. The bridge did cross a river and the river was pretty deep. Jerome Fandor's dive was a beauty. In he went head first. Then with a vigorous kick he rose to the surface, struck out and swam triumphantly for the bank. Five minutes more and he had touched bottom and scrambled out on terra firma, delighted at the success of his venture.

"Of course," he told himself, "for a 'very nice' young man, I do look a bit like a tramp. The river was a precious muddy stream… Bah! with the breeze that's blowing I shan't take more than a couple of hours to dry. Once presentable, I will make for the nearest railway station I can come across. It's very certain Fantômas won't have dared to report my disappearance. So I'll just take a ticket for Paris, and in twenty-four hours at latest, Juve and I will be able to take action."

He had stripped off three parts of his clothing and was busy wringing them out with all the dexterity of a professional washerwoman.

"A touch of the iron would do these no harm," he noted, "but there, one mustn't be too particular. By the way, I'd gladly give a brace of sous to know what my wardress will say when she finds me vanished from my little bed. I fancy she'll find some slight difficulty in accounting for my disappearance!"

Jerome Fandor had guessed right. When, twenty-four hours later, he got out at Paris, his first care was to buy a paper, even before visiting a café near the terminus of the Paris, Lyon, Méditerranée in search of an early breakfast.

"What's the news?" he asked himself, and gave a start of surprise as his eyes fell on the first page. It bore in enormous letters a "scarehead" to the following effect:

*Dreadful Tragedy. A madman escapes from a train, after hurling from the carriage window the hospital nurse in charge of him. The bodies of neither of the two have yet been found.*

"Oh, ho!" he chuckled, "the good lady must have left the train at some intermediate point—and when they found the compartment empty, they made up this pretty story!"

Presently as he was breaking up a croissant in the cup of black coffee he had ordered, Jerome Fandor went on with his soliloquy:

"And to think that poor Juve will read this without understanding the facts. Well and good! I go on to the Prefecture immediately, but I'll start first by buying myself a new suit. I don't want to shame him—and then, I have visits to pay."

## 9. To Reappear Is Well—To Disappear Is Better!

Two hours later Jerome Fandor was disconsolately pacing the broad pavement of the Avenue Mozart in the peaceful district of Auteuil.

"Nobody in at Louis Rippert's!" he was growling. "Nobody in at Henri Tardoux's! Clearly my luck's out today… Yes, that's just the charm of a reporter's life—to have every door he knocks at slammed in his face!… Well, anyhow, I'll go and see the de Vautreuils. If I can pull off an interview with the resuscitated aunt, that will always be something interesting."

He was quickening his pace when suddenly he started round. At his ear a voice, pitched in a discreet key, had murmured:

"So you'd be keeping your eye like on Mlle. Josette, eh? For my part it's the cook *I* want to marry!"

Facing swiftly round, Fandor threw up his hand to heaven in sheer astonishment.

"Bouzille!" he cried wonderingly, "Bouzille, is it?"

"None other!"

"But what are you doing here, you scamp?"

"M'sieur Fandor, by your leave, sir, but you insult my dignity as a man and a citizen!"—and then, without a trace of rancor, he offered a friendly hand to the journalist.

A strange character, this Bouzille. In old days a common tramp roaming the country roads, now an old man of sixty, a scamp if ever there was one, yet honest withal according to his lights, the very type the police harass, judges condemn and jailers lock up, but for all that everybody's good friend, a genial, jovial loafer. Jerome Fandor well remembered his first coming to Paris, his appearance at Père Korn's tavern and the calm nonchalance with which thenceforth, a human wreck, he had haunted the lowest purlieus of the Great City.

An accomplice of Fantômas'? No! Jerome Fandor knew this

was not the truth. Bouzille had known Fantômas; he had even done him services; he had cultivated the society of members of his gang… But many a time he had given a helping hand to Juve and the police too. The poor wretch, forever on the prowl after a five-franc bit, was undoubtedly capable of many cunning tricks, but then he was as simple and irresponsible as a child with it all.

"When people pays me, I keeps faith with 'em!" was one of his sayings. The fact was that after extracting one franc he was always ready to ask yet another of his victim just to tell him he was betrayed after all!

In a flash Fandor recalled all these little details, the while he was shaking the old fellow's gnarled hand with a cordial grip. Then he asked himself, his instincts as a hunter of news already awakened:

"Now why should Bouzille mention Mlle. Josette? Does he know her then?"—and already he was mentally planning out a line of investigation, and at once started with the question:

"But what's become of you, Bouzille, all this long time nobody's set eyes on you?"

"M'sieur Fandor, no offense meant, it's you we should put that question to."

"Granted, Bouzille!… But I asked first."

"Yes, M'sieur Fandor, yes! But I'm thirstier than you."

"That means you want a glass?"

"You're fly enough, M'sieur Fandor! You know what talking means!"

"Off we go then, old sot!… And, you'll tell me your news,"—and disregarding what respectable folks might say, the journalist carried off the old vagabond to a neighboring drinking den. There Bouzille gave full vent to his loquacity:

"What am I doing, M'sieur Fandor! Bless you, I'm doing business, as a man should! Industry, commerce, all that runs in my blood. M'sieur Citroen and me, we're a match!… I'm a Jack-of-all-trades!"

"All trades, Bouzille? and what does that mean?"

"Well, I chop wood… I recover lost property. I bury dogs

that die in pupping… more by token, I fetch them as *is* croaked back to life again…"

"Oh? what's that you say?"

In spite of himself Fandor gave a jump… no doubt he knew perfectly well you must never hustle Bouzille if you wanted to draw interesting secrets out of him. But he was equally well aware that the old fellow, for all his simpleton air, was far from being a fool. If Bouzille threw out casually statements so extraordinary as the one he had just made, for certain he knew something… and wasn't minded to make a mystery of it.

The tramp meantime, pretending not to notice his companion's surprise and interest, was hammering on the zinc counter with his fist in a lordly way!

"Another of the same, eh, M'sieur Fandor?… and it's you stand the racket again, M'sieur Fandor—no offense meant?"

"Righto, Bouzille!… But you were saying…?"

"That I was a dog's undertaker? Yes, so I be. I even dream odd times of making a bigger business of it. What I ought to have, M'sieur Fandor, is a handcart—with tears painted on it, you know. Then for sure, I could raise my prices. You wouldn't care, M'sieur Fandor, to join in as partner like?"

"Bouzille, old man, too much palaver!"

"Good and well, I'm boring you then?"

But it was no use trying to change the conversation. Fandor stuck to his point:

"You were telling me, Bouzille, how sometimes you brought your dogs back to life again…"

But the journalist was cut short. Bouzille had clapped a peremptory finger to his lips.

"Hush!" he whispered. "If I said so, I did wrong."

"Why?"

"Because, M'sieur Fandor, I'm getting old, and to think of them things just knocks me out of time… If I'm to talk of that, I must eat a bit o' something, to keep up my spirits like."

"Bouzille, you are the limit! Yes, eat if you like to, but speak!"

"So I will, M'sieur Fandor… But I may give the order—and you'll pay again, eh?"—and he shouted:

"A crusty loaf, landlord!... And a whack of cheese, ripe old Camembert, eh? the sort that walks off the plate all on its own... A garlic sausage—to keep the flies off... And a pint of brew! That won't break you, M'sieur Fandor?"

"You'll ruin me, Bouzille! But there, I fancy you're going to tell me some very interesting things."

"All I know, my word and honor!... Come a bit to one side, no call for eavesdroppers!"—and smiling happily Bouzille took his seat at a table face to face with Fandor, who asked himself anxiously what surprising details he was going to learn from his picturesque guest.

*      *      *      *      *

Alas! the journalist was not at the end of his troubles. To make Bouzille speak out was never an easy thing, and on this particular day the old fellow was more than usually disposed to be secretive:

"M'sieur Fandor, I respect treaties, I do. *I'm* not like the Boches. I promised you I'd tell you what I know, didn't I? Well, here you are. The fact is, I know nothing, not a thing! I don't understand one blessed thing about that story of coming back to life. And you can say so, if you like, in your paper. It's God's truth..."

"But come..."

"Wait a second then! That's the outline of the story, the gist of the thing, so to say. But, you understand, there's details. I don't see much in 'em myself... but you and Monsieur Juve... By the by, he's quite well, Monsieur Juve, is he?"

At that moment, had it not been for his knowledge of the individual, he would gladly have wrung Bouzille's neck for him! As it was, he cursed the old wretch's reticence, and the idle, meaningless remarks he indulged in as if on purpose to exasperate his auditor.

Anyway, Fandor succeeded in refraining from actual violence.

"Juve is very well, Bouzille," he said. "But..."

"But what? M'sieur Fandor?"

"But I don't recommend you to go near him. He'd run you in, my lad, right enough, to teach you not to hide things from your friends. So there!"

But Bouzille only burst out laughing and replied in a bantering tone:

"Oh, ho! you want to frighten me, M'sieur Fandor, do you?… It's a fact you've not improved your character by being dead ten years!"

"Bouzille!"

"Now, now, don't get angry! But look, a thing like this here's well worth a louis. Just a louis, M'sieur Fandor, and I'll tell you all I know—details and all, every damned thing in fact!"

"Bouzille, I'll give you five francs—and quite enough too."

"Paid in advance, M'sieur Fandor?"

"Paid afterwards, Bouzille—with a bonus of another five francs if you tell me something really interesting."

"Oh, M'sieur Fandor, but you're on the stingy side, you are, and mighty suspicious… But no matter, here goes for what I know,"—and the old fellow, no doubt thinking he had made a very good bargain of it, resolved to tell all he really knew about the mysterious resurrection at Auteuil.

"First," he began, "what I've got to say, to begin with, is that the pup was dead, oh! as dead as dead could be. Besides, I was going to sell his skin for to make fur tippets for ladies what likes them classy things."

"And then?… So you didn't sell after all?"

"No, seeing as how he was over lumpy, that spaniel dog. My knacker he lives at La Villette, and there the animal was at Auteuil. Over a toddle for my old bones."

"Very good!… Then what did you do?"

"That, M'sieur Fandor, that's my secret. That should be paid for separate like."

"And the bonus, Bouzille?"

"Righto, then I'll drive ahead. Well, no offense meant, I ought by rights have gone and buried the beast in the Bois de Boulogne. That was part of the bargain, that was. But the Bois, hmm, at nighttime, I tell you I chickened out. It's a shy neighborhood in the dark. Was I going to risk my precious life, anyhow? Tell me, M'sieur Fandor, tell me frankly what *you* think?"

"What the devil do I care, my good man, about all that?… Come, what *did* you do with the dead dog?"

"I pitched him into the river, M'sieur Fandor, a stone tied round his neck. One, two, three, and plump he goes into the Seine."

"Very good! And then?"

"Then?… of course I mustn't tell you that. It'd do me harm, customers wouldn't trust me… Well, well, M'sieur Fandor, I'll out with it. Then, sir, hands in my pockets like a gentleman, I trots back to M'sieur Rippert's, for to punch an extra tip like, because digging up the soil in the Bois does give a man a thirst, that it does!"

"But I thought you'd thrown your dog into the river?"

"Oh! if you're going to interrupt!"

Bouzille brought out an old clay from his pocket, lit it and then, both elbows planted on the table, went on, very much at his ease:

"So I trotted back, as I told you. I was just coming to the door when a cab pulls up at the curb. Tell me this, what would you have done yourself? *I'm* not afraid of a job of work, I'm not. So I runs up to open the door… Well, yes, I did hope for a sou or two, of course I did."

"Well?"

"Well, there wasn't no sous, but instead of that, why before I'd time to open, out through the window comes a dog, they chucked bang into my arms… 'He was lost,' a voice called out, 'take him home!'—and off goes the rattletrap."

"Then, Bouzille?"

"Then, M'sieur Fandor, that's all… The dog they shoved on me was the dead dog—only he was alive… So there, you understand, don't you? He'd just come to life again—by what the folks say of it!"

Fandor made no remark, loath to put out the old man by questions, when he was evidently speaking truthfully for once.

After a moment's silence Bouzille started afresh:

"So then, either it was the dead dog, only come alive again… or it was the dead dog what had never been dead at all. Just think of me, sir, standing there, and a face on me, good Lord! before the animal! But there, when I says before, it's behind I should've said! because why he'd bolted, no offense meant, that pup had!"

"He'd run away?"

"Oh! not far—only up to the door, the creature! There he was, wagging his tail and barking and yapping! He was asking to be let in in fact—like you, M'sieur Fandor, he was fed up with being shut out like,"—and Bouzille banged down his fist on the table in appreciation of his little joke.

"So then," he concluded, "I couldn't hesitate, could I. I'd buried the animal—in the water. My conscience was clear. But seeing as how he was taking of himself home, why, I'd best do it for him, eh? What'd you have? *I'd* recovered him, hadn't I?"

The tramp could not help himself. He burst into another guffaw as he explained unblushingly:

"All was needed was a bit of string, you see. Once I'd got hold of the dog, the rest was simple… I pull the bell, and the slavey opens the door… Well, I did think I was going to be thanked. But there, they were all like to lose their heads over the animal, and not a soul thought to congratulate me… The door was still open and I just hooked it. Games of that sort ain't all smooth sailing… But what do *you* think about it now?"

But what precisely Fandor thought of it he was not proposing to confide to Bouzille. Of the narratives he had been listening to he chose to remember such details as seemed to be indisputable—at least provisionally. To begin with, the dog had undoubtedly died; Bouzille declared he was sure of it—and, besides, the way he had buried the animal by pitching it in the Seine was proof enough. Yet it was the very same dog that had turned up again alive. How otherwise account for the creature's going and barking at "his own" door?

But there was someone from outside had had a hand in the thing. Who, for instance, was the individual who had brought back the "resuscitated" animal in a cab and given it into Bouzille's keeping, instructing him to return it to its masters?

With a waggish air Fandor questioned:

"Look here, Bouzille, *I've* no opinion to give, but you, you, old man, who were there on the spot, you've got some idea of your own about it all?"

"Times, yes!" Bouzille admitted.

"Tell us then!"

"Tell you, eh? Hmm. Fact is… well… damn, M'sieur Fandor, fact is the idea I've got, is… is a loony's notion!"

"Tell us it all the same," insisted the journalist. "A loony's notion is quite in my line. I've been in that way of business!"

"Then, M'sieur Fandor, stand us another pint, eh?… But no, I'll trust to you. My notion is… is in fact well, it's like this here. I thinks in my head, 'Believe a dog what's dead can come alive again?' no, that I can't. That's a bit too thick. Then, there's only two things to choose between—either it was not the same dog that came back, or else the dog never died! I can't get out of that, M'sieur Fandor, it's one or the other, any simpleton can see. Only the difficulty that beats me is that, on the one hand, I could take my Bible oath I saw the damned pup dead—on my honor, sir, I did!—and that, the other hand, the animal that come back was surely the same dog, seeing as how the beast recognized his own home and his own master and all the damned show!"

"And so, Bouzille?"

"And so, M'sieur Fandor… And so, damn it, I say there's some trickery to it, a plant of sorts, you might say. And that makes me ask another question: Can *He* too have come alive again meanwhile?"

No need for the old man to name the terrible personage he alluded to. The mere sight of his twitching face and the way he had dropped his voice had been indication enough. Yes, Bouzille too had thought of Fantômas. Bouzille too had found the only possible explanation of the grotesque mystery in this tragic name, this name of terror, that by its mere utterance made the impossible seem possible!

"You haven't actually seen him, Bouzille?" Fandor asked to make sure.

"No, never once!"

"And in the ken?… They still talk of him?"

"Oh, yes! there's always some say he'll come back. Yes, plenty talk always!"

"Well, Bouzille, if he does come back, we'll fight him, Juve and I will, and that's all there is to it!"

"So you will, M'sieur Fandor, sir, so you will… and I do think…"

"Yes?"

"I do think as how the battle must be begun already. Oh! I ain't such a fool as I look… Just now, when I spotted you in these parts, I said to myself, I did: 'Seems as M'sieur Fandor's busy like with things. A very nice young man he is, and if he's in it, there'll be trouble, never fear. Go to his side, my lad!' Wasn't I right, eh?"

Fandor contented himself with nodding his assent. For the second time his interest and surprise were vividly stirred… Bouzille had just called him a "very nice young man"; surely the old fellow could not have invented the phrase of himself! And it was the very same description Fandor could fancy himself hearing again on the hospital nurse's lips… Was it not fair to conclude that the old vagabond was in touch with her? Above all, was it not logical to argue that Bouzille knew more than he choose to tell about Fantômas' resurrection?

But alas! it would serve no good purpose to question or threaten the old man. Better to take him on the soft side. In his own way Bouzille was a philosopher who laughed at all threats and all offers of reward. Jail? But jail had no terrors for him! If he was liable to fear at all, it was much more the fear of Fantômas than that of Justice. Money? But the old tramp could frame no wishes of that sort beyond the few francs he needed for his protracted sojourning beside tavern counters. No, nothing had any hold on the happy-go-lucky, smiling old fellow, wide-awake always, if a trifle crack-brained—and completely independent.

"The game is to go easy!" thought Fandor, "that's what we must do, and patiently, one thing at a time, collect the tiniest scraps of evidence. That way we shall get to the bottom of these mysterious resurrections. That way, above all, Fantômas' reappearance will be proved to be an actual fact, and so the villain will be collared and unmasked and beaten."

Jerome Fandor turned over in his mind the details he had just learned. The dog appeared to have died, really died, before its reappearance. Moreover it seemed certain, it was the same dog. And this animal, now come alive again, had been brought not by Bouzille, but by an unknown individual. "However," the journalist summed up, "all this only confuses the issue, instead of clearing matters up,"—and he rose from his seat:

"Now, Bouzille, I'm going to leave you. Look, there's your ten francs, my man."

"Thank you, M'sieur Fandor. You're as honest as the Bank. May I stand you a glass?"

"No, I'm in a hurry."

"To your fiancée's good health, come!"

"I am not engaged, Bouzille."

"Well then, to mine's good health?"

"*You're* engaged, are you, Bouzille?"

"Why, of course I am, M'sieur Fandor... Oh! yes, a woman very high up, the sort I likes—Mamzelle Victoire, the de Vautreuils' cook. Oh, oh! yes, she gives me a taste of the broom-handle when I talk of marrying her. But that don't prove nothing. The ladies they do love to say 'no,' when they means 'yes.' Ain't that your opinion too, M'sieur Fandor?"

The journalist did not answer. Bouzille was an inexhaustible talker. Once launched on his unprofitable clatter, there was never a chance of stopping him.

"I wish you good luck, Bouzille," Fandor cut in, "but I must say goodbye. I repeat, I am in a hurry," and so saying, he shook the tramp by the hand and made his escape.

Verily and indeed he was in a hurry now! Forgetting all about his own adventures, his whole, attention was fixed on the mysteries he must unravel in order to get on the track of

Fantômas. What dark and dreadful scheme was it the Lord of Terror was concocting? To what end had he set going these odd, incomprehensible happenings? Yes, the essential point was to discover his real object, his eventual purpose, in resorting to these puerile proceedings. At the same time he could not but recall the fact that the Comte de Vautreuil was in charge of jewels worth a prodigious fortune.

"Yes, the mysterious writing on the wall demanded a consideration. Come now," he thought, "all this hangs together, it's all of a piece!"

Hurrying away, he made straight for the diplomatist's house. He was resolved to renew and carry out the investigation interrupted in so extraordinary a fashion at Marseilles by his terrible adventure in the cellars of the hotel. After that he would devote himself to finding Juve, who, on his side, would no doubt have been at work and would, like himself, be in possession of new details.

The journalist rang a determined peal on the doorbell of the small house in the Rue de l'Assomption.

"Mademoiselle Josette de Vautreuil at home?" he asked the footman.

"Who is it wishes to see her, sir?"

"Be so good as to give her this from me." Fandor had no card with him, but he noticed on a table in the hall a supply of envelopes and letter paper, and he wrote quickly:

*Jerome Fandor would be glad to see Mademoiselle de Vautreuil personally. He is desirous of putting her on her guard against certain dangers and informing her of some interesting facts.*

"There," he thought to himself, "that should gain me an interview. If you're unlucky enough to say you wish to make inquiries, why, you're just shown the door. But if, on the contrary, you announce you have come to give information, then you're all right. Curiosity is always the surest means of rousing interest."

Evidently he had argued well, for two seconds later Josette

de Vautreuil in person walked into the little smoking room into which the servant had shown the visitor.

Josette de Vautreuil seemed greatly agitated and her pretty engaging face was deadly pale.

"Sir," she began naively, "I am willing to see you because of your name, though I had promised my fiancé not to speak again to anyone of the tragic events you know of… What is it you wish to tell me?"

Jerome Fandor found it difficult not to give a start. For a mind like his, alive to police matters, the lightest words may have a serious meaning! Josette, it seemed, had promised to see nobody, and she had given this promise *to her fiancé!* So, it appeared this man Henri Tardoux was set on having things kept dark.

However, without a trace of excitement and postponing all consideration of the point, Fandor replied:

"Before giving you the promised information, Mademoiselle, I should like to know first if you have not noticed any fresh development in Mlle. de Vautreuil's behavior? Does not her condition show some improvement, however slight?"

"Alas, no, sir… And besides, I see her very rarely."

"How's that? She is in this house surely?"

"Certainly. But the doctors have advised keeping her almost completely isolated, this isolation being indispensable for resting her nerves. And then my fiancé, disturbed at the idea of my being agitated by seeing her, has asked me not to enter her room."

"Oh! ho! What a careful young man!" thought Fandor, his suspicions growing stronger. But aloud, he merely added:

"So Mlle. Eléonore is looked after by someone else. She never speaks? never writes? She can tolerate nobody close beside her?"

"No, sir! But all this is nothing new… Your message…"

"Quite so! But I don't know if I ought to speak now. Perhaps your fiancé would deem it out of place. I should have wished…"

But at that moment Jerome Fandor's words were cut short by a hideous uproar that made itself heard all over the house. It sounded just as if the furniture was tumbling about the place, as if a pitched battle was in progress. Shrill screams, a woman's screams, cries of rage or terror, were clearly audible.

And there was a man's voice too, a hoarse, muffled voice beseeching:

"Hold your noise, woman! Keep quiet, for God's sake! What a vixen it is!"

*     *     *     *     *

For a second or two Josette de Vautreuil and Jerome looked at one another in sheer amazement. The hubbub they heard was so terrific there was no accounting for it by any everyday incident. Undoubtedly something serious was happening… But what could it be?

Josette gave a scream, clasping her bosom with both hands as though to restrain the wild beatings of her heart. Jerome Fandor seemed little less dumbfounded. "My word, it's bedlam broke loose!" he cried. But then, seeing the girl's distress, he made haste to reassure her:

"Don't be afraid, Mademoiselle, I beg of you! I am here, ready to defend you… But I must know…"

The truth is, Fandor was in ordinary circumstances a very lighthearted, if a rather frivolous personage, but danger held such an attraction for him that instantly he became a reasonable, deliberate, almost phlegmatic human being when it was a question of facing it.

"Now," he proceeded, "will you wait for me here? Or will you go with me?"—and as he spoke, he crossed the room, opened the door, ready to dash off in the direction of the uproar, which still continued with unabated violence.

Josette de Vautreuil, however, was no coward, and then anything seemed preferable to the idea of remaining all alone under such circumstances. "I will go with you," she declared decisively.

In two strides Fandor was across the deserted entrance hall and had reached a back stairway that led down to the basement. Still followed by his young companion, Fandor stumbled headlong down the kitchen stairs. At the bottom he came upon a passage, halfway along which was a closed door, and it was plainly behind this the fight was going on. For a battle royal it most certainly was. The sound of blows and howls and yells could be clearly distinguished.

"Mademoiselle," ordered the young man, "stand to this side,"—and he tried to open the door. Impossible! The door was locked on the inside.

"What next!" the journalist growled, then, come what might, he shouted:

"Hold tight! I'm going to bust in."

But at that moment the door opened, and, fiery-faced and disheveled, looking like an angry goddess, big Victoire, the massive and majestic cook, appeared on the threshold of her domain.

"Oh! the men!" she groaned. "They're sure to kill each other... The old man is mad with rage, the little one is as cunning as the devil himself!"

Her words needed no commentary. In the kitchen two men were fighting savagely, so tightly locked together nothing could be made out but two bodies interlaced and rolling over and over each other. On the floor a kitchen dresser had half fallen on top of a sack of coals, and this it was doubtless that had hindered the journalist from opening the door at first. But these details the latter had found no time yet to verify when behind him Josette screamed out:

"They'll kill each other! Separate them! Oh! separate them!"

"Bah! that'll only be so much vermin the less!" declared the cook... "Mademoiselle doesn't think it was my fault?"

But that was not the point at issue. Fandor had run in, and gripping each of the combatants by the shoulder and hauling them apart by main force, managed to separate them.

"Are you mad, you fools?" he demanded. Then in sudden amazement: "Bouzille," he cried, "what, is it you, Bouzille?"

"Myself, M'sieur Fandor! It's that blackguard there I wanted to wallop, because why he's making love to Mamzelle Victoire, my girl, he is!"

"The impudence of the fellow!" protested the cook, as Fandor meanwhile was scrutinizing the other combatant. The "blackguard" that Bouzille had attacked so ferociously was a man of rather small stature, whose features were so buried under a thick beard and a heavy moustache it would have been difficult to describe his face. Smudged with coal dust into the bargain, black from head to foot and panting from the desperate struggle he had just been engaged in, he did not seem in the least intimidated! In fact, in his eyes there lurked a roguish sparkle, and he appeared thoroughly well pleased with himself.

Josette now intervened. "I do not want any scandal here, Victoire!" she said sternly. "If my father was in the house, he would give you notice… I shall say nothing, that's understood, but send these two men away,"—and she was on the point of leaving the room, after asking Fandor to accompany her and apologizing for the tragicomic episode, when the coalman took a step forward and said quietly:

"Mademoiselle, your servant is not to blame. There is only one culprit—and that is myself… And I would wish to express my regrets to you in a few minutes' talk… Fandor, will you please introduce me?"

If Josette at that moment experienced a feeling of amazement that came near depriving her of her senses, be sure Jerome Fandor for his part was opening wide eyes that bore witness to his utter and complete bewilderment. He made a startled exclamation, and then laid a masterful hand on the astonished girl's arm and led her quickly from the room.

"Come, Mademoiselle, come with me. Let us go back to your salon. I know this man. He is a friend of mine!"

Amazed, but guessing that surely she was confronted with yet another mystery, Josette could only obey the young man's suggestion, and returned to the little salon, followed by the journalist, who was himself followed by the coalman.

The coalman? Not so! When Josette turned round, it was no longer the "blackguard" who had just now been exchanging fisticuffs with Bouzille she saw. That mysterious person had with one sweep of the hand torn off beard and moustache.

If he still retained his sordid raiment, it was nonetheless a fact that with his clean-shaven, intelligent face, his keen eyes and the lips curved in an ironic smile, he now showed all the outward tokens of a man of the world. Moreover Fandor had that very moment exchanged an affectionate greeting with the ex-coalman.

And now he was introducing him to Josette de Vautreuil.

"Inspector Juve," he announced, "of the Criminal Department Headquarters... the King of Police Officers, Mademoiselle!... and my best friend!"

"Juve! Juve!" stammered the girl, "but...?"

"But he was dead, Mademoiselle? Yes—and so was I! At this time of day that doesn't go for much..."

Involuntarily Fandor broke into a short laugh, as he went on:

"Juve was no doubt pursuing an investigation in your house. Bouzille, who gives himself out as your cook's fiancé, took him for a rival. That's how it went, you may be sure. Am I not right, Juve?"

"Almost, Fandor! You're no fool."

The tone of the detective's voice alone would have sufficed to reassure Fandor. For Juve to have spoken as he did, almost gaily, showed very clearly that the investigations he had been making had afforded him some pieces of information that were greatly to his satisfaction.

"You say *almost,* Juve," Fandor now asked. "What, only *almost?*"

"Yes... for if Bouzille fell upon me, that was because I went out of my way to provoke the battle!"

"What do you say?... why, with what object?"

"An object I don't care to confess... Well, he got on my nerves! I wanted to see which was the better man, Bouzille or I! So there!"—but the police officer seemed to be struggling with an impulse to break into a great shout of merriment. Then he proceeded:

"So, Mademoiselle, you must pardon your cook. The poor woman is not in fault... Besides that, she's a woman of sound common sense, not the sort to believe in resurrections from the grave! Listen, Mademoiselle, before Bouzille came, she said—I give her exact words: 'Dogs that come alive again—no, I don't believe that! Such a thing's never been known—and what's never been seen before that never is, and never will be seen!' There, what do you think of that for an axiom? a trifle discouraging to inventors, what?… But…"

"But," interrupted Fandor impatiently, "but you're just talking through your hat, Juve. What the devil does this cook woman's opinion matter? The mysteries we are concerned with appear to be authentic. If you don't believe in them, then explain how things did happen. And then, why do you tell us it was of set purpose you excited Bouzille's jealousy."

Fandor was not speaking at random. Tipping him an all but imperceptible wink, Juve had invited him to go on in the same vein. Was it that the detective wished the view to be put strongly to the girl that the story of her aunt's reappearance was just a sheer impossibility? Did he think she knew something that she was keeping back? Did he wish by the display of his skepticism to force her into making some startling revelation?

All the while the police officer was so smiling and looked so *arch*—it is the only word to meet the case—that Fandor was positively boiling with impatience. But his impatience was to be still further justified. Juve calmly went on:

"Ah! yes, Mademoiselle Eléonore, who is in mid-Atlantic is at the same time here on the spot? That's true, I was forgetting the fact! Listen, Fandor, and you, Mademoiselle. Mark me, there's one point that's most important, most important… and that is…"

He was not to be hurried, Juve. After a dramatic pause, he announced sententiously:

"To reappear is well… to disappear is better!"

Hardly had he completed this oracular pronouncement when a fresh event befell that further increased, and that to the highest degree, the surprise Fandor already felt.

Without so much as a warning knock, the door of the little salon flew open and pale, livid, trembling from head to foot, a maidservant appeared.

"Mademoiselle! Mademoiselle!" she panted.

Josette sprang to her feet. "Honorine! what is the matter? Whatever is the matter?"

"Mademoiselle!" the girl repeated wildly, "your aunt's gone! Mademoiselle Eléonore has disappeared!"

Almost before the servant had finished speaking, two sounds rang out in the little room, a great oath from Fandor—surely excusable under the circumstances, and a cry of anguish from Josette. Then the girl darted forward and sped to Mademoiselle Eléonore's bedchamber, and at her heels, Fandor.

Alas! two minutes later it was only too plain the servant-girl had spoken the truth… But this afforded no explanation of what had gone before. Following Josette, Fandor found himself in a large room, comfortably, even luxuriously furnished, a good wood fire burning cheerfully in the grate and heavy muslin curtains admitting a pleasantly softened light. It was a calm and cozy retreat, the downy nest of a comfort-loving old maid petted and spoiled by her fond relations.

But all that really affected Fandor in the aspect of the room was the one outstanding fact—that it was empty, not a soul within its four walls!

"Gone!" he muttered, "Mademoiselle de Vautreuil has mysteriously disappeared! Has she been carried off? or did she go of her own free will?"

Casting the swift glance of one well used to appraise the importance of the smallest no less than of the most significant details, he noted:

"Only one door, opens on the main staircase… A window, insecurely fastened… But the window gives on the garden—and a woman of her age could never climb the walls… The devil's in it!"

Then, half involuntarily, he turned and asked:

"Juve, can *you* see anythi…"—and got no further. Juve was not there!

Fandor wrinkled his brows in perplexed thought. To account for the detective's not being in the room, the scene of yet another mystery, the only possible assumption was that he had found it more to the purpose to hasten elsewhere. Had his amazing perspicacity then already led him to form a definite suspicion? Had he hurried off on the track of the vanished aunt?

"This disappearance," Fandor noted in a swift flash of thought, "has been no surprise to Juve. He was expecting it. The phrase he pronounced just now proves as much. For certain Juve is on the track of the fugitive."

Josette meantime had sunk into an armchair and was sobbing hysterically, naturally enough unnerved by all these agitating events, while Fandor turned and left the room, returning to the ground floor. If Juve needed help, Fandor was not the man to leave him in the lurch. He would come to the rescue, never fear! Arrived in the entrance hall a quiet voice reached his ears:

"I am here, Fandor. You're looking for me?"

The voice came from the small salon, and Fandor darted into the room, to behold a sight that made the young man ask himself if he had not lost his wits for good and all, if he were awake or dreaming.

Seated quietly on a sofa, Juve was reading a Review he had picked up from the table, and which he replaced on Fandor's entrance.

"Well?" he asked.

But Fandor was struck dumb. At the very time the plot was visibly thickening, the very moment after the aunt's mysterious disappearance, Juve remained so impassive, Juve was so unfazed, that he never even moved from the room and sat there turning over the leaves of a paper!

"Well?" repeated the detective, in the calmest possible tone.

"But whatever are you after there?" stormed Fandor.

"What am I after, eh? Why, I'm just waiting!"

"Waiting! you're just waiting?"

"Of course!"

"But who? what?…"

"Look here, my good fellow, I'm waiting for you—you and Mlle. Josette. We were talking… you went away… I'm waiting for you to come back! What else would you have me do?"

Fandor sat down. He wanted time to recover his calmness, to set his ideas in order. Forcing himself to speak composedly he asked:

"Juve, tell me, old man, why did you not go up to the bedroom, the place Mademoiselle Eléonore had just disappeared from?"

Juve this time actually shrugged his shoulders, as he laughed:

"Ha, ha! but that's a good one! You tell me yourself the old lady has disappeared, so what the devil do you want me to go and do up there—where there's nobody anymore?"

"But the disappearance is extraordinary surely? unaccountable?"

"Lord! how you do worry yourself!… Yes, to be sure, I told you, didn't I?—'To reappear is well, but to disappear is better!' Don't you see, it's all perfectly simple,"—and getting up, and stretching like a tired man, Juve added:

"Now, suppose we take our departure, eh? After all that's happened, I feel we're perhaps in the way. Don't you think so? I'm sure you do. So let's be going, young 'un! We'll ask one of the servants to make our excuses… and say we shall be coming back again,"—and without the smallest sign of hurry Juve made for the entrance hall. Then, after entrusting Honorine with a message expressing his regret and announcing another visit before long, he left the house whistling and as calm as he had ever been in his life.

But, as was only to be expected, the police officer had not gone twenty yards before Fandor was impatiently questioning his friend.

"Well?" he demanded. "Tell me, what you make of it. You've gathered…"

"Hmm, yes, I've gathered one little thing!…"

"What's that?"

"Of no great importance…"

"Still, tell me! Don't make me drag your words out of you!"

"No, no! but it's so silly what I've found out… Well, here it is anyway. I've found out, Fandor my lad, that people who act miracles are not very brave!"—and, seeing Fandor ready to protest at the light tone he adopted, Juve added:

"But I am serious, dead serious! What, you don't believe me? You don't see that, if Mademoiselle Eléonore has disappeared, that's because she was afraid to hear me quarreling with Bouzille?"

And the strange thing was it really seemed that at that moment Juve was not speaking lightly at all!

*        *        *        *        *

Whether Juve was speaking seriously or no, however, in maintaining that Mlle. Eléonore de Vautreuil must have vanished simply and solely because she had been terrified by the dispute that set a coalman and Bouzille by the ears, Jerome Fandor cared not a fig. If granting indeed the police officer had made important discoveries while under the de Vautreuils' roof, Fandor was of opinion that he too for his part had not been wasting his time.

Certainly he never hoped to beat Juve on his own ground as a police officer. He recognized as an indubitable fact that the King of all Detectives possessed a consummate adroitness he, Fandor, could make no pretensions to. But for all that, it was quite true that on several occasions his individual investigations had been successful where Juve's efforts had proved partial or even complete failures. Able as he was, Juve was after all but a man, and does not an ancient and well-approved proverb declare that "to err is human"?

Rather huffed by his companion's attitude, Fandor resolved there and then to take a turn at piquing the detective's curiosity.

"Bah!" he announced by way of provocation, "for my part it's not Mlle. Eléonore and her goings-on, whether due to fear or not, that hold my attention."

"Really?"

"Yes, really and truly! There's somebody else seems to me much more open to doubt."

"Come, come!"

"Oh! I've not let anything out. But I quite think that you, you

Juve, have the same suspicions as myself."

"Well, well, and why not?"

"Suspicions that bear upon a man…"

"Why, certainly."

"On a man who makes a vital necessity of shrouding all his affairs in darkness and mystery."

"If he's the criminal, Fandor, that's only natural surely?"

"I don't deny it, but he's clumsy. Three times over his fiancée mentioned his name."

"His fiancée? He is engaged then?"

"Why, of course he is, Juve. So you think you're getting ahead of me with your discoveries. A mistake! Juve, in four days, in five perhaps, you'll arrest this somebody."

"You flatter me, Fandor."

"And the somebody in question is Henri Tardoux."

"No!… It is Fantômas!…"

And as Fandor gave a start of surprise, Juve quietly resumed:

"Why, yes!… It is Fantômas!… You didn't think it was?"

"Juve… Henri Tardoux isn't Fantômas?"

"Oh! dear, no!"

"And yet Henri Tardoux is mixed up in it?"

But Juve was shrugging his shoulders, and Fandor saw the action.

No, Juve was not the man to make any bones about expressing his opinion in the frankest terms.

"Listen to me, Fandor," he said, "and try your best to understand me. It's simply silly what you're saying, and sillier still what you're doing… or what you're going to do."

"What I'm going to do, Juve? But I'm not going to do anything at all."

"Oh! yes, you are. You're by way of letting your imagination run away with you against poor Henri Tardoux."

"Granted! But what makes you think that so foolish?"

"Hold hard, Fandor, my lad! No running off the rails!… Tardoux is a very honest man."

"What is there to prove it?"

"What is there to prove the contrary?"

"The pains he takes to prevent…"

"To prevent his fiancée going near Mlle. Eléonore. But come, that's only very natural. If you were in his shoes, you'd do the same. Come, come, don't allow your nerves to get the better of you… And now, let's talk of something else. We've done enough work for today. Let's go back home."

"Fact is, Juve, our home is the hotel… Where are you putting up?"

"Where? You ask me where? Why, Rue Tardieu of course. Yes, Rue Tardieu same as before. Never fear, nobody knows of it, or ever will… To M. Havard himself I'll explain one of these days that I've rented a flat Montparnasse way… But for you, my boy…"

"Why, Juve, you surprise me. You've got hold of your old place again? After ten years?"

"Yes, yes indeed! I've even secured my old servant Jean again! Come, come, never look so amazed! It's quite a commonplace business. See here, my lad. By way of providing against accidents always possible in a life like mine, I took the precaution of paying my rent for twenty years in advance. Jean too has his wages paid up once for all. Thus, dead or alive, my home and my domestic await my pleasure. You see, we've only stayed dead ten years, so I've found everything in quite a good state of repair. More by token, my landlord pulled a long face over it. He couldn't raise my rent!"

"Jean must have had the surprise of his life!" observed Fandor. "He supposed you dead, I imagine, like everybody else? What did he say?"

"What did he say? He said: 'Monsieur hasn't brought back the portmanteau he took with him on the *Gigantic?* Monsieur has no luggage?'"—and without giving Fandor time to express his amusement at the old servant's phlegm, Juve hailed a taxi, and opening the door:

"Anyway, you'll soon see him. You're coming to my place?… So get in!"

Fandor accordingly, stepping past his friend, got into the vehicle—and then the door slammed to behind him! "Rue

Tardieu," came the order in Juve's voice. But he had not got in himself. No, as Fandor fell back on the seat as the taxi started with a jerk, he saw that his companion was not beside him.

"What the devil!" grunted the young man. "Why…"—and he tapped quickly on the window, stopped the cab, and putting out his head, asked the driver:

"Where's the gentleman who was with me? He didn't get in? Did you see him go?"

"The coalman, eh?"

"Yes… the coalman."

"He stayed on the sidewalk…" but on the sidewalk there was nobody to be seen! Juve had simply vanished.

"He did it on purpose," thought Fandor. "I know him too well to doubt that if he told me to go to his rooms, he means me to wait for him there… Yes, no doubt about that. But the beggar might have let me known beforehand."

Nothing remained but to give the word to drive on, and Fandor at once decided to do so. At the same time he was thinking to himself:

"Most certainly Juve is right: 'To reappear is well, but to disappear is better!' How he must be laughing in his sleeve at me at this moment!"

## 10. Pull Devil, Pull Baker!

No, as Fandor drove off in his taxi, Juve was far from being in a laughing mood. Not that his disappearance had anything mysterious about it or could not be quite simply accounted for.

Taking advantage of his companion's back being turned as he got into the cab, the detective had quietly hailed another taxi, into which he jumped, shouting to the chauffeur:

"Drive on, straight ahead!"

Then, fifty yards further on, he had changed his order: "Avenue de Clichy, my man. Stop a bit after the crossroads, corner of the Rue Legendre."

In the taxi, now rattling on at a rapid pace, Juve was thinking:

"No, I regret nothing. In the first place I'm not sure if I shall succeed. Then, secondly, where I'm going, I have no right to take *him*. Fandor is a journalist. A journalist is a fellow who writes for the papers. Very good! He has no other obligations except to 'hatch out,' as he calls it, the best stuff. I'm different. I am a policeman, and must act as such. To me therefore, or I'm much mistaken, the hard knocks—and to Fandor the glory of describing them. Every man to his trade!"

"Fandor," he went on, after lighting a cigarette, "has hitherto exposed himself overmuch. He has been in every danger, taken every risk. Well, that's got to end. Yes, it must end! It's quite enough already that he's got a ten-year hole in his life. After dying once, he has come to life again, and I won't have him dying a second time—for good and all!"

In fact, if Juve left his friend with some abruptness, if for a good while before he had vouchsafed him only obscure and oracular replies, this was simply and solely because he was about to undertake some perilous adventure and did not wish Fandor to run the risks he was prepared with admirable coolness to confront himself.

Presently at the corner of the Rue Legendre the cab stopped before a big ironware shop and Juve got out and crossed the crowded pavement. Dismissing his driver, he entered the shop, where he bought a strong light chain and had two pieces of iron riveted crosswise to the two ends.

"Why! they're wrist-gyves you're having made?" asked the shopman curiously. "You're in the police, are you?"

"If anyone asks you questions, you have my authority to say you know nothing at all about it,"—and leaving the young man a good deal taken aback, Juve paid at the cash desk and left the shop.

"There!" he said to himself, "I am 'rigged out,' as the sailors say. In five minutes I shall be in the thick of it. In two hours, in all likelihood, either I shall be dead again—for good this time—or I shall be victorious... Bah! care killed a cat. Forward's the word!"

He went on down the Avenue de Clichy to its termination, then turned off to the right and reached the shy neighborhood of lanes and alleys on the far side of the Cemetery of Montmartre.

"It's this way," he told himself, "if the information given me at the office is correct.... Ah! there's the place. My instinct has led right. It has just the sort of look I expected."

Calling a halt, he proceeded to scrutinize from a distance, without appearing to do so, a tavern of an uninviting exterior, one of those establishments that seem to be always half asleep, one of those evil-looking drinking-shops where you ask instinctively what sort of customers frequent them. On the signboard in black letters picked out with tarnished gilding, was described:

*"Successor to the Père Korn."*

"There you have it," observed the police officer. "A house invoking the name of the saintly Korn, the biggest scoundrel I've ever come across, can be nothing more or less than a haunt of the gang—yes, I mean Fantômas' gang."

Boiling over with excitement though he was, Juve mastered his feelings and forced himself to review the situation calmly.

"No," he thought, "I am on the right track, I am not acting at random. Only yesterday afternoon I induced M. Havard to have the whole staff of servants at the de Vautreuils', Henri Tardoux's and Louis Rippert's sent about their business. Now one or another of these fellows, supposing them accomplices, is bound to come back here to see his comrades. And, as a matter of fact a watch was set and I have information that Mary, Louis Rippert's maidservant, frequented this same drinking den. Why yes, it's all as clear as daylight. The woman's a member of the gang!"

The information was so important he was bound to try to turn it to the best possible advantage. Louis Rippert's servant was a frequenter of the tavern of the defunct Père Korn. Therefore he must visit this tavern to discover whether among the habitués was not to be found one of the lieutenants of the Lord of Terror. Fantômas was certainly not likely to show himself in public. At least he would hardly turn up under his own name. Yet who could tell? He was such a daring ruffian!

But Juve was no less daring than his adversary. Crossing the ill-looking alley, he approached the drinking-shop. In his coalman's clothes he was hardly likely to attract attention, he thought, if he slipped quietly into Père Korn's old den. On the other hand, would not this same disguise give him away perhaps to the men he was after. Was it not in the cards that by now the gang—if a gang there was—had been warned of his visit to Josette de Vautreuil's?

"Now for it," he made up his mind. "We shall soon see!"

A shady locality—and a thieves' kitchen, no doubt of that to a policeman's eye. The furniture gave the place away—heavy tables, scored with odd-looking scratches, wooden benches attached to the walls by ropes, to hinder their being used as weapons of offense in pitched battles, an overpowering smell of absinthe—in defiance of the law. The landlord, behind his counter, was a colossus. He could boast of possessing the physique demanded by his trade, the fellow could! His sleeves were tucked up, and the muscles stood out on his sinewy arms. The man stank of vice, with his little blinking eyes, deep-set under a low, square forehead, and his brutish face.

All this Juve had seen at the first glance—all this including a group of five drinkers, the only customers, who were joking with a woman, a servant-girl perhaps.

"Drawn blank!" thought the detective, "nobody here I know."

However, he could get out of it now. So, sitting down at a table, he shouted in a jovial tone:

"A go of brew, Père Korn No. 2!"

It actually seemed as if these words, coming from his own mouth, were the signal the men were waiting for. Hardly had Juve finished speaking before he was answered by a howl:

"Down with the cop! Death to the damned spy!" Simultaneously the five scoundrels set upon him, while the woman, making a dash to the door, was trying to lock it. A man thinks rapidly at such a moment—and acts quicker still! Juve did not waste an instant. He saw he was doomed, but he was resolved at least to sell his life dearly. He darted forward.

"No knives!" cried a voice, "we want no blood about!"

Juve shuddered. "That voice, those grave deep-toned accents, whose were they? and the slim form of this sixth assailant who seemed to have sprung from nowhere? Yes, it was *his* voice surely, *his* form! It was He!... *He,* Fantômas!"

With a hook of the leg the police officer brought his first assailant to the ground. Then he sprang at the man he thought he recognized. "Now, the wrist-gyves! quick!"—and he slipped the thing on.

The rest meanwhile had hurled themselves upon him, but he shook off the grim swarm of clustering humanity, with a yell, "Make room, by God! make room!"

His prisoner struggled desperately, but instinctively the detective twisted the wrist-gyves tighter and tighter, so as almost to crush in the bones, and dragged him towards the door.

There the woman stood, barring the way. With a blow of the fist he felled her to the floor. He knew that, once out in the street, he would be safe, and fighting ferociously, kicking and butting with his head, he drove back the miscreants who were striving to beat him to the earth, brandishing cudgels and loaded sandbags.

To blindfold his prisoner he had snatched a cloak hanging on a nail and thrown it over his head, and now, stumbling through the open door, the two rolled together on the stones of the lane outside.

*     *     *     *     *

Juve was down, rolling on the pavement, but quick as lightning, in a quarter of a second, he was on his feet again and savagely twisting the wrist-gyves, which he had never lost hold of, till the chains ate into the very flesh of his prisoner.

"Come on!" he yelled, and started running, the other perforce running beside him with hoarse bellows of agony.

It is difficult to conceive what a fearful instrument of torture this simple contrivance is. Merely by twisting a little harder on the chains encircling the wrists—sometimes one wrist only—of the poor wretch he is taking along, a detective causes his captive such intense pain the man is infallibly brought to heel. The worst brutes, the most callous murderers, the most desperate criminals, are cowed.

Juve's captive was no less incapable of resistance as he was dragged panting along. Behind them could be heard the sound of the pursuers' feet, as they poured out of the drinking-shop, but the police officer had a good start and soon turned the corner into the Avenue de Clichy. With a cry of "Saved!"—followed by another—a shout of triumph this time: "Taken! *He* is taken!"

No, Juve felt no doubt of that. For an officer of his experience the veriest trifle sufficed for the strictest identification. True, he could not boast of ever having seen Fantômas face to face under his real aspect. When the brigand was abroad on one of his sinister enterprises, he invariably wore his black mask. When, on the other hand, he was assuming the character of some seemingly honest individual nobody would ever suspect of evildoing, he could disguise himself with marvelous skill, actually changing the hue of his complexion by injections of coloring matters, actually altering the very shape of his features by the employment of methods of plastic modeling, an invention of recent years, such for instance as the use of stearin introduced under the skin so as to modify the outline of nose, chin, cheeks and forehead, even!

No, neither Juve nor any man alive knew Fantômas' true face. The malefactor showed a score of different countenances, had a hundred different aspects.

But, in revenge, Juve knew his voice—and that voice he had just heard!

Yes, it was Fantômas, and Fantômas was his prisoner. Fantômas was on the road to the scaffold—only too mild a punishment for his atrocious crimes and the reign of terror he had inflicted on all the world. The grim battle then was over, thought Juve, the desperate duel decided, and his soul was drunk with the strong wine of exultation!

The police officer was a kind man generally, and would have felt compunction at treating an unfortunate man with brutality. But mercy was out of place with Fantômas. No pity can be felt for a wretch who is preeminently and above all a monster, an outlaw, a vampire! Each order he gave in a curt, harsh voice was emphasized by another twist of the dreadful instrument.

At first Juve had thought of claiming the help of a couple of constables and dragging off his prisoner to the nearest police station. That is how Inspectors of the Department proceed. That is the recognized rule and custom in cases of arrest without special warrant. But he had changed his mind. With Fantômas he felt impelled to act in direct defiance of routine. This was the surest means of checkmating the crafty devices the brigand might, with his terrible aptitude for crime, have contrived to prepare beforehand. Fantômas was bound to have foreseen that he would be conducted to the station, *therefore* he must be taken elsewhere. Fantômas was bound to have calculated that his arrest would be carried out in such and such a way, *therefore* it must proceed in some quite different fashion.

With his usual promptitude of determination, Juve came to an instant decision. No sooner had he reached the broad Avenue de Clichy where the passersby hardly so much as turned to look, far from imagining that an arrest was taking place under their eyes, and even farther from suspecting its tragic importance, the police officer called a cab luckily passing at that moment on the prowl.

"Get in!" he commanded the prisoner. Then turning to the startled chauffeur: "Criminal Department officer!" he informed the man… "To the Prefecture—and drive your hardest!"—and the door banged shut behind him. Once inside the confined interior of the vehicle, which started off at a good round pace—Juve's orders brook no demur—the detective was alone with the Lord of Terror, his heart leaping wildly in pride and satisfaction. The thing was done! *He* was captured! A few minutes more and the door of a prison cell would close on the worst of all the thieves that ever lived.

Fantômas sat there without a word, as if exhausted. What were his thoughts? What sudden panic was perhaps at that moment assailing the man who had deemed himself invincible? Juve felt a devouring curiosity to know these things. He longed to see the scoundrel face to face, to read in his eyes the fear in his heart, the avowal of his defeat. Above all he would fain have seen Fantômas' features, which were still concealed by the cloak the detective had thrown—like a falcon's hood—over his prisoner's head. Should he not remove it and enjoy the spectacle of his captive's despair? Had he not a right to do this? But Juve resisted the temptation. "No, no!" he said to himself, "not now! An instant's heedlessness and he might escape. Later on, when he is in his cell."

Never had Juve imagined taxis traveled so slowly. Under ordinary circumstances the sworn foe of cabdrivers, whom he looked upon as reckless fellows, this time he would fain have had his vehicle go its hardest and pass every other conveyance on the road. But at last the taxi reached the riverside quays. There the driver slowed down in doubt, not quite sure which door of the great building gave entrance to the Headquarters Department.

"Drive on," shouted his fare. "This way—now straight on!"

The vehicle drove under an archway and stopped in a small,

gloomy courtyard.

"Porter," yelled the detective, "shut the gates! Nobody to go out without a permit!"

It was a quite unusual precaution, but, after all, was such anxiety exaggerated?

Juve ordered his prisoner to get out, and following with perfect docility behind his captor, the brigand moved forward cowed by the dread of those terrible chains that all the time tortured his macerated flesh.

"Step up! Stairs here!"—he had to be led like a blind man.

But now, where to take him? After a ten years' absence Juve no longer knew his way around the once familiar building. Partitions had been removed, new passages constructed. Still, the Chief's office was sure to be in the same place. Still holding tight to his man, Juve turned down a well-remembered corridor.

At that moment in fact two officers were passing along it, likewise escorting a prisoner wearing handcuffs. Juve hailed them, and when the men turned about, he announced himself: "Inspector Juve!"

He did not know them—they had joined after his time. But by the start they gave and their deferential bearing he felt very sure they were at any rate familiar with the name of the King of Police Officers, whose reappearance, besides, at the Prefecture even more than elsewhere, was the subject of universal discussion.

"Tell me," Fantômas' captor demanded, "are there still special cells here for dangerous criminals? Where are they? Everything's been altered…"

"Why, yes, Monsieur Juve! There's one just behind you."

"Very good!… And this fine fellow you're taking along is an important cop?"

"Oh, Lord! no!" one of the two inspectors replied, "a common pickpocket, caught in a roundup."

"Entered on the lists yet?"

"No, not yet!… But why?"

Juve hesitated for half a second before he spoke. Then: "You're to let him go… yes, let him go! He'll have another run for his money before he comes to the gallows!… You're going to let him go, for I need your help… There, off with his handcuffs, and clap them on my man… That's right… No, I shan't remove the wrist-twister… Catch hold—and mind, no mercy! Screw up fit to break his wrists, if he tries on any tricks! Now show the gentleman into a special cell! Yes, that one!… Go in along with him!… Excellent!… Gentlemen, I shall lock you in with your prisoner… Just the time to see the Chief, and I'm with you again… There, you understand, I presume? The man is a terror—a holy terror! You're responsible for him. Don't lose sight of him for one second—for one quarter second. And don't, under any pretext whatever, take off his handcuffs, nor the wrist-gyves either… And if he makes a single movement… see, there's my revolver! You take me? you quite understand?"

Juve was obeyed to the letter. Fantômas, handcuffed and gyves on wrists, was pushed into the cell indicated. One of the Inspectors grasped the torturing chains, while the other stood back to the wall and revolver in hand, never taking his eyes off the miscreant. Yes, an exaggeration perhaps, this wealth of precautions—an exaggeration to all appearance. But Juve was well satisfied. At any rate he need not worry.

So the King of Detectives went his way, double-locking the door of the dungeon behind him and pushing to the heavy bolts.

"My prisoner!" he repeated, "my prisoner at last!" adding in a voice feverish with excitement.

"And now to inform Havard! Oh! but I'm going to give him the surprise of his life. I won't tell him who it is I've arrested. No, I'll merely find out if he's in his room and ask if I may bring in my prisoner,"—and Juve hurried off along the corridor.

Suddenly a laugh rose to his lips. "What of the poor devil I made them let go?" he thought. "Why, he'll only be stopped by the porter after all. What a disappointment! The whole place is in a state of siege, it appears?"

A window stood open and Juve leaned out to look. In the courtyard the great gates had been shut and the porter stood before them on guard in faithful compliance with the orders received.

"Good!" observed the detective, "and if my protégé is nabbed again, why, I'll put in a word in his favor. A promise *is* a promise, and I said he was to go free!"—and with this reflection, Juve proceeded on his way.

At the far end of the corridor an usher was on duty, who rose deferentially on seeing him approach:

"Good morning, Monsieur Juve!"

"Good morning, Joseph!… The Chief is within?"

"Yes, Monsieur Juve, but he's busy with someone."

"Who is it?"

"I don't know, Monsieur Juve, but when he sent for you…"

"Eh? He sent for me?"

"Why, certainly, a moment ago… Didn't they tell you?"

"No, I've only just come…"

"Well, the Chief told my mate: 'Go and see if Juve is there! Tell him to come right away. Say it's most important.'"

"Very well, I'll go in."

"Righto! Monsieur Juve… I think it's to do with a gentleman, an electrician… a scientist… I don't know what all, who sent in his card. I showed him in a second ago…"

"Very good! Excellent!"—and Juve knocked, and without waiting for an answer half opened the door. Important as the communication might be his Chief wished to make to him, he had news more important still to tell his superior!

And yet Juve had started at the old usher's words, struck by a sudden intuition. Monsieur Havard was closeted with a man of science, physicist—and was not Henri Tardoux something of the sort? Might it not be he, possibly, the Head of the Criminal Department was in conference with?

His first glance, however, convinced the newcomer of his mistake. The visitor was a man of years, wearing a long white beard, who bore no resemblance to Josette's betrothed…

M. Havard introduced the stranger:

"Dr. Smith Eric Walton, of Chicago, my dear Juve. I sent for you because the doctor has expressed a wish to speak to you as well as to me. He brings us the scientific explanation of the trick by which the Auteuil mysteries were worked."

"Bless my soul!" was Juve's noncommittal reply.

"Oh! it's very simple!" the stranger declared with a smile. "But it has its tragic side too."

"Will you excuse me a second?" Juve broke in, and darting from the room, he ran to the usher Joseph.

"Hey, friend!" he said, "will you do me a service? Go quick to the duty-room, and ask in my name for a couple of Inspectors, the two most senior on the roster, to take post outside special cell No. 3. They're not to let anybody leave the cell. I have a most dangerous prisoner there! Tell them so… Now, I've got to give five minutes to the Boss…"

With a smile on his face at having thought of this additional precaution, a really exaggerated one this time, he returned to M. Havard's room:

"Here I am, Chief… here I am, Doctor… So you say the Auteuil mysteries can be scientifically accounted for?"

*       *       *       *       *

In declaring that he was ready to hear the scientific explanation of the baffling mysteries all Paris was discussing Juve had spoken with a perfectly grave face, but nevertheless his voice had something of a bantering, ironical tone about it that Doctor Walton could not but observe. In fact, turning to the police officer, the savant protested:

"My claim strikes you as preposterous, sir?"

"Not the least in the world!… There is bound to be an explanation… So…"

"So it only remains to judge if mine is adequate?"

"That is precisely what I think!"

"Well, I shall hope to convince you… However, I will avoid over-technical details, and only give you the net result of my discoveries. We will go into particulars after that, if you demand to hear them… Of course I may count on your discretion?"

"Of course!"

"Well, gentlemen, to begin… But, first of all, let me ask you a question: Are you agreed that the seasons are turned upside down? There is no longer now hot in summer, no longer cold in winter? In a word, that something has gone wrong with the celestial machinery?"

This exordium could hardly fail to mystify M. Havard and Juve. What had the temperature to do with the matter in hand? Still, they bowed politely, while M. Havard observed:

"There is something in what you say. Some late winters, in particular, have been as rainy as autumns."

"Capital! You follow me perfectly… Well, gentlemen, there lies the whole problem… why, yes!"

Smiling in his turn with a touch of irony, Doctor Walton went on:

"The only thing is to think of it… Now *I* have had the illuminating thought. It was a flash of genius! Ah, ha!"

Juve and M. Havard exchanged looks of surprise. One and the same idea had crossed both their minds…

But the savant proceeded:

"At school, gentlemen, you were taught, no doubt, and if you weren't dunces, you have remembered, the fact, that you make water by producing an electric spark in a gassy medium containing oxygen and hydrogen… Electricity, it follows, can upset the weather… Is that plain?"

Juve and Havard again exchanged glances.

"But to leave that point for the present," the Doctor went on again. "I'm coming to something more important… Gentlemen, the seasons have been modified by the abuse of wireless telegraphy and telephony! All these waves have led to the formation of storms… And I accuse Henri Tardoux…"

"Eh?" cried Juve, starting violently.

"Silence there!" thundered Doctor Walton, springing up. I am speaking seriously… I accuse, I say I accuse, Henri Tardoux, scientist, of having changed winter into summer and summer into winter by his experiments. Yes, and I accuse him further of having produced the illusion of Mlle. de Vautreuil's presence and that the dead dog's reappearance by help of the wireless telegraphic waves…"

Doctor Walton burst into a cackling laugh and resumed:

"The transmission of pictures to a distance! Why, everybody knows that science is on the point of realizing it! Therefore, conscious of my rights and of my duties, a devotee like Pasteur of the good of humankind, I have come here to invoke your help… Yes, Henri Tardoux is a murderer!… But I offer myself as avenger of his victims!… Give me a revolver, and I will go and kill him! I will free humanity of a monster!… You understand? You do understand?"

For the last five minutes, as a matter of fact, Juve and M. Havard had both understood only too well. They were in the presence of a madman!

Alas! it is so everyday an incident at police offices, the arrival of a maniac, that it causes but little surprise. On the occurrence of any sensational event of the day, unhappy creatures of the sort are sure to present themselves.

But now the mad American was losing every atom of self-control. Like all victims of a fixed idea, he had up to that moment expounded his theories with sufficient calmness. But he was reaching the stage of super-excitability, pacing up and down the room, tossing his arms, uttering hoarse tirades:

"The ministers refused to see me!… I tell you, Tardoux has me followed!… But I will kill him! I will kill him, I say!"

But meantime M. Havard had quietly rung a particular bell, and turning to the poor demented creature:

"I'm asking them to bring you one of our new brownings…"

Then, as two men in hospital uniform entered, M. Havard went on:

"Look here, the gentleman wants a weapon of the best make to shoot a great criminal he has just been denouncing to us. Will you take him to our armory and provide him with what he wishes."

"Certainly!… Will you come with us, sir."

The madman was gone in a flash. Then, as the heavy door closed behind him, Juve asked:

"And what will the Department Infirmary do with the poor devil? There's no new regulation, I suppose?"

"Oh dear, no! They'll just dispatch him to Bicêtre, or to

some other asylum. Besides, he has quite likely escaped from a paying home for the insane. But no matter for that. What I find surprising is how he gained admittance here. He sent in his card and I received him on his merits—and also because he told them to say he could throw fresh light on the mysteries… Anyway that's of no importance… You had something to say to me?"

"Why, yes, sir!"

"Oh, ho! your eyes sparkle! Anything serious?"

"Serious enough!"

"Regarding the Auteuil mysteries ?"

"Exactly!"

"The devil! Anyhow *you're* not mad?"

"Chief, I'm not joking!"

"So! Speak out in that case!"

"Not here, sir!"

"Why not? what do you mean?"

"I'll ask you to go with me…"

"Far?"

"Two steps only. As far as cell No. 3…"

"Oh! but then…"

Monsieur Havard had turned pale. He knew Juve too well, in fact, to make any mistake as to what the detective's looks portended. Everything about the latter's attitude announced some sensational piece of news.

"Juve," he proceeded, "it isn't…"

"It is, sir! It is Fantômas… He is my prisoner!"

"Mercy on us!… Is this the truth?… But where is he? Who is on guard?… Are you sure?"

"Sure he cannot escape? Yes, I am. He is handcuffed, and the gyves on his wrists into the bargain; and then two Inspectors stand over him in the cell where I locked him in, and one of them carries a drawn revolver, while two more do sentry go outside the door!"

"Come on! Let's go!" cried the Chief, stamping with impatience.

"And that's not all," continued the detective, laughing in

spite of himself as he said the words: "I've likewise declared a state of siege! The gates are shut and not a soul can leave the Prefecture."

"Excellent! But come on, let's be off!"—and Juve and M. Havard left the Chief's room and hurrying along the corridor Juve had traversed a few minutes earlier, the pair soon stood before the doorway of cell No. 3. The police officer drew the key from his pocket and throwing open the door, invited his Chief to enter.

Next instant Juve, the decorous Juve, let fly a mighty oath, his voice strangling in his throat with surprise and consternation—surely not without good and sufficient reason!

The cell was empty—absolutely empty! Fantômas had vanished! and the two Inspectors with him!

Thereupon, ironical, furious too, and more than all unfair, M. Havard—who at odd times was a trifle jealous of Juve and his celebrity—remarked sententiously:

"Well, but… it's of a piece, eh?… Diamond cut diamond, you know,"—and with the words, swung round on his heels and went back to his private room.

## 11. To Arrest Is Well... But To Release Is Better

There was nothing, it seemed, in the cell likely to reward investigation or of a nature to indicate a clue.

Juve before the eyes of the two genuine Inspectors who looked on in consternation, began by picking up the cloak that had been used to blindfold Fantômas and which, the latter had of course left behind. Underneath it, however, he made an interesting discovery.

"Why, what's that?" chorused the two Inspectors in surprise. The find consisted of two strips of leather provided with copper buckles and laces, resembling the wristlets acrobats wear for fear of straining the tendons in their "strong man" acts.

"So?" muttered the detective, examining the articles, and said no more.

"Gentlemen," he announced, "the fellow's escaped, and far away by this time!... You can go now."

But, as he spoke, his keen eyes sparkled strangely. Juve, in a flash of thought had just seen it all. A single detail sufficed to reveal the whole mystery of what had occurred.

"So?" he repeated, as he stood alone in the cell, "so Fantômas had that on his arms? In that case my gyves never hurt him at all, and the cries of pain he mimicked were simply meant to take me in! Oh! but it's typical of the fellow! Yes, Fantômas had taken his precautions!... Consequently, he expected to be arrested, consequently he allowed himself to be arrested,"—and Juve smiled dolefully.

"Yes, I've behaved like an idiot!" he concluded. "I thought I had caught him. Not so! He got himself caught on purpose. I thought I was conveying him to prison; I was doing exactly what he wanted! And he has got away with all the ease in life!"

Thanks to this one clue the detective had fathomed the truth; nor could the part played by the two Inspectors leave much doubt in his mind. The two men and the self-incarcerated prisoner were of course accomplices, as was shown by the disappearance of all three together.

But suddenly another point occurred to him, and frowning in perplexity.

"Come now," he muttered, "let's think a bit. Yes, I can guess what must have happened. Fantômas has departed, escorted by the two bogus Inspectors. That much I can ascertain by questioning the porter… But Fantômas and his two warders, that makes three people. Now there were four inside the Prefecture, the two sham Inspectors, Fantômas—and the pretended pickpocket. What's become of the last named?"

"Hmm!" he continued, pondering the probabilities, "the fourth ruffian must have hidden himself somewhere. The Prefecture is an immense building; no doubt the fellow's waiting quietly in some corner or other till the gates are free again!"

Firmly convinced of the correctness of his theory, Juve marched down to the porter's lodge, but here a fresh surprise awaited him.

"What was the prisoner like?" stammered the porter, much upset by the thought that he had unintentionally connived at a criminal's escape, in answer to Juve's questions. "Why, I can tell you that much. I saw him as plain as plain—a little man, quite a little man, a bit potbellied, quite a fat fellow in fact, with a face…"

"A *little* man?" Juve broke in.

"That's what I said!"

"And the two Inspectors in charge of him?"

The man's description was both full and precise. A former police officer himself now retired, he possessed the quick, accurate eye of a professional, and Juve had no illusions left now as to the true state of the case. The three individuals who had marched boldly out of the gates were the three accomplices, but Fantômas was not one of them.

"What has become of him then?" Juve asked himself once more, while his heart recommenced its feverish beating in his breast. "Is he still in the building? Can he have the effrontery to hide in the very Prefecture itself?"

No, that was too unlikely, and naturally enough the detective came to the conclusion:

"He has left the place, but left it in such a way as not to attract attention—and has gone after doing what he came to do!"

For this was what was worrying Juve now. If Fantômas had got into the Prefecture by means of an arrest he had manifestly planned and prepared and contrived himself, this was evidently with an object, a definite, but secret object.

"What was it?"

"He was running a tremendous risk," Juve reflected. "A man doesn't play a game like that without a motive. But what motive could he have?"

Suddenly a fresh idea struck him.

"In any case," he told himself, "I'll have the building searched from cellar to garret. Were it to last two days, no one shall leave the place without my seeing him first."

But no sooner had he made up his mind to these drastic measures than a new notion set him quivering from head to foot.

"Fool! fool that I am!" he stammered. "The motive, the motive I was looking for—why here it is!"—and Juve fell to striding feverishly up and down the courtyard, quite regardless of the inquisitive looks the worthy porter kept casting in his direction.

"Why, yes!" he repeated to himself, "here is the motive Fantômas had in getting himself arrested and then mysteriously escaping. He knew very well I should be dead set on capturing him again. He knew very well that, if I could not discover how he had got away, I should inevitably jump to the conclusion he was still here, and so spend my time in hunting him up and down the building. Then he would have a free hand to be at work elsewhere!"

Juve looked pale and harassed. So conscientious was he that his most natural mistakes appeared to him in the light of grave derelictions of duty. By letting Fantômas make a fool of him, was he not thereby exposing those whom it was his business to defend against the villain's nefarious schemes to untold perils?

"Yes, Fantômas knows I am kept busy here," he muttered. "His trick keeps me here, and meanwhile he is free to betake himself to Auteuil and murder Léon de Vautreuil and Josette there!"

But was he on the right road? Was he not perhaps by way of making yet another mistake?

"By God!" he swore to himself half out loud, "if he did leave the place, it is my first duty to find out how."

In two strides Juve was across the little courtyard and again questioning the porter.

"Tell me," he demanded, "either before or after the exit of the three we've just been talking about did nobody go by you? You must have opened the gate for other employees I suppose?"

"For one person only, Monsieur Juve!"

"Someone you know by sight?"

"Why, certainly! a Deputy Head of the Secretarial Department—an *ex*-Deputy Head, I should have said, for he has resigned… seems he's found a marvelous fine post in a business house. But there, you know him, Monsieur Juve, don't you?"

"What name?"

"Monsieur Louis Rippert."

"Oh, yes! I know him."

Juve was nonplussed. If Louis Rippert and no one else had passed through, how explain Fantômas' escape? But Juve had hardly put the question to himself before he broke suddenly into a great laugh.

"Oh, ho! but… but why not?" he chuckled, and he started tramping to and fro again.

"So Louis Rippert passed through," he reflected. "But Louis Rippert has resigned… Why precisely did he resign. Hmm that's what I should like to know… Again why, having resigned, did he come back here? To recover his papers, his personal belongings no doubt? Just to think how it all fits in together once again!"

For the third time Juve returned to the porter's lodge:

"Monsieur Rippert carried an attaché case in his hand, didn't he?"

"Yes, I think so."

"What time was it he came here first?"

"That I can't tell you, sir. I did not see him pass."

"And as a rule you do see him?"

"Yes, as a rule, yes! He bids me good morning. But today he didn't speak to me at all."

Juve clenched his teeth together to keep in the words: "Of course he didn't!"

Yes, truly, as he had just observed, it was all fitting together at last in a wonderful way. Mad, preposterous, startling to the last degree, the idea that flashed across the police officer's brain, the thought that was forming at the back of his mind.

"I have no proof," Juve was reflecting. "I cannot and I must not say anything for certain, but how logical it all seems. How it all hangs together…"

Louis Rippert, Deputy Chief in the Secretariat, had for certain gone away, whereas he had never been seen to arrive!… Louis Rippert, after his resignation had paid a visit to the Prefecture in order to carry away sundry private papers of his in an attaché case, Louis Rippert on the other hand was mixed up in the Auteuil business, inasmuch as he was the "resuscitated" dog's master…

"Then again," Juve added, struck by a new idea, "isn't he the maidservant Mary's master, the girl who I've been lucky enough to discover frequents the late Père Korn's dubious establishment?… Who can be sure even that Mary didn't slip off on purpose, just to decoy me to the tavern in question?"

Juve's mind was soon made up. So often in the course of his long battle with Fantômas had he unmasked the fantastic incarnations of the grim Lord of Terror that he felt intuitively, knew with an almost miraculous prescience, what the truth must be:

"Louis Rippert! not a bit of it! There *was* no Louis Rippert, and there never had been!… Louis Rippert was Fantômas!

"While I was dead, along with Fandor, Fantômas, to make the world forget him, must have taken this incarnation, for who would ever have dreamed of looking for the wretch under the guise of an Official of the Prefecture of Police?... Then he learned through Tardoux of the immense value of Léon de Vautreuil's diamonds, and he was tempted to embark on a fresh criminal enterprise. Oh God! nobody saw him arrive today, because he came in the shape of Fantômas—in my custody! He passed out undetected, because he made his escape in the shape of Louis Rippert—a person above suspicion!... And he has done all this, because tonight, at this moment, while I am messing around and wasting my time, he is at work, the scoundrel!"

By this time Juve was pale with agitation.

"I shall verify the facts at once," he resolved. "If Louis Rippert is really Fantômas, I wager he's not at home tonight. If, in fact, he merely came back to recover his papers, he would have come back as Louis Rippert. If, on the contrary, if he chose to arrive as Fantômas it was because he wanted Fantômas' disappearance to keep me busy here, so as to give him a free hand elsewhere... Well, the fight's between us two! The night's not done yet! I shall get there in time, I think!"

Juve was recovering his spirits. He had suffered a defeat, so much was certain! But the battle was far from being ended—and what general was there never lost an engagement? What counts, what constitutes the greatness of leaders, is it not most frequently the energy they show in repairing the reverses they have met with, the skill they display in changing failure into success?

For the last time, Juve returned to the porter's lodge. "The orders are countermanded," he informed him. "The gates are free to all."

"Very good, sir!"

Then, wheeling about, Juve went up again to the upper floors of the Prefecture where the rooms appropriated to the Chief Inspectors are situated. Since the previous day when he had been officially restored to his old position, Juve had one of these for his own use.

"I'm going to try out my telephone," he said to himself, "and if I'm off in another five minutes. I won't say a word about it to Havard. He can send what communiqué he pleases to the Press, I don't give a damn!… Henceforth I shall only inform him of definite and undoubted results. If I capture Fantômas, if I arrest Rippert, I'll see he's listed in on the prison register before saying anything to the Chief. That'll teach him a lesson!"

But at that very moment he caught sight of the Head of the Department advancing along the corridor.

Beaming with gaiety, M. Havard stepped up to the Inspector:

"Well, Juve, nothing fresh, eh?"

"Nothing, worse luck!"

"No news of the fugitive?"

"None, unfortunately!"

"Well, well, never say die. You'll be more careful, and more successful, another time."

"Certainly, sir!"

Two minutes later Juve was in his private room at the telephone asking to be put through to the Deputy Head of the Secretariat. This done, and while the young ladies of the Exchange were making the connection with the subscriber asked for, Juve again found his heart beating wildly in his bosom.

"Would Louis Rippert be there? Would he have left home?"

A maidservant—Mary no doubt—answered very politely:

"Monsieur wants to speak to the master? The fact is he's not at home… gone on a journey… for several days. Who is it asking for him?"

But Juve had already hung up the receiver. Gone away, "for several days," had he, this Monsieur Rippert? Oh, ho! say rather—for always! run away! bolted!

A quarter of an hour more and Juve was leaving the Prefecture, giving the taxi he had called as address the corner of the Rue de Ranelagh and the Avenue Mozart. From there he could reach the Rue de l'Assomption without risk of interference. Once there, would he encounter Fantômas, would he unmask the pretended Rippert?

So preoccupied was Juve that at the moment he took his seat in the vehicle, he never noticed a man who, crouched in a recess in the wall, was watching his departure with the evident intention of following him and now, seeing him get into a taxi, hailed another for himself.

*  *  *  *  *

One of the ablest police officers of the day, Dr. Locard, Director of the Police Technical Laboratory at Lyons, one day made a remark—thinking it may be of Juve—an observation the truth of which every detective has had occasion to verify:

"No detail is trivial in matters of police investigation. The most apparently insignificant fact may prove to be of prodigious importance. Everything should be noted and everything taken into account."

It was, in fact, quite a trivial detail that in the present case was destined to have the most important consequences... The man who was shadowing Juve and who had issued from his hiding place at the moment the police officer left the Prefecture had followed the latter's example and also hailed a taxi. Hurriedly he gave the man his orders:

"Quick! follow that red cab in front. Don't pass it, whatever you do, follow at a distance."

But the driver seemed a dull-witted fellow!

"Follow the red cab?" he asked. "Which red cab?"

"That one, good Lord!... there, the one turning the corner."

"Right!... so Monsieur is going to where it goes?"

"Great God! yes, man!... off you go!"

"But Monsieur hasn't told me the address. Suppose I lose sight of it."

"Bah! you're a born fool!" growled his passenger between his teeth.

He was already inside, but quicker than ever, he leapt to the ground, prepared to run behind the other taxi, to do anything rather than lose sight of it, at any rate till he had found another, more quick-witted driver. But he had not taken two steps before the chauffeur was after him, shouting:

"Stop him! stop him!"

Passersby were turning round to stare, and our friend halted with an impatient:

"What's up? are you gone mad?"

"But, sir," retorted the chauffeur, "I lowered my flag. You owe me for hiring…"

The unknown made a gesture of despair.

"I owe you something else," he said savagely. "I owe you the veneration the Arabs pay to imbeciles!… There, it's good money, keep the change… And do try to go to night-school evenings… So long!"

The speaker was Jerome Fandor!… But, for all his bantering speech, Fandor was positively boiling with rage.

"Juve 'plants' me Place des Ternes," he growled, "Juve packs me off willy-nilly to the Rue Tardieu… Well, I'm not a fool, I can see very well that to act like that, Juve must be planning some great scheme he wants to keep me out of, by way of sparing my precious carcass… So, of course, I start out to checkmate him… They tell me at the Prefecture Juve has just come. I'm always fly enough, and I bustle away and hide myself to watch for my man. A three hours' wait, and out he comes. I'm just going to accost him—very prettily, when he stops a taxi. 'Very good,' I say to myself, for Juve to be spending money like this, there's bound to be a snake in the grass. And *I* stop my taxi too—and if that same taxi doesn't stop *me*, and spoil my little game! Haven't I every right to be in a fury?"—and walking on, slowly now, Fandor reflected:

"Where to go? Rue Dupert? To the Institut Pasteur? They'll give me treatment there perhaps?"

In fact, the question the journalist was asking himself seemed insoluble. Juve's taxi had disappeared at the turning and was gone to some unknown destination. How impossible to find it again in the wilderness of Paris! Still, Fandor was not the man to sit still and do nothing. Accordingly he proceeded with his reflections:

"Come now, to think things out calmly and quietly, Juve is off somewhere… But where? obviously where he can carry on investigations. Now, where can he best do this? Where mysterious matters are afoot. Ha, ha! I begin to see daylight."

With a wave of the arm Fandor hailed a fresh taxi. Cautiously he scrutinized the driver's face, then convinced the man belonged to the intelligent and clear-headed race of Parisian mechanics, he gave him his instructions:

"Look here, my friend! I don't know where I'm going to! Yes, that's so! To start with, you're to drive me to the corner of the Rue de l'Assomption and the Boulevard Montmorency. There you'll pull up! I'm leaving you something on the fare. If in a quarter of an hour I'm not back, consider yourself discharged. If on the other hand I do come back—well, then we'll go somewhere else. You take me?"

"Must be an owl not to!" retorted the fellow with a laugh. "Monsieur isn't sure about catching somebody at home and prefers to go and see on foot?"

"You've hit it, my lad!… So off we go!"—then, as the vehicle got underway, Fandor put his head out of the window to shout:

"Put some pace on, anyway! If you get into trouble for excessive speed, you can go tomorrow to the Prefecture and ask Juve to take off the fine again. I'll leave you my card."

Five minutes later, however, Fandor was almost sorry he had made any such incautious suggestion! Electrified by the name of Juve—a name of which all the Parisians were at present talking, the driver went off at such a headlong pace that the journalist was terrified.

"The devil!" he thought, "at this rate, I have every chance of getting there quick—but in small pieces!… Ah! the truck!… Whoa, there! that fat old gentleman had a close shave that time!…"

Nevertheless, though it went like a racehorse, the taxi reached the Rue de l'Assomption undamaged.

"A record, eh, sir?" cried the gallant chauffeur.

"A super-record!" declared his fare. "I'll hire you to cart around all the good people I'm hoping for a legacy from!… There you are—there's twenty francs. Wait for me a quarter of an hour!"

"Righto! But your card?"

"Here it is!"—and Jerome took himself off. His merry humor

deserted him the moment his back was turned, giving place to a gravity and preoccupation he took no pains to conceal.

"Shall I find Juve?" he kept asking himself. "My cab must certainly have overtaken his, still he had a good long start, so he can't be very far off—*if* he is coming here."

Meanwhile Fandor was moving on at a sober pace. As usual in this Auteuil district bordering on Passy, the street was deserted at an hour like this and poorly lighted into the bargain by widely spaced gas lamps. Not a passerby was to be seen, not a trace of a constable discernible.

"A charming landscape!" Fandor observed. "A man might cut his throat here in perfect tranquillity. The news would 'transpire' next morning.… Hmm, let's keep our eyes open!"

He opened them the wider, did the good Fandor, inasmuch as he was greatly exercised by Mlle. Eléonore's disappearance—and wider still, because, feeling convinced that Juve was coming, he told himself—with every appearance of sound logic:

"If Juve does come here, it isn't to indulge in moonlight reverie. So evidently something must be going to happen."

Yet everything seemed perfectly peaceful. The dead silence reigned that characterizes the aristocratic districts of Paris at night. At long intervals a tramcar could be heard rumbling along the Avenue Mozart, or the horn of an automobile. Now and again the whistle of a train recalled the proximity of the "Ceinture" railway.

Slackening his pace yet more, with hands in pockets, and as a precaution pushing back the safety catch of his browning—a recent acquisition—Fandor presently arrived before the de Vautreuils' residence.

The house, facing the street and having a garden beyond it over which towered a high six-storied building, lay no less calm and silent, doors and windows tightly closed. Not a gleam of light showed behind the shutters. With one swift, comprehensive glance Fandor took in the state of things.

"Fast asleep all along the line!" he muttered to himself—"and so much the better! After all, that proves nothing… Damn!

there's a gas lamp very inconveniently placed—right in front of the house, and I can't see a corner anywhere to hide in. He did not stop, but walked on, scrutinizing right and left the general aspect of the street.

"But I *must* hide somewhere!" he reflected. "In the first place, supposing Juve comes, I want to treat myself to the pleasure of giving him a surprise. In the second, if my worthy friend is after game, I mustn't be walking up and down and scaring the quarry. That's so, but where to stuff myself in? A mailbox? But they make 'em so absurdly small… or I'm so absurdly big! Must find something better than that."

But it was no easy job. From one end of the Rue de l'Assomption to the other small private houses succeeded one another, separated at intervals by taller and bigger buildings, forerunners of the "improvements" the speculative builder was threatening the district with.

"Of course I could slip into a garden," thought the journalist, "but then I might hit on a house where they keep a dog, and it's never an agreeable job explaining a nocturnal visit to beasts of the sort… Now where *am* I to hide?"

But Fandor gave a sudden jump:

"Why, what a fool I am! Don't the Le Rouxs live close here?" These Le Rouxs were two good-natured young fellows, old friends of Fandor's, who assisted their father in the management of a big business in the garden trellis and rustic-seat line. The journalist could remember paying a visit once to their place and the vast workshops that formed part of the establishment.

"Yes, the Le Rouxs, that's the ticket!" Fandor decided. "I'll swarm up on the roof of their workrooms. If they hear me, I'll tell them who I am. I only hope they won't go shooting at me without warning!"

However, Fandor was not the fellow to be deterred by any risk of that sort. Creeping cautiously down a passage or covered entry, he found himself in a small yard in which were stored in symmetrical piles, planks and balks of timber. Noticing a stout beam, Fandor set this up against the coping of the roof and using knees and hands started to clamber up it. An acrobatic feat of this kind was nothing to the young man. He soon reached the roof, along which he stepped cautiously forward, stooping down as much as possible as he advanced.

"Let's find a good place," he said to himself. "Something in the nature of an orchestra stall is what I want, or a seat in the grand circle. Here we are, this is first rate! From here I shall see everything." He was indeed in luck's way. He could look down not only into the Rue de l'Assomption and see the de Vautreuil's abode, but even discern the garden and the roof of the little house…

"If anybody comes—Juve, or…"

He broke off in the middle of his sentence, and his heart stopped beating, so intense was his surprise and excitement. "If anybody comes," he had said, and lo! before his eyes at that very moment someone *was* coming—and coming in such a fashion the journalist could only gasp and stare. On the roof of the de Vautreuils' house, hoisting himself up, no doubt, by means of the wild vine and ivy that covered the back wall, a man was trying to climb, *was* climbing upwards.

The moon unfortunately was set. Fandor could not make out the features of the unknown, who now stood up, resting his weight on the coping of the roof, his shape relieved against the dark background of the sky. To make up, the journalist could perfectly well discern the man's stature and dress.

"Who the devil is it?" he asked himself. "Certainly not Henry Tardoux! He is thinner… Certainly not Fantômas! He is taller. Certainly again, not Juve! Juve would not be dressed like that. In fact, the man appeared to have donned a kind of close-fitting tights such as acrobats wear, whereas good old Juve had left the Prefecture clad in a very ordinary sort of jacket and an equally commonplace overcoat."

"Who can it be then?" Fandor reflected anxiously. "I can't see, and I can't guess." Then he had another surprise.

This mysterious and alarming figure that had just scrambled on to the roofs of the de Vautreuil's house was cautiously moving forward. Stepping up to the cluster of chimneys that broke the ridge of the rooftree, he bent down in turn over each of them in the attitude of a man listening.

"Can it be some spy wishing to discover what is going on in the house, or some miscreant using the chimney flues as a speaking tube for communicating with an accomplice already inside the place?"

Instinctively Fandor had drawn his revolver to be ready for anything that might happen.

"In any case," he resolved, "I'm not going to lose sight of him, and whenever the good man chooses to begin, I have him by the ears. Five seconds to scramble down off my own roof, dash across the road and rouse the de Vautreuils, and the man's ours. He simply can't escape!"

But at that moment Fandor had another shock of surprise. The unknown had turned round to face him. Crouching as he was in the shadow of a neighboring house, the journalist knew he was invisible, but perhaps the polished barrel of his weapon might have been seen. Anyway, the man he was watching dropped flat on his roof and began to crawl up to a chimney pot, and reaching it, stood motionless.

Fandor let fly an oath. "By God! I mustn't let the beggar see me, that would be too idiotic. Anyway, he's bound to move off sometime, and then I'll catch him…"

But hours, long, dreary hours, passed, and neither the unknown nor Fandor stirred. Neither seemed the least inclined to leave his post.

"And no signs of Juve!" thought the journalist. "That's the queerest part of the whole business! Where the devil can he be?… But there, after all," he reflected further, "perhaps Juve *is* here? There's nothing to hinder his being in a better hiding-hole than mine, nothing to prevent his too, like me, having seen the villain I'm shadowing."

But Fandor felt himself more and more at a loss: "Who was the wretch?" Then, as a new idea struck him: "By God! can it be Louis Rippert? I don't know him, I have never seen him. Come now!"—and arguing from point to point, Fandor by degrees reconstructed almost the same chain of reasoning as Juve had already done. He could not indeed take into account at present the events that had occurred at the Prefecture, inasmuch as he knew nothing about them, but he thought of all the other circumstances directing suspicion on the young man.

"He is a friend of Tardoux, to start with," he told himself—"and Tardoux, I mistrust the man! Again, he is the owner of the dog that came alive again. And then Juve doesn't know him either. Juve has never set eyes on him at the Prefecture. Can he have been keeping out of his way on purpose?"

But evidently the journalist could come to no certain and definite conclusion. It was all merely conjecture.

"Bah! I'm wasting my time!" he exclaimed suddenly. "Guessing won't lead to much. What we want is to know. Well, there's a sure way of knowing—and that is to find out!"—and his eyes still riveted on the spot where the unknown stood motionless, Fandor reflected:

"Am I to go on waiting? After all, that strikes me as risky. Who can tell if my man won't slip between my fingers, supposing I leave him the initiative? On the other hand, who can be sure, supposing I make a dash at him now, I won't take him by surprise? All said and done, nobody has any right to fool about like this on the housetops, so I have a legal motive for intervening."

To intervene, to do something, to be quit of this tedious inactivity, was altogether to Fandor's taste, patience being anything but the young man's leading characteristic, and in a moment he had decided on a plan daring to the verge of recklessness. Taking advantage of the darkness, he would come down from his point of vantage, and scramble up himself on to the de Vautreuil's roof.

"Obviously the fellow will either throw himself upon me or he will take to his heels. Very good! That's just what I want. If he springs at me, I will defend myself, if he bolts, I will give chase... In twenty minutes from now I will know this night bird's name—or I will have no further use for mine!"

Jerome Fandor was not the man to hesitate, once he had made up his mind, and then and there he set about realizing the plan he had fixed upon.

To scramble quickly down from the observatory where he had spent such weary hours of waiting, to cross the street in a couple of strides, to climb the fence and leap down into the garden, all this was mere child's play to the young man.

"My friend must be thinking I am still on my roof," he reflected. "From where he is I don't suppose he can possibly see me. That's all to the good, so let's get to work! Ha, ha! the fat's in the fire now!"—and overjoyed at the notion that perhaps he was going to make some sensational discovery, Fandor set about the last climb he had to make, the escalade of the de Vautreuils' house.

If the man the journalist was after had been able to negotiate the ascent, evidently the feat was a comparatively easy one. And so it proved. Ivy and wild vine covered the walls and their interlacing branches formed a rudimentary stairway conducting to the top. But unfortunately these proceedings could not long remain silent. Of necessity, as he gripped at the branches, Fandor kept knocking away bits of plaster, that rattled down on to the ground of the garden walks.

"Hmm!" he muttered, "if my man isn't stone deaf…"—and at that moment the fellow showed that he was not so afflicted. Fandor had not reached the second story, in fact, when, to his very natural annoyance, he caught sight of a man's shadow thrown on the high white wall of a tall building at the far end of the garden.

It was easy enough to guess what was happening. Having heard the noise, the man must evidently have leaned over and seen, if not recognized, his pursuer. And then and there, no doubt, he had realized the disadvantage of his situation. A struggle on this narrow roof must inevitably rouse all the inmates of the house, and his arrest could hardly fail to follow under these conditions. Accordingly he was evacuating the position.

Simultaneously Fandor, on his side, seeing the shadow cast by the flickering light of the streetlamp in front of the house, hesitated no longer. "Ah, ha! capital!" he exclaimed, half laughingly, half anxiously. "So the gentleman's making off? How I do admire courage! But, after all, what does it matter? The next scene will be played in the street—and why not?"

Undoubtedly the man was climbing down by help of a drainpipe, but being anxious not to make a noise, and probably afraid of some belated passerby seeing him, he was moving quite slowly. Fandor on the contrary scrambled down from his perch as quick as ever he could, and the instant he reached the ground, started running round the house, hoping to be in time to give battle there and then.

But alas! his hopes were vain. As he turned the last corner, he had just time to make out two hands clinging for one second to the coping of a wall bounding the garden on the side of the Rue de l'Assomption. The vision was gone in a moment. The fugitive had instantly let go, and the sound of flying feet could be heard on the asphalt of the roadway.

"Better and better, my fine fellow!" grinned the journalist. "I didn't win the 'hundred' for nothing in my day! I'll show you what sprinting means!"—and quick as lightning, he sprang forward, leapt the wall and plopped into the street.

There the young champion was to meet an unpleasant surprise. In vain he looked to right, in vain he stared to left. There was not a soul in sight!

"Made off?" growled Fandor. "Impossible! Vanished! Gone up to heaven?… Oh God! in the Rue de l'Assomption that would be something very like sacrilege… But devil take me if I know where he *has* gone!"

"By God!" he swore presently, "I'm very sure he hasn't flown away! So he can't be far off… yes, but where?"—and involuntarily, while his eyes searched every dark corner, the young man thought of the long minute when *he* must have been perfectly visible standing there under the gas lamp, and now he offered the finest possible target to any resolute marksman.

"Very obliging to let myself be killed like that!" he soliloquized. "But I must look out. I haven't the smallest desire to carry home a coat with a bullet hole in it… All the same, I do wish Juve was here!"

But Juve was most certainly not there. If that police officer had been anywhere in the neighborhood and had seen what Fandor was after, he could never have stood by inactive. He would have flung himself upon his friend to reproach him for risking his life so recklessly.

Suddenly Fandor broke into an oath. A hundred yards ahead in the direction of the Boulevard Montmorency, just over the top of an iron gate giving access to a garden he had caught sight of a man's head—the man he was chasing. More daring than his pursuer, or rather perhaps urged on by fear, the fugitive had faced the risk of encountering a watchdog, and had entered private ground, from which he was keeping a wary eye on the enemy. Instantly the journalist's spirits rose.

"Ha, ha! my fine fellow!" he laughed, "so there you are! Well, I've got a nice little present all ready for you!" Without taking his hands out of his pockets, so as to hide what he was doing, Fandor had opened the spring-catches of a stout pair of hand-cuffs he had taken the precaution of borrowing from old Jean, Juve's factotum.

"Not a pretty bracelet for a young lady," he was saying to himself, "but for a ruffian who goes climbing by night on the tops of houses where old ladies appear and disappear at pleasure!…"

For all that, joke as he might—it was an inveterate habit with him—Fandor was very well aware of the gravity of the issue involved. The foe had run away—but he had not fled far. Did this mean he was afraid? or was it the maneuver of a murderer waiting the favorable instant to spring at his victim's throat?

"Yes, the beggar has all the look of watching out for me," thought Fandor. "Well, so much the better! I'll give him a run for his money, never fear!"

He had taken his cigarette case quietly from his pocket, and well in sight, like a man who supposes himself alone, having abandoned the abortive pursuit, he now struck a match and lit up.

"Now the fellow's persuading himself, I haven't seen him—and that's all to the good for the plan I've got in my head."

It was true the young fellow had determined on a plan, but

a plan so wildly reckless it came close to the verge of madness. Crossing the street at a walking pace, strolling along head down, as if lost in thought, Fandor moved off in the direction of the Boulevard Montmorency, that is to say, straight for the low wall behind which he knew the man watching him was ambushed.

"Yes," the journalist reflected, "I am playing a game of double or nothing with my man, that's what it comes to! Soon as I come level with him, I shall be in range of his revolver, no doubt of that. If he wants to shoot me, there's nothing to stop him… But will he want?"

The question was one that might well have deserved more consideration than the intrepid young man gave it. In a moment he had answered it to his own satisfaction:

"But he will not shoot! No, he will not fire, because a revolver is a thing that makes a noise… and we are barely a couple of hundred yards from the Avenue Mozart." Then, with a short laugh, he went on:

"He won't fire. Instead, he'll leap his wall and come after me. Well, after all, that's just what I want,"—and as a matter of fact, that was precisely what he was aiming at. His plan, like all good plans, was quite simple. Convinced of the impossibility of dislodging his quarry from the garden he had hidden in, the journalist had devised a scheme to entice the man to come after him of his own accord.

"I shall go on slowly, never looking behind me or doing anything to excite his suspicions, as far as the Rue du Docteur Blanche. Then, still strolling in a leisurely fashion, I shall turn off to the left—and he will follow me. In five minutes he will reach the corner too—and that's where I'm going to wait for him! To crouch close against the wall, to spring out suddenly, and grip him by the collar, to clap on the handcuffs, that's a mere trifle. The great thing is to catch him napping!"

As he indulged in these sanguine anticipations, Jerome Fandor came very near dubbing himself a genius.

"Ha, ha!" he chuckled, "but this'll be one in the eye for old Juve this time!"—and still without the least hurry, that was an essential point, he moved on.

Nor can it be denied that just then the young man's heart was beating somewhat faster than usual. It is the mark of true courage not to deny the danger or refuse to believe in it, but on the contrary to have a clear conception of its nature and gravity—*and* to face it with a scornful smile.

"Warm work!" Fandor told himself. "The danger zone begins here. I am well within range, no doubt of that. Now, is he going to shoot? Not yet perhaps? A little further on then, maybe? Anyway I shall hear the click of the hammer." But all was silent so far.

Then, to demonstrate his perfect self-possession to himself— and to the watcher behind the wall, he stooped as if to tie a shoelace.

"Well, fire away then. Fire, if you're going to!" he muttered, tasting the joy only valiant hearts know, the fierce joy of defying imminent and immediate danger. Twenty steps away, in the dark, revolver in hand, holding his life at the pistol's point, was a scoundrel who hated him for sure.

But nothing happened, and presently Fandor stood up again and proceeded quietly on his way; and, strangely enough, it was then, as he moved further away from his adversary, that his nerves began to tingle, as he told himself:

"By God! a man of iron! What self-control to resist the temptation when revenge was ready to his hand! It *must* surely be Fantômas. Till that moment he had been in doubt, half believing it to be an accomplice of the arch-villain, and even imagining that this accomplice had taken no action because he was waiting in vain for the arrival of Fantômas, detained perhaps by Juve somewhere or other…"

But suddenly all uncertainty vanished. He *knew* the man could be no other than Fantômas. Who, if not the Lord of Terror, the Genius of Evildoing, could possess the coolness to behave as the unknown had just done? Who else would have dared to clamber to the housetop when Juve might very well be watching the building? Who, above all, if not the cruel and callous Torturer, could have suffered Fandor to pass within range of his weapon without firing, waiting for a more propitious moment to spring at his enemy's throat?

"Come, come! there can be no doubt about it. It is He, He and no other, who is tracking me down!"

He was sure now. If he mimicked the leisurely gait and behavior of a stroller without an anxiety in the world, if his whole manner testified apparently to the fact that he had abandoned the pursuit he had but now undertaken, this by no means hindered his nerves quivering in a paroxysm of agitation.

Now he was approaching the turning of the Rue du Docteur Blanche, the spot where he had resolved to take up ambush and lay his snare.

"Slowly round the corner," he warned himself, "very slowly. There, that's excellent!"

But once out of sight of his pursuer, the journalist's demeanor changed instantly.

Where to hide? What position to take up so as to be sure of leaping at one bound at the villain's throat?

One glance was sufficient. In a second his mind was made up. At the street corner was a wooden palisade, a dilapidated and worm-eaten fence enclosing probably some bit of wasteland or a tennis ground, such as abound at Auteuil. The line of this fence, constructed of uneven planking, was out of the true and in one place bellied a little inwards.

"First rate!" the journalist declared. "If I crouch in the hollow, my man will never see me till he's right round the corner and I'm on him before he can say knife."

Only one more doubt ended in a second: Which had he better do? Keep his browning in his hand, or the handcuffs?

"If I am armed and ready, and he resists, I shall fire," he thought. "But have I any right to shoot the fellow, after all?… No, best have my handcuffs ready. Besides, we must take Fantômas alive. I shall hand him over to Juve. *He* must have the honor of the capture."

Here ended Fandor's reflections. Henceforth, every sense on the alert, he stood listening, his whole frame quivering in the darkness and silence. Was the other coming? How long he was about it! Perhaps he wanted to give his enemy time to increase the distance between them? Or had he decided to strike the first blow himself?

Suddenly the young man felt a conviction that the crisis was imminent. A second more and the man would turn the corner—half a second more and he *must* arrive…

Fandor choked down a furious oath—the fellow had *not* turned the corner! Warned, it may be, by some mysterious instinct, he had crossed over to the opposite pavement, and was continuing straight on down the Rue de l'Assomption, passing the opening of the Rue du Docteur Blanche without apparently deigning to cast one glance in that direction.

So then he was not chasing Fandor? He was not so much as thinking of attacking him? Instinctively, obeying a purely reflex impulse, the journalist fell back a pace and bent low over the ramshackle fence. He was sure the man could not distinguish him in the surrounding dark, but, to make up, *he* could see the other distinctly… Fandor felt the blood rush to his head. In the man's hands something glittered—a weapon for sure! Then the strange costume he wore! Surely it was a complete suit of tights, tights of grey silk, a color doubtless chosen to match the slates of a house roof. How fail to guess, in view of this carefulness of detail, the skillful hand and nice precision of Fantômas?

Fandor's patience was at an end. The man had passed the crossroads and was almost out of sight. At all costs he must catch up to him and leap upon him—and so thinking, the young man set off at a run. He dashed across the side street, reached the opposite pavement, turned the sharp corner of the Rue de l'Assomption—and next instant gave a frantic exclamation:

Copying Fandor's own tactics, lying in wait for him behind the street corner just as he had himself done, the man's threatening figure rose up before him.

"Fantômas!"—and an echo repeated the dread name.

Then two sharp clicks… followed by two rapid oaths. Fandor had applied his handcuffs. With marvelous coolness and quickness he had clapped them on the man's wrists. But, simultaneously, the latter had clapped another pair on Fandor's!

Then, arms interlaced, bound fast to one another, each thinking he had made the other prisoner, the two men rolled together on the ground.

Hampered by the handcuffs that made of them a pair of inseparable Siamese twins, they were soon on their feet again. The two adversaries could see each other at last, and two cries of mutual recognition rang out together:

"Juve!"

"Fandor!"

The two friends had been chasing each other, each a victim of the same mistake!

*     *     *     *     *

On seeing it was Juve, his "good old Juve," he had just arrested and that Juve on his side, committing an identical mistake, had similarly handcuffed him, Fandor burst into a great shout of laughter. And never surely had he had better reason to give free vent to his gay humor.

"Ho, ho!" he stammered out, shaken by convulsive gusts of merriment, "whatever were you after here, Juve?"

"Why, I was after Fantômas, by God!... and you?"

"I was in the same boat! In fact, I was dead certain I'd recognized my man!"

"You suspected someone? Henri Tardoux, I suppose?"

"No! I was almost thinking it was Louis Rippert."

Juve, as he heard the name, gave a violent start, but quickly checking himself, he merely observed:

"Still, all this doesn't tell me how you came to be on that roof."

"And you, Juve, on yours? and dressed up as a human bat!"

"Do be serious, man!"

"Can't do it, Juve! The thing's impossible!... But, first take your handcuffs off me."

"Eh?... first take yours off me!"

"But I can't, Juve, the key's in my pocket."

"You're a sweet boy, Fandor, but my key's in my pocket, too."

"Then there's no way of getting loose?"

"Oh God, no!"

"Well, this is the limit,"—and, with another laugh, Fandor mimicked the tones of a street hawker selling some choice article:

"Here y'are, the most astute detective of modern times and the cleverest of reporters! Here y'are! To be sold in one lot! They can't be parted!"

"Hold your tongue!" Juve begged. "It's just too idiotic what's happened us!"

"Too silly for words! And then, I'd like to smoke a cigarette."

"You'll just have to go without!… But come, we must think of something."

"So be it, Juve, let's think!… Would it meet your views if we took a seat—on the curb, for instance? I'm dead beat… And I can't sit down unless you do too."

The situation struck him as so farcical he was quite amazed to hear Juve suddenly exclaim:

"Great heavens! but we're just mad!"

"Why?"

"Remember, man, we're in a locality Fantômas is bound to frequent. Think of his delight if he caught us like this, the pair of us, at his mercy? Not even capable of defending ourselves!"

"The devil! Yes, you're right, Juve. Shall we cut and run?"

"Run where to, pray?"

"To get our bracelets taken off?"

"And who's to do it, my boy?"

"Why! why, the policemen at the Auteuil station, to be sure."

"So that tomorrow Havard may make a to-do over my clumsiness? No thank you! I have my feelings!"

"Hmm! yes, I understand… Only… But, look here! I have an idea. I know who to apply to…"

"Who?"

"To Bouzille, Juve! He lives at the Point du Jour. Going by the Bois we can get there without being noticed, just looking as if we were taking a stroll together arm in arm."

"Come along then, your notion's a good one,"—and they set off. On the way Juve questioned his companion, and drew from him a detailed account of his adventures. Then, in receipt of this information, he proceeded to relate how he himself had come to be on the roof.

"You understand," he declared, "that if you got to the Rue de l'Assomption before me, it was because I gave myself time to change. I made a point of the tights so as to be less easily seen… But, devil take me if I dreamed it was you when I saw someone lurking in ambush."

"Exactly my case! I'm hanged if I suspected you for one second!… I thought you were too fat."

"Yes, to alter my figure, I padded myself."

"And too short."

"No heels, my boy!"

"And I came precious near firing my revolver at you."

"Same here! When you went past my garden gate…"

"Say, Juve, why didn't you turn the corner?"

"Bah! didn't take a wizard to guess your trick! I preferred to take ambush myself. You were dead sure to follow up my tracks."

"Well, you caught me, Juve, eh?"

"And you caught me, Fandor."

"Yes, and that's proof of one thing, Juve."

"What's that?"

Fandor put on his most sententious tone to reply:

"Well, it proves this, that to clap the handcuffs on anyone is not the last word in the policeman's art!… To arrest is well, but to release is better!"

This time Juve's face relaxed in a smile. Then he went on more seriously:

"Anyhow, Fantômas didn't come. And devil take me if I know where he is… I admit it's a disappointment. I was convinced…"

"Look there," broke in the other, "there it is! That's Bouzille's palatial residence, not a doubt of it. He told me: Diogenes and I are a match! My tub's as good as his, only mine's a vast sight bigger, ain't it now for sure?"

It certainly was! Juve and Fandor had just come out on the banks of the Seine, and there, on a stretch of waste ground, they beheld an enormous, a gigantic barrel, last relic of some wartime munition works.

"Let's knock him up!" suggested Fandor. He gave a kick, and instantly a voice answered:

"Clear out, you pack of blackguards!"

Then the journalist resorted to a harmless bit of humbug.

"Out with you, my man!" he ordered in a peremptory voice. "It's a police raid. You're our prisoner!"

"Prisoner? Not a bit of it! I'm caretaker of the yard. I'm not a vagabond at large, my good sirs!"—and, with a pale scared face, Bouzille appeared outside, draped in a gorgeous dressing gown, made out of an old eiderdown, girt about his person with bits of string.

"I'm no vagabond!" he protested indignantly. "I'm in charge of this here barrel. And I've other trades too. I'm a telephonist, to start off with… and a dogs' undertaker too… I fish out folks as is drowned… I recover lost property…"

But he got no further. He had recognized his visitors.

"God o' mercy!" he cried. "M'sieur Juve!… M'sieur Fandor!… And if they ain't tied up together like! Oh, ho!"

"Bouzille, take 'em off us, that's the ticket now! Here, get the key out of my pocket!"

But Bouzille was gazing at Fandor with solemn looks:

"Me rummage in your pocket? But I'm an honest man, I am! It's just enticing me to petty larceny what you're asking me to do. S'pose I made a mistake and first pinched forty sous out of your purse…"

"Take your forty sous, only release us, do!"

"Forty sous, M'sieur Fandor, for waking me up in the middle of the night! and for helping you escape! No, can't be done! With victuals as dear as they be, it's no sort of payment! But there, you didn't let me finish… s'pose I did take forty sous, as I was saying, it ain't enough… now three francs, three paltry little francs…"

"Bouzille, hurry up, man! You shall have five francs. But if you play the idiot, Juve's going to run you in for pitching in the river the dogs you're paid to bury. That's commercial swindling, that is!"

"Righto, M'sieur Fandor!… Look here, what I'm doing isn't for the ten francs, mind you!"

"The five francs, Bouzille."

"The eight francs, I repeat, the same's you promised me. It's along of our being colleagues…"

As he talked, Bouzille had been groping in the young man's pocket, found the key of the handcuffs and set Fandor free, who in turn liberated Juve. The old fellow now went on:

"Why yes, we're colleagues, so we be! I report for the Haven Agency. It's a new line of business…"

"What's that you're telling us?"

"It's God's truth, M'sieur Juve. Look, here's how it is… But first pay me my nine francs."

"Your five francs, Bouzille!… Here they are… You were saying…?"

"Well, I was saying, this here business, how you've come to hunt me up, I'm going to telephone it up tomorrow. That'll stand me in another five shiners."

"And who's going to pay you for the information?"

Juve and Fandor exchanged a rapid glance. The name was what they were burning to hear, the name of the individual who was interesting himself in their doings!

"M'sieur Louis Rippert," announced Bouzille, "the owner of the pup that was so set on living,"—and out of the corner of his eye, the old man was watching to see the effect of his words. But neither Juve nor Fandor had moved a muscle.

So the old tramp continued:

"M'sieur Rippert's just gone away, gone off to Chartres, at five o'clock… 'If there's anything new turns up about that dog business,' he told me, 'telephone me.' I'm not going to spoil the game. I'd tell him you were making inquiries and you've discovered nothing… That's not giving nothing away, for sure?"

As the old fellow spoke, Juve was digging his nails feverishly into the palms of his hands. At first, on hearing Louis Rippert's name he had felt a thrill of intense satisfaction. If it was a fact that Louis Rippert was anxious to know about Fandor's and

Juve's doings, was this not pretty well proof positive, that Juve was justified in suspecting him to be Fantômas?

But now, his delight gave way to something very like despair. If Rippert had left for Chartres at five o'clock, was it not manifest, on the contrary, that Rippert was *not* Fantômas? Juve had held Fantômas prisoner till long after that hour.

In a quavering voice he questioned:

"Are you certain, Bouzille, that Monsieur Rippert left at five o'clock?"

"Why do you ask, M'sieur Juve?"

"Answer my question. I want to know."

"Then, don't wish to force you, but make the five francs a bit more! M'sieur Fandor's not been generous."

"You shall have ten francs," Juve promised, "if you give me your word you're telling the exact truth."

"Hand over the shiners then, M'sieur Juve. Here's how the thing was. It was my own self carried his trunk to the railway, for the price of a cab fare. More by token I just took a common handbarrow for the job.… And M'sieur Rippert, he went off by the seven after five train. I shut the carriage door myself. Them's things you can check if you so please, M'sieur Juve, things as is sure and certain…"

Juve was convinced and said no more. He gave a gesture of discouragement and weariness. Then, turning to Fandor:

"Come, let's go home! Tomorrow we shall see clear daylight…"

"And that's a bit of ill-luck for me," protested Bouzille. "If only there was an eclipse, business would look up, it would! I hire out smoked glasses for to look at the thing through. But it's a trade that's pretty slack most times!"

Juve and Fandor, however, were not listening. After a careless shake of the hand to the old man, they went their way and presently in the Boulevard Exelmans took a taxi. Juve gave the word, Rue Tardieu, and they set off for home.

For once the great detective felt himself beaten, badly beaten. Fantômas had played his game out exactly as he had intended. Fantômas had done just whatever seemed good to him, and his adversary had found no way to hinder him. With a shudder, Juve asked himself:

"What news shall I hear tomorrow? What has he been doing tonight while I was incapable of checkmating his designs?"

But Juve was not destined to wait for the morrow to hear a sensational piece of news. Home again in his flat in the Rue Tardieu, which had witnessed so many extraordinary adventures before now, the police officer was bidding his friend good night and wishing him sound repose after the fatigues of their day when he noticed a look of surprise on his servant's face.

"What's the matter now, Jean?" he questioned the old man.

"Monsieur isn't going to look at his letters?"

"Letters are there?"

"A dispatch by pneumatic, sir."

"And you never told me, stupid!"

"You never asked me, sir."

There was no more to be said: Jean was fidelity personified, but sometimes he was taken with whims it was best to take no notice of. Jean was a Breton, and that accounted for many oddities.

"Give it here!" Juve said curtly, and tearing open the envelope, informed Fandor: "From Josette de Vautreuil. I'll read it you!" Then he gave a cry of stupefaction, and presently began to read:

"Sir," the letter ran—"In gratitude for the sympathy you and Monsieur Fandor have shown me, I think it my duty at once to put matters on a right footing and disabuse your minds of the impression a most baffling incident may have caused. We all believed that my poor aunt, Eléonore de Vautreuil, had disappeared as mysteriously as she had previously mysteriously reappeared in Paris. It was nothing of the sort. An hour after you had gone, on going up to the attics to find a trunk my father is taking away with him on a journey, our servant Louis saw my relative hidden behind a pile of articles put there to be out of the way. Mlle. Eléonore, terrified no doubt by the noise of the disturbance that occurred in our kitchen, must have fled upstairs to this attic, where nobody even thought of looking for her. I may add that her condition appears to be in no way modified… Yours, etc.—the usual phrases," concluded Juve. "By God, it's above bearing! The instant I make out a theory, something knocks it to pieces! The aunt was discovered at the very time I held Fantômas prisoner. It follows…"—and without finishing his sentence, Juve wheeled round:

"Good night, Fandor!"

"Good night, Juve! Get to sleep quick…"

"Oh! I'm dying to go to bed."

But this was a falsehood. Juve was not sleepy at all. He was far too anxious, too agitated to be capable of enjoying one minute's repose. Instead of going to bed, Juve threw himself into an armchair and, his everlasting cigarette between his lips, fell into a profound reverie.

Suddenly the police officer sprang to his feet:

"Why, bless my soul! but the thing's obvious. It's sure and certain, manifest, self-evident! But how came I never to think of it? I'm getting imbecile surely, decrepit, past my work!"

A surprising idea had very certainly flashed across his brain…

Almost at the same moment his telephone rang, and Juve ran to the instrument.

"Hello!" he cried. "Yes, it is I, sir!… Why! what! Why certainly, I'll come. I'll come right away… You're perfectly right. Of course my battle with Fantômas can't relieve me of my ordinary duties… You've done quite right to summon me. In ten minutes I'll be with you," and he hung up the receiver.

Then, hurrying from his room and dashing across the passage, he banged with his fist on Fandor's bedroom door.

"Get up, lazy bones!"

"Eh? what?… is the house on fire?"

Fandor had been sound asleep, waking with a start, he asked again:

"Is the place on fire, Juve? Whatever's up?"

"Yes, there's a fire going, that's so—but not here!"

"Then, what do you want me to do?"

"There's a fire, and we're off there! Quick, I tell you! Dress, man! I give you three minutes to be ready."

"But, after all, Juve…"

"Hush! listen to me!… Your browning, eh? and three clips of cartridges in your pocket… Yes, there is a fire afoot, my boy. You can see for yourself that means hot work, can't you?"

In truth Juve seemed to have completely recovered his good humor.

## 12. "Goodbye!"—But Is It Really Goodbye?

"Say, Juve, can you be going mad? Here you are 'doing' fires, like a raw beginner!… My word! do you think you're a fireman these days?"

Fandor was grumbling, as was his way whenever Juve thought fit to keep him in the dark about even the most trifling of his designs. A matter of no moment, anyway, for it did not in the least prevent the young man's dressing in all haste, and with unquestioning obedience to orders, slipping his browning into his pocket.

"Here goes!" he announced presently. "But, oh God! I've no helmet… and no hatchet… and no buckled belt! no uniform to wear in fact. But there, you'll lend me one, I suppose?"

"Don't talk so much!" was all the answer Juve vouchsafed. "Ready? then away we go!"

"Away where? No place in particular, eh?"

"Orders are: follow me!"

"Peremptory, but a bit vague! Say, are you making a long trot of it at this rate?"

The question was natural enough. Juve had shot down the stairs like a meteorite, and once in the street, was tearing along at a breakneck pace. Five o'clock in the morning had just struck. The Square d'Auvers was deserted and not a vehicle was to be seen. But the detective knew his whereabouts too well to hesitate a second. He made at once for the Place Pigalle. There the two friends found a long line of night cabs on the rank, and Juve instantly hailed the one that looked the fastest.

"Where to?" demanded the chauffeur, alert and ready in a moment.

"Rueil, the Rueil Asylum! I'll help you find the way. Quick as you can go!"

Juve was already inside and Fandor, still bewildered, took

his place beside him.

"Rueil!" he was growling. "We're going to Rueil? to the Madhouse? I give it up! You're sure they won't keep you there, Juve?"

"Let me get my wind, and I'll explain…"

When, five minutes afterwards, poor Juve had a little recovered his breath, he turned to Fandor, all smiles.

"No," he declared replying to the journalist's last question, "no, they won't keep us there. The great thing, mind you, is to get there in time."

"In time for what, Juve?"

"Why, to remedy the consequences of my stupidity!"

"Which means?"

"My lad, the Asylum is on fire…"

"Very good!… or very bad!… But I don't see…"

"The Asylum is blazing, Fandor, to allow Fantômas to perish… and do what he has sworn to do…"

"Fantômas?"

"Why, yes, Fantômas! Fantômas who is the madman we listened to like a pair of school children, Havard and I! Oh! I shall never forgive myself for not having guessed it all sooner."

*     *     *     *     *

Two hours after his arrest, Doctor Walton, the unfortunate lunatic captured in M. Havard's private room at the Prefecture, after furnishing the Head of the Criminal Department with sundry incoherent explanations regarding the Auteuil mysteries, had duly appeared before the Senior Physician in charge of the Prison Infirmary.

A brief memorandum from M. Havard obviated all need for medical examination such as is customary when the insane fall into the hands of the police, in the American doctor's case.

"Pseudo-scientific insanity," announced the physician, "mania of invention and perhaps tendency to mania of persecution,"—and with the two words, "Rueil Asylum," he sealed the fate of the unhappy man. Accompanied by an imposing bundle of official forms, he was conducted to one of the big yellow and buff vehicles that convey patients to the Paris hospitals and soon was on his way to the Department Asylum.

In the vehicle Doctor Walton sat perfectly quiet and inoffensive. He seemed indeed utterly exhausted, as the insane generally are after a violent outbreak or when a similar outbreak is imminent. No sooner arrived at Rueil than the House Physician, whose duty it was to assign the various types of madmen according to the particular section of the House they were to occupy, noticed the new patient's depressed condition.

"Dangerous perhaps, this fellow?" he hazarded. "The papers he has brought with him are pretty vague… Very good! Put him provisionally in the padded room. Tomorrow we'll see about classifying him."

Five minutes later he was locked in in room 18. Once inside and the padded door shut on him, the madman instantly lost the dull, heavy look he had worn hitherto. Assured that he was alone and unobserved—the peephole in the door was shut—he broke into a laugh:

"So there we are!" he chuckled, "Juve, at this very moment, must be hunting for me all over the Prefecture! When he's tired of rummaging the place from top to bottom, he'll start off to Passy to investigate there! Then he'll go back home and go to bed. Oh, ho! I think my little plan is working out perfectly. Barring accidents, I shall be at liberty round about three or four in the morning. The motor will be waiting for me. It'll take me a quarter of an hour to get back to Paris… And I shall be all the safer as the devil's in it or if Juve don't come rushing here, when he finds out what's going to happen presently."

Alas! if only Juve could at that moment have scrutinized, were it but for a second, Doctor Walton's face, if he could have seen clearly those hard, cold eyes, if he could have lifted a corner of the man's wig, he would not have felt one moment's hesitation in recognizing him there and then.

Doctor Walton? No, Fantômas… if indeed Fantômas was the man Juve had arrested at the tavern of the late lamented Père Korn.

The wretch, as calm as if he did not know himself confined in the most terrible of prisons, the miscreant who had but now announced: "I shall be free at three o'clock in the morning or thereabouts," stretched himself at length on the padded floor of his cell and shutting his eyes, fell into a peaceful doze.

*      *      *      *      *

Would he have been so calm and unconcerned had he been aware of the events occurring at the late Père Korn's tavern at the very same time he was being locked up in the padded cell at Rueil?

About seven in the evening a couple of workmen had entered that establishment, workmen of a decidedly raffish appearance. One fellow, with a long beard and long, straggling hair, displayed a pair of patched, down-at-heel shoes untidily laced up with bits of string. The other, carrying a plumber's toolbox, a peaked cap thrust well back on the head, his shirt open at the throat, was chewing the butt of a cigarette.

"A glass of the stuff for me and my mate!" he ordered, addressing the man behind the counter. "You're the boss, are you?"

The landlord nodded yes and demanded in his turn: "What d'ye want with me, eh?"

"You've got beds to let by the night?"

"That depends…"

"It was Julot from America told us about your place… Quiet quarters are what we want."

"For one night?"

"Just to give us the time to look round for work, y'know… We've hoofed it from Lyons."

"Come in then… I'll show you the way."

The dialogue between them might have been overheard by anyone without exciting particular attention. Nevertheless it contained two passwords—"Julot from America" and "Lyons." The tavern-keeper's doubts were satisfied.

"A crib for the two of you, I 'spose?"

"Righto!"

"Here y'are then. It's fifteen sous the night. You pay in advance…"

"Of course, of course!"

Guided by the landlord, who was replaced for the moment at the bar by a waiter, the two workmen had entered one of the squalid dens that are the furnished apartments of the "submerged tenth" of Paris. They examined the state of things like men familiar with such localities, then they asked:

"And the exits?"

"Ah! I see you're the right sort!" the landlord laughed. "Prudence is a virtue, anyhow. But the cops never set foot in my place. Look here! to start with, there's the same way we came in, passing through the shop, and then, another way out this road—you open this door, and the stairs come out on the other passage…"

"Righto! we'll take the crib. Here's your fifteen browns."

"You're going to 'doss' right away?"

"For sure! Tomorrow, must hook it bright and early, along of 'business.'"

"Good night then, mates!"—and the landlord withdrew. Keeper of a dosshouse by the night, he was not so simple as to ask newcomers to give their names, deeming himself well enough able to invent out of his own head the cabalistic vocables he never failed to inscribe scrupulously on the police registers. He knew very well that folks who made such a point of knowing the exits from the house would never trust him with their true designations.

Hardly was the landlord out of the room before the two workmen exchanged a grin. No indeed, they were not even thinking of turning in! Standing up very wide-awake and looking at each other's fingers, they began gesticulating at an amazing speed, talking in fact in the deaf and dumb alphabet.

"What do you think, Theo?" asked workman number one in this silent language, "does the landlord suspect anything?"

"Lord! I don't know, Henri old boy. One never can tell. Anyway, as we've promised Juve to keep good guard, let's do as he said. If he ordered us to note down hour by hour whatever happens in this crib, you may be sure he has his reasons for it!"

In fact, the two workmen who looked so disreputable and

behaved so strangely, were no other than the two Inspectors Theo and Henri of an earlier chapter. After the mysterious disappearance of Fantômas at the Prefecture, Juve had not failed to observe the consternation depicted on the faces of the two officers, and realizing at once that he could count on their absolute devotion had given them orders to keep an unceasing watch on all that occurred at the drinking-shop once kept by the worthy Père Korn.

"Are you taking first watch?" asked Theo.

"If you like?"

"Very well! Now to fix up the little instrument, eh?"

And Inspector Theo proceeded to open his toolbox and extracted certain delicate electrical contrivances.

"Best turn in," he advised his companion. "Lie down on the bed, eh? If the fleas are only reasonably voracious you can always doze. In case of alarm, I'll give you a nudge…"

"Righto! I'll relieve you at midnight."

In two minutes silence reigned in the room. Theo was evidently asleep. As for his comrade, he was lying on the floor, a cigarette between his lips. He had put on a pair of earphones and arranged beside him a sort of little box or casket on top of which glimmered faintly two little metallic lamps. Was he playing some game, or was he really engaged in a serious and important occupation? The little box, as a matter of fact, was a wireless telephone amplifier, and simply enabled the police officer to hear, many times magnified, all sounds registered by an extremely sensitive microphone placed in contact with the floor. By means of this simple apparatus, one within the powers of any amateur to construct, he was able to overhear with the utmost ease whatever was said in the tavern room that lay directly underneath.

In that room, at that very moment, were gathered some fifteen persons listening, it seemed, with deep attention to what a young woman was telling them—and this young woman was no other than Mary, Louis Rippert's pretty maidservant!

"You will each of you," she was saying, "take a tin of petrol. Then you trot off, you know where to. The orders are to be obeyed to the letter. At two o'clock, at latest, the fire must break out everywhere at once—not a little flash in the pan, mind you! but a mighty blaze that'll burn the whole place to ashes. You take me? Once the house is fired, you're to hook it."

"And you, my girl?" a voice asked.

"I! never worry your head about me, Paulet. I've the Master's instructions."

"But we're never going to see him, the Master you prate of?"

"Oh, yes, you will! He'll come—at his own time."

"But, say, is he really Fantômas?"

"Idiot! blockhead!… You'd better ask him yourself!"—and turning to another of her audience, a man very correctly dressed in the livery of a chauffeur, the girl demanded:

"And you—is your trap in running trim?"

"Of course it is!"

"You're to take me along, my lad! and set me down where I tell you… and you'll bring back the person injured. You understand, eh?"

Mary could see by her hearer's nods that the directions she had supplied had been duly noted. Then, darting away with a supple swing of the hips, she ran to the counter behind which the landlord had just taken up his post again.

"Well?" she questioned.

The man did not hesitate for a moment:

"You were right—they're cops, and no mistake!"

"Men Juve has sent?"

"Looks like it to me…"

Mary shrugged her pretty shoulders, and going back to the other men, warned them:

"Look out, my lads! Seems there's a brace of cops upstairs—spies of Juve's."

The words were hardly out of the girl's mouth before the whole group round her sprang to their feet with an instinctive movement of alarm. One and all were crooks, notorious criminals, "apaches,"—but the mere name of Juve froze them with terror!

And next moment a voice suggested:

"Spies, spies of Juve's! What say to knifing them?"

*     *     *     *     *

But Mary peremptorily forbade anything of the sort. "You're talking sheer nonsense," she declared. "You must know the Master won't have us act without first consulting him. The great thing now is for you to be able to get away unhindered with your tins of petrol. After that, the cops can just do what they please… I'll see to them. So," the girl went on authoritatively, "you're just to lie low. In an hour's time you must be off. Till then you can smoke, but no drinks, mind! The Master in fact has given the necessary orders,"—and pretending not to notice the frowns that greeted this last recommendation, she beckoned the chauffeur and left the room in his company.

Who was this woman really, this supposed waiting-maid, who now acted as the grim criminal's lieutenant? This no man knew, save Fantômas, the mastermind.

And then, who was Fantômas? Was Juve in the right in his momentary suspicion that Louis Rippert was he? Or was Fandor more clear-sighted in accusing Henri Tardoux? The fact is that in this respect the two friends had, and could have, only vague suspicions resting on very feeble evidence.

Whoever she might be, however, Mlle. Mary made no long stay in the tavern parlor. Disappearing for a moment in a secret passage, she quickly came back for the chauffeur.

"Stand by!" she ordered the man. "We must go quick, just time for me to change and make our way yonder,"—and the two went out as she spoke.

*     *     *     *     *

At the same moment, having lost only a word or two of the conversation in the room below, Inspector Henri got up, his face a trifle pale, and laid his hand on his colleague's shoulder:

"Wake up, Theo! I've got something to tell you,"—and once more the silent language of the fingers allowed the two to exchange confidences without any risk of being overheard. Rapidly Henri put his comrade in possession of the information he had just acquired.

"Look you," he explained, "these scoundrels are going to set fire to something at Rueil. Yes, but what? and whereabouts?… must we warn Juve?"

Theo pondered a moment before he replied:

"No, not yet! To do that, we'd have to leave the place to go and telephone. But, once outside, we couldn't get in again. No, best wait till the gang's gone. We'll shadow the blackguards and find out where they're going to. Then one of us'll go and telephone while the other keeps his eye on them."

"Right you are, Theo. Mustn't go too fast. Juve don't like bunglers!"—and the Inspector resumed his position on the floor and putting the receiver to his ear, began again listening in to the talk, commonplace enough now, going on in the common room of the inn.

*     *     *     *     *

Whoever he was, this much is certain: Doctor Walton was gifted with boundless audacity and imperturbable coolness. After a few moments' thought when he found himself alone in his padded cell, he had calmly closed his eyes and gone to sleep like a man unbothered by the smallest anxiety. Presently, however, he reopened his eyes, a smile hovering about his lips, as he listened for any sounds indicating that his orders were being carried out.

Suddenly he sprang to his feet, straining his ears harder than ever. In the distance, deadened by the thick padding, a low crackling could be heard. At first the sound was faint and intermittent. It was hard to say exactly what it was, but soon shouts and screams mingled with it and the trampling of flying feet, while the howls of patients suddenly awakened added to the din.

"The play's beginning, it seems," laughed the Doctor, and coolly lay down again.

"The panic is bound to be appalling," he reflected with satisfaction. "There's a great number of patients, while the staff sleeps at the far end of the courtyard. If my orders have been properly carried out, the fire must have broken out in full fury everywhere at once,"—and he laughed more gaily than ever.

Truly, at that moment panic terror reigned in the Departmental Asylum. In the very middle of the night, after the second and last round of inspection, flames had suddenly shot up in a score of different places, wherever they were likely to find the most inflammable materials to feed their rage. In one second the attendants, male and female, had realized the tragic magnitude of the disaster. The dispensary, crammed with drugs and chemicals, bandages, ether, explosive and combustible substances of all kinds, was already a blazing furnace. The linen storeroom the same. So too the general store, where stocks of petrol and grease were kept, and the laboratories containing bottles of acetylene bound to explode with dire effect. And the conflagration was spreading from block to block of the vast building like a river in flood no dam could stay.

On all sides rose frantic shouts. "Save yourselves!" cried some. "The patients! save the patients!" yelled doctors and attendants, roused from their beds in wild haste. Already it seemed impossible to approach certain blocks. Already the whole terror-stricken population of Rueil roused from their slumbers by the alarm bell, were hurrying up to lend a helping hand in the work of rescue.

"The patients!" they told each other, "the patients! The poor wretches will be burned alive!"

Yet how could they release them, let them escape? Who could tell what atrocities they might not commit, some of them, excited to frenzy by the danger they ran.

But alas! the time was past for discussing what should be done and what not done. So fast had the fire spread that by the time the firemen arrived, the whole asylum was nothing but one fearful furnace into which no man could venture and hope to live. Overwhelmed with distress and consternation, the Director was personally superintending operations risking his life at the post of most imminent danger.

"Get the staff together," he ordered, "and let me know which blocks have been cleared. Quick! quick!" Then calling a house-physician to him: "Have the Police in Paris warned. Some of the patients have no doubt escaped. They must be recaptured. The rest should be conveyed to neighboring asylums… Oh! and give the alarm to the Paris Fire Brigade!"

But these steps had already been taken. The Captain of the Rueil Brigade, a young and energetic man, was seeing to things.

"The motor engines are just coming!" he announced. "M. Havard is coming too. He has phoned me that he is bringing with him the famous Inspector Juve… But stand away, Doctor, stand away! this piece of wall is going to fall in!"

At that moment the house-physician came back at the double. His face was white, despite the red glow of the flames.

"Well?" demanded the Director, "what have you to report?"

"All the blocks are cleared… All except the observation cells."

"How many patients were there in them?"

"Five, Doctor!"

The Director shuddered, horror-stricken, and the other hastened to add:

"The fire regulations were all duly observed, but nothing could be done. From the very first start, it was impossible to go near the observation building."

The Director could only shake his head in despair, repeating:

"Five! there were five of them! Poor wretches, to be burned alive! Horrible! horrible!"

"And the staff?" he asked.

"All safe—as far as we know… The rooms at the Mairie, and the classrooms at the Communal School have been commandeered. The patients are being conveyed there."

At that moment a short man, dressed in black and armed with an eyeglass, came on the scene, shouldering his way through the press with an air of authority. It was M. Havard, Head of the Criminal Department. Well used as he was in his official capacity to scenes of devastation and disaster, the Chief started back in horror when he heard how five human beings were still imprisoned in that fiery furnace that was blazing more fiercely every minute.

"Poor creatures!" he faltered. A terrible death—if they're not smothered by the smoke, that is, before the flames reach them."

Then, his thoughts instantly turning elsewhere, he inquired:

"And about escapes? Haven't you held a roll-call of your inmates?… And Juve? has he come?… Not yet? Why what can he be after? Oh! of course he thinks himself too great a man to trouble his head about such a trifle!… What he likes better is arresting Fantômas—and then by his confounded folly letting him slip through his fingers!"

The gibe was entirely unjustified. Juve could not possibly be there yet. At that very moment scorching fast and furious along the Rueil road.

But M. Havard got no further. A half-smothered cry from a hundred throats, a wild shout of terror and amazement was heard.

"What now?" groaned the Director, hurrying forward. "What next?" cried M. Havard, "what the devil's happening?"— and both men rushed off towards the crowd that seemed ready to burst the barriers holding them aloof and gesticulating frantically at sight of some fresh horror.

Breathless with excitement, the Captain of the Fire Brigade informed them:

"A woman… a nurse… yes, one of the female attendants, has just dashed into the flames, to save the burning wretches—an act of sheer madness, gentlemen! She can never reach them! She'll never get back alive!"

Then all were forced to beat a retreat. The wind was driving before it such whirlwinds of smoke that the place became absolutely untenable.

*     *     *     *     *

In the block accommodating patients "under observation," the block that had not been cleared, the grim-faced Doctor was no longer laughing. The building was ablaze, everywhere flames were licking the walls, the heated surfaces of which produced a fiery temperature in the cells that made the air even more unbreathable than did the acrid fumes of the smoke that filled them.

"Damnation!" swore the pretended lunatic, listening intently with frowning brows, the veins on his forehead swelling and a hard, fierce look in his eyes.

"In five minutes the job must be complete, else I shall be burnt to a cinder myself. But there, my calculations were correct, they *must* be correct. Mary no doubt did what was wanted to set the watches right, and I told her distinctly 'sixteen minutes after the first spark.' Anyway, it's high time to be up and doing!"

Another man would have been choked by now. The Doctor only stood up the straighter and with a great laugh.

"Time to show the signal!" he grinned.

An amazing, an incredible proceeding followed. The man stretched out his right hand and with his left simply tore out a finger! Yes, the doctor did actually and veritably tear out a finger, but there was no harm done. On his right hand up till then he had really had six fingers—which shows conclusively that number six was bogus. An elementary dodge in fact, one practiced by conjurers and never so much as suspected by persons not in the secret. A sixth finger made of goldbeater's skin cleverly modeled and painted and fastened to the hand between the first and middle fingers by a glued flap concealed by a little coloring matter, so easily escapes the eye that as a matter of fact no one *had* noticed it when the newcomer was searched on his first arrival at the Asylum.

No sooner was this false finger detached than the Doctor—Fantômas, without a doubt, hurled it through the skylight of his cell, the glass of which had been shivered by the intense heat. And instantly a dazzling green light flashed out—this sixth finger was neither more nor less than a bengal-light!

Almost at the same instant the door burst open and, her face blackened with soot and the clothes half burnt off her back, a woman rushed in.

"Master! I am here," she stammered, scarcely able to articulate.

"Very good, Mary! You are punctual to the minute… Everything has gone as it should?"

"Quick, Master! quick! quick! The place is an inferno! We shall never get out alive!"

"Come now, what nonsense! You've brought what's wanted?"

The nurse seemed half unconscious, but she was just able to draw from her bodice a thin roll of a strange-looking material.

"Here it is!" the girl panted.

"The asbestos shirt, eh? Very good !… and the overall?"

"Master! I have it on…"

But, as she stammered out the words, Mary, Louis Rippert's pretty servant, fell fainting to the floor. The girl's strength was utterly exhausted.

The skylight was open and the door ajar, and the draft now swept the flames into the room, and along the padded walls, which were already catching alight when Doctor Walton at last showed some signs of haste. A passive spectator hitherto, he now fell to work with preternatural energy.

"The asbestos shirt!" he was muttering, "yes, an admirable invention! The fireproof fabric employed by cinema actors in America when they have to brave a fire. With it I am sure of my escape… Ah! but the hospital overall, so as not to attract attention? But she is wearing it… Oh! but I've no time to waste! to work!"—and stooping, he lifted the fainting girl in his strong arms and sprang outside.

An appalling spectacle confronted him. On all sides the walls were crashing down. Fallen beams barred the way, forming a tangled forest whose branches writhed like serpents endowed with a hellish life as the flames devoured them.

"A rough road!" the Doctor growled, but he dashed on regardless of obstacles. Thanks to the asbestos shirt he had donned—Mary doubtless wore another like it—he ran no risk of his clothes catching fire, though the flames were curling round him and licking his face with their fiery tongues.

"Warm work!" was his only word, in the calmest of tones.

He was outside the building now, but there it was worse. So dense was the smoke that even the gleams of the flashing fire could not pierce it.

In the darkness he stumbled, and with an oath:

"I must get on at all costs!" he muttered, "but the woman is too heavy for me! I'm going to…"

But the atrocious, cowardly speech was left unfinished. Behind an eddying curtain of smoke, he had caught a glimpse of the boundary wall lying in ruins, its spikes littering the ground, and the crowd beyond tossing in fierce excitement.

"Saved!" he cried. "Now for a bit of 'gallery'!" And this is what the crowd saw: from the very heart of the conflagration, bounding over piles of blazing debris, a man, an unknown stranger, was tearing towards them like a demon, carrying in his arms the fainting form of the nurse who had dashed into the fiery furnace a few moments before.

At the sight a great cry of admiration arose, swelling like a stormy sea. M. Havard himself hurried up to the gallant rescuer.

"Sir! sir!" he vociferated, "your name, sir, for the cross!"

But the man haggard, distraught, beside himself—or so he seemed, fled on, haunted no doubt by the terror of the fiery death he had so narrowly escaped.

"Make way!" he was shouting, "make way!"—and the press parted before his onrush, some thinking to see him trip and fall, some yelling "bravo! bravo!"—others doubting their own eyesight…

But with a sudden dart the man made for a motorcar halted at the corner of a street—the car of some official personage, so it was supposed. The rest followed with lightning rapidity, so fast no one had time to interfere. The man sprang into the vehicle, tumbling in headlong with the woman he had saved.

Bystanders heard him give the order:

"The Hospital! drive to the Hospital!"—and the car started off at breakneck speed.

As it flew by, it passed another car just arriving. In this were seated Juve and Fandor!

*      *      *      *      *

It was obviously impossible for Juve, be his genius what it might, to have guessed the events occurring amid the flaming ruins of the Asylum, so that it never even crossed his mind to consider who was the occupant of the car his own had just met. Indeed his attention was too much occupied with other and grave matters to trouble his head about such a trifle.

"Quick, Fandor," he instructed his comrade. "Get out quick. Look! there's Havard yonder. He's bound to know where the patients are. An examination must be held at once… Fantômas has of course disguised himself, made up his face to look like one of them ready to make his escape now that discipline is relaxed owing to the catastrophe,"—and springing out of the car, Juve hurried up to his Chief.

"The patients?" he demanded, "where are the patients?"

But M. Havard was half dazed by all he had witnessed and could give no answer. Turning suddenly upon the detective and Fandor: "You are too late," he told them, "to see the finest thing I have ever beheld, a veritable act of heroism, a rescue that seemed impossible…"

But the one word "impossible" had given Juve a start, and he was frowning ominously. Who else, indeed, was capable of doing impossibilities as if it were a game of play? who else but the wretch he was there to track down and whose mere name made him blench?

"You mean to say?" asked the police officer.

"I mean to say this," snapped M. Havard, "there are fine fellows in the world, anyhow, and brave fellows! A man, come from I don't know where, snatched from the flames a nurse who had attempted to save some poor creatures in danger of being burned alive. After which, while the applause was still ringing in his ears, the rescuer jumped into the motorcar you passed…"

"Oh! damn it all!" swore the detective savagely. Then eagerly:

"The car?" he shouted, "did anyone see the car he went off in?"

"Why, Juve, my dear man," protested M. Havard, "what's the trouble with you now?"

But Juve did not hear a word. He had dashed up to a fireman, left in charge of a reel and who, standing where he did, must have seen every detail of the scene.

"The car? the chauffeur? Tell me this, how long had they been here. How did they get through the barriers? Speak out, do!"

Startled by this torrent of questions, the worthy man could only roll his eyes in bewilderment.

"But… but," he stammered, "I don't know, not I! It was an official car, for sure. The driver wore a cockade…"

"A cockade! a cockade! Good Lord, and nobody here has a coachman with a cockade, I suppose! It was *he!* it *was he!*"

Juve was by this time racing to his own car, Fandor sprinting along behind him. Tearing after them, Havard, who had quite lost his head, was yelling behind them:

"Answer me! answer me! What the devil's up? Juve, who was it?"

He received the reply full in the face—like a blow:

"Fantômas!… and you've just been applauding him to the echo!…"

No explanation, however, was to be had at that moment from the detective. Fandor and he, in fact, had reached their car by now. As the driver was not to be seen, having gone off somewhere to see the fire, the journalist sprang to the wheel:

"Get in, Juve! Quick's the word! We shall catch him yet."

Fandor was a first-rate driver, as he soon showed. He did not know this particular make, yet he lost hardly a moment in starting up, testing the gears one after the other, and getting away on the high road to Paris at a pace that soon exceeded every possible limit of safety.

"We shall catch him, Juve! We shall overtake him! He doesn't know we're after him, so he'll never drive like this!"

At his side on the driving seat Juve was coolly examining his browning and cocking the weapon.

"You know, my lad," he breathed, his voice barely audible in the fierce wind that whistled round their ears, "no pity, no mercy on him—or on ourselves! If we come up with him, you'll smash into him, upset him. We may kill ourselves, but we kill him too!"

"Agreed!"—and neither said another word. Presently, after passing the crossroads at Les Bergères, they made out a cloud of dust a long way ahead.

"That's our man, perhaps?" Juve's voice rattled in his throat as he spoke.

But at that moment a confused sound of shouting reached their ears, now shrilling high, now sinking to a deep, low note.

"The firemen from Paris! Have a care, Fandor! Pull to one side!"

"By God! they're going apace, too!"—and the vehicles, going under full power of the engines, were on the point of meeting and passing when suddenly Fandor's car seemed to rear up on end, half overturned and lurched violently aside. Simultaneously, a hundred yards ahead of it, the foremost Fire Brigade car, the staff car, also skidded disastrously and swept across the road, ending up by hurling itself against a tree.

"Done for!" cried Juve.

"Damnation!" swore Fandor, and stopping his engine, while by a miracle, the car righted itself, the young man leapt to the ground.

"Tires burst!" he announced with another oath. "Both front tires gone, and back tires punctured!"

"Glass on the roadway," Juve was vociferating at the same moment, "pounded glass!… And nails! By God! he knew very well I should be after him."

No further explanation, indeed, was needed to account for the twofold catastrophe that had at one and the same instant befallen the firemen's vehicle coming from Paris and the police officer's car making for the capital. Yes, Fantômas had foreseen that he might well be pursued, and he had taken his precautions. He had scattered over the road handfuls of nails and pounded glass, knowing that, in this way, he must inevitably bring to a dead stop every motor vehicle following on his heels.

Fandor stood helpless, wringing his hands in despair.

"Still, there *is* another road," he suggested presently, "by way of Mont Valérien. But it will take time to change the tires…"

"Oh! but there's no call for hurry now! No," growled Juve,

"no need at all! The game's up,"—and he went on gloomily in a shaking voice:

"Fantômas has got his way, look you! In ten minutes he'll be in Paris, and he knows quite well we're stuck here helpless. He has a free hand to do whatever he chooses!" Then turning to his companion:

"Come on, Fandor, it will be daylight in an hour. We'll leave the car here, and our driver will recover his property all right."

"But what of us, Juve?"

"Oh! the battle's not over yet, my boy!… We'll get on afoot. By the time we reach the fortifications we're sure to come across a conveyance of sorts to take us home,"—and the two set off at once. Presently they passed the powerful fire engines of the Paris brigade, which, less speedy than the staff car, were only just coming up. Provided with solid tires instead of pneumatic they could defy the nails littering the roadway. Eventually the pair found a market gardener ready and willing to give them a lift in his cart.

Arrived at the Barrier, they thanked the man and giving him a right royal pourboire, took a cab.

"Rue Tardieu," Juve gave the order, "Rue Tardieu, No. 1."

"We are going home then?" asked Fandor.

"Yes, human endurance has its limits. Besides, who can tell what tomorrow has in store for us? Who knows what news we shall have in an hour's time?"—and involuntarily Juve shuddered. Then sinking down in his corner, he shut his eyes and refused to speak another word.

Oh! but the sleeping city Fandor gazed at as he stood leaning out of the window, smoking his everlasting cigarette, too tired out to rest like his companion, the mighty city of Paris filled him with a sudden terror—the terror that comes over a man for some dear one he knows to be in mortal peril and whom he feels himself powerless to protect. Yes, it was true, Fantômas was within its walls, alive once more, free, triumphant. It was true that, shaking off his pursuers, as a hunted wild beast shakes off the pack that snaps at its haunches, he was back again in Paris ready to carry through at his own good pleasure the villainous purposes he had resolved to accomplish.

"Fantômas!" the young man said over to himself the dread syllables. "Fantômas! Fantômas!" he repeated like a man helpless and tortured in the clutches of a horrid nightmare.

A hand fell on his shoulder. "Come, my boy! we are almost there. Wake up!"

"I've been dreaming—a beastly nightmare!" the young man growled. "Say, Juve, I'm just longing, you know, to creep between the sheets."

"And so you shall, my lad!"

"But not you, Juve?"

"Oh! yes, I shall too, you may be sure—unless…"

The two men, after paying off their driver, had crossed the entrance lobby and were hurrying up the stairs when, in the silence of the sleeping house, at this preposterously early hour, an electric bell sounded.

"The telephone! my telephone!" exclaimed the police officer, and dashed forward, climbing the narrow stairs as fast as he could. But Fandor was nimbler than the older man and reached the door of the flat first. After fumbling a moment, he found the keyhole and opened. With one bound he was across the anteroom and in Juve's den.

To unhook the receiver was the work of a second. "Hello! hello!" he shouted. But no answer came. Raging with impatience the young man shook the instrument wildly to and fro.

"Hello!" he vociferated, "hello! Speak, can't you?" But nobody seemed to hear. He was on the point of pitching the instrument to the devil when at last a voice from the exchange reached his ear.

"Hello!" the girl was saying, "North 36-00, is that you? Oh! you're there at last? Are you through?"

"Why, no!" protested Fandor. "Just cut me off."

"Well, hang on. They'll ring you up."

"Same old song!" muttered Fandor. "Yes, they'll ring me up—or they won't ring me up!… And it might be something important…"

He was going to put down the instrument for good this time,

knowing as he did the futility of any complaint, when a final word of the operators left him stunned with surprise:

"Oh! never fear! Oh! yes, they'll ring you up all right. For the last half-hour or so they've been calling you every two minutes. They've even had us put them through to the head office to ask if you were 'out of order'!…"

So it was a question, as Fandor had declared on the chance, of some very serious communication.

"You heard that, Juve?" asked the journalist, for the other had now arrived and had seized a receiver.

"Certainly I heard."

"Then we'd better wait, eh?"

"Evidently."

"I suppose it's M. Havard?" suggested the journalist.

"Yes, very possibly."

"Or perhaps Theo or Henri?… Or our driver? after all, we never paid the poor devil, did we?"

"Yes, again."

"Juve, you strike me as not thinking much of my suggestions… Say, are you expecting a message?"

"I'll take my oath I'm not."

"Then you suspect it's most likely someone…"

"You've got it, Fandor! Yes, I suspect it must be 'someone'! Fact is, it would greatly surprise me if it was nobody… or if it was something, a chair say, or an umbrella, wanted to speak to me!"

But, joking apart, the tone of the police officer's voice sufficiently indicated that he deemed it no laughing matter. Fandor meantime seated himself on one corner of the detective's writing desk, his eyes fixed expectantly on the now silent apparatus.

"Oh! but it's tedious work!" he sighed presently, "terribly tedious, waiting like this!"

"Why don't you take a short rest then?"

"But I don't want to rest, I'm not the least bit tired."

"Of course not! That's just what you were telling me in the cab," laughed his friend, bantering him again.

But the journalist had no time to retort. Loud and clear the telephone bell rang out once more.

"Hello! I'm listening!" Juve spoke in a firm voice. Another voice, grave and imperious, replied:

"Hello! Is it really Juve in person I have the honor to speak to?"

"Certainly!… who are you?"—and Juve's voice had taken on a haughty intonation.

Fandor, the other receiver to his ear, looked at his friend in surprise. Why did Juve seem agitated?

He was soon to know. The voice, still pitched in a tone of authority, announced:

"It is I, Juve!… Hello! It is I!… I… Fantômas!"

*       *       *       *       *

How was it that Juve, hearing the voice announce that the speaker was Fantômas, did not drop his instrument in sheer amazement?

Never noticing that he himself did not let go the receiver the police officer had handed him, but rather clung to it with almost frantic eagerness, Fandor thought:

"Impossible! could Juve have been expecting this message? Once he knew someone was going to ring him up, did he guess it was Fantômas who wished to speak to him?"

But such was indeed the case. With the marvelous powers of intuition he possessed, Juve had instantly divined the identity of the mysterious personage so determined to open up communication with him. But it may be he had good reasons into the bargain to account for this perspicacity.

In any case Fandor wasted no time in trying to fathom the causes that had led his companion to form his conclusion. His attention was far too much occupied in listening to the words of the Arch-Enemy which the electric wire faithfully transmitted and whose every intonation shook the young man with a shudder of fear and repulsion.

"Hello! Juve!" the brigand was saying, "yes, it is I, Fantômas speaking. My word! I felt bound to say a word to you. Let me tell you this, Juve, I have the deepest admiration for your talents as a police officer. But no matter, you don't care about compliments from me, I fancy… Hello! hello! don't cut me off! I have serious and important information to give you. You are aware, my dear sir, I know you are, that I and Doctor Walton are one and the same person. So I need say no more on that point. To make up, I feel bound to tell you that, if I condemned myself to spend a very unpleasant night in a madhouse, this was not because I am mad, but on the contrary in full possession of my reason."

A peal of sarcastic laughter that set Juve grinding his teeth compelled the brigand to make a pause, then he resumed:

"Yes, I have my reason—and I had my reasons into this bargain!… Hello! can you hear me all right? The phone seems to be first rate. You catch every word? Yes?… Well, I'll go on."

Under this fire of raillery Juve's face paled visibly. Alas! what answer could he find to make? Was it not better to grin and bear these ironical speeches, in hopes of revenge later on? By his side Fandor too was suffering such agonies at the humiliations poured on his friend that he was almost tempted to hang up the receiver and cut off the communication. But could he do that? Must he not rather allow Fantômas every opportunity to speak freely, in hopes that he would commit some indiscretion leading perhaps to his apprehension?

The wretch meantime proceeded:

"Juve, my friend, you have doubtless guessed—you see I am paying you a compliment—that all this farce had one object only, to get you out of my road and allow me freedom to act. Oh! yes, I don't doubt you cursed me roundly when my nails held you up on the Rueil road. But what would you have? I was bound to attend to a trifling bit of business without having you on my track… If I'm phoning you now, Juve, it's because I have succeeded… and also because I want to do something for you. Why, yes, I'm going to do you a service!"

Again Juve ground his teeth in impotent fury. The torture was almost beyond bearing, but he must drink the cup of bitterness to the dregs; it was his duty as a police officer to listen.

The mocking voice continued:

"Juve, old friend, you know that Comte Léon de Vautreuil was entrusted with diamonds to a prodigious value. No need then to tell you that these diamonds have now changed masters! Thanks to good Mademoiselle Eléonore—yes, that is a fact—I was able to get hold of them… Hmm, well, I need say no more of that… What! I hear you swearing?"

It was Fandor, as a matter of fact, who had let fly an oath. Less master of his feelings than Juve, the journalist had given way to this token of rage—and it earned him a savage glance from his companion.

"Hold your tongue!" the police officer rebuked him. "Do you want to help him gloat over our despair?"

"Come, Juve," Fantômas went on, "never get angry, man! That would be unworthy of you. We have been playing a game, you and I—and I've won. Try to be a graceful loser… Besides, here's something much more to the point. Juve, my dear fellow, you are in bad odor with M. Havard… I don't know how or why, but it's matter of common talk… Well, I'm phoning you on purpose to help you regain his favor. It's only four in the morning, dawn just breaking. Jump into a taxi and away to deliver Josette de Vautreuil, whom I have been obliged, much against my will, to tie down to rights on her bed… There, you see what a kind man I am—for me the shame and dishonor of thieving, for you the honor and glory of the rescuer! Say, am I not tactful?"

Shaking with rage though he was himself, Juve enjoined silence in his companion with a peremptory wave of the hand. Besides, was it all true, he thought, this story Fantômas was telling them with his unparalleled impudence? Was it not his artful way always, in everything, to unite the most subtle false-hood with the utmost apparent sincerity?

And the mocking voice still went on:

"Juve, you are to set the girl free. Then I think we shall be quits. Mark this—I could have killed her, had I been so minded. But I offer you her life, Juve, on one condition, to wit, that you thoroughly understand this point, which is of the gravest importance…"—and Fantômas' voice assumed a markedly authoritative accent:

"Juve, this theft is my last! This conversation we are having is the last of my activities of the sort. I am leaving you in peace, Juve. Abandon your unceasing efforts to hunt me down. My decision is irrevocable—to end my days in retirement. You will hear no more of me. I phoned you, Juve, to bid you goodbye!"

And suddenly, without warning, a sharp click announced that the speaker had hung up the receiver and cut off communication. Fantômas had rallied his enemy to his heart's content and had no wish to prolong the interview further.

For a moment neither of his auditors spoke a word. Then the undaunted police officer, whom no chagrin or disappointment could deflect from the path of duty, sprang up ready for action.

"We must go," he cried. "The risk must be faced at all hazards. That is your opinion, too, Fandor, is it not? Yes," he repeated, "we must take the risk. You have thought over what Fantômas has just told us? It may be he was laughing at us; perhaps he wants to entice us into a trap."

"True! but we must go, for all that—and go at once!" was the young man's answer. "If Mlle. de Vautreuil is really lying bound on her bed, she must be finding the time long… And there's another thing I'm in a hurry to find out," the journalist went on after a pause, "and that is the way the aunt was able to help Fantômas. You have an inkling on the point, Juve?"

"Why, naturally. It's easy enough to see.…"

"Eh?"

"I say, it's easy to understand. Come, just think of this—the fact that the aunt took fright when she heard me quarreling with Bouzille in the kitchen. That should give you a clue to the true state of affairs."

So saying, Juve got up and with an expressive shrug of the shoulders:

"Enough said! Let's be off, Fandor, back again to the Rue de l'Assomption!"—adding softly in a low and significant tone:

"Fortunately for us, there are victories that are defeats. It's a thing that happens from time to time!"

Once more, a quarter of an hour later, the two men were on the road. But they had thrown off almost all sense of fatigue. They had a comforting, a reinvigorating feeling they were at last to hear of some new development, that they were on the way to sensational discoveries.

"For sure, Juve is hiding something from me," Fandor was thinking. "For sure, he has made some find he hasn't told me about… So! I must keep my eyes open!"

As for Juve, he had closed his eyes, and appeared to be dozing. Only a furtive smile that hovered momentarily across his lips showed his brain was awake and that he was enjoying some secret thoughts of his own.

In the Rue de l'Assomption Juve and Fandor found all things in the same state as they had left them. Under the chill light of dawn, in a silence hardly broken by the distant rumble of market carts returning to the outer suburbs from the Halles, the de Vautreuil's little house seemed entirely peaceful.

"Do we ring?" asked Fandor.

"To send in our names! My word, no! We go straight in, and pistol in hand too!"

"Really? Do you suppose…?"

"I suppose nothing… Don't talk! Follow me!" Juve had climbed the garden gate, Fandor after him, without difficulty, and the pair were standing before the front door.

"Are we to pick the lock, Juve," was Fandor's second question.

"No! no need to trouble. I've taken my precautions! A bunch of keys was lying about the other day in the kitchen, so I collared them—you see?"

As he spoke, Juve had cooly drawn from his pocket the keys he had shamelessly robbed poor Victoire of.

"Silence!" the detective enjoined, and slowly and softly he opened the door. Then with a quick push threw it back. Was it not possible Fantômas might be there, ready to murder the men he had telephoned to come.

"In we go!" Juve said decisively—and accompanied by Fandor, who would not let his comrade move a step without him, the detective advanced. He made one stride across the hall, only one—and then he halted sharply, gripping Fandor by the arm.

"Listen!"

From the first floor came a faint groan, a low, pitiful, inarticulate cry.

"Josette!" exclaimed the young man, and, regardless of all prudence, forgetting that Fantômas perhaps was there, lurking in the darkness, watching for the two men who were his bitterest enemies, in two seconds he had mounted the stairs, Juve behind him as reckless as he, as ready for any and every self-sacrifice.

On the landing the two friends saw a light shining through a half-open door, from behind which came the groans they had heard, and they dashed into the room. There an abominable sight met their eyes that left them both standing stock-still on the threshold, frozen with horror.

In the middle of the chamber, her bedchamber, Josette de Vautreuil, half-dressed in disordered garments evidently thrown on in hot haste, lay tightly pinioned on her bed. A gag half hid her delicate features. Her hair, a tawny gold, was half unbound, almost veiling her eyes. The girl was incapable of making the slightest movement, with such callous cruelty had the cords that bound her down been drawn almost to the breaking point.

"Poor little girl!" sighed Juve, echoed in more respectful terms by the younger man. With all haste both busied themselves in cutting her bonds and releasing the girl, who seemed utterly exhausted.

"Whatever has been doing?" Juve's voice was hoarse with indignation and his face a picture of concentrated fury. He was soon to hear the story in a few broken words. Fantômas had spoken nothing but the truth in his mysterious and mocking message. The details supplied by his victim confirmed his statements:

"Father was away on a journey," the girl explained. "Before he left, he gave me the case of diamonds, and I hid them under my bed... My aunt seemed better. Since the day they discovered her in the attic, she used to walk up and down in her bedroom… Well, I went to bed. About two or three o'clock in the morning, hearing footsteps about the house, I got up in alarm. Oh! how frightened I was! Suddenly my door opened, and two men came in, threw themselves upon me and tied me down. One of them, the leader was dressed in a suit of black tights, with a black hood. He wore black gloves and black shoes. Only his eyes glittered behind his mask."

"The well-known figure! The figure of old tradition!" struck in Juve. "Fantômas, by God!"

"The other," Josette went on, "the other, his companion… Oh! Monsieur Juve, I thought I was going mad when I saw him… He was still dressed as a woman, yes, wearing my poor aunt's clothes. He had a wig in his hand, and there were traces of paint on his face… It was, it was…"

"It was Fantômas' dastardly accomplice!" cried Juve in a harsh, savage voice! "I suspected as much!… A mask of gold-beater's skin, a cunning makeup… those pretended fainting fits the moment anyone came near! Oh! we must have been blind not to guess that the so-styled Mlle. Eléonore who vanished as soon as I arrived in the house was simply the brigand's accom-plice!… But finish your story!"

"Then the scoundrels went straight to my bed, seized the diamonds—and took themselves off. I heard them telephoning to you, and… and…"—but Josette de Vautreuil had swooned away.

Then, while Fandor, with the other's help, was laying the girl on her bed, the journalist demanded with every semblance of indignation:

"But, Juve, if you had guessed that the aunt was an accom-plice, why not have collared her? I can't fathom your policy."

"Because you don't think, dear boy!… To arrest his accom-plice was to force Fantômas to take immediate action. I pre-ferred to run the risk of a robbery, and to keep a lookout to try and catch Fantômas himself. To arrest his accomplice, the aunt, was perhaps to drive him to commit a more heinous crime."

"Perhaps! yes, perhaps!… But anyhow, here's the net result,

and a fine result at that, of your astuteness—the diamonds stolen!… The bogus aunt discovered where the treasure was hid and led Fantômas straight to the place—and it's all your fault…"

"You're hard on me, Fandor!"

"Of course I am!… Not to mention that Mlle. de Vautreuil has had a fearful shock that may very likely make her ill, and that her father, the Comte de Vautreuil, who is responsible for the loss of the diamonds, will be ruined… and driven perhaps to do something desperate."

"Come, come!" put in Juve calmly, "you exaggerate. So long as nobody's killed, nothing is past mending!… The whole thing comes to this—Fantômas has merely committed a robbery…"

But Fandor was staring at his friend with startled eyes. No, never, never could he have imagined Juve capable of taking matters with such consummate coolness:

"But what you say is monstrous! A common theft!… Anyway, Juve, I mean to take the field! The diamonds must be recovered—and at any cost! We must notify…"

"Fandor," Juve interrupted the tirade, "you're talking nonsense. The diamonds, I care nothing for the diamonds! They are worth a king's ransom? Granted! But for the money… bah! that's nothing. It's Fantômas, mind you, we must get hold of. Fantômas is a menace to all mankind!"

"Oh! I don't say different," broke in the journalist. "But all that's ancient history. Fantômas has told you himself, that he has got what he wanted, that he is going to disappear. We shall never again find him in our way!"

"A simpleton's argument!"

"Not at all! An argument based on facts. Fantômas has bidden us goodbye…"

"Hmm! hmm! But is it really goodbye? *I* think he only means a goodbye till next time!"—And Juve pretended not to see the impatient shrug Jerome Fandor gave. The young man was now bending over Josette de Vautreuil's bed, holding a bottle of smelling salts he had discovered on a dressing table for the fainting girl to inhale.

## 13. Fandor Owns Up That He Is An Idiot

Three days after this Jerome Fandor was engaged in installing his belongings in a room he had rented at the top of the Rue Dancourt. Presently, tiring of this occupation, he lit a cigarette and subsiding into an armchair, began to think aloud. Jerome Fandor was in the worst of tempers and his reflections were equally black:

"No, I cannot hide from myself that Juve, my dear, good old friend, is taking a line that is preposterously wrong, if not culpable. His ideas are simply insane. To begin with, he, Juve, the straightest man on earth, the police officer personified, is manifestly dead set against Fantômas' having been the thief of Monsieur de Vautreuil's diamonds... Number one. Then he will have it that Fantômas, who, with his own mouth, has announced his departure, is more to be feared than ever! *Why* to be feared, I should like to know. Hasn't he got what he wanted?... Number two! Lastly, and thirdly, he maintains that the Auteuil mysteries are explained by the reappearance of the aunt now proved to have been an accomplice of Fantômas. 'It was one of the gang made up to look like her,' he said himself. And this accounts for everything, the whole blessed thing!... But I'm positive it explains nothing whatever, and I'm not crazy, I'm not! Devil take it, the dog, the dog that was dead and came alive again, *he's* not an accomplice, I imagine!"

Sore and angry, Fandor sprang up and began striding up and down the room. And verily the kind-hearted young man had every reason to feel surprise, if not utter bewilderment. What he noted was quite true. The three points he had signalized in Juve's behavior were indeed such as to cause surprise. For three days now Juve had done nothing about the theft of the diamonds. He proclaimed loudly and emphatically that Fantômas was more to be dreaded than ever. Thirdly and lastly, he only gave a shrug whenever the Auteuil mysteries were mentioned. He argued that there was no mystery any longer!

Moreover, what specially ruffled Fandor's feelings was the fact that, without admitting it to himself, he had a distinct impression that their divergence of views was leading Juve to give him the cold shoulder. Not that it was a coldness amounting to a quarrel, but it was one that was already making their relations less confidential and less friendly.

"And yet," the young man told himself, "it's no fault of mine! All the same I cannot pass over with a smile this theft of the diamonds, which I could swear is giving Mademoiselle de Vautreuil the most desperate chagrin."

Lost in these melancholy reflections as for the hundredth time perhaps he recalled the lack of cordiality that had marked their departure from the Rue de l'Assomption and how since that day he had barely caught a fleeting glimpse of his old friend, who was always away on some expedition or other, without ever saying where, Fandor suddenly stopped dead in his feverish pacing of the room, his face paling and his legs actually trembling under him.

"But it's impossible, insane, this idea that's flashed across my mind! I'm cracked to dream of such a thing! The mere thought of it is too horrible to be entertained!"

Then dragging himself painfully to an armchair, he sat, motionless, elbows on knees and head in hands, concentrating all the powers of his mind on the terrible problem. Presently, in a low, muffled, barely articulate voice:

"Suppose…" the young man shuddered… "suppose Juve… was not Juve?"

Was it utterly inconceivable that the Juve whose words and behavior so troubled him was not *the true* Juve? Was it *quite* impossible to imagine that *the true Juve* had fallen into Fantômas' hands and that the latter had put up an accomplice in his stead—precisely as he had substituted a sham Mlle. Eléonore in place of the de Vautreuils' old aunt, who was really and truly on the high seas and certainly had no notion that she was held to be in Paris at the very same time. Why! in that case it was not to be wondered at that the bogus Juve, put up by Fantômas to play the part of the police officer, could say things *the true Juve* would never have dreamed of uttering.

Yet at the very same time Fandor was up in arms against his own supposition. "How *could* Juve not be Juve?" he asked himself. "Why he has Juve's face!… his voice… his habits and ways!…"

But to each objection he raised the journalist found an answer ready.

"Juve had *his* face?" he repeated to himself, "his face there was no mistaking? Oh! but that proved nothing. Could not Fantômas, with his devilish cleverness, using goldbeater's skin molded to shape, take the impression of a face and produce a mask so marvelously like the original that any mystification was possible? Had he not done this very thing in the case of Mlle. Eléonore? And had he not had ample time to carry through the deceit during the ten years when the police officer, like Fandor himself, had lain at his mercy? So too a voice could be mimicked, while the detective's habits were easy to recognize and copy."

"No!" Fandor told himself next moment. "No, fight as I may against my suspicions, here is the plain truth—nothing *proves* that Juve is not Juve, but there is nothing, absolutely nothing, to disprove that another man has been substituted for him."

At the same time he knew he could have no peace till he had arrived at certainty one way or the other. Moreover the affection he had always felt for his old friend and which still animated him in spite of everything, imperatively urged him to find out, for certain, at any cost, if the true Juve had not fallen into the hands of the Arch-Enemy. His mind was made up. His one and only duty now was to discover if Juve was really Juve!

The journalist had just arrived at this decision as the result of his reflections when suddenly he heard a knock at his door.

"What!" he started violently, "who the devil can know my address already?"—and he invited his visitor to come in. The door opened, and he saw Bouzille's smiling face.

"I've come to wish you good day, honored sir," the old fellow announced, "and to give you a word of warning too. It's not a concierge, nor a portress, nor a doorkeeper, not it! Not a bit of it, M'sieur Fandor, it's a witch, a foul witch!"

"What say, Bouzille? You've noticed that already?"

"I and my friend, yes, we did so."

"Your friend? Where is your friend?"

"At the door! The witch wouldn't let him upstairs."

"He looks like a bad character then?"

"Go on! He's a sight prettier than her! He's thoroughbred, so they tell me. But another thing…"

"Come in, Bouzille, and shut the door—and try to make yourself clear. To start with, who and what is this thoroughbred friend of yours?"

"A pup, M'sieur Fandor."

"Oh! all right! Why didn't you say so? Well, in that case the concierge was within her rights to stop his coming up. But no matter! what was it you came to tell me? And how did you find out…"

"That your digs was here? Why, it was M'sieur Juve told me. Just now, I trotted up as quiet as quiet like, to ask for you at his place… Well, a fine welcome I got, I did! 'Rue Dancourt!' he snapped at me, as you might say, go to the devil. 'Best go and see him at his own place! If he's out of his wits, don't you be surprised! Fantômas has his tantrums, let me tell you!' A fact, M'sieur Fandor, he looked so dangerous did M'sieur Juve, my friend started growling at him."

Fandor shuddered in spite of himself. One detail after another came to strengthen his suspicions: "Was it indeed possible that Juve, the real Juve, could have behaved like this? Was he the man to snub poor old Bouzille? to refuse to pat a dog?"

Mechanically, his thoughts engaged elsewhere, the journalist demanded:

"But all this don't tell me what's brought you to see me. Say, what can I do for you?"

"What I want, M'sieur Fandor, is a bit of a recommend from you. Don't I deserve a decoration like from the government—or anyway a reward from the Society?…"

"What Society, man?"

"Why, I said so, didn't I? the Society for the Prevention of Cruelty to Animals, that's the ticket. Lordy, but it's worth that surely, say, a matter of a hundred francs or so. Look you, that there Mary, Louis Rippert's servant-gal, she's never come back to the house, so the mutt he's been starved, howling with hunger he was! And I fetched him away, because the poor beast's been dead and come alive again, that's no reason he's got no guts. So I took him and I'm feeding him at my own expense. But I'd like to have my decoration, I would, or my hundred francs—the cash for choice of course!"

But there Bouzille stopped dead and stood gaping in sheer astonishment.

With a frantic oath Fandor had suddenly sprung to his feet.

"Great heavens!" he shouted, "but here's the very way to find out! Don't you stir from here, Bouzille. Wait for me. Smoke my tobacco! Read my paper! Do just what you please! I'm coming back!"—and he was gone. Four steps at a time the young man tore down the stairs. Below, in the entrance passage, tied to the door handle by a long piece of string, a magnificent dog stood waiting, his eyes fixed on the spot where he had seen Bouzille, his master for the time being, disappear.

"Hello, old boy!" Fandor addressed the animal, "you and I are going to be chums. Then you're going to help me. Come here, old fellow!"

Instantly Fandor had made friends with the dog. "Come along, my friend," he went on, undoing the string. "We're off on a lark, my beauty. Oh! you want to know where, do you? Listen, we're going to see Juve—Juve or Fantômas—or perhaps Henri Tardoux, *I* don't know. But you, my fine fellow, you're going to tell me."

Wild as it appeared, was it not, after all, perfectly reasonable and clever enough this project of Fandor's? This dog, Louis Rippert's dog, was bound to know Fantômas. Was it not, therefore, an experiment worth trying to confront the animal with Juve, Juve whom Fandor was almost by way of accusing of being Fantômas? If, brought face to face with Juve, the dog manifested signs of an inexplicable dislike, Fandor would not hesitate to provoke an altercation that might perhaps result in throwing light on the problem.

"Nothing ventured, nothing gained!" the young man repeated to himself once more. It was a proverb he invariably abused to justify his recklessness. "If the dog growled at Juve, it's because he has a reason for doing it—and that reason I must discover!"

*      *      *      *      *

The Rue Dancourt is no great distance from the Rue Tardieu, and in a few minutes Fandor was ringing at the police officer's door. But alas! he rang in vain. Nobody came to open.

"Ah!" he remarked, "Juve and Jean are both out, are they? A new departure!… Very good, I'll wait till they return. I still have the key poor old Juve let me have."

An instant later, the dog still at his heels, the young man, in cheerful and excited mood, made his way to his friend's working den.

"Nobody at home?" he called out, by way of satisfying his conscience, but there was no answer. Therefore, as a familiar of the house, Jerome Fandor began to talk to his four-footed comrade:

"Listen here, old man, we're going to play a game on Juve. We're going to rummage in his larder. The devil is in it if I can't fish you out something, and that'll always be something a bit better than the fare Bouzille is likely to offer you."

Letting go the dog, Fandor crossed into the anteroom and made for the kitchen.

But he had not taken three steps when he swung round in amazement. Like a spring suddenly released, at one bound, the dog had leapt into one corner of the passage and was furiously scratching at the carpet, uttering hoarse growls.

"Queer!" observed Fandor. "What the devil does he smell there?"—and he called the dog off:

"Come here, I say! We're paying a visit, my lad! Mustn't tear our host's imitation Smyrnas! Come off, will you?"

But the dog utterly refused to obey, and, as the young man tried to drag away the animal by its collar, it growled louder and even showed its teeth.

"But, anyhow, I don't suppose Juve, the real Juve, is under there?"—and, without another word, he ran for a hammer and a pair of pincers and tore up the carpet. Then, while the dog started to whimper with pleasure, trotting excitedly backwards and forwards and giving every token of the utmost satisfaction, Fandor suddenly felt his heart stop beating. The flooring had been un-nailed and nailed down again! To a practical eye like the journalist's there were unmistakable signs to prove it.

But what the devil could Juve have been hiding like this in his rooms, without saying one word about it to Fandor?

Conquering his agitation, guessing, foreseeing some sinister discovery, some find that would change all his doubts into certainties, Fandor introduced a cold chisel in the crack between two boards and, with a sharp heave, pried up the plank that had been removed and replaced. And this time he gave a hoarse cry—a cry of horror and despair and rage. There, in this secret hiding place, lay a glittering heap of diamonds! It was a priceless treasure that lurked there in concealment! Oh! Fandor could doubt no longer. These diamonds, of an incalculable, a fabulous value, were the jewels Fantômas had stolen from Léon de Vautreuil!

And was it not proof positive that Fantômas was Juve and Juve, Fantômas?… Fandor's brain reeled. He stood stricken helpless with horror!

Then a startled cry escaped him. Behind him—he had heard no sound of his entry—a man was standing with folded arms, a revolver in his right hand—a man whose face was contorted with a terrible grimace of menace and anger.

He demanded: "By what right have *you* taken up this flooring?"

And this man Fandor dared not give a name to! He was lost in agonized doubt. Was he an object for his hatred or his love? Was he the worst of his enemies or the best of his friends?

He had Juve's features… and he was perhaps—or very

surely?—Fantômas.

*    *    *    *    *

For a second that seemed an age, Fandor stood stock-still, his haggard eyes fixed on this Juve he saw before him—and who must not be, who *could* not be, Juve! He had no fear. He was not terrified to stand thus face to face with Fantômas, if it *was* Fantômas, but he felt an unutterable sadness. How know that he was not proving himself frightfully unjust? How be sure he was not committing the most abominable of mistakes?

But involuntarily he dropped his eyes. Once more his gaze fell on the extraordinary hidden treasure-house where the stolen diamonds sparkled—the very proof he was seeking. Alas! no further doubt was possible! And Fandor was on the point of hurling himself on the man looking him up and down when the latter repeated in a voice of grim menace:

"By what right have *you* taken up this flooring?"

Then quickly, with a shrug, the police officer laid his revolver on a table beside him and concluded:

"Well, well! I see it is more serious than I thought. Come, Fandor, come into my room. Come and talk with Fantômas!" and the detective, pointing to the stolen jewels, added in the most good-natured of voices:

"Take it, by all means! Now you have made this noble find, it would be an act of the last imprudence to leave a fortune like this where it is. Come, do as I bid you, take it!… If I laid a hand on it myself, you might very well take your knife to me!"

Juve gave a short laugh. Then, with another shrug, he passed into the next room, while Fandor, gathering up the diamonds as he was told, proceeded to follow.

"Juve," demanded the young man, his voice shaking as he spoke the name, "will you explain…"

"Certainly! But you're to hold your tongue and hear me out.… First let me ask you a question."

"Do!"

"My lad, you accuse me of being Fantômas, do you not?"

"Yes… I think…"

"A point to me! You are not sure!… Now, why do you accuse me?"

"Why! because…"

"Enough! I'm going to tell *you* why. Because I attached no importance to the theft?… And because you suspect it was I committed the theft? Is that the truth?"

"The truth indeed!"

"Well, Fandor, a last question. Say, between ourselves, before you resolved to spy on me, did you not hesitate?"

"Yes, I did."

"Did you not ask yourself if you weren't a fool?"

"Yes, for sure I did."

"And what answer did you give yourself?"

"That I was not an idiot, damn it all! and that everything went to prove it…"

"My little Fandor," interrupted Juve, "it pains me to contradict you, but I'm bound to tell you you're mistaken. You've got to own up—that you are the last word in idiots. Not the second to last, but the very last! You make me blush for you," and throwing back his head, Juve went off in a great laugh at the other's look of chagrin.

No, no! It was really and truly Juve! It could not be Fantômas!

But the police officer seemed to read the young man's thoughts as in an open book!

"Why, yes," he said, "you confounded imbecile! I am myself right enough! And I'll go one better. It is precisely *because* I am myself, I make bold to say, that everything that surprises you has nothing surprising about it."

But the young man was shaking his head, still only half convinced. "I'm waiting," he declared. "When you choose to put the dots on the i's, perhaps I shall understand how it is you are not a thief?"

"But I never said I was not! Why, I *am* a thief!"—and Juve broke into another hearty guffaw. Then he resumed:

"Come then, I'll turn on the light. I've made merry long enough at your expense. Now listen: the first thing that astonished you was the fact that I didn't rush off to track down the aunt who had disappeared the day we all met at Josette's house, now wasn't it?"

"That's so."

"Well, my boy, fact is I had something better to do. My dear fellow, use your wits—just a little bit, do! Look you, we were in a house where, on the one hand, were diamonds likely to tempt Fantômas and, on the other, a person who was there—and who all the while could not possibly be there. Now the said person promptly disappeared as soon as she knew I was on the spot, the moment she learned the police were in the neighborhood. A suspicious circumstance, surely? So then, mind you, instead of running off after her, I said to myself: 'Let's steal the diamonds. That's a sure way to stop Fantômas or the aunt, who is undoubtedly an accomplice, from getting hold of them!'"

"Eh, what?" exclaimed Fandor with a start, "so you already had your suspicions of the aunt?"

"The simplicity of the child! Of course I had."

"But, in that case, when you knew she was back again, why didn't you come and arrest her?"

"I preferred to leave her where she was. That way I was certain to know where Fantômas was bound to come."

"Yes! but by playing that game you were exposing the diamonds you had put back in their place to the risk of being nabbed."

"Oh!… so I had put them back, had I?"

"Why, yes! seeing Fantômas afterwards stole them."

"Not a doubt of it, you've got to own up you are an idiot, Fandor!… Now I proceed: You see now the diamonds were stolen by me. Just tell me then, how *could* I feel excited and put out when I heard Fantômas had stolen them from where they no longer were?"

"Where they no longer were? But… Oh! Good Lord Almighty!"—and Fandor sprang up and threw himself into his old friend's arms, who embraced him cordially.

"So there you are!" grinned the police officer. "You've caught on, my lad! You understand at last why the theft left me so unperturbed! And why you've discovered the diamonds Fantômas stole on my premises!"

Yes, Fandor had grasped the truth at last. "*You* stole the real jewels," he cried, "and you put sham ones in their place. So it's the false diamonds Fantômas has carried off, and you were having the laugh of him finely… And seeing Fantômas was bound inevitably to discover before long the mistake he had made, you were convinced his goodbye was not really a goodbye and that he would come back again…"

"To finish up, my lad, you can add that, knowing all this, it was very natural you should discover in my possession the real diamonds, which are not those Fantômas stole… and that consequently this does not prove me to be Fantômas!"

"Juve, don't rub it in! Juve, forgive me! I own up! I own up!"

"You own up to what, Fandor?"

"Why, that I am the last word—not the second to last, but the very last in idiots! And how pleased I am to know it,"— and the two friends laughed lightheartedly. Juve was the first, however, to recover his seriousness. "Of course," he observed, "when I had stolen the real diamonds to prevent their falling into Fantômas' hands, having clearly foreseen his attempt on them, I took care to inform the Comte Léon de Vautreuil by cable. Do you care to see the receipt?"

"Let me alone, do!" Fandor implored. "You are insolent in your triumph!"

Then suddenly he slapped his forehead, exclaiming: "But my dog, oh God! What the devil's come of my dog? I'd clean forgotten him!… Anyhow, he *has* a way of smelling out things!"

But, five minutes later, Fandor was in despair. Nowhere was the animal to be seen. Finding the door open, the dog had simply taken advantage of the opportunity and bolted.

"Devil take it!" growled the journalist, "whatever will Bouzille say?… Bah! Maybe he's just gone back to find his master."

Then he took a hasty leave of Juve.

"To meet again directly," he said. "We're going to spend the evening together, eh, old man?… If Fantômas *is* still to be feared, that don't stop us having won the first lap… It's paste he's got hold of! just paste!"—and relieved of the weight of anxiety and distress that had oppressed his spirits, the young man took his departure in joyous mood.

Everything indeed seemed to smile on him that day. Right in front of the house door the lost dog was nosing round, his lead trailing behind him. Fandor had nothing to do but collar the truant and take him back to Bouzille.

Later in the evening, after a hasty toilet, the young man, still in the highest spirits, returned to Juve's quarters—alas! only to find nobody but old Jean at home.

"Monsieur has just gone out," that faithful retainer announced, to the journalist's consternation. "Monsieur had that look of his that means big business... Monsieur told me to tell Monsieur Fandor, if he came, he advised him to go to bed early, as he must be tired..."

"The beggar!" Fandor broke in. "Now where the devil can he be off to again?"—and all the young fellow's plans for the evening's amusement fell to the ground.

With renewed anguish he thought of Juve, alone in Paris, of Juve, who refused himself one second's respite, of Juve, who tonight was once more in pursuit of Fantômas, the Arch-Enemy, who was free and no doubt plotting his revenge.

## 14. Juve Finds a Use for a Pneumatic Air Tube

No sooner was Fandor gone off in pursuit of Louis Rippert's dog than Juve quickly dropped his jovial mien and seemed more preoccupied than ever.

"What a gallant fellow the lad is!" he muttered, "always ready to rush headlong into the maddest enterprises, always eager to risk his life, but for all that never anything but lighthearted—and lightheaded!" he added, and as he spoke the last word, the detective could not check a sigh.

"Jean!" he summoned his servant, "my costume Number Three! Quick, I'm in a hurry,"—and with all speed he donned the garments in question.

In five minutes he was out of doors. Strolling at a leisurely pace as far as the Étoile, he jumped on an Auteuil tram, and half an hour later was walking quietly along the Avenue Mozart.

Was he on his way then to pay yet another visit to the house in the Rue de l'Assomption? and what, in that case, did he hope to do? The fact is, Juve was simply putting into application a time-honored police maxim. "There are no such things as clues, broken off," experienced detectives declare. "There are often clues hung-up. The great thing is to string them together again!"—and Juve was entirely of the same opinion.

He knew, beyond a doubt, that Fantômas had haunted the de Vautreuil's house. He was no less aware that, after discovering how he had stolen imitation jewels, Fantômas had nothing further to do there. Nevertheless there it was he must go to try and light on the clue that should put him on the robber's track.

"For certain," reasoned the detective, "Fantômas has set his heart on these diamonds and is firmly resolved to steal them. But he cannot tell where to look for them. In all likelihood he will be at sea on this point, just as I am to know where to look for him,"—and smiling to himself, Juve proceeded to draw his conclusion:

"Therefore, Fantômas is bound to come back to the Rue de l'Assomption, just as I am bound to, he to get on the track of the jewels, I to get on his. We shall surely meet, and that is the very thing I wish!"

A moment later Juve was on the point of crossing the Avenue Mozart, meaning to slip unobtrusively into the Rue de l'Assomption, where he proposed to take ambush, when suddenly he gave a great start:

"Great heavens! Am I going daft?"

But he walked on just the same, not even turning his head or giving himself a chance of observing more closely the woman he had just passed and the sight of whom caused such a shock of surprise he thought at first he must have been mistaken.

"She! could it be she?" he muttered. "Out in the streets? alone? at ten o'clock at night? and dressed up in that fashion? Anyhow, it would be damned interesting if it is the person I suspect!"

Quickening his pace, he turned back on the opposite pavement and stopped before a baker's shop window at the corner of the Rue du Ranelagh. "I shall see her in the glass as she goes by," he told himself, and he was not disappointed. When the lady, never supposing she was being watched, passed behind the police officer, Juve felt convinced he had made no mistake.

It was indeed Josette de Vautreuil he had just encountered! Where was she going?

*       *       *       *       *

For a moment Juve stood still, pretending to be busy examining a display of fancy biscuits and gingerbreads, in reality greatly perplexed and puzzled. Whether Josette de Vautreuil went out or did not go out of nights, whether she was alone or not, was no concern of his. It was not his business to play the duenna, nor was he the man to behave indiscreetly.

But in a moment his policeman's eye noted sundry details that would perhaps have entirely escaped anyone else.

"A veil as thick as they make 'em, by God!" muttered Juve,

"and a mantle as wide and flapping as possible! Hmm, just the getup of someone who wants to avoid recognition. Besides which, a gait showing every sign of extreme haste, and a way of keeping the head down and the eyes peering out suspiciously. Evidently Mademoiselle de Vautreuil is bent on not being seen.… Now, why?"

The detective hesitated between two courses of action that seemed to him equally alluring one as the other. Should he hurry on, overtake the girl and accost her, hat in hand, asking if he might join company with her under one pretext or another? Or, on the contrary, should he slow down altogether and set to work to "shadow" the enterprising young woman?

"Oh, well!" he decided finally, "I shall perhaps be wasting my time, but that's the only risk I run—and I *must* know how Mlle. de Vautreuil spends her evening. It may possibly come in useful!"—and his mind once made up, Juve set about his job of shadowing the girl with his usual artfulness.

It is not such an easy thing, indeed, as many people imagine, to shadow anyone without being noticed. It is in fact a not unprofitable experiment to try. All that is required is, in the course of a casual walk, to pick out any unknown passerby and follow him—without his being aware of the fact—till the time he returns home. How often, in these circumstances, you will find after a short half-hour or so of the game, either the prey will have escaped the pursuer, or he'll start scrutinizing you with the discomforted air of a man asking himself what he has done to deserve the honor of an escort.

Juve, however, was not the man to expose himself to such a misadventure. He was in no wise disturbed even by the fact that Josette knew him by sight. He felt sure of his ability to remain unseen, if he was minded to preserve his incognito. Keeping to the other pavement and allowing Josette a five hundred yards' start, he set off in her wake asking himself:

"Is she going far, or somewhere near? in the district or at the other end of Paris? Is she off to pay an ordinary call? or to keep some rendezvous?"

Finally, after many detours and doubling back that plainly

showed the girl's anxiety to shun observation or recognition and so confuse her tracks as to baffle any possible pursuit, Josette's tram, the second or third she had utilized in her devious course, deposited her with a crowd of other passengers in the Place du Marché at Auteuil, at no very great distance from her original starting point. Juve, who was following in a taxi, arrived at the same spot just in time to see the girl set off at a rapid pace for the turning into the Rue Michel-Ange. Crossing the roadway himself, the detective continued to dog Josette's steps and found himself following her lead along that long and lonely avenue. By half past ten at night the thoroughfares of Auteuil are quite deserted and pretty nearly dark. This aristocratic district, in fact, still keeps to provincial habits and has hardly for a score of years past felt any need to improve the lighting of its streets.

"I have no complaint to make," thought Juve. "It's a convenience in my trade. Anyway, Josette must be a brave girl to be making like this for the purlieus, even more lonely and of far from savory repute, of the Point du Jour quarter." But next minute Juve was yet more astonished. Josette had deliberately turned along the Boulevard Exelmans and was making for the bridge crossing the Seine.

"Anyway," thought the detective, "she's not going to Javel, or to Issy-les-Moulineaux, it seems?"—and abandoning any idea of guessing Josette's destination, he simply followed step by step in the girl's wake, taking advantage of the arches of the railway viaduct to avoid her seeing him. On the other side of the bridge, however, Juve noted an interesting circumstance. Josette had halted under a streetlamp to consult a paper she had drawn from her pocket for further information.

"So," argued the police officer, "she's not sure about the way. That shows she is coming here for the first time, and to meet somebody by appointment… Hmm, but whom?"

He was soon to find out. Fifty yards away stood a block of disreputable looking houses. Before the doors three men, with the air of workmen out of work, three shady looking individuals, were playing pitch and toss.

"Josette will have a fright for once," thought the detective. But he was mistaken. No sooner had the Comte de Vautreuil's daughter caught sight of the fellows than she walked straight up to them and accosted them.

"Ah!" muttered Juve, "the fellows seem to be expecting her!"

Anyhow they were obliging enough, these dubious characters. After reading the paper Josette handed them, they abandoned their game at once and came forward with alacrity to act as the girl's guides. From the corner where he was posted, Juve could see Josette, escorted by the three men, enter a sort of passageway, a filthy alley, feebly lighted by a smoky gas jet.

Then, in a flash, Juve guessed the truth! Good heavens! this was the first act of Fantômas' revenge! Josette had been enticed into a trap and was on the point of falling into the grim brigand's hands! Fantômas had resolved to capture her and hold her as a hostage that would force Juve to any and every concession!

Happen what might, he must act at once, he must not suffer the girl to go a step further, must save her from the dangers that threatened her only too surely—and he dashed off. In two seconds he had reached the alley. Fifty yards ahead, at a turning, he could still see Josette and her satellites, and he opened his mouth to call to the girl.

But it was a cry of rage, a yell of fury, that escaped his lips. A dastardly trick—a rope had been stretched across the road, in which his feet caught, and he fell staggering to the ground. Next instant he felt a savage blow from a cudgel descend with stunning force on the back of his neck.

A roaring filled his ears, his brain reeled and all grew dark. Juve lay there inert, unconscious!

"How long can I have been lying senseless? How comes it Fantômas has not killed me?"

Such were the first questions Juve asked himself on opening his eyes, and he shuddered, as he reflected:

"I am in Fantômas' power—there can be no doubt of that… And it is Fantômas too who has laid hands on Josette… Yes, but to what end has he let me live?… Come now," he went on to ask himself, "where am I?"

Under him the floor was certainly paved with stone. Was he in a cellar then? "But no, cellars have a peculiar smell of their own. Here the pervading odor seemed to be petrol, and yes? india-rubber.... Ah! what's this I've put my fingers in? grease, is it, lubricating grease? Yes, that's it, lubricator for motorcars. So, I'm in a garage, likely?"

He got to his feet with a painful struggle, and being in utter darkness, stepped out cautiously, with outstretched arms and trying the ground with his foot all the time as he advanced. In three minutes he had made the circuit of his prison. Evidently he was in a shed for a motorcar, a shed secured by a strong, solid door, barred with iron. The four walls seemed equally thick everywhere, as he had ascertained by sounding.

"No possibility of escaping!" concluded the detective. "As the furniture is of the scantiest—three empty petrol tins and a couple of old air tubes I found in a corner—and as this stuff can be of no sort of use to me, I think the best thing I can do is to go to sleep and await developments."

Who but Juve could have given such an exhibition of philosophy under the circumstances. He knew himself to be at Fantômas' mercy, and could expect no vestige of pity from the scoundrel. Yet there he was, unterrified and resigned to whatever fate might have in store.

"He or I," he told himself as he stretched himself on the floor, "were bound of necessity one fine day to win the victory. Well, *I'm* not the one! That being so, my best course is just to lie low. If I am to die, as is probable, under some torture worthy of this genius of crime, I prefer to have all my strength to face death coolly. Let us get to sleep!"—and he shut his eyes.

But, for all his resolution, Juve could not get to sleep. In spite of himself, he was boiling with repressed rage, rage at his unmerited defeat—and also, and above all else, at the thought of those he loved, the dear ones he had sworn to protect. What would become of Fandor, left all alone to fight this monster? What fate awaited poor Josette at the hands of the grim and terrible Fantômas?

Thereupon Juve sprang to his feet again. Was he not abandoning the struggle too quickly? Was there not something he could try? Again he undertook a minute exploration of his prison. On his knees he examined the floor inch by inch. But he found nothing—nothing he could put to any use. Mechanically, however, he picked up a piece of paper, which he stuffed into his pocket—if he did escape perhaps he might glean some bit of information from the page—but that was the sum total of his finds.

Then, in despair, he lay down again.

"To sleep!" he told himself again, "I can only wait. I can't even set the place on fire; I have no matches and the petrol tins are empty."

But he had not lain five minutes like this, with closed eyes and to all appearance asleep, when suddenly he leapt to his feet once more.

"By the Lord! why, I'm losing my wits, surely?" he exclaimed in an excited voice. "Haven't I got my fountain pen in my pocket?... And two air tubes to do what I like with?... What more could I wish for, as things are?

Of a truth, the words seemed incoherent enough fully to justify the supposition that Juve *had* lost his wits!

*          *          *          *          *

But Juve was not mad. The insane invariably display a nervous, feverish haste in all their actions that at once betrays their unhappy condition; nothing of the sort, however, was apparent in the police officer's bearing.

Once roused, he advanced, his arms reaching out for the wall, groping for the air tube he had discovered a moment before; then, having found it, he began to whistle as he stuffed it in his pocket.

"My fountain pen?" he exclaimed. "Now, when did I fill it last? Yesterday, was it? Yes, only yesterday. So far, so good! Ah, ha! with a bit of luck, things may yet turn out all right,"—and taking the fountain pen between his teeth, he felt in his pocket and brought out his penknife.

"I'm going to ruin Fantômas' property—and tires are worth

their weight in gold. Oh! but I don't care. The villain is quite ready to make holes in my skin, and my skin's as precious as an old air tube any day, I may say so much without any overwhelming conceit on my part."

As he spoke, he was engaged in a mysterious operation, the object of which only he possibly could conjecture. He was cutting up the air tube, as methodically as possible, and fashioning two rubber rings out of it, the elasticity of which he proceeded to test.

"A bit dried up, this rubber," he observed, "but one must make the best of what one has got. There, that's done, and now to extract the gold pen—they're worth money these gold nibs, and we must unscrew the cap." Then sitting down, he put the two india-rubber rings he had made, one round his foot, the other round his leg. This done, he used them to fasten alongside his ankle the fountain pen, point downwards.

"'Money returned, if not satisfied,'" he laughed… "Well, it's all a perhaps. Perhaps it'll be no good to me… perhaps on the contrary I shall find it of the greatest service. Now, there's nothing for it but to wait patiently."

After all, the police officer had not long to wait. Almost immediately a trapdoor was raised and a brilliant light poured in.

Instantly Juve was up again. Four men, carrying flashlights and heavy revolvers, were pushing their way into his prison. Juve looked the intruders up and down without a word. The first three, dressed like workmen, he had no difficulty in recognizing; they were the same shady individuals who had taken off Josette with them. For the fourth, with one glance Juve had instantly identified *him*—with what a passion of indignation! It was the same figure of tradition that had struck terror into so many hearts. Masked with a black hood, clad in black silk tights closely molding the body, gloved in black, shod with felt-soled shoes that allowed him to move without a sound, it left nothing to be seen save the cruel gleam of the blazing eyes.

Without a word Fantômas—it *was* Fantômas, there could be no possible doubt of that—made a slow, imperious gesture to his underlings. Then, making a sudden ferocious rush, the three men fell upon the police officer and bore him to the ground. Two of them knelt on his chest, and pinning down arms and legs, held their victim absolutely helpless. The third clapped over his face a rough handkerchief covered with a thick coating of varnish.

And in a second, Juve felt he was choking for want of air. Was he then to perish like this? Did Fantômas mean to see him die of asphyxiation before his eyes?

"No, that would be too merciful a death!" reflected Juve in a flash of thought. "No, he is not going to kill me yet."

Suddenly the handkerchief was pulled aside. Naturally and inevitably Juve unclenched his teeth and opened his mouth wide in the effort to recover his breath by a full, deep inhalation.

The next second he understood. With a rapid thrust the man with the handkerchief had slipped a round object into his mouth, something that quickly distended and dilated, forcing the victim to keep his mouth open. There was no risk now of his stifling, but it was impossible for him to utter a cry or speak a word. More surely than a gag, and almost invisible, the choke-pear constrained him to absolute silence.

The choke-pear? Yes, Juve had instantly recognized the instrument of torture so called. Doubtless from some criminal museum of antiquities Fantômas must have stolen this horrid contrivance malefactors of another age were once familiar with.

With mouth immoderately dilated, incapable of making the slightest sound, of uttering the faintest cry, Fantômas henceforth held him absolutely at his mercy. He might, if he chose, leave him to die in some dungeon, to perish there of hunger and thirst in an agony to be prolonged perhaps for days or weeks. Yet Juve hardened his heart. His calmness never deserted him. He was resolved, whatever fate befell him, to meet with contempt and scorn all and every abomination the Torturer might devise.

"Get up!" one of the three accomplices now ordered, emphasizing the command with a kick full in Juve's face. "Come with us! We are taking you where the Master has decided you should go… Now, remember one thing—if you resist, if you attempt to escape, the person you are going to see will be taken and tortured before your eyes.… Ah! you have understood? Let us go!"

All was carried out with the utmost expedition. Seized by two of the wretched minions of the Lord of Terror, Juve, the choke-pear still constraining him to silence, was dragged forward, while the door of the garage was opened. Outside it was still dark night, but the glare of his conductors' flashlights revealed, bound, gagged and fainting, Josette de Vautreuil, whom two other scoundrels now carried into the prison he himself was leaving.

"Remember!" repeated one of Juve's double escort, "one single struggle to escape—and that woman will be tortured before your eyes. So, go quietly!"

But Juve did not need telling. What, indeed, *could* he do? How *could* he escape? How even attempt to rescue Josette? He was asking himself: "What is Fantômas' scheme? What would he be at? Where is he having me taken? What does he propose to do with Josette and me?"

He felt no doubt it was to his death they were leading him, and though firmly resolved to give no sign of weakness and to hold himself well in hand, he could not, for all his efforts, help walking with an abrupt, jerky gait he sought in vain to steady, a gait that caused him to strike the ground with the heel—the trembling step observable in condemned men on their way to the scaffold.

It was pitch dark and Juve could not so much as discover in what direction they were taking him. One roughly paved street followed another in endless succession. Perhaps his conductors were steering an in-and-out course on purpose to puzzle him and hinder him from guessing his destination.

Now and again a passerby would meet the ill-omened procession, but the choke-pear reduced the police officer to silence, while fear for Josette forbade any attempt to escape. So the belated wayfarer would hurry by, never suspecting he had just encountered Juve, the world-famous detective, whom accomplices of Fantômas were haling to his doom, to torture, to Death.

## 15. Fandor Comes to Detest the Cinema

While the unfortunate Juve was shadowing Josette de Vautreuil, falling into the hands of his arch-enemy Fantômas and finding himself carried off he knew not where by the Torturer's accomplices, Fandor, sitting waiting in his friend's rooms in the Rue Tardieu, was bored to death. Installed in a comfortable armchair, smoking cigarette after cigarette, the journalist was firmly resolved to stay there till Juve returned, determined at all costs to find out what the latter could have been doing that night.

From time to time, in the intervals of watching the hands of the clock, the young man would growl out with an oath:

"Now, what the devil is he after, the beggar? Where in blazes can he have gone? What shocking behavior! coming home after midnight, after one o'clock in the morning! Oh! but Juve must reform! He must learn to keep reasonable hours and not make me so anxious about him!"

Suddenly he sprang to his feet. He had heard a step on the stairs, and made sure it was the delinquent at last. Running to the outer door of the flat, he threw it open—to find himself face to face with Bouzille, who was at that moment preparing to ring.

"What! it's you, is it?" cried the astonished Fandor. "You're not come with a message from Juve, by any chance, eh?"

Bouzille, as usual, was all smiles.

"M'sieur Fandor," he began confidentially, "I bear no malice. But for that there M'sieur Juve, no! I won't have nothing more to do with him. He was over rough with me, that he was!… It's from your place I've come. I was fair getting fed up waiting for you when I says to myself you were bound to be here. Anyway, they told me to try here, if so be you weren't in at home…"

"*They* told you? who are *they*? You have a message for me?"

"And urgent, so seems, M'sieur Fandor. But I must explain…"

But so prolix and confused was the old fellow in his explanations that the journalist cut him short:

"Bouzille, I'll strangle you, if you don't tell me straight out…"

"There, there, what a bad temper you be in! Well, it was like this—Mamzelle Josette's maid, she gave me this here note for you. Seems it's important like, very important!"

"Give it here then, for God's sake!"—and Fandor abandoned any attempt to discover how Josette's intermediary had come to entrust Bouzille with the commission. Almost tearing the missive out of the old man's hand, the journalist ran into Juve's working room, leaving the tramp to wait outside on the landing, in order to get some peace to read Josette's letter, which he was greatly surprised to get. But on opening the envelope, he was more amazed than ever. The note was very short—only a few lines in pencil written by a trembling hand, and ran to the following utterly unexpected effect:

"Dear Sir,"—wrote the girl—"knowing the interest you are kind enough to take in my welfare, I venture to ask you to do the impossible to meet me, before three in the morning, at M. Henri Tardoux's, in view of an interview of the highest and most serious importance. I have no doubt therefore that you will come, and I thank you a thousand times by anticipation."

"Ah! but that's coming it a bit strong!" muttered the young man between his teeth, amazed and astounded. Josette to be making assignation with him "before three in the morning," and that at Henri Tardoux's! No, he could not get over it! To begin with, how could the girl be out of doors at such an hour? Then, what could this serious and urgent communication be that she wished to make. In the last resort, what could have induced Mlle. de Vautreuil to apply to Bouzille of all people to carry her missive.

"I must know all these things," Fandor resolved. "Bouzille will tell me…"

But Bouzille was not to be found on the landing. Deeming his task accomplished, he had left the house. In vain Fandor searched for him and shouted his name down the stairs.

"So!" observed the journalist, "things are getting more and more extraordinary! Can it be a trap of sorts? Indeed, I have never much liked this same Henri Tardoux… Juve never would inquire into his antecedents, but I…"

He broke off to stand lost in thought in the middle of his friend's room. Something seemed to warn him that this time he was to be confronted with some formidable mystery. The clock, striking two, roused him from his preoccupation.

"Two o'clock, oh God! I've only just the time to get there!"—and now the young man's mind was made up. One fact at any rate was certain—a woman, a young girl, was appealing to him, demanding his help. How could he refuse the call?

Ten minutes later, a taxi was bearing him to the Villa Montmorency, and it was barely a quarter to three when he rang at Henri Tardoux's door. As nobody came, he rang again, and a third time, and a fourth.

"Oh, ho! there's no one in the house then?… or else… ah! good Lord! can it be…"—a wild surmise had flashed across his brain. Josette had summoned him to her fiancé's house. Now this fiancé, Fandor had always regarded with suspicion, vague indeed, but nonetheless convincing to his mind. Had Josette too discovered some dreadful secret? Could the girl, in her despair, have come to commit suicide at the house of her lover who was proved unworthy of her? Had Josette written the letter demanding Fandor's presence to make sure that her poor corpse would be seen and identified at once and so avoid the hideous necessity of its conveyance to the morgue.

There are circumstances when the nerves are so exasperated that the most improbable suppositions hold the attention. Fandor's tragic hypothesis was preposterous, but the horror of the tragedy he pictured was so agonizing he could hesitate no more.

"At all costs," he resolved, "I must know the truth. I am going in!"

He had no key, but there were few locks could long baffle a pupil of Juve's. For a couple of minutes Fandor worked at the mechanism of the fastening with a picklock he had taken from his pocket, and the door yielded without difficulty. Striking a match and then turning an electric switch, the young man crossed the hall and opened the first door he came to.

"Anyone here?" he demanded, but no voice answered him. Then, in growing alarm, he set about an exploration of the whole house, calling again and again. Nowhere could he see a living soul, and nobody appeared to hear him.

"Yet," Fandor muttered, "the letter is precise, it says 'before three o'clock'… Ah! perhaps my watch is a bit fast? Josette and Henri Tardoux are to come here and have not yet arrived? Yes, that is another possibility…"

The young man returned to the ground floor and entered the room used as a laboratory by Professor Marsonval's disciple, the same room where poor Mlle. Eléonore had appeared under the incarnation of an accomplice of Fantômas.

Next moment the journalist started violently. A motorcar had stopped before the house.

"It is they, no doubt?" he thought. But a bell sounded in the empty house.

"The devil! Tardoux doesn't ring surely at his own front door?"—and he dashed out onto the steps. The dazzling light from two car lamps blinded him, but he could still make out the figures of four persons hurrying towards him.

*     *     *     *     *

"Must excuse us, Monsieur Tardoux," a voice was saying. "We're behind time, but it's no fault of ours…"

This was the last thing Fandor could have expected. He answered the speaker:

"You're making a mistake. I'm not M. Tardoux, and he isn't here… But, who are you?"

Involuntarily the journalist had taken a step back, and no longer dazzled by the lights, he could make out on the man's cap the well-known name of "Gaumont."

"You're from the Gaumont Company?"

"Yes, sir! We're bringing the films, and the projector. You know about it, sir?"

"No, I don't know anything at all about it!"

"Oh! well, no matter for that. We know the house. Monsieur Tardoux will be here soon. Meanwhile we'll get things ready. There, that way, you fellows—into the laboratory."

The last words were addressed to three employees, wearing similar caps with the Gaumont badge, who were coming up the steps carrying a number of big boxes. "Screen up against the wall," the head man continued his directions—"same as last time. Set the projector here. Look, that's the plug you take the current from. Hurry up, for God's sake! Monsieur Tardoux said particularly it was to be working at three o'clock—and it's just on the hour."

Turning to the men again, Fandor asked further:

"What *are* your orders exactly?"

"Sir, it's all quite simple. I was to bring these films along— they were put through at top speed, by special request, and handsomely paid for, I can tell you! Then, with the gear you see I'm to throw 'em on the screen. Seems it's a novel of adventure of sorts and the thing's very important and very urgent…"

"And it's Monsieur Tardoux who's to look on at the show?"

"Monsieur Tardoux—yes, I think so. And another gentleman, I believe—a journalist, I'm given to understand. But I don't know his name…"

"Fandor, likely? Jerome Fandor?"

"Oh no! sir, if there'd been talk of Fandor, that name would have stuck in my memory—he's a celebrity, he is!" But Jerome Fandor only knitted his brows in perplexity, entirely indifferent to the flattering opinion—all the more sincere inasmuch as the speaker was assuredly ignorant of his identity.

"It's all mighty odd!" he muttered. "Anyway, we'd best wait and see."

"But no, sir, that's just what we mustn't do," protested the man. "My orders are to show at three o'clock—even if there's nobody there. Seems it's by way of an experiment. So, if you'll take a seat, I'm going to begin."

"With pleasure!" Fandor agreed. "M. Tardoux won't be long now, no doubt."

He was utterly nonplussed. "What was the show going to be? and what possible interest could a story of adventure have for him?" he asked himself.

Next moment Jerome Fandor's question was answered. Switching on the current, Gaumont's man had lit up his lamp, and in the dark room the screen stood out brightly illuminated, exhibiting the title, "A True Story." Fandor read the words, and then, in a sudden spasm of horror and indignation, panting with rage at what he beheld, he sat spellbound before the hideous, abominable picture.

On the screen he saw portrayed a group carrying shoulder high a man tightly pinioned, incapable of the smallest movement. And the man was Juve—Juve looking like a corpse, his mouth gaping open, his face suffused with blood, suffering the agonies, it seemed, of martyrdom.

Another horror! from the unhappy victim's jaws was extracted an object which a close-up exhibited clearly and distinctly.

"A choke-pear!" shuddered Fandor.

But the show resumed its course. Now, relieved of this instrument of torture, Juve was thrown down on a couch, where, still bound, he lay motionless.

But what was this? Above the detective's head an enormous mass of iron hung suspended. A single cord bore the weight, obviously enormous, of the huge block of metal, just one single cord, and round it was wound spirally a slow match of tinder.

"Oh! but!" groaned Fandor, springing up in his agitation, "if the cord breaks…"—and he shut his eyes, unable to endure the thought. If the cord did break, the mass must inevitably fall on Juve's head and the unhappy man would be crushed to death!

Meantime the whirring of the projector never ceased, and unable to resist the burning curiosity that consumed him, he fixed his eyes afresh on the moving pictures. Slowly Juve had raised his eyes and was looking at the iron weight hanging above his head. Then it seemed he gave a start, as if he heard someone addressing him, and shrugged his shoulders.

Then a yell of fury from Fandor: "Fantômas! it is Fantômas!"—suddenly beside the couch a man's figure had appeared on the screen, a figure Fandor, his heart standing still with horror, recognized but too readily—it was *he,* the Lord of Terror, the Torturer, Fantômas!

He stepped up to the couch. Holding a light in his hand, he proceeded to set fire to the match twining around the cord that held aloft the terrible weight of the impending mass of metal.

Ah! now Fandor grasped the dreadful truth. The slow match, burning away little by little, would set the cord alight, and the cord itself would likewise burn away slowly but surely. Then, in due time, consumed to the very core, it would suddenly break, letting the ponderous mass of metal fall and crush Juve beneath its weight. An appalling death, a death whose gradual approach the victim would be able to watch in agonized suspense from second to second!

Starting back at this nightmare vision, doubting his own sanity, unable to believe in the reality of what he beheld, Fandor turned to question the men from Gaumont's—and found himself alone!

The projector once set going, porters and operator had departed, taking advantage of his horror to slip away unperceived. Alone, yes, the young man was alone! And a startling conviction flashed across his mind:

"No, these men were no employees of the Gaumont Company! It was no tale of adventure he had been brought there to witness! It was… it was just this, a true story, as the title described it. If he had been summoned there to see this cinema performance, it meant that Fantômas, Fantômas who had contrived the hideous scheme, had some fell object in view!"

Pale and aghast, uncertain whether he was dreaming or awake, Fandor fixed his haggard eyes on the screen, on which the moving pictures still appeared in due succession, showing the slow match still little by little burning away.…

Ah! a subtitle. Fandor spelled out the words as they showed up one after the other on the screen:

"Persuade Juve to tell where he has now hidden away the real diamonds! If he refuses to speak, his head will be shattered to pieces,"—and no sooner had Fandor read the words, the menacing, abominable words, than the telephone bell suddenly rang.

The young man dragged himself painfully to the instrument and unhooked the receiver. Instinctively he guessed who it was ringing him up, and he called:

"Hello! Juve, is it?"—and the police officer's voice replied:

"Hello, Fandor, is it you? Then listen…"

*     *     *     *     *

Abominable, barbarous, inconceivably atrocious, this inhuman scheme of Fantômas' that forced Fandor to participate in Juve's death, to be a witness of the final culmination of his friend's agony.

For the film told a true story. With villainous ingenuity, Fantômas had set the apparatus to work, filming scene after scene—the detective's arrival at the place appointed by him, the moment when he was relieved of the choke-pear, the moment when he was deposited under the iron mass that in falling was to dash out his brains.

Standing impassive two paces from the couch, still wearing the black costume of story and tradition, the Lord of Terror explained his purpose to his prisoner.

"Fandor has seen you," he told him with a sardonic laugh. "Now Fandor is going to speak to you. Come, make up your mind! Tell me, Juve, where the diamonds are. Get Fandor to tell the secret, if *he* has them… Speak! If you refuse, I leave you here to die alone. I condemn you to the doom that hangs over you! Speak out, and your life shall be spared."

Juve's only answer was a shrug.

"So be it!" Fantômas resumed. "There's someone else, if not I, will induce you to listen to reason… Hark! do you hear?"

A telephone bell had sounded. The connection an accomplice had called for was made, and Fantômas clapped down the instrument in front of his prisoner.

Hoarse and breathless Fandor's voice come through: "Hello, Juve! Hello!"

And at last Juve broke the scornful silence he had maintained almost from the first moment of his capture.

"Hello, Fandor, you, is it? Now listen… You've seen the film? Yes? Good, then you will know how I died.… Of course, dear lad, I refuse to reveal where the diamonds are… and—I speak in the name of the friendship between you and me—I forbid you to betray the secret. You are to give them back to those they belong to.… No, not a word! I am speaking. The match burns fast and I have not done.… Fandor, dear lad, I am going to die. What matter? but it will be a victory for Fantômas… So then, you understand, you will avenge me. You will never abandon the pursuit, and one day you will triumph. Make that the aim and object of your life. You swear you will? Oh! I can trust you, Fandor!… Hello! hello!… No, not a word! You cannot surely advise me to play the coward! You would be dishonoring our friendship!… Silence! In two minutes it will be ended. Bah! I am not afraid… Fandor! Fandor! hush, hush! I forbid you to go on!… Where am I, you ask. I do not know. Now, will you stop trying to persuade me! I'm breaking the instrument,"—and with a sharp heave of the body, Juve threw the telephone over onto the floor, where it broke to bits.

But instantly Fantômas bounded to his prisoner's side. No less breathless, he had followed the dialogue he had invited.

Yes, Fandor had besought Juve to speak. Yes, Fandor had frantically adjured his friend not to throw away his life. But, if he knew where the diamonds were, he had not told—even as Juve, face to face with Death, in the very presence of Death, obstinately refused to betray the secret.

With closed eyes, the police officer lay waiting for the end.

"Juve, Juve! are you mad?" vociferated Fantômas. "Do you suppose for one moment I should hesitate? Do you not know I am without pity? Can you not see that now, for no consideration on earth, will I spare you? Juve, Juve! speak! speak! The match is burning—and the cord!"

Juve shrugged again. "I am well content," he declared simply. "Fandor will avenge me!"

"Goodbye, then, Juve!" the brigand spoke with an odious callousness. "The threats of a dying man leave me indifferent.

Farewell! Peace to your ashes. I will have you buried tomorrow… Farewell!"—and slowly, step by step, he withdrew. It may be he still hoped that Juve, seeing him go, knowing himself abandoned to his fate, would call him back.

But Juve spoke no word. Still stretched on the couch, beneath the cast-iron mass that in a few seconds more would dash out his brains, Juve was now alone—alone with Death drawing nearer and nearer, alone with the tiny red flame that, as it gnawed at the cord, was gnawing at his life, nibbling away his existence, dooming him to the grave, second by second, strand by strand…

But now, after lying a moment with closed eyes, listening to the silence, noting the sinister quiet of the place where he was to die, Juve suddenly broke into an uncanny peal of laughter.

"How much more time?" he asked himself. "Forty to forty-five seconds, I suppose—say forty, not to run any risks… Yes, the cord will break in forty seconds—thirty-five now. When the flame reaches that point I have fixed upon—well, it's perfectly simple, five seconds before then, I shall go away… five seconds before—not an instant sooner!"

But what could he mean? He went on:

"And, thanks to my air tube and my fountain pen, given a trifle of luck, by God! it will be my turn to wish Fantômas peaceful repose in the tomb!"—and Juve gave another half-stifled laugh.

Did he think to escape? He was still pinioned, incapable of moving a limb, of stirring a finger… His wild words, alas! might well lend themselves to a different explanation. Do we not read of heroes whose gallantry is beyond cavil, yet who have gone mad to see Death slowly but surely drawing nearer and nearer?

*　　*　　*　　*　　*

For a moment longer Juve lay rigorously still. Then as the flame reached the point in the cord he had fixed upon, the police officer began a slow and deliberate series of movements, the object of which was entirely incomprehensible—to all appearance. He was bound with stout solid ropes, capable of defying any human muscles. And yet, slowly but powerfully Juve began to stiffen his arms making the muscles stand out strongly, just as if he hoped by this means to burst the bonds that held him prisoner. A vain hope surely? No, a perfectly reasonable one!

There was a slight cracking sound, and lo! the ropes, broken, or rather cut clean through, fell off and left him free. In fact, miraculous as the thing seemed, its explanation was of the simplest, the most logical.

To tell the truth, Juve had been in no wise embarrassed by his bonds. Never for one second had he counted himself a prisoner! He had merely, with amazing coolness, been waiting for the moment he deemed most favorable for exercising the maneuver he had now carried out. Indeed the police officer had long feared he might one day fall into Fantômas' hands. He had long known that such a fate might befall him and that in that case the redoubtable Torturer would not fail to secure his prisoner with strong, solid ropes.

So he had taken his precautions accordingly, and had had made to his order a pair of leather wristlets in which were inlet safety-razor blades. Easy to see how by this ingenious device the police officer was able to regain his liberty. At ordinary times the wristlets remained invisible under his coat-sleeves, but, if bound, should he wish to cut through his bonds, all he had to do was to swell out his muscles. Then the blades, sharpened to a keen edge, coming in contact with the cords sliced through them in a moment.

Now, his arms once free, one may be sure Juve was not long in liberating his legs and next minute had leapt from the couch.

"There!" he cried. "If Fantômas has not heard me, all goes well. If, on the contrary, he has caught some sound, or if, when the iron weight crashes down, he chooses to return to see my corpse, well, I shall only have to show him I still know a bit of jujitsu! I can undertake to bring him to reason!"

As he spoke, Juve had sprung to the door by which Fantômas had left and by which, in all probability, he would reappear if he thought of revisiting his victim. But a moment later Juve abandoned all expectation of that day coming face to face with Fantômas. The great block of, iron had fallen with a terrific crash, shattering the couch and half demolishing the floor—and neither Fantômas nor another soul had come.

"Precisely what I thought!" exclaimed the detective, no longer even troubling to lower his voice. "He must have left the house. Upon my word, I'll do the same. But, oh God! where am I?"

Very softly and cautiously, Juve pushed open the door behind which he had been lurking.

"Nobody?" he said to himself. "No, nobody there! And there'll be a window? Well, I'll get out by the window… I'd like to have a look around the room first. Suppose I light up!"

With the utmost coolness and an audacity almost beyond belief, already bent on resuming his investigations, Juve struck a match. Then with a cry of amazement:

"Ah! but I'm at Tardoux's place. So Fandor was right. Tardoux must be in the plot, an accomplice of Fantômas!"

Yes, Juve felt certain he was making no mistake. The furniture he was looking at assured him of that. Evidently he was in the laboratory of Professor Marsonval's young assistant. He had been there once before, and perfectly remembered the carved wood armchairs, the table overloaded with scientific instruments, a blackboard, other details his trained eye had exactly noted.

"So I'm at Auteuil, in the Villa Montmorency, it seems? So much the better. I shall easily find a conveyance…"

He threw away the match, which was beginning to burn his fingers, and crossing the room, threw open the window.

"Oh God!" he muttered, "it's still night and as black as ink… I only hope it isn't raining… though now… Anyway, let's jump down into the garden. I'm on the ground floor, so…"—and, confident there was no great height to fall, he let himself go.

Next instant the police officer gave a yell. He had fallen plump into water, deep water. A strong current was sweeping past, carrying him swiftly away downstream.

## 16. Fandor Is Told the Story of "Tom Thumb"

As Fandor stood listening in horrified suspense to the last words his poor friend would in all probability ever speak to him, when Juve, to cut short a heartrending scene, had broken the telephone Fantômas had handed him, the journalist was on the verge of madness, the madness of despair.

For him Juve was more than a friend, more than a brother, almost a father. As far back as his memory could reach—even to that far-off time when his name was still Charles Rambert—Jerome Fandor was conscious of having always loved and admired Juve.

And, in a sense, he had but now been witnessing his death agonies! He had heard his friend dictating his last wishes to him, leaving him as a sacred duty the task of avenging his death.

Jerome Fandor felt well-nigh heartbroken. Was this, this ignominious death, the reward fate awarded Juve for so many struggles, so many strenuous efforts, so many acts of sublime courage? Was the police officer to be done to death by the Criminal?

"And I can do nothing!" sobbed the unhappy young man. For indeed, what *could* he do? Where was he to go? How was he to meet and confront Fantômas? And where was Juve? *Somewhere* in Paris in the hands of the outlaw. And Paris was so vast! and there were so many dens of iniquity in the great wicked city, so many haunts of crime completely unknown to the Police!

But gallant and impulsive natures are quick to throw off depression and brace themselves to instant action. In less than three minutes Fandor had quitted Henri Tardoux's house and with never a thought of his own concerns, forgetting all about Josette and her mysterious summons, he was running breathlessly for the nearest cab rank.

"Quick, my man! and drive your hardest!… the Prefecture of Police!"

Once there, at the headquarters of the Criminal Department, could he not mobilize the whole posse of Inspectors and then and there begin investigations?

Unfortunately he lighted on a youthful Inspector, the only one on duty, and that functionary, a raw recruit, lost his head when he heard the astonishing story.

"But what do you want me to do?" he asked with a bewildered gesture. In three minutes Fandor had summed up his man. He was good for nothing. At Juve's name he had grown helplessly excited, while that of Fantômas had frozen him with terror.

"So be it!" thought Fandor. "I'll go and see Havard… He doesn't like Juve perhaps, he is jealous of him, but he's a man of action, anyhow. He won't shirk responsibility…"

Hailing another taxi, he reiterated once more his exhortation to top speed, and the chauffeur started away at a breakneck pace and quickly landed him at the Chief's door.

But the journalist was pursued by ill-luck. M. Havard was not at home.

"The Chief is taking the chair at a banquet to ex-soldiers," he was informed. "You'll find him in the Restaurant Voyot."

There Fandor hurried, resolved to leave no stone unturned. He felt it was all in vain, he could never save Juve's life. But how could he resign himself to abandon his friend, to attempt nothing—even were it useless or impossible?

"He went on foot," the hall porter added. "Oh! yes, and I heard him say: 'I'll drop in at the office. I shall be glad to see if the night duties are going all right'… I didn't catch any more."

"We must have crossed each other," thought Fandor, pale with disappointment. "But I'll catch up with him at the Prefecture."

He was driven back there, and leaping out of his taxi, he burst like a bombshell into the porter's lodge.

"M. Havard? has he gone again? He came here, didn't he? Is he here still?"

But, before the man could answer, a mocking voice rebuked him:

"Good Lord! don't make such a rumpus!… Better come and treat me to a whet of brandy at Montmartre. I'm half frozen, my boy! I'm just out of the Seine!"

"Juve! Juve!" stammered Fandor, and he threw himself into his old friend's arms.

*     *     *     *     *

An hour later, in a private room at a quiet restaurant—often as that room had been the discreet witness of confidential secrets, seldom could it have been the scene of so extraordinary a conversation—Juve and Fandor were seated before an appetizing menu, especially chosen by the younger man.

"So there," the police officer concluded his narrative of events, "I was wondering what on earth had happened. I was in the water, and a torrent at that! the last thing I expected! Then, of course, I just gave up thinking for the time being, and struck out. My swimming's got fine and rusty, I can tell you, my boy!… Anyhow, I touched bottom the other side of the viaduct, and that told me I was actually in the Seine. The river was in flood too, as is its way… No matter for that! I just took a taxi back home. No Fandor to be seen! Then I guessed you'd be at work trying to save me, and naturally that took me straight to the Prefecture—and there I found you."

Juve poured himself out a glass of champagne, swallowed it with manifest satisfaction, then resumed:

"And now for serious matters. You are in a condition to think coherently, Fandor?"

"Why, certainly I am!"

"Then will you explain, if you can, one thing I cannot yet understand."

"To wit, Juve?"

"Now, my boy, give me your full attention. Well, as I've just been telling you, on leaving Fantômas' house, the place where he thought to murder me, I tumbled into the Seine…"

"Yes, well?"

"Well, Fandor, but that is impossible."

"Because?"

"Because, Fandor, this house where I was, I recognized it. I know what house it is—and this house is not anywhere near the river!"

"What! what cock-and-bull story is this you're telling me?"—and Fandor now eyed Juve with a roguish air. Might not his friend's words, in fact, lend themselves to a supposition not altogether unlikely under the circumstances?

"Juve, the champagne?" suggested the young man.

"Hold your tongue!" protested the detective. "I'm not joking… I fell into the Seine—that's a fact. But I know the house where I was—and that's a fact too—and that house is Henri Tardoux's house."

"Eh? what? You were saying?"—and Fandor sprang from his seat.

"Juve," he went on, "what room in that house were you in?"

"I escaped by the laboratory room."

"How long after our telephone talk?"

"Seven or eight minutes, I should think."

"In that case you are making a mistake. I tell you so straight out. You were not in Tardoux's laboratory."

"But I was! I tell you I recognized…"

"You're mistaken! entirely mistaken!"

"But why so?"

"Because I was there myself—and I did not see you!"

"What? what do you say?"—and Juve too leapt to his feet.

"I am positive," he declared, "absolutely certain I'm not deceiving myself… I was in the laboratory."

"Juve, I go the same. I am sure, absolutely convinced I was in that laboratory myself…"

The two friends were looking at each other with scared faces.

Neither one nor the other was jesting. Neither one nor the other had succumbed to the libations, very modest libations in fact, they had been indulging in. Yet one or the other must inevitably, of necessity, be either lying or making a mistake.

"Juve," Fandor spoke again, "I was at Tardoux's house! It

is you who are deceiving yourself. Your tumbling in the river proves it…"

"In good sooth," Juve acknowledged, "anyone would say you were right, yes, they would say so—but, all the same, I am making no mistake. So that's that!"

Then suddenly without giving Fandor time to answer him, Juve went on:

"Anyway, all this is of no importance… You're not tired?"

"No! why?"

"Then ring for the pageboy… I'll tell you later on…"

Fandor did as he was bidden, and almost immediately a small boy appeared.

"Young man," Juve gave his orders, "you will be so good as to go and stand in the middle of the Place Pigalle. Once there, you will please cast a look at the sky. Then you are to come back and tell me if it's fine or bad weather, if it's likely to rain or not. Off with you!"

Too well used to the eccentricities of intoxicated customers to be surprised at anything whatsoever, the lad bowed respectfully.

"I can tell Monsieur that now," he declared, "the weather is just perfect. It's daybreak, and it's going to be a superb day."

"You are sure of that?"

"Sure and certain, sir."

"Then here's something for you. Go and ask for our bill and coats and hats, and call up a taxi."

No sooner was the lad gone than Fandor began questioning his friend afresh.

"Juve, I don't understand. What connection can the weather, good or bad, have with the locality where Fantômas held you prisoner?"

"A direct connection, Fandor!"

"You surprise me!… And you were saying it was of no importance our finding out which of us, you or I, was making a mistake?"

"Yes, that is what I think."

"Well, do please explain how you come to think so!"

"You're mighty impatient. But there, I'll tell you. It is of no importance now to decide the thing one way or the other, because, if it isn't raining and if it doesn't rain for another hour, we shall be fixed up for certain…"

"But how? Is it a charade?"

"No! it is the result of the judicious use of a fountain pen and the air tube of a pneumatic tire."

Then, as the headwaiter came in, bringing in on a plate, discreetly folded in two, the bill, which Juve immediately impounded—he had taken care to borrow a little money of the Prefecture doorkeeper—Juve proceeded to put the copestone on poor Fandor's bewilderment.

"A little patience!" he whispered in his ear. "I'll tell you everything in the cab—including the story of Tom Thumb! Why yes, one must know the story of Tom Thumb to understand how a fountain pen and an old air tube may be put to use when one is up against—you know who!"

And, dropping his voice, Juve concluded:

"By the way, it won't be Perrault's *Tom Thumb* I'm going to tell you. It will be something, not so pretty certainly… but a deal more modern!"

*       *       *       *       *

Comfortably ensconced in a corner of the conveyance the pageboy had fetched, his feet resting on the opposite seat, Juve sat smiling at Fandor's anxious look, and dissembling to perfection his own excited state, began in this wise:

"Once upon a time, my child, there was a police officer called Juve, who, by his clumsiness no doubt, found himself the prisoner of a redoubtable brigand. They had confined him in a shed at a garage and he was telling himself sadly that for certain they would be carrying him off somewhere else, to a place it was very important for him to find again, if he could escape by help of his leather wristlets…"

"Well done, Juve!" broke in Fandor. "But wouldn't the police officer be quite well able to see where they were taking him?"

"This police officer," Juve went on, "had a friend by the name of Fandor, who was the limit for addle-patedness. But he, Juve, was no addle-pate. So he knew the wicked ogre Fantômas would never be such a fool as to let him discover the position of his robbers' cave, and foresaw the villain would do the impossible to baffle him…"

"The devil! but this Juve was a clever one!"

"Like all the heroes in fairy tales, Fandor! But please don't interrupt!… Well, in his prison-house, poor Juve was thinking: 'Oh! if only I had some white pebbles—or blue, or red, or green ones—in my pocket! I could drop them one by one as they were haling me off, and that would let me easily discover, later on, the place I'm to be taken to… Why, yes! but then he had not a single pebble.…"

"So, Juve? So…?"

"So Tom-Thumb-Juve puzzled how he could devise a substitute for the pebbles he had not got…"

"But that was impossible, Juve!"

"And, as this Tom-Thumb-Juve was not such a simple oaf as his friend Fandor, he did hit on something—something quite easy! He knew where he had been captured; the whole difficulty, therefore, lay in knowing where they would take him to afterwards. All he had to do, accordingly, was to blaze his trail from this known place to the unknown place…"

"Why, of course! Go on, do go on! I'm dying of curiosity!"

"That's because my tale's so interesting… Then, Fandor, Tom-Thumb-Juve noticed an old air tube of a pneumatic tire, cut two india-rubber rings out of it and used them to fasten his fountain pen on his ankle, point downwards… Now, do you understand?"

"No! proceed!"

"And, that done, always supposing it didn't rain, he was quite sure of finding his way back—because at every step they made him go, he would have taken care to plant his foot sharply on the ground, stamping hard, as if marching with a measured tread—which each time was bound to jerk out a drop of ink!… There, not such a bad dodge, eh?"

"Juve, you're a stunner!" exclaimed the younger man with

an offhand familiarity that made his admiration all the more expressive. "Juve, there's nobody in this world to match you!"

But Fandor stopped of himself. Perfectly calm and unruffled, Juve had dropped off into a sound nap! Little he cared for compliments! Even Fandor's left him indifferent. Juve was keen only for the fight—and soon the struggle must start afresh.

It was not long before the cab stopped at the entrance to the bridge of the Point du Jour, and in a second Juve was awake, had paid off the taxi and dismissed the driver.

"Now for it, Fandor!" he cried. "We can only count on ourselves, and act as swiftly as possible. To pick up the clue offered by the ink stains, follow it up and discover Fantômas' haunt, to make out how it was both of us, you and I, could be at one and the same time at Henri Tardoux's—there's what matters now…"

"And to find Josette?" stammered Fandor.

"Certainly!… Though… Hmm, I have a notion of my own about that."

Fandor gazed inquiringly at his friend, but asked no further questions. Indeed, since the police officer had told him his adventures and explained how it was that, while following Josette de Vautreuil, he had fallen into Fantômas' hands, Fandor's curiosity had been strangely excited.

To begin with, how came it that Juve, so devoted to duty, so generous-hearted, seemed to pay so little heed to the girl's unhappy plight? He knew she was in Fantômas' power, and showed no anxiety! A mere allusion to the subject was all he had vouchsafed. And then, what did Josette's own behavior mean? Why had the girl made appointment with him, at three o'clock in the morning, at Henri Tardoux's—where she had never appeared? Why, again, had she gone so mysteriously to that shady district where she accosted, without a qualm, fellows who were assuredly accomplices of Fantômas?

"Juve cannot have been mistaken!" he thought. "He shadowed her, he saw her. So it was she, it must have been… But in that case, how understand…"

He dared not complete the sentence. The suspicions that filled his mind, in spite of himself, horrified him. It was unthinkable that the poor girl was another of the brigand's accomplices. The monstrous supposition was utterly improbable from every point of view.

However, the journalist had little time to pursue his lucubrations further. Taking him by the arm, with the air of a harmless stroller chatting to an absentminded companion, Juve was drawing him towards the alley where, a few hours before, he had been the victim of a dastardly assault.

"Look there!" the police officer suddenly cried under his breath, "look at the curb of the sidewalk there… Do you see? do you see?"

Fandor with difficulty checked a cry of exultation. There, on the smooth stone could be clearly discerned a drop of blue ink!

"The first link in the chain!" declared Juve. "Let us follow up the clue! Yes, I've surely been along here. Look at the pavements…" and there, at intervals, showed up the little ink stains, testifying to this modern Tom Thumb's ingenuity. In places, however, they disappeared, wherever they had fallen on ground that rendered them invisible—on sand, loose earth, liquid mud—but further on they always began again.

"We shall do all right!" grunted Juve. "My notion was a good one. It's only a question of time… Only, it won't work if it should rain, by God!"—and at last Fandor understood Juve's reason for showing so keen an interest in the weather. It was plain enough, in fact, that a mere shower would have been enough to render his dispositions fruitless by washing away the telltale spots.

Nothing of the kind, however, was to be feared. The sky was crystal clear. And, anyway, the pursuit could not last forever. Juve was conscious of having walked three-quarters of an hour at most, and had certainly not covered any great distance. Moreover, in all likelihood, he had passed and re-passed by the same localities, for Fantômas was pretty sure to have tried confusing the trail. Without a doubt the place of Juve's imprisonment and torture could not be far off.

By this time the two friends were entering a newly built street, very clean and quite empty, where the ink spots showed up with perfect distinctness. Suddenly Fandor, pointing to the far end of the street, burst out with an angry curse.

"Juve, there! There! Look!"

"Ah the villain"—and both, with one impulse, dashed forward at a run. At the corner they had caught sight of Bouzille, though the old tramp had evidently not seen the two friends. He was far too busy! On his knees on the sidewalk, a bottle half-full of water by his side, Bouzille was solemnly scrubbing away at the flagstones. Impossible not to realize the old man's infamous purpose in this seemingly idiotic task!

In an instant Fandor had the old wretch by the collar and was dragging him to his feet.

"Scoundrel!" he thundered, "what are you after?"

But Bouzille, after a start of terror very natural under the circumstances, for he was far from expecting any such violent interference, opened wide eyes of bewilderment and injured innocence.

"What am I doing, M'sieur Fandor. But you, gentlemen, might've bid a fellow good day first, seems to me! It's M'sieur Juve's been telling you more lies about me, for sure! You do look that angry!"

"Bouzille, I'm not joking! Answer me!"

"Answer what, M'sieur Fandor? Ain't a matter of money, eh? I don't owe you ought, do I?"

But at this point Juve took the affair in hand. He had stepped on a few yards and noted that the ink stains stopped dead, in fact that Bouzille had broken the clue short off. He was in no laughing mood.

"Have a care, my man," he pronounced coldly. "If you anger me, you'll pay dear for this!"

"Beg pardon, M'sieur Juve, but I can't pay nothing! Cleaned out, I am! stony!"

"I'm not playing a game, Bouzille!"

"No more am I, M'sieur Juve. I'm working."

"Well, who for?"

"Who for? for a woman. I can tell you that much. I let the wench cajole me, I did! So, I'm cleaning up…"

"Bouzille, yes or no, will you speak out?"—and as he spoke

the police officer drew a pair of handcuffs from his pocket. And, to tell the truth, nothing more was needed to make the old tramp as talkative as a magpie.

"M'sieur Juve, I don't understand," he protested volubly. "I'm doing a bit of cleaning up. That's not forbidden, is it? It's a woman—the one I told you about, she asked me to do the job. Any law against that, eh? She'd broke a bottle of ink and don't want folks to know. Ain't I got a right to rub out the marks? Ain't it my own business, anyhow? Must be reasonable, M'sieur Juve!"—and Bouzille, who spoke in tones of the most guileless simplicity, added after a short silence:

"First go, it was a louis I got off of Mam'zelle Marie…"

"Louis Rippert's one-time servant?" broke in Juve sharply.

"So she was. But she's in another place now, they tell me. Well, it was a louis I pocketed, I did… You give me another louis, and I'm quite ready, you know, to break a few more of them ink bottles, if that's to your liking."

It was impossible to tell if the old fellow spoke seriously or no. He could feign stupidity perfectly, whenever he thought good. One thing was quite certain, that he was always the devoted servant of the most openhanded paymaster.

But Juve had turned pale. Louis Rippert's servant? So it was she, this girl Mary, who had ordered Bouzille to rub out the ink marks! And had not Juve known ever since his visit to the tavern of the late Père Korn that the pretended maidservant was neither more nor less than an accomplice of the Torturer? So then, Fantômas had sent Mary to Bouzille. The brigand had already fathomed the ingenious trick Juve had employed.

"Not an instant to lose!" calculated the detective. "If Fantômas knows I am out to find his den, he will see to it I never get there. He will destroy it first. Then he turned to Bouzille again and in a peremptory voice:

"Bouzille, my friend," he said sternly, "I ask you for no explanation. Only, you are to lead us, Fandor and me, to the point where you began your cleaning up, as you call it. It is an order I am giving you! and I give it you in the name of the Law!"

Juve had spoken in a tone Bouzille could no longer disregard.

"Old friends like you!" he protested nevertheless, "to go talking of setting the Law at me, that fashion! But there, I'll take you to the place—and, for sure, you'll give me another forty sous, eh?"—and, out of the corner of his eye, he watched first Juve's face and then Fandor's. Seeing both looking stern and determined, he too grew serious again:

"Follow me," he invited them, "follow the guide! We shan't spoil much shoe leather in getting there. It's just alongside the river yonder—where the fire was this morning…"

"Eh? what do you say?"

Juve had given another violent start… "So the place was burned down? Had Fantômas fired it? Already?"

Bouzille proceeded: "And a pity it was, too, to see the house blazing. It was chock full of pretty things, that there crib was… what with the set-pieces and all…"

"The set-pieces?"

"Why, of course! the set-pieces for the cinema, y'know!"

A quarter of an hour later, Juve and Fandor were on the move again, not without having first given Bouzille a word of warning how they strongly suspected him of helping Fantômas and threatening the old scamp that one fine day he would find himself disastrously mixed up in an ugly business.

But what cared they what fate was reserved for the old fellow, better fitted after all to excite amusement than indignation. Had they not just made important discoveries, which Juve now proceeded to sum up?

"You see, Fandor, it was all perfectly simple! A cinematograph set-piece! *I* was confined in a set-piece of the sort, faithfully copied from Henri Tardoux's house, where *you* actually were last night. Hence the bewildering feeling we had of having been both of us together in one and the same place without seeing each other. Hence too, my mad adventure, when I jumped out of my 'property' window, why, of course I tumbled into the water, seeing the contraption was built alongside the Seine. Hence, again… think! just think!"

For a second Juve stood silent, his eyes sparkling with eagerness. Then he resumed: "Hence, too, the affair of the dog! why, of course, that dog that came alive again!"

"Good Lord!" cried Fandor, wondering. "How ever do you make out that the discovery of a cinema set-piece accounts for the resurrection of a dog?"

But Juve was quietly shrugging his shoulders: "Oh! don't go talking like a child! There was no resurrection. Rippert's dog never did come alive again—any more than Josette's aunt was in two places at once. Now, listen!"

Juve lit a cigarette and proceeded:

"It's all as simple as 'how-d'ye-do'! The only thing was to think of it!… In the matter of the dog's resurrection, what bothered *me* was not the fact that Rippert recognized his dog. He might have made a mistake. That can easily happen—at a pinch the resemblance can be helped a bit, only a matter of a little faking. No, what nonplussed me was this—admitting Rippert could have been mistaken in recognizing 'his' dog, I could not admit that the dog on his side, recognized his house, resumed 'his' old habits, made much of 'his' master, if it was not the same animal, the one that was dead… Whereas now…"

"Now, Juve?"

"Oh, now it's as plain as plain. Assume—as was the fact—that Fantômas wanted to steal M. de Vautreuil's diamonds. To that end he must have someone in the house to help him. So he decides to send an accomplice in the guise of Mlle. Eléonore, supposed to have reappeared in Paris.… Hardly a likely story, by itself! he thinks to himself; we've got to persuade folks to believe in this extraordinary reappearance of the aunt. So he resolves there's to be a 'resurrection.' Oh God! that's the thing to inspire confidence! And then and there he thinks of a dog. But what to do? how to set about the job? Why, it's as easy as A B C! Mary, another accomplice, has been fixed up as maid at Louis Rippert's, to supply information about the de Vautreuils, friends of her master's. Mary is to be of further use. Going by what the girl tells him, he has a set-piece constructed in exact imitation of Rippert's dwelling, and in this he rears a dog. The animal knows Mary, knows his 'home,' noses, I suppose, some of Rippert's wearing apparel, on somebody else's back, somebody else who's in the secret, the clothes being provided by Mary, who carries them back home after each rehearsal. After that, Rippert's own dog is poisoned—and the other brought on the scene!… Say, Fandor, is it to be wondered at if the new dog makes a blunder, as I did myself? Is it surprising if, on arriving at Rippert's, he thinks he is at home, in the bogus house where he was reared?… *He* was no trickster, the honest beast!…"

"Juve, you're a wonder!" Fandor broke in. "How simple it all is—once you know the explanation!"

Whereupon Juve smiled a little knowing smile.

"Why, yes!" he said, "and it's like that always… And it won't be any different when I have finished unmasking Fantômas!"

"Finished, Juve? *finished* you say?"

"Certainly!" returned the police officer. "Come, let's take another taxi… These taxis are ruination… But I'm in a hurry to get to Tardoux's."

"Oh!" exclaimed Fandor, in some surprise.

"Before going elsewhere!" Juve concluded with a smile.

## 17. A Good Defeat Is Better Than a Bad Victory

When declaring he meant to pay a visit at Henri Tardoux's "before going elsewhere," Juve had once more adopted that cryptic tone he was so fond of, but which never failed to exasperate Fandor to the last degree. Indeed, whenever his friend spoke in this strain, the younger man knew it was perfectly useless to ask questions. So he merely nodded. "Very good! keep your secrets to yourself," he said crossly.

"Thank you for your kind permission!" scoffed the police officer… "But, anyway, there's no great secret left, is there? We know pretty well how it was possible for us to come to life again. I told you as much at Marseilles… We know perfectly well how it was possible for Mlle. Eléonore to be in two places at once. The supposed aunt was nothing more nor less than an accomplice of Fantômas… We know how Rippert's dog…"

"Yes, yes!" Fandor interrupted him, "we know all that!… But there's one thing we do not know—where Fantômas is, and how to arrest him, rather an important point, that?"

"I never said it wasn't!" retorted Juve, who had meantime stopped a taxi, and given the address of the Professor's assistant, looking all the time as smiling as Fandor looked out of temper.

After a moment's silence the latter resumed:

"Then there's another thing we don't know—what has become of poor Josette? Juve, I cannot understand you! how do you find it possible to show so little anxiety on her account?"

"My dear Fandor, you are a very good boy, but it somehow strikes me it's the business of those who feel an interest in Josette to find the girl."

"You mean me, Juve?"

"Go along! her fiancé, of course!"

After this the young man relapsed into absolute silence. Of

course he knew Juve too well to suppose he really meant what he said. Better than anybody he knew the police officer was not the man to ignore the girl's peril. Better than anybody he recognized his friend's utter devotion to duty. It followed that Juve had his own reasons for acting as he did.

But what were those reasons? As the cab bowled along the Boulevard Exelmans on its way to the Villa Montmorency, Fandor cudgeled his brains to guess the truth. For certain, Juve suspected someone. Beyond a doubt he thought Fantômas was hiding under the guise of an adopted personality.

"But whose?"

For a moment he was for accusing Rippert. "But there, it cannot be Rippert. His maidservant has left him. He was obviously deceived himself about the dog's coming back to life. Yes, Rippert is clearly above suspicion. Moreover, he is actually out of Paris, and this alibi would alone suffice to prove his innocence, inasmuch as Juve, only last night, was at grips with Fantômas. Who else then is open to suspicion?

Involuntarily Fandor spoke a name. "Henri Tardoux? Could it be Henri Tardoux? But neither does he fall under any genuine suspicion… He was the first to see the mysterious aunt on her return to Paris, true, but that proves nothing… He was deceived, true, but he was by means the only one… He does not wish his fiancée to be mixed up in these sensational incidents? Well, Juve was right—in his place I should have felt the same. So then?…"

At that moment the taxi stopped at the young scientist's door, and two minutes later Fandor was listening eagerly to what Juve was saying to Josette's fiancé—remarks that set him staring in bewilderment. Received without demur by Henri Tardoux, the detective proved himself quite the polished gentleman. Without making the smallest allusion to the sensational discoveries he had just made, including the real circumstances of the dog's "resurrection," Juve began in these terms:

"My dear sir, if we disturb you like this at this early hour, Fandor and myself, it is because we wish to tender you our apologies…"

"Apologies?"—this with a start of surprise.

"Certainly. We have both of us, both Fandor and myself, been taking intolerable liberties with you…"

"But, I don't see!…"

"The step we are taking is a very natural one, though I may add that in acting as we did, we were only carrying out an imperative duty. We meant no disrespect—but police investigations, you know…"

"Monsieur Juve," Henri Tardoux interrupted this flow of excuses, "let me assure you I don't understand one word, not one word you're saying! I am unaware of any grievance I can have against either you or Monsieur Fandor."

"Mademoiselle Josette de Vautreuil has told you nothing then?"

"My fiancée? When? What about?"

"And last night you didn't find your house in a state to make you shudder?"

"I must repeat, Monsieur Juve, I don't know…" And Henri Tardoux really did not know. After attending the dance at which he had vainly hoped to meet his fiancée, and waiting there till the very last moment, thinking she might have been accidentally delayed, he had afterwards spent some considerable time in aimless wanderings about the deserted streets. When eventually he reached home, it was already daylight. He had gone straight upstairs to his own den, the room into which Juve and Fandor were presently shown, without even glancing into the laboratory, the scene of the nocturnal cinema performance at which the journalist had been present. Thus the detective's references to Josette and to the state in which, as Juve supposed, he had found his house were so much Greek to the young man.

"You don't know? In that case," Juve continued his apologies, "I must confess my sins—our sins, I should say, for Fandor is as much to blame as myself"—and, smiling more and more blandly, Juve pretended not to see the frantic signals of distress and denial Fandor was making him.

"What the devil is Juve going to do next?" thought the young man. "He's never going to tell this Tardoux I received an equivocal summons from his fiancée? Things like that are not done! And then, why explain how I came to his house last night, at Fantômas' instance?"

Then suddenly he paled visibly. No, it could not be! Juve was not, by any chance, actually charging Tardoux with being, if not Fantômas, at least an accomplice of the brigand's? Were all the officer's polite speeches to end in an arrest?

Juve was still talking: "As to Fandor—he took the liberty of spending the night in your house, doing a cinema there, picking the lock of your front door…"

"Eh? what? you tell me?…"

"And as to myself, about eleven at night, my dear sir, I made bold to follow Mademoiselle de Vautreuil… to spy on her in fact."

"Sir, you go beyond all bounds! Once for all, I beg you to explain yourself clearly. I have no use for such pleasantries—a very poor taste, let me tell you."

Henri Tardoux's voice was shaking with anger. But Juve went on his way, more smiling than ever.

"But I'm not joking. I'm speaking seriously. It is in all sincerity I am offering you my apologies. If Fandor spent the night in your house…"

"But this is preposterous! You came here, to my house?"

At this point, feeling bound to intervene, Fandor made up his mind to speak.

"By God! yes!" he admitted, "I came here…"

"And you picked my lock?"

"I did!"

"And you were present at a cinema show? But, good Lord! I haven't got a cinema!"

"Nevertheless, I did see a performance…"

"Will you please, once for all, explain yourself."

"Certainly—in three words! Employees from the Gaumont Company. Hmm! I may add it was surely a lie they told in saying they came from that firm—last night brought to your house a reel of films and the necessary apparatus to throw them on the screen. Having nothing better to do I sat and watched the pictures…"

"But, but how came you to be there?"

"Why, because… because I had received a letter summoning me to your house."

"A letter from whom?"

"The mischief!" muttered Fandor. "After all, the truth must come out… The letter was from Mlle. de Vautreuil. She begged me to come…"

"You lie, sir!"

"But, my good sir!"

"And I must ask you to withdraw your allegation here and now!"

"My good Monsieur Tardoux, I don't choose, sir, to be spoken to in that tone!"

"I take what tone I please with a confounded blackmailer!"

"Oh, come!"—and Fandor, without more ado, was in the act to box Henri Tardoux's ears, who stood there pale with anger, when Juve, still smiling, at last intervened.

"Now, now!" the police officer said soothingly. "Calm yourselves, gentlemen. You're never going to quarrel over a misunderstanding. Fandor, show the note you received."

Instantly the journalist drew it from his pocket.

"I speak the truth!—and *there* is the proof of what I say! Do you hear?"

But Henri Tardoux was trembling visibly. "Certainly it is Josette's writing!" he stammered, "and the hour corresponds. What *can* it mean?"

He broke off to hear what Juve was saying.

"Now you see Fandor had some excuse," the detective went on. "Anyway, Mademoiselle Josette did not put in an appearance at the place appointed. She preferred to obey *your* summons… But, heavens! what a shady locality you asked her to come to!"

"I'm going mad! raving mad!" stammered the young man of science, and beating his brow like one possessed, he asked:

"So *I* made an assignation with Josette, you say?"

"Assuredly! I followed her as she was on her way to meet you."

"And you saw her with me?"

"No!… At that moment Fantômas laid hands on me. You start—but I tell you plainly, Fantômas captured me. In fact, that is one reason, my dear sir, made me think you so imprudent. You had invited Mademoiselle Josette to a distinctly dangerous locality, and…"

"But, forgive my asking, how do you know…?"

"That you did invite her? Why, in a very simple way. In the garage where I was imprisoned by Fantômas I picked up a piece of paper. It was your letter. I have just discovered it in my pocket. It was by reading it I came to understand where Mlle. Josette was bound…"

"You have the letter?"

"Certainly! here it is,"—and the detective put into Henri Tardoux's hands the crumpled sheet of paper. The latter glanced through it, and stood as if paralyzed. At last he got out:

"It is indeed my writing… and my signature! And Josette…"

Then he broke off and went on in a hoarse voice:

"Monsieur Juve, and you, Monsieur Fandor, I apologize for the quick temper I showed just now… Things are driving me insane. The letter is perfectly clear and precise—*but* I never wrote it! I never invited Josette to come to Grenelle…"

But the inscrutable Juve was again smiling.

"To proceed," he said—"and Fandor's letter, was it from Josette? No, surely!"

"But I say yes. At least I think so. At least… Oh! I don't know now! I cannot tell!"

Then, with difficulty articulating the words, Henri Tardoux added:

"Yes, gentlemen, I feel I am bound to tell you—I dare not pronounce Monsieur Fandor's letter a forgery, for it was agreed long before that Josette and I, yesterday evening, at the precise hour of the rendezvous arranged by her, were to meet at the house of friends who were giving a dance that night."

"And your fiancée did not come to this dance?"

"No, Monsieur Juve, she never came… Which would lead me to suppose she really intended to meet Monsieur Fandor."

For a moment Tardoux was lost in thought. Then he burst out again:

"But why this strange summons? and why to my house? No, no! it is obvious the letter is a forgery."

Yet the young scientist had hardly uttered the words before he blanched again.

"But then," he cried, "Josette has told me a lie! Yes, a lie! Ten minutes before you came, I phoned to her."

"At her house?" Fandor interrupted to ask.

"Of course! To ask her why she had not come to the dance last night."

"And she told you she was ill?" suggested Juve.

"That she had felt tired… How do you come to know… And then, why this falsehood? If she went out in compliance with a supposed letter from me, a forged letter, summoning her to Grenelle, why did she not say so?"—and Tardoux sank overwhelmed into a chair.

"Oh! I am afraid," he confessed, "I am afraid!"

But Juve smilingly reassured the unhappy young man, and Josette's lover felt convinced that the great detective was ready and willing to prove his fiancée guiltless of any blameworthy action.

"You know something then?" he asked eagerly.

"Perhaps I do! and I believe I am going to do you good service. But first I must have you swear to say nothing, not one word, whatever happens, whatever you may hear Josette say to me…"

"Say to you?"

"Yes, I am going to telephone to her. I have your word of honor?"—and Juve's voice grew serious. "I beseech you, sir, trust to me! I do assure you I am entirely in earnest, and you will never regret the step I am taking."

Then, on receiving a nod from Tardoux in token of his consent, Juve took up the instrument and gave the de Vautreuils' number.

"Hello! hello!" he began to speak after a few moments' delay, "is that Mademoiselle de Vautreuil? Hello! It is I, Juve, speaking. My respectful compliments, Mademoiselle! Hello! I am telephoning you on behalf of my friend Fandor, who is very anxious about you. Why that appointment yesterday, which you did not keep? And why tell a lie to Monsieur Tardoux?"— and with a reassuring smile, he handed a second receiver to the girl's fiancé, so that he might hear her answer.

Alas! the reply was decisive, though betraying evident agitation. In a shaking voice, as though hurt and wounded to the quick, Josette replied, hesitating as if picking her words:

"Monsieur Juve, I do not understand what you mean!… I ask you by what right you interfere between my fiancé and me… I told Monsieur Henri Tardoux what was only proper for me to say… As for Monsieur Jerome Fandor, I do not understand one word of what you say about an appointment I made with him… I know nothing of the matter you speak of!"

"But…" protested Juve.

"Let me finish!" Josette de Vautreuil cut him short. "In any case I have had enough of these everlasting investigations, these police inquiries. They are uncalled for and indiscreet!…"

The girl's voice quivered with a sob, as she concluded: "Moreover, my mind is made up. This morning I received a letter from my father—which I was going to communicate to you… My father wishes me to join him immediately in London and to bring him the diamonds you recovered… He proposes to sell them there… Be good enough therefore to let me have them as soon as may be… I am waiting for them."

The girl's labored breathing testifying to her agitation could be plainly heard over the wire, as she resumed:

"And I beg you also, if you see them, to inform Monsieur Tardoux and Monsieur Fandor that I do not wish them to trouble any more about me… Their behavior is an insult!… I should refuse to see them, if they came!"

At the cruel words Henri Tardoux's hand shook so grievously he dropped the telephone on the floor, thereby cutting off communication.

"Angry! Josette is angry with me!" he groaned.

"Well and good!" broke in the imperturbable police officer.

"I have a sort of notion in my head I shall be kissing her, your Mademoiselle Josette, on both cheeks before the day's much older!… Why, yes, on your wedding day, my dear Tardoux. She'll owe me as good as that, surely!"

Then, paying not the slightest heed to the bewildered looks of Professor Marsonval's demonstrator, Juve added:

"Your hat, Fandor—and yours, Monsieur Tardoux! Why, certainly, we're going out,"—and he made for the door, muttering between his teeth:

"By the Lord! I thought as much! Last night put me on the track!… Oh, ho! owl as I am, I can get the evidence now to prove it. Fortunately!"

*     *     *     *     *

"Juve, you are never going to surrender the diamonds…?" demanded Fandor.

"Certainly I am!"

"Juve, you don't think that would be madly imprudent?"

"Oh! yes, I do!"

"Well, then?"

"Then, dear boy, will you tell me, pray, in virtue of what right I could refuse to restore them to Mlle. de Vautreuil?"

With Henri Tardoux stumbling at their heels, exhausted, overwhelmed by the angry words Josette, his gentle fiancée, had spoken regarding him, Juve and Fandor proceeded arm in arm, conversing in subdued tones. From the first the young man had protested against this return demanded by Josette of the famous jewels so ardently coveted by Fantômas, but the detective's last words lashed him into a positive fury.

"Why, Juve," he cried indignantly, "you take one for an imbecile then?"

"Which means?"

"Which means you think I do not understand?"

"Understand what, Fandor?"

"Why, that you accuse Josette of being Fantômas' accomplice."

The young journalist spoke in a muffled voice that shook

with anger. The strange attitude adopted by his friend, what he had himself seen, what he had heard at Henri Tardoux's—all these things combined had forced Fandor to this definite conclusion, and more emphatically than ever, he concluded:

"So we must never, whatever may happen, however things may look, we must never surrender the diamonds to Josette. She will only convey them to Fantômas—her Master!… Oh! yes, of course I know it is against the law to refuse. I know very well Josette can compel us to give back the jewels… But there, you are not Juve for nothing, by the Lord! She must be brought to book! Josette's complicity must be made manifest…"

"There, there!… You're short of memory!" Juve broke in on the tirade, hailing a taxi passing some way off, and then, as the vehicle drove up: "You're short of memory," he repeated—"and short of logic! You charge me with suspecting Josette to be Fantômas' accomplice?… seriously?"

"Why…"

"Then you simply forget that not five minutes ago I assured poor Tardoux, who is making himself miserable quite unnecessarily—that he would soon be marrying his fiancée… So, you think I want him to marry a criminal, do you?"

"I think… what you wanted was to put him off the scent, eh?"

"Ah! well, my lad, best get into the cab, eh? That'll be more useful than standing there talking foolishness!"—and still smiling and shrugging lightly, Juve stepped aside to make way for Henri Tardoux.

"You too, my dear sir! I'm particularly anxious your reconciliation with Mademoiselle Josette may not hang fire. It's a matter of a couple of hours or so, in any case,"—and he gave the driver the address and followed the others into the taxi.

"Rue Tardieu—and as quick as possible!"

"Rue Tardieu, Juve?"

"Yes, of course—to get the diamonds, you know."

"You really mean it, then? You're actually in earnest."

"Absolutely in earnest!… I see no way of keeping back the stones."

"But, to hand them over to Mademoiselle de Vautreuil is to expose them to Fantômas' attempts."

"Bah! she starts for London tonight… And then, Fantômas will not always be free—I hope."

But Fandor was shrugging his shoulders now. He found himself less than ever able to understand Juve's behavior. Yet the police officer had never seemed so unruffled, so assured of a victory he had no warrant to hope for.

"Whom does he suspect? whom does he suspect?" Fandor asked himself wildly. "It is not Josette, it seems, nor Rippert, nor yet Tardoux? Is it myself, by any chance?"

While the journalist, silenced by Henri Tardoux's presence, kept his lips rigorously closed, Marsonval's demonstrator seemed suddenly to lose control of his emotion.

"Monsieur Juve, a word with you, if you please!" he requested.

"By all means!"

"You believe in my fiancée's innocence, do you not?"

"Yes, fully, unreservedly!"

"So you think the letter written by her to Monsieur Fandor…"

"By her or by another!"

"Will be explained?"

"Just as the one you wrote to her will be—or more correctly, the one you are *supposed* to have written her."

But the taxi was pulling up at the house in the Rue Tardieu, and Juve broke off to admonish his companions:

"Stay where you are! Five minutes to run upstairs to my rooms and get these precious diamonds from the new hiding place where I concealed them, and I'll be with you."

He sprang lightly to the ground, remained away ten minutes, then reappeared carrying a small bag which he held in both hands with the greatest circumspection.

"Rue de l'Assomption, Passy!" he directed his driver. Then, taking his seat again in the cab, he half opened the bag and tilting it over towards Fandor:

"Look and see if they are the genuine diamonds, will you— St. Thomas that you are!"—and the journalist could doubt no longer.

He was in fact in such a state of bewilderment he felt unequal to saying a word or paying more than the vaguest attention to what Juve and Tardoux were saying, when the taxi pulled up for the second time at the de Vautreuils' door.

Juve's voice was trembling a little as he invited his companions to alight. Involuntarily Fandor turned to look at his friend and saw his face was pale.

"Juve," he suggested in a whisper under his breath—*"Browning?"*—and the other doubtless understood, for he nodded his approval, adding in the same subdued voice: "but the handcuffs will suffice!"—and he rang at the door…

For the moment Fandor again felt convinced that his suspicions were well founded. Surely Juve was preparing to arrest Josette? Had he not, in fact, confessed as much?… But how *could* the girl have become Fantômas' accomplice?—and his doubts began again.

Then, as they stood waiting for the door to be opened, Juve turned to Henri Tardoux.

"My dear sir," he advised him, "keep cool. Whatever happens, remember one thing—I give you my word your fiancée is innocent of all wrong. I swear she is worthy of you. I…"

He did not finish, for the door was opening. But the tone in which the police officer had spoken belied the possibility of any kind of subterfuge. No, Juve was telling the truth. He entertained no suspicions of Henri Tardoux's fiancée.

"The gentleman would wish…?" the manservant Louis asked the visitors.

"To see Mlle. de Vautreuil. And be so good as to tell her it is Monsieur Juve."

"Certainly, sir!"

The three were shown into the small salon where Juve and Fandor had already interviewed Josette, and left to themselves.

"Now, my friends, you are going to obey me implicitly and exactly. I'm in deadly earnest this time! You'll wait for me on the landing—outside the door of the bedroom!"

"The bedroom?" objected Henri Tardoux, "what bedroom?"

"Do think!" Juve snapped. "Your fiancée said she was ill, so naturally she will receive us in her bedroom."

He had not finished speaking when Louis returned: "Will Monsieur come with me?"

"Certainly!" Juve assented. "My friends are going up with me as well. They want to give Mademoiselle de Vautreuil a little surprise. They'll wait for me outside her door."

"Very good!" was all the well-trained servant said, strange as he may have deemed the arrangement—and thereupon the three visitors climbed the stairs to the first floor.

"This way, sir!" the servant invited, knocking at a door. Meantime, with a rapid gesture, Juve had directed his allies to their posts.

"Don't stir from there under any pretext whatsoever!" he whispered earnestly to Fandor. "The room has only two exits. You stay to guard one, I shall be at the other. The window is already watched."

"Already?"

"Hush! yes!"—and Juve made his way into Josette's chamber. Once within the door, the usually well-mannered police officer's behavior underwent an extraordinary change. Instead of making his bow to the young lady, who lay on a couch inhaling a smelling bottle, he strode across the room—*ran* would be the better word—to the second door that gave apparently on a backstairs. Setting his back against this door so as to bar all egress with his body, the detective turned to the recumbent figure.

"Mademoiselle…" he was beginning when the girl broke in indignantly.

"What is this, sir? what does it mean?"

"Mademoiselle," Juve started afresh, "here are the diamonds. They are in this bag… But I must beg you not to insist…"

"It is useless, sir, to go on! My mind is made up… Please give me the jewels… Besides, I cannot think what should make you uneasy. Fantômas has sworn he means to disappear—and I trust his word…"

"I do not!" Juve shouted back and at one bound, he sprang

towards Josette with a ringing cry:

"Fantômas! In the name of the Law…!"

The sentence was never finished… Quick as lightning Josette was on her feet and had tossed her smelling bottle into the fireplace. Instantly a stench of sulfur filled the room, then flames broke out, setting alight the carpets which had evidently been soaked in some inflammable liquid.

"Fantômas! Fantômas!" yelled Juve, and leapt to grapple Josette.

But he recoiled with a cry of horror. Josette too sprang back and tore down a curtain and there, behind it, pinioned, gagged, appeared another Josette—the true Josette, for certain, round whom the flames were already licking cruelly.

"Help! help, Fandor!" screamed Juve, hoarse with alarm. He had dashed to the prisoner's side. Seizing her in his arms, he tore her from amid the flames and threw her on a bed at the other end of the room.

But this, this act of rescue, was precisely what Fantômas had counted on—Fantômas who was the other Josette. Pouncing on the bag of diamonds and snatching it up, he sprang into a press and disappeared. Beneath this cupboard the ground had been dug out and its flooring cut away, so that the miscreant dropped to the ground-floor level.

By this time, however, Juve was smashing open the window with his fist.

"Theo! Henri!" he yelled, "look out! Fantômas is escaping!"

From the Rue Tardieu, where he went to get the diamonds, Juve had telephoned to summon the two Inspectors, ordering them to come instantly and take post to right and left of the house, ready to intercept any fugitive.

"Here, Chief!" came two answering shouts.

But it was too late! Stripped of his woman's clothes, clad in the traditional costume, a slim, black figure that defied capture, Fantômas was out of the garden in a flash, and in two strides had crossed the road.

In the pavement, directly opposite, a sewer trap lifted. An accomplice held it open from below, and through this trapdoor the wretch dived and disappeared!

The police officer had foreseen everything, he thought, had guarded every possible way of escape—but Fantômas' devilish ingenuity had outwitted him! Impossible to continue the chase in the labyrinth of the Paris sewers!

The trap fell back in place, pitted with shots Juve and his Inspectors let fly. Was the scoundrel hit? But what mattered that? He was free, triumphant… He was unmasked, but victorious!

*　　*　　*　　*　　*

Ten minutes later, her head lovingly pillowed on her fiancé's arm, the true Josette was able to tell her tale.

"Yes," the girl explained, "I went out yesterday to meet Henri… Oh! that letter in which you asked me to join you at Javel frightened me so!… I hesitated, I could not believe it came from *you*… And yet it seemed so impossible you could be doing wrong that I took all sorts of precautions so that no one should follow me and see me meet you in such a place!… Ah! what was my despair when I found myself a prisoner in Fantômas' hands and he swore Juve was his captive too!"—and the girl shuddered at the recollection of past danger as she continued:

"This morning I woke to find myself in this room. How had Fantômas conveyed me there I cannot tell. He kept me in a state of abject terror. When you telephoned me, Henri, he held a dagger to my heart and forced me to tell you a lie! So too he dictated my replies when Juve called me to the instrument. Oh! how I longed to have the courage to refuse to claim the diamonds back! Again and again I told myself, 'I am a coward! I ought not to ask for them. He is going to steal them! and the poor refugees who want to sell them and are in such sore need…!'"

Then Juve took up the word. "Mademoiselle," he asked, "at what amount did your father value these jewels?"

"Eight million francs, or thereabouts."

"Then my defeat is as good as a victory!… Mademoiselle, you will be so good as to hand this check for ten million to the Comte de Vautreuil. It is the price of the diamonds… Take it!"

Could the police officer have made a more startling, a more astounding declaration? Fandor was on his feet in an instant.

"Juve, the stolen diamonds were imitation like the others?"

"Wrong! They were good, sound, genuine—Fantômas would never have let himself be done twice over. If I had brought paste a second time, he would have known of it. No, they are actually the Russian diamonds that he has just stolen!"

"But, that being so…"

"That being so, the explanation is quite simple… When it became a question of Fantômas having come back to life, the insurance companies against theft took fright. Naturally their risks were augmented… And their Amalgamated Committee applied to me, instructing me to establish clearly and beyond dispute if the brigand was or was not alive again. My answer was I must have a bait… a sensational robbery. I said to myself, you see, Fandor: 'Either I shall arrest Fantômas, and that will end the thing, or he will escape me. But in the latter case, then nobody can henceforth throw doubt on his actual existence'… So I asked the companies to buy these diamonds! to leave them in my hands! I was to have carte blanche to stake everything on one bold hazard, win or lose… They agreed to take the risk— what is ten millions to the Amalgamated Committee of all the companies? It is open to it to raise its premiums, once the fact is indisputable, once it is sure and certain that Fantômas is alive again!"

Juve's tale was told. Suddenly clapping Fandor on the shoulder, the great man merely added with a genial smile:

"So, my good lad, nobody wants to hear another word from you! Henri and the true Josette have something better to think about, I wager, than the diamonds. Let us leave the lovers together… We have other work to do!" And a sigh escaped from the police officer as he went on:

"The conclusion of all this! But, Fandor, you know what it is! Fantômas is free! Fantômas is wealthy with the proceeds of his crime! Fantômas will resume his nefarious exploits!… It is War! the battle begins afresh between the Arch-Enemy and us!"

Fandor nodded his head in grim assent.

"Yes," he cried, "he is alive again! Yes, he is free! free to start anew on his hideous career of cruelty and abomination!... If only we could know *when...*"

"In a month, in a week, tomorrow—this moment! When and where he chooses!... I am ready, Fandor!"

"And I!..." said the journalist simply.

Then, by one common impulse, Juve and Fandor clasped hands in a grip that told of their great, their deep, their eternal affection.

Somewhere, somewhere in Paris, under his sinister mask, Fantômas was perhaps already plotting some fresh atrocity!

But the two friends were there, scornful of danger, their faces open to the day, eager to accept the wager of battle—ready, yes ready!


THE END